# COFFEE  LOFT COLLECTION

# Contents

# Pardon My French Press

J.P. Sterling

# Contents

*To my friend, Peg, who has the best sense of humor, and always has a joke for me when I need one.*

# ONE

## Christian Hanson

"I'm sorry, sir." The hotel receptionist clicks her ridiculously long and stabby nails on her desktop keyboard, glaring at me through her obviously fake eyelashes. "We don't have a reservation for a Christian Hanson, and we are fully booked for the night."

"Are you sure?" I shift my weight from one sneaker to the other while shuffling my worn leather backpack to the center of my back. My whole body aches from the most grueling commute ever. My flight from Boston to New York had been delayed, and eventually canceled, due to a winter storm. Of course, I only found that out after sitting at the airport for hours. I tried to rent a car. Any car would have done. I would have driven an electric scooter if I had found one to rent. All the car rental companies were booked from the influx of flight cancellations.

But lucky me, I found a bus ticket. It should only have taken about five hours to get here, but with the reduced speeds from the road conditions, it took eight. I won't mention I had to sit by a gum-popping woman who didn't know the meaning of personal space. It had been a grueling day. All I wanted was my hotel room and a bed.

I let out a defeated sigh. In hindsight, the bus ticket was a good thing. It only set me back thirty-five bucks, which I didn't really have to spend anyway. A car would have been another dent on the credit card.

I don't doubt that I will pay it *someday*.

That someday due date is largely what contributes to the recent knot in my gut. I'm on a mission to make it smaller, not larger. It's all part of my plan to realize my dreams of true financial abundance. "I'm certain I booked a long stay. A whole month, in fact. Can you check under the name Christy? I know it's weird, but it's close to Christian and sometimes that happens."

Her eyes widen, fanning her spider-leg lashes. "Just one moment." More clickity clicks with her knife nails. "I'm sorry, Sir," her automatic not-sorry tone resumes. "We don't have a reservation for *Christy* Hanson. Last I checked, most of the hotels and shelters on the east side of the city are full, as they pulled homeless off the streets for the night. The weather forecast is for record lows tonight."

I rake my hand through my hair as tension pools in the back of my brain. I clearly recall making the reservation when I booked the flight. It is . . . well, maybe not clearly. I almost vaguely remember making the reservation. I pull out my phone, tap my emails, and scroll.

"Is there anything else I can help you with, Sir?" Spider lashes rushes me.

"Well, hmm, I'm looking for my confirmation number." I scroll, knowing the email is here. "Maybe you could try Christian *Man-son?*"

Her lips tighten together, not even twitching as she resumes her clickity clicks, this time with more force. "I'm sorry, Sir—"

"You know," I hold up my palm, "it's fine. Thank you for your assistance. I'll call around to another hotel." I had heard her say all the hotels were full, but standing here is a waste of time. Tomorrow is a huge day, my first day at my Coffee Loft store. With the excitement brewing, my nerves twist into a tighter knot thinking about it.

My Coffee Loft is located in the middle of Station Square on Long Island, a historic building founded in 1906, with a Tudor roof resembling something straight out of Europe. It was a fantasy location, which I was lucky to be able to snag when a local coffee shop sold out.

I started working at a Coffee Loft franchise in college as a barista. I would have never dreamed that five years later I'd own my own. The Coffee Loft franchise has been good to me. I loved it so much. Now that I own my own store, it is fulfilling my dream of building an empire. Sure, it takes huge sacrifices right now. It's worth it to show my family, especially my grandma, everything I did on my own. She'd be proud of me. She might even smile as big as she used to before my mom passed.

I push off from the counter and roll my single suitcase back toward the exit, scrolling my phone for hotels. Nothing on this part of Long Island. Just as spider lashes said. Everything on the east side of New York is booked. I sure didn't have the funds to take a cab to Jersey, and I couldn't handle another bus. A brief glance from the lobby window shows thickening snowfall blowing at a near-horizontal slant.

I wish I had the money to secure a long-term Airbnb, but it might be a month or two of working before I have money to do that. I need somewhere to lay my head for a few hours until I can look for something nicer tomorrow.

I had carefully selected this hotel because it is the cheapest on Long Island, and it is only a block away from the Coffee Loft. My eyes arc around the top of my lids as an idea fills my brain. I mean, it is *my* store. It's a block away, and it would give me a respite for the night. It's not a Holiday Inn, but it's warm, has a bathroom, and a sofa I can crash on in my office . . .

I flash my phone screen, confirming it is nine. All the staff should be gone. It's not like anyone will even see me sleep there.

*Why not?*

I shove my phone into my coat pocket and head out the exit.

My feet crunch in the new layer of snow as the sidewalks are nearly empty—a rare scene for a city normally so bustling even at this time of night. I pull my wool jacket collar up, hugging it against the bottom of my ears, but it barely takes the sting off. I am not dressed for a winter walk. I pace faster, shoving my hands in my pockets to keep my fingers from freezing.

At the corner, I wait for the crossing light. It's too cold to stand still, so I shuffle my feet in place, trying to keep warm. Across the street is a small grocery store that's been closed for the night. A soft light glows in the window, displaying some of their bakery items.

A flitter of movement next to the building catches my eye.

A homeless man is standing under the awning, with nothing more than a light jacket on. My first thought is to look away, and

I check on the crossing light. Still red. My mind returns to spider lashes saying all the shelters and hotels are full for the night.

He'll freeze.

The subway exit is right behind him, and it gives me an idea as I reach in my fleece-lined pocket and pull out my wallet.

A few bucks, and my credit card.

The light finally swaps to green, and I cross the street, walking the cash over to him. With a weary smile, I offer it to him. "Do you think you can get on the subway with this to stay warm?"

His eyes grow softer when they catch mine. "God bless you."

"Don't mention it." I reach around his back, giving it a pat. "Stay safe."

"You too." He grabs his lone backpack by his foot, and shuffles away.

I pivot and marvel at the most magnificent building I've ever seen.

*My Coffee Loft.*

# Two
## Portia Grant

I ogle the open Coffee Loft pantry. All my morals are being tested.

One Oreo.

My favorite snack. The only thing better than an Oreo, is an Oreo with milk. Or ice cream. Yeah, an Oreo ice cream blended treat. You could add sprinkles on top, too . . . like for kids. I giggle to myself as I'm almost thirty and clearly past the age of sprinkles unless I *need* to eat them. Then I would. Like if someone put a gun to my head and growled, "eat these colorful sprinkle treats, or else." *Of course, I'm going to eat them in that situation.* Sprinkles are an option. For other people. A vibrantly colorful and delicious option.

My stomach churns ungracefully, reminiscent of those old-fashioned hand churned-ice-cream makers, but with the handle off kilter and in need of some fresh grease in the gears. It pains in the worst way, making a dying noise, reminding me of all the meals I didn't eat today.

We use Oreos in our blended drinks, and I opened this pack a few days ago. I eyeball the Oreo. One cookie isn't enough to make a drink. *Besides,* it's likely a tad stale. Not spoiled rotten, just approaching its use by date.

*I'll have to throw it out in the morning.*

I check over my shoulder, expecting someone to stop me. Of course, I'm solo. Being short staffed today, I barista'd without a dinner break. A grumble erupted from my stomach, the call of a blue whale reverberating all around.

I eye the trash can in the corner, still overstuffed, waiting for me to tie the bag and take it out back. It didn't really have room for an Oreo.

I'd need a fresh trash bag for one lonely Oreo. That is wasteful. If I did put it in the trash, it might even attract rats. New York has a huge problem with rats, and I don't want to contribute to that. Would it really be stealing if it was going in the trash in the morning?

My fingers nearly tremble as I snatch it. Saliva musters at the tip of my tongue. Adrenaline surges, as I have never stolen anything in my life.

This obviously isn't stealing.

I nibble off the edge with my front teeth. *A tad soft on the outside, but mostly still crunchy.*

A childish giggle escapes from the back of my throat as I unscrew the two sides and scrape off the creamy filling with my teeth, melting it on my tongue. I relish every second of this drop of heaven. This cookie was a lot like me. The perfect metaphor to describe the state of my life. Although I had developed my first row of crows-feet in the corners of my eyes, I was in my prime on the inside. Not expired at all. Certainly, still worthy of a fairytale love story.

I replace the two halves together and bite the cookie, taking most of it into my mouth. Man, I'm starving. I hardly chew it. *So good.* My churning stomach screeches out for more.

Really, I deserve a free Oreo.

It is the least this place could do for me. I'd worked since noon without a break, which is *illegal*. But short staffed or not, I'm not about to let our customers down—I have too great of a work ethic for that even if I hate this place a little more each day.

This coffee house had always been a family-owned shop. Recently the owners retired, selling out to some new guy who is transitioning the store to a Coffee Loft franchise. At first, we were all excited, thinking we'd get big raises. Coffee Loft has the best coffees, but right after the sale went through, the jerk owner sent an email stating nobody was allowed to get more than twenty hours a week. That meant we had to work every shift by ourselves. He also said something about a new pay scale that would be applied after an in-person evaluation is completed. That didn't sound like big raises to me. Everyone except me, and one newer gal, Jade, had quit. They didn't want to have to prove they knew how to do a job they'd already been doing.

I'm confident in my abilities. Since I was the person running this place for the last year, he needs me. When everyone quit, he gave me special permission to work as much as I needed to until he gets here. Since I worked so hard, I should get a huge raise. Add in the corporate insurance, and it is too hard to say no—at least for right now.

I have goals. I'm not going to work here *forever.*

Because I really hate it here.

I ball my hand into a fist and pound on my chest, as I nearly choke on that scathing thought.

I can't even imagine the crow's feet I'd have after working this slave labor job forever, or even five more years. That's why I'm devoting all my free time to building my own match-making business. Sure, it's not making a profit *now*, but things take time. And until it takes off, I must put in the long hours here to be able to keep my apartment.

Nope. I'm only staying long enough to get my matchmaking business in the black. Another year, tops. I shove the last of the Oreo into my mouth.

This part is mostly stale. It was only a little fresh on the outside. A façade to trick me into putting the whole thing in my mouth.

Fighting the reflex to gag, I stifle all thoughts of how the Oreo has instantly become a personification of everything wrong with my life. The underappreciated days of working here, ghosts of failed attempts to turn my life around—the latest being my app. And the fact that I always have been, and always will be single.

A shuffle from behind alerts me—my eyes pop open, and I stare at the growing shadow on the pantry wall straight in front of me.

*A rather large shadow of a human figure.*

My breath catches in my chest.

That's not *my* shadow!

My shadow is cute and petite. Never reflecting a pound over one twenty-five. Okay, maybe one forty-five, but I'm not a teenager anymore. Plus, I just wolfed down an Oreo! This shadow is much too shadowy to be one hundred and twenty-five—*okay, forty-five pounds*. It was more like two hundred with broody shoulders.

But I'm alone.

I had locked the front door, even pulling on the handle to double check it. I have had nightmares about this very moment. It always started the same. Me, a beautiful woman trapped alone here.

Which means . . .

*Someone broke in!*

My legs buckle while my adrenaline surges through my veins and all my senses are heightened.

*I'm getting robbed!*

"Are you eating company Oreos?" the shadow asked, not sounding the least bit concerned about my recent near-starving situation.

Oh no! My throat closes from panic, cinching my esophagus, and putting pressure on my airway. With my mouth still full, everything backed up. I can't breathe through my nose. I swallow the Oreo, but it isn't chewed enough. My hand flies to my throat as a gurgling noise crooks out.

This is bad!

*I need water!*

I stumble backward, gurgles crackling out of my throat as I bolt to the sink.

Where's a cup?

My eyes rapidly inventory the shined stainless-steel sink and counter. The bare counter sparkles with perfect shine from the cleanup I had recently completed. Not one single stray cup. I do spot my French press in the center of the counter. *That's going to have to do!*

I gurgle again. It's not an attractive sound at all. Feet shuffle behind me, and the voice calls out, "Are you choking?" I wish with *everything in my soul* I could answer that with a giant sarcastic, *no,* but I can't force out even a peep. Now woozy, I need to do something! Panicking, I spin on my heel and flail forward.

A set of strong arms swoops in from behind. Hands lock below my ribcage. My last breath wrings out of my lungs like a dish rag twisting. I was either being attacked or Heimliched. With no breath left inside of me to fight, my body goes limp.

My ribs crackle from a gut punch. I'm still unsure if this is an attack, or the Heimlich.

Never had either.

A puff of air, I didn't even know I had, rushes out of my lungs with enough force that I cough. My Oreo heaves out.

*Hallelujah,* I'm alive! I inhale deep breaths, falling to my knees to aid the process as I hold my chest.

I nearly died.

How's that for karma for stealing?

I'm never doing that again!

But I'm rescued by this perfect stranger sent to me.

Is he an angel?

A paranormal paramedic of some sort?

I rub my throat as I continue to draw in air, catching my bearings. I slowly raise my head. I must know who he is.

My jaw drops as he's *gorgeous.*

Not just a little gorgeous, but I've never seen anything like him.

A steaming cup of hot cocoa hot! The narrator's voice in my head doesn't shut up, tracking all his most impressive features. A chiseled jaw line dominates his face in all the best ways. Dark hair with a rebellious front spike, most likely caused by an unruly cowlick, but he wears it well. Eyes a perfect hue of blue, wavering from the colors of deep-sea water all the way over to light gray.

Fascinating.

Who is he?

Unbidden goosebumps dot my spine, and I pinch my brows together as I ask the first thing that bleeps out, "Are you robbing me?"

# THREE

## Christian

My heart rate tames as I place my hand firmly on her back. My insides freeze, and I hold my breath. I've never been good in emergency situations—which is why I went into the coffee business—not first response. "Just relax." I focus on measured breathing, taking my own advice. "You're okay."

She stands with her hand propped on the counter, wearing a Coffee Loft apron. She's clearly an employee, but the fact that she's here hours past closing is confusing. Her blonde hair is tied up in one of those disheveled buns that oddly looks put together, accentuating her high cheekbones. As her breath evens, her gaze shifts to me. Her eyes are colored like wild July-sun-ripened blueberries so electrifyingly beautiful they vortex me right in. There's a magnetism that's instant.

Shuffling her feet backwards, she adds distance between us. "Are you robbing me?"

I burst out laughing as my head springs back. "No, I'm not robbing you." Pausing, I consider how strange my being here might look. It was hours past closing time, and I had to look like a homeless person lugging my suitcase. Yet, she was the one eating *my* Oreos when I walked in. I can forgive one cookie, but I'm going to give her a hard time with it. I point a finger gun at her, lightening the mood. "It looks like you were robbing me."

"What?" Her T is extra sharp. Clearly, she got her breath back. She eases along the wall, lifting the fire extinguisher from its hook, and aims the nozzle at me with her hand secured on the trigger. "What are you doing here? And you better speak fast before I call the cops."

"Whoa." I throw my hands up as if I'm under arrest. "I'm Christian, the new owner. I didn't break in; I have a key." I emit another series of chuckles as she can't be serious.

"Wait." Her eyes shift side to side before locking on me. "You're the new owner?"

"I am." My lips twist into a grin which I hope convinces her not to soak me.

Her hand flops forward, and she drops the fire extinguisher to the tile as she emits an explosive sigh. "Why didn't you say something instead of sneaking up on me like that. You nearly killed me!"

"Me?" Jabbing my thumb into my chest, I connect the pattern where she shifts the blame to me, and my defensive senses rise all the way to my neck. "I saved you! You were choking. If I hadn't performed that heroic life-saving maneuver, you'd be toast." I guffaw in disgust. "You should be thanking me."

"Thank you?" Her jaw drops and she makes a face as if she's going to vomit. This woman was clearly not in control of her bodily functions. Nearly choking to death, and now dry heaving, all in the span of five whole minutes. Not sure what that suggests.

Maybe she needs a chiropractic adjustment?

Laughter rushes out, her breath is warm as a summer breeze as a wave of it meets my nose. It also smells like Oreos. "What's so funny?" I ask. She swipes at her eyes, wiping tears, with continued waves of laughter. This woman is clearly unhinged. It's a good thing I caught her eating my Oreos now, or who knows what she would have stolen from me. "Ma'am—"

Her laughter drops off, and she deploys an accusing finger at me. An extra pointy digit, with a not-even-close-to-conversational slant at my mouth. "Don't ma'am me."

Sweat beads on my forehead. Why do I feel as if I'm breaking the law in my own business? "I'm so confused right now. Why am I the one in trouble?"

"You snuck up on me, tried to kill me, had the audacity to accuse me of stealing, and you called me ma'am."

"But you are okay now, right?" I force an even tone, trying to infuse a calmer environment. "Or should I call a paramedic?"

"I'm fine." She crosses her arms over her chest, and sharply angles her hip away from me. "That's not the point."

"What is the point?" I ask softly, lowering my voice even more, as I see my moderated voice is bringing down her anxiety. "What are we arguing about?"

Her brow dips into a low V, and she emits a huff so quiet it is barely audible. "You are saying what?"

"Nothing really." My shoulders fall, releasing tension as we are finally about ready to have a normal conversation. "Maybe that I'm Christian, your new boss." I throw out my hand, offering a handshake. "Nice to meet you. I'm glad you lived. What did you say your name was?"

Her chin raises, and she receives my hand, her skin is smooth as Ivory soap. "Portia. I'm the one you spoke with over email. Everyone but me, and one other gal, quit."

I bobble my head a few times as this isn't exactly pleasurable news. Apparently, she is one of my only trained staff. If I want to keep this place going without closing, I'll need her. At least until I hire and train someone else. It is the week before Christmas, though, and adding new staff now would be impossible. Better to be nice to her. "Thank you," I manage through my racing thoughts as my to-do list continues to stack up in my brain. I hadn't planned on needing to hire and train a whole new staff. Training can be costly, and I don't have any spare funds.

She triple blinks. "You're welcome." Her words are quick, mirroring a child who was being forced to have manners.

"Now that we established you lived," I scan the room, everything appearing to be in its place, except for the fact she is here hours after closing, "is there a reason you're here. Do you need a ride?"

A sigh rumbles in her throat before she finally pushes it out with force. "I'm here because I am working. It took me forever to clean since I was by myself all day."

"Okay." I chain nod about six times, as this reminds me of talking to my little sister. The attitude. "Well, I appreciate that. I'm here now and can finish up." I want to say, will you leave so I can sleep, but that won't win me any respect.

"I did everything, but you're welcome to inspect if you think it needs it." She paces to the employee coatroom, calling back, "I haven't had a day off in three weeks. Would you mind me taking the weekend off?"

Now it is my turn to nearly choke, as she springs back out of the coatroom and beelines to the door. Of course, I never expected anyone to work three weeks without a day off. I didn't know this place had been so depleted on staff, or I would have just shut the door completely until I got here. In our email correspondence, she always sounded as if everything was fine. The knot in my throat swells another notch as overwhelm consumes me. I had no idea I'd have this much immediate stress. "I'll handle it," I grumble.

# Four

## Portia

In my tenth-floor studio apartment, I lie on my secondhand futon with a white, goose-feather down comforter pulled over my face, blocking the burst of sunlight coming in from the bottom of my cracked open window. I could easily reach over and close it, but I'm too lazy to do that.

Plus, I don't have control over the heat in my place. It's an old system, and only the building manager has temp controls. Once he cranks the boiler on for the year, all the heat rises to the top floor. The bottom floor people complain about freezing all winter, while the top floor roasts in smoldering heat. Even though it's December on Long Island, if I leave my window closed it will rise to almost eighty degrees. It's a good thing my gas bill is included in my rent, or I'd be looking for a different apartment.

I yawn, pulling the pillow over my head to darken the room more. Finally, a day off! A text bleeps on my phone. There's no way I can answer that.

Another text. Still not answering that.

I adjust the pillow to cover my ears.

And another one.

This better be an emergency, or I will quickly make it one.

I snake my arm out of the covers, and grapple for the phone on my nightstand slash end table. I don't even have the screen to my face yet, and it vibrates with another text. One eye peels open.

**Jade: Did you know the new owner is here? I came in a few minutes late this morning, expecting it to be you, and it was him. He's all over my case about my clock-in times.**

**Jade: Why are you not here? You didn't quit, did you? Please don't quit. I can't afford to quit, too.**

**Jade: I don't like him.**

**Jade: He bobbles his head when he talks.**

I stretch my hands way over my head and arch my back, setting off a chain reaction as my cat, Mr. Noodles, joins me in our morning cat stretch. This used to be the most joyful part of my day, snuggling with Mr. Noodles. Today, I had to tend to this. I grumble, flop over onto my back, hover my phone over my face, and type.

**Me: I met him last night. Sorry, it was so late that I forgot to warn you.**

**Jade: He has some sort of OCD or something because he's literally doing inventory on everything. Instead of helping me make drinks, he is counting Oreos. It's so weird.**

A snort blurts out of my lips, and I can't help but take pride in that. Mr. Noodles paws at my arm, signaling it is time to fill his bowl. I drop my phone on my comforter and get up, not taking a moment to straighten my bed. I have zero plans to make my bed today. After I get some food, it's back to bed with my laptop to do admin work for my matchmaking business. Heaven!

Well, the bed part is heaven. The work part is okay. I love my little matching business, but it turns out it's harder to make a profit than I thought. To funnel people into the site, I give them a free match. Clients are meeting partners and dropping off the site at record speeds before they even sign up for a paid membership-hence why I am not making money. I'm in major need of recruiting new people. That I can't do from my bed.

Since I'm at emergency lows with potential dates on my website, I say sure when my dad calls around noon to ask if I want to go to Home Hardware. Dad is a retired carpenter with a lower back to prove it. He doesn't do much handyman stuff anymore, but he claims to miss the ambiance of the hardware store. Saturday outings are a regular thing for us. I tend to think it isn't so much about the ambiance as it is his need to get out of the house. It is evident that my parents still love each other after nearly forty years of marriage, but it is no secret that retirement is bringing them a little *too* close together.

My mom used to enjoy her days doing craft projects and quilting. If you had come home in the middle of the day, the kitchen table would be covered in whatever she was working on. Now that Dad is home, he sits at the table and plays online racing games on his tablet. I don't see the harm in it. He could do a lot worse things, but Mom says the fake engine noise gets on her nerves. I guess I can understand that.

Back to Home Hardware, I'm terrified of anything sharp and can't lift a thing over thirty pounds, but it turns out it has another product I need. The store is loaded with hunks. Dad knows how headstrong I am. He has long since given up arguing with me, instead insisting he come with me. Nobody can say my dad doesn't support me.

While Dad spends an hour talking about the weather to the guy in the paint aisle, I push the cart up the light bulb aisle and scout each guy I pass. Wedding ring. Wedding ring. No Wedding ring. Also no teeth. Oh, no wedding ring and a full set of teeth! I nonchalantly cut in front of him, reach for something on the shelf above my head, and wiggle my fingers, signaling I can't get it.

"Let me help you with that." He falls for my plan, rushing to my aid. "I got it." His fingers brush against the LED light bulbs, a pack of eight. "Is this the right one?"

Since I only have two fixtures in my entire studio, I have no clue what I will do with all these lightbulbs. The branding on the side of the box says, "Each bulb lasts twenty years." I quickly compute the math. If I live in my two-fixture studio forever, that pack of bulbs will last me for the next hundred and twenty years! I can't back down on my plan now. "Yes, that's exactly the one I need. Thank you." I take the box from him and place it neatly in the corner of the cart. Then I raise my lashes back to him and sweetly say, "I bet your girlfriend appreciates how tall you are?"

He adopts a flirty smile, picking up on my banter. "No girlfriend. I actually just got back from a military deployment."

"That's amazing. Thank you so much for your service." Batting my lashes again, I slide a QR code card out of my purse. "You know, I don't normally do this, but I have a matchmaking business. It's very exclusive. I have a waiting list, but I'm overcome with such an appreciation for your kindness. I would love to offer you a free match. Will you accept this code?" I smile, hoping he can't tell I'm lying through my teeth. Not only do I not have a waiting list, I also only have four available female matches currently.

His gaze slides to my card, and he smiles a little suspiciously. "Matchmaking?"

"Yeah, it's called, Your Last First Date. It differs from other dating sites because it focuses on personality matches. There are no profile photos until you unlock that feature. You don't get a name until after you chat with someone. It's a lot of fun." I pull my lips into the tightest grin I can. "It's the least I could do to thank you for your service." I cross my toes. I'm not a contortionist, it's clearly a saying meaning I cinch my toes together. Waiting.

"How do you match people without letting people select?"

"I love that question." I run a hand through my long hair, tucking it behind my ears. "I have a series of required personal questions. If you want, you can go into further personality quizzes, things that take your Myers-Briggs category into consideration. Then the algorithm does the rest. It's a lot of fun."

He takes the card from me. "My name is Liam, by the way."

Of course, his name is Liam! Every hot, single guy on this side of the Brooklyn bridge is always Liam. He's so perfect for my site. I can't wait for him to meet his dream girl. "I'm Portia. Nice to meet you, Liam." I hold my grin, backing away with my one hundred-and-twenty-year-light supply and steer my cart back toward my dad while I wave. "Well, I better let you continue your day. Thanks again." Now, to find some more women for my site. With Liam as bait, it shouldn't be a problem. I need to leave Home Hardware for the ladies, though.

I round the corner, nearly crashing into Dad. His gaze slides to my one-hundred-and-twenty-year supply of lights, and a proud dad smile lands on his lips. "Ah, you caught one, huh?" The first time I recruited with him, I thought it would be cringe. It turns out he viewed it like fishing, and kept score for me, too.

"Military, and very polite."

"That's not too bad." He sneaks a look at his drugstore wristwatch. The leather strap has long been worn out, but somehow, he keeps it together by punching new holes in it each time it snaps. I swear he's had that watch since I was five. Being an all-around handyman, he doesn't believe in throwing anything out that can be fixed. "It's not even one o'clock yet. You have time to get another one. Do you want to cruise the car lot?"

A smile glues to my lips because Dad's the kind of dad who'll do anything for me, and clearly *does* do most things for me. "I don't know if I can handle the car lot with you today." That's the one place I have to keep an eye on him, as he might come home with something he's not supposed to. He's always had a passion for cars—hence the name Portia. "Nah, I'm not a fan of the car lot men. I might see if I can borrow Mrs. Nelson's dog again later, and pretend to lose him at the park. She's been letting me walk him since the elevator broke. It worked well last time. The guys at the park tend to be fit and outgoing, matching the fastest."

"You know, Portia." Dad places a hand on the cart handle, slowing it down as I turn and catch his gaze. His blue eyes match mine. They haven't clouded even a spec over the years, still holding that same mischievous spark that used to take me on all the adventures when I was a kid. "One of these days, you might catch a hunk for you to keep."

"You know what I always say, Dad. Always a matchmaker, never a match." I sigh, wistfully. I'm not embarrassed to talk about my dating life. Mostly because there isn't anything to talk about. Plus, my dad is the easiest person to talk to about anything. Although I would never admit it, I would love to meet my own match. I force a smile, hoping he can't see the worry cloud my eyes.

One of my greatest fears in life is living my whole life in auto mode, working a job I don't have a passion for, doing the same routine without feeling anything and without finding my true love. I want to find love, but I'm also building a dream. It's a hard balance to juggle. At least for right now, I'm fine pouring my heart into this app while I wait for my last first date.

Besides, if I have a boyfriend, he won't be okay with my cruising for dudes with my dad, and this seriously is the most fun I've had. I know my dad would miss it as much as I would. Then we'd have to find a new hobby together. Something like real fishing, and fish are stinky.

# FIVE

## Christian

"What happened to my French press?" Portia stands on her toes, peering into the top cupboard. "I always leave it on the counter next to the espresso machine, and it's gone."

"I threw it away." I loiter in front of the microwave, nuking my left-over takeout pasta from last night. The same takeout pasta I've had *every* night for the last week since I arrived here. I don't love pasta. In fact, I'm getting sick of it. The mere smell of the cheese makes my stomach curdle, but it comes in a box from the neighboring grocery store for super cheap. Anything I can do to save a dollar is worth it. I don't doubt I'll be on a noodles and air diet for weeks—if not months—at the rate business is going.

Slowly she pivots and locks her gaze on me. "Why would you do that?"

"Coffee Loft doesn't sell French press coffee. We sell gourmet espresso at top shelf prices."

"I wasn't going to make one to sell. That's what I prefer to drink." She shuts the cupboard, and parks one hand on her hip. "You could have asked before you threw it away. That was *my* personal French press."

"I'm sorry I didn't realize you left personal belongings laying around." I shrug, knowing this transition is going to be hard for her. "I thought it belonged to the previous owner, and since I bought this place, it would be mine."

Her eyes pace to the pantry, and back to the ingredient canisters on the counter. "Did you also throw all the Oreos away because I can't find those anywhere?"

"Ah, we must be out." I wince, pretending not to care, as it doesn't make sense to tell an Oreo thief where I hide the Oreos. The microwave dings. I grab my pasta, and head back to my office. In the rush to open the shop this morning alone—because Jade was late again—I had no time to eat until now. Jade couldn't have caught me at a worse moment.

I'm not proud of what I did. When she came in late, I was so overwhelmed, I ended up letting her go. Jade was never on time, and you'd think for having a new boss, you'd at least try. Sure, today is Christmas Eve, and terrible timing, but she'd need to go eventually with her performance. I might as well give her the holiday off.

I'm not a jerk.

The stress added up too fast.

Now, there's this constant constriction in my chest, and I'm having trouble breathing. I still haven't found a hotel that doesn't cost a kidney. I finally got a rental car dropped off, which gives me more options for a hotel. As soon as I have time, I'm going online to book a room. It had been a week since I slept in an actual bed, and it is wearing on my mental health. Not to mention the kink in my neck.

That isn't even the worst pain I've had. It turns out the previous owners didn't provide accurate records. I had requested three years of tax returns at the time of closing. Now that I can see the actual sales, it is clear they were fudging the numbers to prepare it for sale. There is no way they were making the kind of money they said they were banking. Either that, or all their customers left when they sold the place. Sometimes that happens. Customer loyalty is a real thing.

There is the typical morning rush you'd expect for a coffee shop, but that only lasts an hour, or so, and it quickly dies down to nothing but a slow drip of random people throughout the day. There is no reason we'd ever need two people working simultaneously. Not to mention the bad habits of the two people I had. Plus, they were both being paid inflated management wages. I don't need management anymore. I need cheap labor. There's no way they'd stand for a pay cut. I know I wouldn't.

I'm coming to terms with what needs to be done. I hate this situation, but it's better to let my overpaid management go. They can draw unemployment. I can regroup with new people. After the holidays, I'll have a huge grand reopening ceremony to introduce the Coffee Loft brand.

I shovel pasta into my mouth and stare at the deposit slip I filled out. Twenty-three bucks and eighteen cents. Not worth even going to the bank. Sure, most people pay with plastic or digital these days, but even that won't keep this place running. I must assume the old owners used this place as a tax write-off of some sort, but I can't do that. I'll lose everything. I barely got financing for this place. If it wasn't for my grandma putting up her own business as collateral to obtain a personal loan, I wouldn't even be sitting here.

No, I don't need to go to the bank, but I'm going to walk there anyway for some fresh air and a chance to clear my head. I shove the deposit slip in my pocket and emerge from the office to find Portia leaning over the counter with a coffee cup in one hand and a Sharpie in the other. Her hair is pulled up into twin messy buns, and her smile is bright and inviting. Despite all the sass, she really is beautiful. "So, you said your first name is Brad?" She writes the customer's name on the cup. That part I don't have a problem with. It's what spews out of her mouth next that makes my mocha boil. "Tell me, Brad. Are you getting a drink for your girlfriend, or is it just—"

"That's enough!" I step in front of her and steal the cup. My blood pressure spikes, and I remind myself to take deep breaths. "Stop hitting on the customers," I grumble as I place the cup next to the espresso machine while I run shots.

"I wasn't *hitting* on him," she hisses under her breath. "I'm trying to find out if he's single."

"I don't care if you were buying him a winning lottery ticket," I hiss. "It's not appropriate to harass the customers like that." I empty the espresso shots into the cup and seal the lid before handing the cup to Brad. Portia and I watch silently as Brad leaves, but as soon as the door closes behind him, we resume the same fight we've been having since she came in at noon. "You need to start being professional, or—"

"Or what?" She parks her hand haughtily on her perfectly rounded hip. "Go ahead and tell me that I'm getting fired, because I'd really like to see you run this place without me."

"Don't even test me. I already let Jade go this morning."

"What? You let Jade go?" Her jaw unhinges, flapping all the way down until I can see the dental filling in her lower left side. It's nothing disgusting but hints of a sweet tooth. "You're bluffing. Why would you do that?"

I toss a shoulder up into an *I'm-bored-of-this-conversation* shrug. "It wasn't anything personal. I reworked the budget, and I need to revamp things to save money. She was paid management wages, and I don't need a manager as I'm here. Add to it, the fact she's been late every day for the last two weeks."

"You weren't even here the last two weeks. You have no idea how hard we've been working." Her eyes narrow until there is nothing left but tiny slits. "You are a jerk."

"That almost sounds like disrespecting your boss." My words were low, hinting at a warning. Judging from the looks of the books, I have to assume that Jade and Portia had been running this place into the ground, and I don't feel bad about needing to take this place in a new direction. A direction that makes money. It's not personal. Well, a little personal because I really didn't care for her sass, but it is also business.

"Go head, and fire me," she huffs as she juts out her chin. "You wouldn't last one week without me. You'd lose all your business. Nobody is going to buy coffee from your bobble head."

"Oh, really?" My head tilts, partially from the kink in my neck, but even more than that, it's what happens when my ego weighs in. It's a minor flaw that happens sometimes. "Not only will I 'handle' it by myself without you and Jade," I insert finger quotes around the word handle. I'm so worked up from the stress of everything, I'm acting completely out of character by feeding into her attitude, "It'll be my best week ever."

Her voice drops so low, it's hardly above a whisper. "What are you saying?"

My lips twist into a sinister grin. Maybe from the stress of sleeping on an ancient sofa that smells like sweaty feet. Maybe it's ego. Something gets into me. "I'm saying you can leave. I don't need your attitude. I certainly don't want to keep my Oreos on lockdown anymore."

"Well." Portia sticks her leg out, tapping her foot as if it is helping her to keep from running her mouth. "Just you wait, and you'll see I'm right. You'll come crawling back."

"Doubt it." I nod to the door. "Leave your apron, and I'll send your check in the mail."

"You're serious?" She whips off her apron and balls it up. I duck, assuming she's going to hurl it at me, but she maintains her composure and stuffs it in the hamper on her way out. "Just wait until I tell everyone you painted over black mold!"

"You can't do that!" I yell, pacing after her toward the exit. "That's slander!" I doubt she hears me, because the door is already shut. I brush my hands together, feeling a job well done. Problem number two is solved. Now that I don't have her harassing my customers, I'll surely get *way* more business. I can focus on my grand reopening, and everything is going to be amazing from here on out.

I scan the empty foyer, tracing the unfilled aisle to the counter. Nothing but emptiness. The clock ticks loudly on the wall behind me, and for the first time since I've been here, I notice a hum from the light in the dessert display case. I walk back to the office, yank out a sheet of printer paper, and scribble Help Wanted. When I come back to tape it in the window, I scan up and down the street. Empty. "It *is* Christmas Eve. People are with their families. Just give it a couple of days until people realize this place has a hip new owner, and a fresh look." I tell myself. "Then it'll be packed."

# Six

## Portia

"Dad," I huff through the phone as I steer Mrs. Nelson's English Mastiff through the jogging path in Central Park. Well, actually one look at the size ratio and you'll know who is steering who. The size differential is what makes this recruiting endeavor so fruitful. "I got fired from the coffee shop."

"You did?" The lack of shock in his voice tips me off that he was expecting something like this. "Were you recruiting on your shift again?"

"That's not the point." I yank the leash to the side of the path, pulling Oliver into the grass while we pass a trio of Shih Tzus. Oliver is smart, excellent at following directions, but he never understands his size. He wants to play with everyone, often scaring away every breed smaller than him. "The point is that Christian is a jerk. And he threw out my French press. He had the audacity to say I was hurting his business, and he'd be better off without me."

"I don't know about that. You've got the best sales skills I've ever seen." Dad's even voice was laced with a chuckle. "It's a bit of a cliché, but you could sell ice to an Eskimo. When you put your mind to something, you go after it."

"Exactly." I tug on the leash again, directing Oliver away from the hot dog cart. I'm not against feeding him street food, but I usually reserved such treats for a reward after he brings me a hunk.

"So, what are you doing now?" His voice takes an inquiring tone. "Is the app making any money?"

"That's the thing." I halt on my heel as I pass a single jogger with no wedding band. A look over my shoulder confirms he's fit and definitely fast enough to run after Oliver. I cradle the phone between my ear and shoulder as I use both hands to unhook Oliver's leash, while discreetly pointing to the man jogging away. "That's the one we want, boy. When I say go." Oliver dances in place, doing his I-found-a-hunk-excited-tail wag while I pause, letting the jogger get a good length away.

This works best when it looks as if I don't have a chance to catch Oliver. While I wait, I continue my conversation with Dad. "The app's algorithm is successful. Which sounds like a good thing, and typically it is, but I can't keep people long enough for a second date. With the first one free, it's like one date and they're off to happily ever after. It never fails. A perfect match every time."

"That's amazing the algorithm works that well."

"Not really, because I got most of my female recruits from the coffee shop. Now that I can't go there daily, I'm not sure how I will keep up with the supply."

"Who said you can't go there every day? He doesn't own the whole block."

"What are you saying? Just recruit on Christian's doorstep." My voice trails off. That is the *perfect* idea. It would also annoy him like crazy, and I'm all for that. I'll have to think about that another time. My hunk is a good quarter mile away. It is time to put my plan into action. "Gotta go, Dad. I've got a hunk to catch." I hang up before I give Dad a chance to reply. I point toward the man and instruct Oliver. "Fetch!"

Oliver bolts forward with lightning speed. I grab my foot and pull it behind my leg, stretching. It's been a while since we'd been hunting in the park, and I need to limber up. I grab the other foot and give it a good tug as Oliver rounds the corner on the jogging path. He's about halfway between the man and me now, and I start a slow jog to warm up some more. When Oliver's about to pass the man and not a moment too soon, I call out, "Oliver! Come back!"

I dig in and pull speed, running as if my life depends on it, and scream for help. "Somebody, please stop my dog!"

The shrillness in my cries for help even startles me. I have this routine down to a science, and as I'd hypothesized, this man is fast. He jolts forward, taking a mere ten seconds to snatch Oliver by the collar. Now is not the time to stop crying. I learned it is best to carry on a little longer while I worked up a few crocodile tears. "Oliver!" I cry out. "Why do you do this to me?"

The man holds Oliver's collar, jogging him toward me. I continue my script, "Ah, thank you so much! I'm not sure how he got off his leash." I grab Oliver's collar and hook his leash while scratching his head with my free hand. Now that I am this close to our catch, I can see he's definitely a ten. He's over six feet, fit and could mirror Patrick Dempsey when he was younger. "I don't know what I would have done if you weren't here." I bat my lashes and smile at him sweetly. "He's not even my dog. I'm walking him for my neighbor. Your *girlfriend* must be lucky to have such a dashing and quick man around."

"I don't have a girlfriend." His lips curl up, ready to banter.

My smile curls even more. *I hooked another one.* I pat Oliver's head and quietly promise to get him a hotdog on the way home.

Now, to figure out what to do about losing my best recruiting spot.

# SEVEN

## Christian

It's the day after Christmas. I spent yesterday alone in my hotel room, finally resting in an actual bed. It might have been depressing to some people, but a real bed is the best Christmas present I could have had. I slept the day away, not even missing a big family gathering.

Today, I drum my fingers on the Coffee Loft counter, staring at my grandmother's name in my phone contact list. Even though she hated the idea of me buying this place, my grandma made a personal loan to me for it. She didn't give me any special privileges though. I have a strict loan repayment plan with an interest rate that was in her favor. My first loan payment is due next month, leaving me hardly any time to make money to pay her.

The store's low sales weren't the situation I had planned on. I also never planned on starting over with staff either. Although I do believe it's the best choice going forward, it's taking time to become profitable.

My grandma is wealthy. She mostly gets her wealth from real estate investments, but she also owns the construction business that my late grandfather spent his life building. Not a prestigious luxury home-building one, rather a dirty road construction company with big noisy trucks, of which she is so proud.

From the time I was a baby, they had me in a hardhat, sitting in the dump truck next to Grandpa. They did everything they could to train me in the ways of a "blue-collar, working man." I always loathed it. I had allergies, and the filth and dust would make my eyes crust over and my nose plug up. I never complained, though, because passion oozed out of their smiles.

Grandma had held onto the dream that *someday* I would carry on their business for the next generation. She would have handed it over to me on a silver platter, complete with a ribbon-cutting ceremony. It's all I remember her talking to me about when I was little. "Someday, you will own Total Trucks Construction, and you can drive any truck you want." I never admitted it, but I merely pretended to enjoy playing with trucks when I was little, to see their pride shine.

My grandma even sent me to one of the best business schools in the country to get a formal education. For that, I'm grateful, and will never forget her gift. I didn't use it the way she had hoped. It's an understatement to say I broke Grandma's heart when I asked her for a loan for my Coffee Loft franchise. She gave me the loan papers with white knuckles.

I hope in time, after she sees my success, she will see this is a better fit for me.

More than that, I strive to make her proud.

Unfortunately, my timeline isn't working the way I need it to. I put the cart before the horse on a few things. A colossal cart that won't budge. I worked all morning and only four people came in. One didn't even order a drink, but asked to use the restroom. I don't doubt that Coffee Loft as a franchise has the tools it needs to help me turn this location around, but it could take time.

Time is expensive. I won't have the money to pay Grandma this month, but I don't want her to think I'm using her. I need to explain the situation now, so she isn't upset with me.

I drop my forehead into my palms and rub at the tension that's been there all week. No amount of peppermint mocha will help.

I'm out of options.

I press on my grandmother's number and hold my breath, counting the rings. One. Two. This won't take long. My grandmother sits next to her phone. If anything, she is probably playing Candy Crush on it. She has been a loyal addict of that game—and only that game—since it was first introduced. She must be on level one million by now. I count rings until it goes to voicemail. My insides freeze. She ignored my call. Then my internal organs add another layer of ice.

*What am I going to do? She's going to think I blew her off and took advantage of her if I don't pay her.*

I rake my fingers through my hair. I already paid an enormous amount of money to have mailers sent out to people in the neighborhood for free promo drinks next week. I've got commercials running, and radio ads booked. Short of begging on the street for people to come in, I don't know what to do to drive up business. It takes time for word to get out that this isn't the same old run-down coffee place it was.

*How does this place have literally no customers?*

For the first time, my denial wanes, and now anger bubbles in my gut.

*Is the road blocked off?*

*Something is up.*

I furrow my brow and stride to the door. Something must be going on in town to take all the people. A concert or a holiday parade. That must be it. I'm too new to town. I didn't even think to look at the schedule of events.

I place my hands on the glass door, gazing down the street. Traffic. Pretty boisterous, if you ask me. Why is nobody stopping in? My sign says open. I even double-check it, flipping it to closed and back again.

I turn my head to check the other direction. What I see startles me so much that my eyes immediately swell and bug out of my head, while my brain sets off a countdown to an explosion.

My hands ball into fists, and I struggle not to slam my hand through the glass. *I'm about to flip my froth,* but I don't need a repair bill.

Portia—my annoying ex-employee—is standing right outside my door. Her cheeks are rosy from the icy air, but she's bundled up in a heavy winter coat with a red and white striped scarf around her neck. Aside from the fact that she looks more festively beautiful than any actress in a Christmas movie, I can't stand to look at her. She is holding a French press by the handle, drinking coffee straight from it through a loopy straw!

*Clearly, she is doing it to taunt me.*

Was she serious about telling people I have mold?

She's running off all my customers!

*This must be illegal.*

*It's clearly not ethical.*

*It's sabotage!*

My brain flashes to her saying I won't last a week without her. Now I know her plan.

She's unhinged! Like an oversized barn door flapping in the wind, teasing for the next giant windstorm where it goes flying out to kill someone. She's dangerous!

She's getting revenge on me for firing her. *Oh.* I rub my hands together, working up my own plan. Something to steal her—or rather MY—customers back.

It must be fast.

It has to be cheap.

I don't have time to waste. I'm bleeding money, and she is lying to all my customers.

I rub my temples as I think of a way to stop it.

*I've got it!*

# EIGHT
## Portia

I clamp down on my bottom lip, fighting with every ounce of my soul not to burst into laughter. Christian is pacing back and forth in front of the huge Coffee Loft window, and if looks could kill. Ah, my stomach wrenches from holding in my giggles.

I should not be this joyful, but it's the day after Christmas and is my best recruiting morning ever. I've handed out hundreds of QR cards this morning, and I already got a full baker's dozen of recruits into my apps. I've been so happy all day, I shimmy when I walk.

Dad never disappoints me, giving me a brand-new French press in my stocking yesterday. I'm so happy to see it, I'm drinking coffee straight from it. Of course, there's no coffee grounds in it. That would be weird. Dad bought coffee from the shop down the street, as I'm not going to patronize Christian. I giggled when Dad passed over my favorite childhood loppy straw, and I couldn't resist. I may look completely looney drinking coffee from a loopy straw, but I'm happy.

It didn't surprise me that Dad stayed to help. He rolls his eyes at my recruiting, but he's secretly proud of me. I couldn't have a better partner in crime. Not only does he not flinch when I recruit, but he's always a source of motivation. He reaches forward, offering help. "Give me a stack of QR codes."

Before I can answer, Christian whips open the Coffee Loft door and wails in protest, "Oh, no, you don't!" Christian pokes a slanted finger at me. "You're not standing here. It's private property."

I'm in such a good mood that not even Christian can ruin it. His previously bright blue eyes were wavering toward gray now, hinting at sadness. I tilt my head, inspecting them from a different angle.

Maybe not sad.

More stress and exhaustion.

Do I feel sorry for him?

NOPE. He fired me on Christmas Eve.

I stride closer to the street, making sure my shoulders are back. The sun is at high noon, making it brighter than usual, but something catches my eye. I squint, catch my breath. Before my heart sinks, I straighten my spine and develop a plan. Who does Christian really think he's up against?

I'm great with people.

All people.

Including this handsome police officer he's obviously called on me. Christian is still lurking in the shadows under the Coffee Loft canopy when the officer approaches. "Good morning, Officer," I bat my eyelashes. "Lovely day for a walk, isn't it?"

Christian snorts so loudly it draws the officer's sideways gaze. He must have felt the heat of the officer's stare, because he immediately goes on the defensive, blurting out, "Officer, she must be breaking some code. She's right in front of my business, bothering all my customers."

"It's not against the law for someone to walk." He motions down the sidewalk. "However, if you loiter, and harass citizens, that's an issue, and that's the report I've been given."

"Ah, no, sir." I widely wag my head back and forth, maintaining my innocence. "I'm simply enjoying the fresh air, but if it's a bother, I'll be on my way."

"That might be best." The officer's gaze drops to my giant coffee with the loopy straw, and the cards I'm clutching, but he doesn't ask about them. "You seem to be having a nice day. Maybe avoid this area if you can. You don't look like you're here, causing trouble."

Christian emits one of those screeches that's meant to be explosive, but he obviously suppresses it, leaving his face to flush a deep crimson as he runs back into the Coffee Loft. I pinch my side hard to stop cracking into laughter in front of the cop. I don't want him to get even a hint that this was anything more than a coincidence of location. "Thank you for your assistance."

"Absolutely." The officer takes a slow step away, and I call back with an air of flirtation while jerking my thumb over my shoulder at my dad, "Don't worry about me. Dad keeps me out of trouble."

He nods goodbye at my dad, then smiles one of those flirty sideways smiles at me before he turns around to leave. I'm giddy as I quickly turn back to my dad, who is lurking behind me. The fact that he's vouching for me to police officers warms my heart more than anything. No daughter on the planet has as much support as I do. Getting fired is stressful enough, but thanks to my dad who developed this plan, it turned into the most successful recruiting event.

Dad shoves his hand in his jacket pocket. "Well, honey, it might be best to move across the road for now."

I eye the business across the street. A family-owned pizzeria called Pappi's. I don't eat there often. They have excellent pizza, and the family is one of the sweetest in the area. They wouldn't mind me there, but I only have the desire to bother one person. I certainly didn't want the cop to circle back around to find me still standing here. This was only going to work if I was *smooth*.

"You know," I start, then pause. I've gotten more recruits today than I usually do in three weeks. I call the day a success. "I'm getting ready for a break. We can go home."

"Sounds good to me." Dad's lips curl into his proud dad smile, and we fall into step together and head toward his car.

"Afterall, I can come back tomorrow."

# Nine

## Christian

My phone's on silent mode. I don't want to deal with any calls right now, but I catch it lighting up. It's Arielle, my little sister, who is attending her first semester of college, and hasn't exactly been attending classes. My gaze wafts through the Coffee Loft, not a soul in sight. I unlocked the door, but I need to check my doorstep. I don't doubt something is *up*, but I can wait a minute and welcome the distraction. "Hey, El."

There's hesitation on the other line before I hear a quiet and out of character, "Heeeey."

My brows pinch together as I adjust the phone to hear better. "What's wrong?"

"Can I come stay with you for a while?"

"Here?" I straighten my spine, my attention lasering in on this conversation. "You mean, in New York?"

"Yeah, I can sleep on the floor. It's not a big deal."

"Wait a second." I pace forward, sorting out previous conversations we'd had. Nothing we'd spoken about sounded as if she was in trouble. Still, my big-brother alarm sounds. "What's going on? Why would you leave college in the middle of the year?"

"Let's say college isn't my thing."

"El," I press her name firmly. "You know I'll do anything to help you. Be honest. Why are you quitting school?"

"I didn't quit." A crackle of air blows into her phone, projecting loudly on my end. "I sort of lost interest. Now, there isn't a point."

"El," I say softer this time, echoing her sobriety. "I won't judge you, but are you sure you want to quit this close to the end? You never know. Sometimes it looks worse than it is. You already have half of the year done. It's worth it to wait." I swallow, waiting for her to fill in the conversation with her usual chatter, but nothing comes. "El?"

My sister is a talker, and the only reason she'd ever be quiet in a serious conversation is if she's fighting back tears. I'm more practical than her. I would be stubborn and finish school, but I understood her nature. If she had already quit with her heart, there was no point in her body staying there.

"Ah, sure. You can stay. I'm in a tiny hotel room, but I'll call the desk to change to a two-bed." I want to ask her if she has an idea of how long she was staying. However, the lack of her usual chattiness tells me she isn't in the mood to talk. "When should I expect you?"

"Like ten minutes."

I check my watch, even though I don't need it to compute that math. She could not drive or even fly from Massachusetts that fast. "Are you teleporting?"

"Nah, I got an early start." She pauses for a beat. This is the part where I would normally tease her, but her tonal inflections warn me not to. I wait for her to offer further explanation. Even after the longest silence—one that was so stale, it made me cringe—the only thing she whispers is, "Thanks, Christian."

"Yeah, you bet," I mumble into the phone. Not because I wasn't sincere, but I am doing my best to hide my concern. "See ya soon."

The conversation falls into silence, and I set my phone down. The tension in the back of my head immediately swells. I'm unable to support myself. I've dug a deep hole with this Coffee Loft, and there is no way I can help her, too.

But *not* helping her is not an option either.

I rub my temples, wishing for a pressure valve I can crank to release the strain in my head. It does nothing but make me feel overwhelmed. I force a positive thought. "Well, if anything, Arielle can work the counter while I get a job that actually makes money." I laugh, not in a funny way. My fingers jitter with anxiety, like they want to play a piano. I've never played in my life. That's new. Maybe not the best sign.

Perhaps a coffee can help?

I walk behind the counter, ready my shot glasses for espresso, deciding to switch to half-caff, hoping the reduced caffeine will be better for sudden new jitters. There's no way I can switch to decaf cold turkey. My counter is perfectly shining, and my grinders are packed to the top with beans the way I left them yesterday when I closed. Nothing is out of place, even though the store's been open for almost an hour. I hate how clean it is. I haven't had one customer. I checked both sides of the block when I switched the sign from closed to open, and Portia wasn't there *yet*. I assume it's only a matter of time.

I'm at a loss for what to do with her if she comes back. What are my options? Maybe file a restraining order for harassment? I can't sit back and let her ruin my business.

A cold breeze wafts through the air, drawing my attention to the open front door.

Immediate surge of adrenaline.

*Not a customer.*

"Boy, you must have been sitting in the parking lot." I smile genuinely as Arielle stomps between the narrow pass of tables. A knit beanie sits on her head, with her not-showered blonde hair hanging out at the bottom. She's wearing that scowl she became famous for. The one that says, I'm-not-a-morning person. Now that I see she's safe in one piece, I can't resist teasing her. "Who stole your puppy?"

She plants her feet on the other side of the counter, glaring as if she whole-heartedly believes I stole her make-believe puppy. She has so much disdain clouding her ordinarily bright blue eyes, I'm thinking I need to check the backroom for a dog. "What did I do?" I seal my coffee cup lid and take a sip. "Are you going to tell me what's going on, or do I call Dad and tell him that you're here—"

"No." Her hand flies up in a stop motion. "Don't call Dad. Not before I get a job, or he'll make me come home to work for him."

"Then you better start talking." Completely understanding her dread of not wanting to work for a construction company, I motion to the table behind her. I pull out a chair for her, taking the one across from it for myself. "Are you in trouble?"

She sinks into the chair, dropping a sigh that borders on a whimper. "No trouble. Just sick." Before I have time to scan her for symptoms, she plants her gaze right on mine. "Heartsick."

My shoulders drop as everything makes sense. Of course, this is about a man. That's why she's here. She expects me to enlighten her about my species. As every time before, I have nothing to do but shrug. "Who do you need me to beat up?"

A tiny curve tips upward on her lips as she knows I talk a big talk with my big ego, but I can't punch a fly. "Trust me, I wish that was an option."

I wave my hand out, putting my empty lobby on display. "I got nothing going on here. Might as well take it out on some sorry loser."

"He's not a loser." Her quick defense reveals more than she planned, and she bites her bottom lip, as if trying to take it back.

I take a sip of coffee, and then stare out over the empty chairs and tables. Something about having Arielle sitting here with me makes sense. Maybe that's what I need? A partner. She sure looks like she could use a friend right now. We always made a good sibling team, getting into trouble, or rather out-of-trouble together.

I am in trouble this time. If anyone can help me get out of trouble, it will be her. "Well, I'll let you stay on one condition." I point a disciplinary finger at her. "You have one week to tell Dad. I don't want this coming back at me."

Her jaw drops as I wave my finger at her, and she doesn't even stutter out a broken rebuttal. "Yeah, that's fine. Whatever." As if trying to force a change of subject, her gaze dances around the room. "Why is no one here?"

Now it's my turn to glare, as I push back my chair, ready to investigate on my own. "I'm wondering the same thing. Let's go see why."

# Ten

## Portia

Unable to stop humming, I steer Mrs. Nelson's dog back to the apartment building from our morning recruiting walk. My app is exploding with new users. After yesterday's promotion, the word finally got out, and I'm getting organic signups. *Paying ones!*

I'm late to the coffee shop, but not fretting because my app is literally running itself. Every time I log in, there are new users and I have no idea where they came from. Finally, being one step ahead of the process is a much-needed stress relief.

I let out a sigh as we climb the stairs. Me, two steps at a time. Oliver, four steps at a time, as he has massive bandwidth. His nails scratch the cement, and his dog tags jingle as we round the final corner to his home. I knock on his door, calling out. "We're back."

Mrs. Nelson is hard of hearing. She doesn't admit it, but I suspect she's also hard of seeing. The evidence being, it doesn't matter what time of day I show up, she always has one random sponge curler in her hair which she seemingly overlooked. I pound on the door because it's the only way she hears me. "Mrs. Nelson, Oliver's home!"

Pressing my ear to the door, I hear nothing. Not even the pop of her recliner chair folding back up. "Mrs. Nelson!" I rise to the tips of my toes, nearly smashing my nose against the pane while I peer through the lace curtains on the tiny top door window. Everything is dark. She's not home. One would think it odd, but I don't even shrug. She's awfully forgetful. It's not the first time, or even the second or third, she has forgotten I have Oliver, and she leaves to run an errand.

Usually, I don't mind because I can certainly take him for another lap to top off my recruits. Today, I'm anxious to get to the coffee shop. "We're here!" I holler at the top of my lungs and twist the doorknob, hoping it will budge enough for me to slip Oliver inside. The knob is as tight as my dad's pickle jar lids.

Speaking of Dad, I sure wish he were here. He'd take Oliver until Mrs. Nelson returns, but my parents have a weekend wedding out of town. They left this morning. I check the time on my phone. It's well past Coffee Loft opening time. If I don't get there for the morning rush, there will be no point. My website is busy today, but how long will it last? I surely can't get cocky because I have one good day. I need to keep recruiting.

I tap my foot, weighing my options. Before I talk myself out of it, I spin on my heel and head down the stairs. Oliver's going to hang out with me today. He's probably ready for a nap. He'll be fine.

I giggle as I pull my lips into a dubious grin.

Christian will *love* him.

I'm whistling by the time I steer Oliver to Coffee Loft. There is a small line of people lingering on the Coffee Loft sidewalk. Not in front of the door waiting to get in. Most of them appear to be waiting to go down the subway entrance. I sidestep, avoiding getting in their way, and giggle, visualizing Christian's glowing scarlet face peering out the window to see me.

I'm not a mean person. I've never met a person I didn't like. Well, until Christian. It's not to say I hate him, more I hate what he did. I'm not afraid to stand up for what was right. It isn't right for Christian to fire both Jade and me on Christmas Eve. Especially after we ran that store for weeks by ourselves without even a day off.

Plus, this is the best location for female recruits because of all the high-end fashion boutiques in the area. Unless I want to go into New York City, this is the perfect place for me. Also, it's a teeny bit fun to taunt him with my presence. I slowly pass in front of the glass door but resist the urge to press my face to the glass and wave like a crazy person. Instead, I paste on my stoic expression and raise my chin.

"Good morning!" I call out to everyone. "Would anybody like a free match on my dating website? It's called, Your Last First Date, and I have a 100% match success rate."

I snap for Oliver to sit next to me, and he's obedient enough. Mostly because he's tired, and he lays down with his giant tongue almost grazing the ground. "Are you ready for the weekend?" I ask Mr. Donold. He's a retired accountant who lives alone, but steps out every morning for a fresh bagel from the grocery store. I have no idea how long he's been single, but he dresses fairly nicely with tan trousers, and a button shirt every day. He could certainly attract a woman. No matter how often I insist he try my app, he refuses. For some reason, he hasn't told me to bug off about it yet. With an encouraging smile, I tack on, "I can get you matched for a date today."

He tsks, but I'm not offended. This is what he does. It's a game we have. "Someday," I go on, "I'll get you signed up." Now that I've caught my breath from rushing over here, I glance down at Oliver, who suddenly stands in alert, doing his signature I-found-hunk-excited-tail wag.

"What do you see, boy?" I raise my gaze, but it is too late. I don't have a tight grip on his leash, and he takes off. His force is too strong for my unprepared hands. I grapple at the end of the leash, but my hands are full, and everything jumbles together. It's useless. All my cards scatter to the ground, and Oliver is *gone*.

# Eleven

## Christian

Out of nowhere, a massive beast of an animal swoops in from behind me and jumps on my chest, knocking me off balance. I stumble back, flailing my arms. He's so massive, he blocks my view. I take one too many steps back, and my heel teases the edge of a subway staircase. I windmill my arms backward, fighting the urge to fall, but it's no use. I tumble, taking the beast with me. I wail out in pain as my back twists in an unnatural way, and my head pounds against each concrete stair ledge over and over. One, two, three steps, and I finally stop rolling, but I drop down a fourth step from the sheer weight of this creature on top of me.

This is undoubtedly a premeditated attack.

Someone is trying to kill me.

As I plop down yet another stair, my cheek is met with a warm, velvety tongue and slobber. Cringing, I open my eyes. "Stop!" I wail out, and stretch my neck, trying to free my face from his washing, but the beast must think we're playing. "Get off me!" I yell, finding my lungs again. "I can barely breathe." Surprise. He doesn't listen. I find my bearings enough to shove him off me as I totter to a standing position. Dizzy, and not at all feeling the way standing should, I've developed a bit of a hunch from the spasms in my lower back that won't stop rocketing all the way down through my leg. I brace one palm on my back while grasping the stair rail with my free hand and hiss, "Go home, doggie."

He sits his massive furry bottom on the top stairs, taking watch over me, not moving. I don't waste time talking to him again, but there's a niggling in my brain wondering where he came from. Something could have happened to his owner. A shrill voice meets my ear, "Not that man, Oliver!" Portia's standing at the top of the stairwell, her jaw hanging low.

"I'm so sorry." She hobbles down the top two stairs, grabbing the beast by the collar with one hand and securing the end of the leash in her other. "He's trained to run after hunks—I mean, *men*. I had no idea you were even here." Her gaze skirts to the side. "Are you okay?"

Straightening my back as much as I can with my new hunch, I mutter, "Yeah. I'm totally fine."

She opens her mouth to speak. Nothing comes out. Then she tries again. "You don't look well?" Her cadence sounds more like a question.

I pivot, wincing as my back spasms, and I suck in a loud gasp.

"Wait a second." Stepping forward, her brows lower. "You're hurt."

"I'm f-fine," I squeak, my voice a tad high. Clearing my throat, I try again as I readjust my hand position lower on my back. "Just a little back pain. Nothing a little rest won't solve." The world is spinning, as I clearly hit my head harder than I thought. I slide my foot up a step, gluing a plastic smirk on my face. All the while, I'm crying for my momma in heaven on the inside, with pain imploding in my back.

"Are you sure?" She moves down another step closer, the dog still on the leash, but he's sitting quite well for her. I turn my face, desperate to hide the beads of sweat I can feel forming on my forehead. "Did you break something?"

"Nope. Everything's good as new." I slide another foot up, faster this time to prove my point. "Nothing I can't shake off. Bye now. Have a nice life." With a death grip on the rail, I suck in air, and snake my foot up another step, all the while trying not to howl out in agony. There's no way I can let her—of all people— see me cry. I wobble as the world continues to spiral around my head.

"I don't mean to pry, but you look broken." This time her hand meets my shoulder, and a lightning bolt splices through my arm. If I hadn't been malfunctioning before, this completes the job. I immobilize, resigning myself to the fact that I'll be stuck on this stair forever. "You took a good tumble down these stairs. Maybe you should get checked out by someone?"

Her hand moves down my arm, meeting my hand that's braced on my back. Even though her hand is tender and warm, her touch pricks my skin, sending tingles back through my arm. "I'm f-fine." I shake off her hand. "It's not like you're a nurse."

"No, I'm not a nurse, but I can tell when someone is injured. You are hunched over, and you never used to stand like that."

I slip a toe on the top stair and straighten my back as much as I can, but my back spasms from the tiniest movement. I push through it. I need to get out of here before I do—or say—something stupid. I certainly don't need her touching me again.

"You look unstable. You need to lie down. Let me help you back to the store—"

"You can't come back to my store!" I blurt out. El will be curious about Portia and concerned about me. She doesn't need to be either. That can never happen. There's no way I can ever let Portia into my store again. There's a reason I had to let her go because she's—

My mind goes blank. Portia's hand is on my arm again as she takes the rest of the steps, closing the gap between us. "You have the most soured expression on your face. You're either in massive pain, or something else is bothering you. What's wrong?"

"Nothing's bothering me." I shake my head, but that throws off the last little balance I have, and I'm back in orbit, spinning around. So dizzy.

*Run! But I can't run. I can't even hobble, but I desperately want to leave, and she won't leave me alone.*

"Wait a second." Her head does that tilting thing it does when she's thinking. I don't like it. "You don't look well."

"Nope. Sure don't." I inhale deeply, my stomach dropping a full inch as the stairwell continues orbiting. "Uh." I need to sit down. Everything is whirling around my head. I grip the rail harder, focusing on my inhalations. Even though I'm sure she's holding her hand steady, my vision is so off kilter, her hand appears to wave in front of me like a white flag.

I need a white flag.

I also need to get out of here. "Whatever," I mutter as I fumble forward. I must get out of here before I pass out from pain. I take more steps.

I kept waiting for the world to go dark, but somehow I pace the twelve steps back to my store safely-one painful step at a time.

Then everything goes dark.

# TWELVE

## Portia

"Don't you have someone you can call?" I stand over Christian as he lays flat on the sidewalk after collapsing. Oliver sits next to me, arching his gaze up. I can smell his expectation for me to congratulate him on catching a "hunk." I bite my cheek. Christian is *not* a hunk.

Christian's not doing well.

His karma from firing me brought real pain.

Or maybe it's not karma. I stare at Christian wincing in pain. *I* failed to control Oliver. Maybe it's a very expensive lawsuit if he decides to be litigious?

I'm not happy about this one bit. Even if it's the single person who fired me on Christmas, I must help him because the accident is Oliver's fault. Since Oliver is my responsibility—*it's my fault.*

"I'm fine." He mumbles over the double chin he creates when he winces. He rolls on to his side while bracing his lower back with one hand.

The Coffee Loft door flies open, and out comes a literal model. Blonde hair wafting down her back, and alabaster skin so flawless it was smoother than French silk. "What happened?" Her words burst with importance.

"Ah, he fell down some stairs and tried to walk. He might have a concussion."

"I'm fine," Christian's high-pitched demand bellows from below us. It gets even worse when he tries to pull himself to a seated position. His death rattle rolls out, causing me to gasp in shock.

"Let me help you." The model swoops in, bracing up Christian as he stumbles to his feet. I cower with my eyes wide as they waddle together back to the building.

He's seriously injured, and Oliver did that.

Fear swooshes through my body.

I don't want to get Oliver in trouble. Or worse, Mrs. Nelson. I'm the one who taught Oliver to run after hunks—*men*. The recruiting game is an innocent thing we do. Oliver wasn't supposed to hurt anyone. *This is my fault!* "Can I help?" I stammer, stepping forward to open the door. Before my palm brushes against the handle, Christian hollers loudly, jolting my nerves.

I jerk my thumb over my shoulder, taking an alarmed step back. "Maybe I should just go?"

"Stop screaming." The woman wraps her arm all the way around him. "You sound like you are dying."

"I'm not dying." Christian's weakened voice wafts out. "It's just my back. I sprained it."

I'm screaming in my head while my feet plant on the floor. *Don't go inside! It's a trap. Since when do I help people who fire me?*

The woman speaks so gently, as if she's taking care of an infant. "Let's get you to your office to lay down on the couch."

My stomach wrenches, and I combat the urge to grab it as I try to remain tough. There are a lot of things in life I detest, but high on my list of "things I can't stomach" are people in pain. Against all my better judgment, I cower in the doorway, vowing to not let even a toe inside ever again.

*It is a betrayal to step inside this place!*

Christian's huffing out heaving breaths each time he exhales.

The woman's perfect-mother-hen voice rolls out. "Maybe you broke something?"

"It's not the pain that's bothering me." Christian's lips purse into a perfect O while he blows out an even breath. "I've blown out my back before. It takes days to be able to walk. I can't work on my feet. Eventually I'll be fine, but my store will be bankrupt by then."

My gaze skirts the empty Coffee Loft lobby. Life's been more than a little crazy lately. There isn't much I am sure of, but something jiggles inside of me. I need to protect Oliver and Mrs. Nelson. "Don't worry about getting back to work," I rush, persuasively. "I can help out."

"Thanks, but no thanks." His sarcastic tone cackles out.

The woman nods toward me. "Do you know her?"

"Ah, she used to work here," he mumbles over his double chin again.

"Oh, that's perfect." Her posture springs up like a zipper cinching along the spine. "She knows what to do, and she can help out while you rest."

"No. Nope. Not perfect—"

"I'm Arielle." Her excitement bubbles out with her gaze locking on me, all the while she speaks over Christian, "I'm Christian's sister. We'd love it if you will help us." Now she's stroking Christian's back as if he's a long-haired cat. It helps to keep his sarcasm at bay as they continue to the office at a snail's pace.

I finger tap my chin, hating this whole thing. What choice did I have? I caused this mess. I need to fix it. A scuffle at my feet reminds me I'm still trailing Oliver. He's pulling on the leash, like a moth fighting for freedom from its own spun cocoon. "Let me run home first, and drop him off, and I'll be back."

"That would be wonderful," Arielle calls back.

*Or maybe I won't come back!* My eyes are about to bug out of my head.

*Why do I have all the bad luck?*

"Yeah." I run a hand through my hair, tucking it behind my ear. "I mean, I can help for an hour or two while he rests. Maybe for the rest of the day—"

"Perfect." Arielle leans over, practically heaving Christian further through his office door. "That would be amazing. Thank you so much!"

I can't hear anything else. My ears are bleeding, and I walk forward until my feet meet the doorframe. Slamming my forehead against the muted-eggshell paint, I suppress a scream.

Is this happening?

Is my luck really getting even worse?

First, I was fired. Then the dog I borrowed to run my business—so I don't go homeless—broke the jerk who fired me. I just offered to *help* him!

I throw up my hands as my shoulders bounce, preluding to sobs I'm holding in with all my strength. I've got to hurry and get Oliver home. Maybe if I can cover Christian's customers, he won't threaten to sue me or Mrs. Nelson?

*This is the worst possible thing that could have happened today!*

# THIRTEEN

## Christian

"Why did you do that?" I whisper harshly to my sister. "That woman is my nemesis, and you invited her into my space."

Arielle always has an uncanny ability to be best friends with everyone. She's a Labrador of people. I knew better than to let her talk to Portia, but it's not like I had a choice. Portia was spying on me. Now I'm stuck. Literally, and figuratively. I sprawl out on the couch in my office, and I can't even wiggle my big toe.

If I tell Portia she can't help, I'll look like a total jerk. Plus, I know from the last time I threw out my back, I'm going to be off my feet for at least a day or two. Arielle isn't trained to run the store. But Portia could train her. Maybe if Portia can show her the ropes this afternoon, I won't need any more help from her?

"Christian, relax." Arielle peeps back into my office door from the lobby. "Nobody's here yet. You're not losing any business."

"That's not helping the matter," I grumble.

"But look what I found lying on the ground outside." El flashes a postcard in front me. "It's a QR code for a free match on this new dating website called, *Your Last First Date*. You should sign up. It would give you something to do while you're lying there, and it might help that mood thing you've been having."

I flash a look at the ceiling. There's nothing wrong with my mood. I'm not signing up for a stupid dating site. "That's the dumbest thing I've ever heard."

"Come on." Without waiting for an invite, she takes a giant step inside the door, crossing the room to snatch my phone off my desk. Then she plops to the floor, sitting next to me. "There's nobody here, and it will kill time. It might be fun."

"Not doing that—" Shuffling my feet from annoyance, I wince when it pulls my back muscle.

"Great!" El cuts me off while pulling up a bright pink website on my phone. It's the most disgusting thing I've seen all day, but it doesn't even phase her as she types. "I've been worried about you. This is the perfect thing to take your mind off all the stress you have here."

"That's the last thing I need."

"Look at how cute the website is," El gushes, ignoring my defenses. "And look." She points to the screen, her lips twisting into a giddy grin. "You can pick your preferences!" She adjusts the angle of my phone, her whole face lighting up from the glow of the screen. "Let's see...what do you like? Kindhearted. Professional. Family oriented, and we'll add good looks for fun."

El's clicking buttons I can't see from my spot of slamming the back of my head against the armrest. I don't doubt she is making me look like a giant tool on there. Again, Arielle's always been social with everyone. This is right up her alley. "You should be the one making the profile."

"Oh, no, I'm not on the market at the moment, but you totally are."

I can't stand to be here, wasting my time with this, but I can't move, so I'm out of options.

"Look!" El peels her eyes from the screen, sliding it so I can see it. "You got a match!"

"I did?" I hesitate, straining my gaze to see what she looks like but there's no photo. "Where's she at?"

"You don't get a photo until you unlock that feature after a successful chat. Let me send her a message for you!" El beams at me before her fingers glide back over the keyboard. "This is going to be so perfect."

*Not perfect. It's the definition of insanity that I would let my sister do this. I don't need to chat with anyone. I don't need a date app. All I need is my back to feel better so I can get off this floor and run my business!*

# Fourteen

## Portia

I dab the tear in the corner of my eye while squinting at the scathing review one man left on my website. I had stopped inside my apartment after dropping Oliver off, and couldn't resist logging into the back office of my site for a quick check. Now I wish I hadn't.

*Reviewer - Waste of time. Don't bother. I signed up and kept getting error messages before it even gave me a match. It's a scam.*

A line of perspiration beads on my lower back. With all the organic traffic on my app yesterday, I had an influx of men. The men were matching, taking the woman out of the match portal. There are *no women left*. Men are getting error messages. This has never happened before. I've always had enough people to at least give them one match to keep them busy chatting.

*What am I going to do? I don't have time to find more women. I promised Christian I'd come back to the store to help him. If Dad were here, I could send him out. He doesn't come home until tomorrow. By then I could have more bad reviews!*

A horrible thought creeps into my brain.

I can make a fake profile and chat with these men until I get more women.

Should I?

I inhale deeply, weighing that option. It's not the right option. It can backfire in the worst way. But then again, how will anyone find out? A lump rises in my throat, but I swallow it down. I'm not scamming people. That's not what my company stands for. I would rather the app goes on hiatus for a few weeks than do that.

But if it went on hiatus, I might not be able to redeem it. I might get so many bad reviews it would never recover. Not to mention, this is my time to fly this ship. Yeah, I know ships don't fly. Sail it. Whatever. I need this app. I sank all my savings into it. It's my one shot at becoming financially independent and finding freedom from my drudgery at the coffee shop.

Sure, Dad can give me money until I find something else. I don't want to do that anymore. I'm nearly thirty. There's something about being thirty and needing to ask your dad for rent money that feels dehumanizing.

My app flashes another error message. Someone tried to match, and it didn't work. It is Thursday, one of our busier days, as people match for the weekend. I stare at my wall, feeling as if the room is shrinking, closing in on me. This is bad. I must figure something out.

Without thinking twice—I don't have time for guilt—I go to the new client scene, racing to create a profile. Yep, my mind is made up. I must save all my hard work.

I don't need to lie, because it doesn't ask for my name or photo. I quickly select preferences from the drop-down menus of what I'm looking for.

Male.

Career oriented.

Family values.

Good looks.

Kind-hearted.

That got me into the portal, where there are a series of more detailed questions to narrow down the search. I don't narrow it down. I want to match with as many men as possible to keep them on my app until I can get real women.

Sweat pools in the center of my palms by the time I click the Match Me button. A heart thumps on the screen while it finds my matches, and I let out a heavy breath.

I can't believe I'm doing this.

But what choice do I have?

Just this once, because Dad's out of town, and I don't have any time to get ahead. If this doesn't qualify as an emergency, then I don't know what does.

The screen switches to one that looks like a Guess Who board, filling each square with a match. Twelve! I matched with twelve. That's good. Not enough. There's still going to be some men who won't get matches.

Why did this have to happen now?

My computer chimes with a message!

*Already?*

Boy, that was fast. Now I must message back.

What am I going to say?

Forget what!

*I need to leave before Christian gets even madder at me.*

Oops, another chime.

And another.

My adrenaline surges all the way to my neck. I can't chat with all these men! What did I just do? I opened a tsunami of ethical issues.

A knot in my throat swells, making it hard for me to breathe. If I tell all these men I'm too busy to chat, they will want another match at some point. All this did was buy me a little time. Not much time. This can't be happening!

The lump in my throat pulsates, but this time when I try to swallow it down, it lodges tight, not budging.

Everything I have worked for this last year and all the savings I dumped into this app flash through my mind. If I don't get the ratio balanced soon, I'll be inundated with bad reviews. Reviews that stay online *forever.* My app is too new to absorb all those bad reviews. I'll be buried by them.

I want so badly to yank my hair because I'm frustrated. Instead, I scream out, overwhelmed as tears flood my eyes.

Don't panic. I breathe into a new thought. I must stay positive.

I didn't make it this far to fail now.

I quickly swap my status to say I'm interested in chatting but busy. Then I race to the coffee shop, vowing to respond to all of the messages in between customers.

# Fifteen
## Christian

With my gaze pinned to the floor—thanks to this lovely new back hunch—I hobble out of my office into the lobby and brace a hand on the wall. "What did I miss?"

One of Arielle's penciled on brows rises above the other. "Absolutely nothing. This place is a dive."

"Thanks, sis."

"I watched a ton of YouTube videos teaching me how to make these coffees. Oh!" She flashes a jug at me. "Which reminds me, you're down to your last almond milk."

"So, let me get this straight. Not only are you not making any money, but you are using all my resources. Perfect."

"Well, I have to practice somehow. I had two lattes already, and I'm buzzed. I think you should try one of these almond milk lattes." She points to the nutrition label on the side of the jug. "Look at how much less sugar it has. It's a lot better for your insulin levels. It may help stabilize your mood."

"Nothing's wrong with my mood, or my insulin." I scoff. If I could walk, I would run over there, grab that jug and chuck it to prove my point. I don't need anything special to help my mood. I'm not moody. She's moody. Why is she even talking about moods? "Are you a doctor now?"

Arielle backed up against the counter, lifting herself to sit directly on it, with her feet hanging down. I glare at her. "Nobody wants your butt on the place you put their drink."

She cringes, muttering, "Almond milk will fix your mood," as she slides off the counter. "How is your back?" My heart tanks to a whole new low as I toss a discreet glare out the front door, watching the people walk *past* without even looking inside. "Fine."

"You're not fine." Arielle tilted her head, giving me an angled stare.

"How would you know?" I button my bottom lip, not wanting to leak even the slightest clue that my back is erupting in pain at this very moment.

"I can tell because your brows are beaded together. That lady should be back any minute to help." She checks her watch. "Then you can rest. What did you say her name is?"

I scowl at El. It's absurd she's even suggesting I receive help from someone who was literally running off my customers only moments earlier. Nobody on the planet has that level of patience. "Her name's Portia, and I fired her. She steals all my Oreos and was sabotaging me."

"I hope she doesn't sue you."

My eyes slide side to side as I mull her comment. "What do you mean?"

Arielle readies the espresso machine by wiping off the steamer with a damp rag. "Her dog had an accident on *your* property—"

"Public property," I cut in. "The cop even confirmed the sidewalk is public property, and I have no right to kick her off. Nobody can claim the subway."

"Hmm." She presses the espresso button for shots and pours milk into the steaming cup. "I almost wonder, though, if she couldn't fight that. You know, it's like how you must shovel snow from the sidewalk of your business, but you don't own it. You can get sued if someone slips. Did you notice if the dog was hurt?"

"Nah. It's not icy. It's nothing I did." I shake my head vehemently. "There's no way she can blame this on me. She was trespassing." My thoughts recoil in my head, while Arielle noisily steams the milk. Somewhere in the last hour she taught herself to run that machine fairly well, and I sit back, observing. Maybe Arielle coming to visit wasn't such a bad idea? She can help me work until I can get back on my feet.

Arielle divides the milk into two cups, adds the shots, and seals the cups with their lids. "For your mood." She hands me a cup, tacking on, "Just try it."

I'm famished, craving something to take the edge off my tumultuous morning. One little sip won't hurt. I press my lips to the lid, doing a temperature check. Who knows if Arielle actually knows what she is doing? However, the temp is perfect, and I lift the cup until the first taste meets my tongue, and it is a little liquid heaven. Delicious. So smooth, with a little nutty undertone, giving it a hearty flavor. "That's good."

"Told ya." She takes a long sip of hers before lowering her cup and trapping my eyes in a lock.

"What now?" I eye her cup, remembering how two minutes ago she said she'd had enough coffee, and now she is downing a third latte. She is expensive to keep around.

"She's pretty. I wonder if she's single?"

"No!" I bleep out, but then play dumb. "Who are you even talking about? Who's pretty? Maybe you should go get me some more almond milk since you're drinking all mine, and the delivery truck doesn't come until next week."

She watches me coyly over the lid of her cup while taking a long sip. "I don't have my license."

"What license? You don't need a license to buy almond milk."

"Driver's license. I'll have to take a bus or something. It would be way complicated, especially since I have no idea how this city's laid out."

"There's a grocery store next door. Wait a second . . ." I set my cup down. "How'd you drive here without your license?"

"I never said I drove. You said I drove. I took a cab from the airport."

"Okay. How you'd lose your license?" I study her face. She never lies to me. Not that she hasn't tried, but I can tell because her left eye twitches. It isn't moving now. It's beaming forward, completely unwavering.

"It's kind of dumb, but I had a bunch of parking tickets from parking on the street at school. They were out of parking permits by the time I went to buy one. There wasn't anywhere to park unless I wanted to walk a mile. Apparently, when you don't pay your tickets, you get a court date. I didn't know I had a court date because my car registration went to Dad's address. Since I never call home, he didn't bother to let me know. Since I didn't know, I didn't show."

"You're kidding." Scratching the back of my head, I wonder if I missed some family drama. Neither El, nor I had ever avoided Dad. "Why haven't you called home?"

"No, big reason. I wasn't ready to tell Dad about school, and I knew I could never lie to him."

"He more than likely has figured it out, but he is probably giving you space until you come to him. You know he's not confrontational."

"Right." Her gaze pulls to the floor. "I didn't want to stress him out while I try to figure out my life."

"El, what's going on with you?" Momentarily forgetting that I'm the hunchback of Notre Dame incarnate, I step forward, but immediately halt while I emit a loud hiss and grab my lower back. *Not doing that again.* I'm still concerned about El. "This isn't like you."

"I know." She inhales deeply before pulling her lips to force a lopsided grin. "I lost myself at school, but I'm trying hard to get out of this funk. I need to get away from that town for a while. You know, since it's my hometown. I think I could heal here."

The pressure valve on my headache cranks up to double speed. I'm drowning in this Coffee Loft. I can do that because I only have myself to take care of. I did that on purpose because I have goals. That sounds selfish, but I don't want anyone else to sacrifice the way I'm forcing myself to do. I want so badly to tell Arielle not to worry. She can stay here if she needs to. With zero sales, I don't know how long *I* can stay here.

I can't tell her that.

"It's going to be okay." I pull my lips into a complicit grin. "You can stay here if you need to."

# Sixteen

## Portia

"That's awful, Mom." I take long strides back to the coffee shop with my phone glued to my ear, and I glare at the overcast sky. This winter has been brutal as it dumps snow every day. I hoped to hear my parents had made it home. "I'm sorry the airline is jerking you around like that. You're right to rent a car to drive."

"Yeah, it'll be a long haul, but we're tired of waiting." Mom's surprisingly optimistic tone rings through the phone. "If everything goes well, we should be in late tonight. Is everything still okay there?"

"Yep," I quip as fast as I can. "Everything's . . . excellent."

"Good. Did you and Oliver catch anything this morning?"

Christian flashes in my mind, causing my breath to hitch in my chest. I'm not sure why I'm uneasy. It's something Oliver and I do all the time. What will my parents think when they learn I hurt someone? "Ah, just one guy, but he isn't interested in the site."

"Really?" Mom audibly scoffs. "That's too bad. Well, when we get back, Dad will take you to Home Hardware. That always works."

"Yeah, it sure does." I hover my finger over the End Call button. Leaving out the major details about what I'm really doing brings a wave of nausea to my gut. "Gotta go."

"Love you," Mom sings into the phone.

"Love you, too." I end the call, feeling hopeful about my afternoon at the Coffee Loft. Hopefully Christian is resting, and not monitoring me, because I need to reply to these messages.

The Coffee Loft hardly looks open as I pass through the empty cafe, each table neatly put together without so much as a coffee ring stain. The lights are on, and the soft music station hums in the background, but there is no sign of customers anywhere. I adjust my French press while straining my neck to see behind the counter into the office. "Boy, I really did steal all of your customers," I jokingly call out, still pacing forward before I have eyes on Christian.

A cacophony of crashing sounds explodes from behind the counter, and a few random plastic drink cups roll, followed by Christian's front hair spike slowly peeking over the ledge. His already round eyes swell larger when he sees me. "What is that thing you are holding?"

I halt. Maybe this is a bad idea? "Uh, pardon my French press." I set it down on the table nearest me. "It's my favorite way to make coffee, and if I'm going to work all day, I need a fresh cup."

Christian's narrow face grows even longer as his jaw drops. "I told you Coffee Loft doesn't make French press—"

"Portia!" Arielle flies out of the backroom, swooping into our conversation, cutting off Christian. She's already standing next to me with an uplifted brow of concern pinned on her face. "We're so glad to have you back." She waves me back behind the counter. "Grab an apron, and I'll make you a drink on the house. We just unpacked the Coffee Loft special blend. You have to try it. It will make you toss your French press for good."

Christian's mouth flaps open. "You—"

Arielle gives him a stony glare and speaks over him. "Christian's been telling me how awful he feels about letting you go. It's been a big misunderstanding. He's truly ecstatic for the second chance." She breezes behind the counter. As she walks past Christian, she places her hand on his jaw, physically closing his gaping mouth. He doesn't crack a smile, but I stifle a giggle.

"What would you like to drink?" She positions herself behind the bar, hand hovering over the stacks of cups, waiting for my instructions.

"Ah, it's fine. I can use my French press."

Christian's head jerks back, as he immediately goes off balance, lifting his foot. My guess is Arielle stomped on it because his voice squawks as he grumbles, "No, I insist. You're helping. It's the least I could do to *pay* for your drinks."

Giving up, I guess I could try their *special* blend. "Let's do a skinny, cinnamon dulce, half-caff since it's afternoon already."

"Absolutely." She snatches the large cup—the one we call Lofty—and sets it on the counter. "That's Christian's favorite flavor. You two have so much in common. I can already tell you'll get along fine now that everything is behind you."

Christian robotically pivots, hunching over as if gravity is too strong for him to fight. He silently hobbles to his office, and pulls the door closed behind him. Another cacophony of noise rumbles out from behind his closed door. Arielle pauses, locking her eyes on me, and giggles. "He takes some warming up, but I promise he'll be fine once you get past this stage. What kind of schedule do you like?"

I meander up to the bar, waiting for my coffee. "How about a shift when Christian isn't here?"

"If you want to open tomorrow, that would be great. I was going to do it, but I would love to sleep in. I hate morning shifts." She presses the lid on my cup and hands it to me over the bar.

"Thank you." I receive the drink. "That's perfect."

"Christian changed the code for the keypad, but I'll text you the new one." She waves her hand over the coffee brewing station. "Everything else should be the same."

"Sounds good."

"Alright, if you are okay here then, I might slip out and run to the drug store to get Christian some pain meds." She flashes her hand up. "Unless you need anything?"

I can't believe I'm about to work for Christian, but I don't want him to retaliate against Oliver. "I should be fine."

"Sounds good." She spins on her heel, heading toward the door. "I'll see you in a jiffy."

"Absolutely." I wave my hand, knowing fully well Christian's head will explode if he sees me running this place alone. I stare at his closed office door. It's clear he's staying locked in there as long as I'm here. My gaze paces the lobby, and there's no one here.

That's probably my fault since most of my customers confessed to staying away since I was fired.

I smash my lips into a thinking cinch while pulling out my phone to stare at my app.

Might as well chat with these guys.

I have about a dozen choices. Since I'm only at level one, I can't see any photos or even their names. Nobody sticks out over the others. That's one of the features I built into the app. Scrolling for something to stand out, a message pops up from one of them, and I tap on it.

**Heyyyyyy Profile 421! How are you? Fun fact. The more Ys people have in their greeting, the more interesting they are.**

I snicker at the cheesy joke that reminds me of my dad's jokes and reply.

**He**

I press send and drum my fingers along the counter, waiting to see if this dude has a sense of humor.

After several minutes of no reply, Arielle breezes back through the door with a grocery sack. "See, I told you I would be fast."

I stuff my phone in my apron pocket, and slap on a cheery smile. "You didn't miss anything."

"He's not that bad." Arielle's peacock blue eyes trace the closed office door. "He's under a lot of pressure with the Coffee Loft and family stuff. Underneath this moody facade, he's got a heart of gold."

I sputter out a cough, then throw my fist in front of my mouth to fake another cough, covering up my ill reaction to her description of her brother. *Nobody with a heart of gold fires someone on Christmas Eve.* "You don't have to explain anything on his behalf."

"That's the thing." She unpacks the milk cartons, stowing them in the fridge. "I think I do. I'm not making excuses." She shakes her head as if she's rejecting shame. "What he did to you was terrible.

I don't agree with it at all, and I intend to help him see that he was wrong. He's been in this hating people stage for a while." Lifting both shoulders up, she pauses while she takes a deep breath and exhales out the last part, "ever since our mother died."

"Oh." I pin a stoic expression on my face, unsure why I need to know about Christian's personal issues. I'm not insensitive, but it's clear we aren't friends. Still, I'm not one to be rude when someone is opening up to me. I keep the conversation going. "Sorry to hear that. Was it recent?"

"No." She pulls one side of her lips up into a disgruntled expression. "Like almost twenty years now. I barely remember her, and we each dealt with it differently. Seeing how short life was made me want to live life to the fullest. Christian had the opposite reaction, swearing off people. He'll never admit it, but it's an act. He's afraid to get close to anyone because he doesn't want to get hurt. I almost think the worse he treats someone, it's like an inverse barometer to gauge how much he could like you."

"Well, then he must love me," I sarcastically belt out, ready to laugh until my stomach hurt but Arielle's expression didn't waver from her serious one. "What?" I ask in my cynical tone.

"It's not love, but I definitely would say you have an effect on him."

Ice runs through my veins, and I sputter out another cough. I must be coming down with something. I didn't expect her to reply so thoughtfully, as I had been joking. Swallowing, as the mere suggestion of Christian not hating me made me queasy, I push the idea out of my head, redirecting my sights to the lobby.

Nobody here.

"Are you hungry?" Arielle shoves the grocery bag in the trash and pulls out her own phone. "Today has been crazy. I got Christian some pain meds. They'd be better on a full stomach. Can you stay for pizza if I order it? Christian's treat."

She paces to the office, cracks open the door all the while still scrolling on her phone. "You should treat us to some pizza since nobody ate today."

I don't see him from my spot behind the counter, but I can hear his forlorn reply. "That sounds like a terrible idea."

"You need to take some meds, and you shouldn't take those on an empty stomach."

"It won't be empty. I have two ketchup packets in my wallet I'm saving for tonight," he grumbles from behind the crack in the door.

I snicker and look away. I get he hurt his back *but come on!*

"Christian. This is important." Arielle steps inside the door, closing it almost all the way. Harsh whispers bicker back and forth until I hear Christian's gruff sigh.

"I *guess,* I can order pizza from that place across the street," he mutters. "It's just pizza. *And my sanity.*"

"I can run over there and grab it." Arielle offers as she tugs open the office door, heading out the exit before Christian has a chance to rebuttal. "I'll be back."

About half an hour later, Arielle returns with a single box of pizza. "I didn't realize that place closes so early. I got the last one." She sets the grease-soaked box on the counter. "I hope you like plain cheese, because that's all they had."

"That's fine." I'm so hungry I could eat the whole pizza myself, but I didn't tell her that.

She helps herself to plates and dishes out slices of pizza, handing one to me and then sets two more on a table, and calls out to Christian who is still locked up in his office. "Pizza's on the table!"

We stare at the door as it slowly creeps open, and Christian emerges with a polite nod to her while he hobbles over. "Tell me something." His gaze catches on mine. "Is this place always this dead?"

"Not when I worked." I stare at my pizza on the plate in front of me, waiting for him to connect the dots.

"Do you know what happened to my customers?" Christian lowers himself softly to the chair. I don't tell him that chair tends to be unstable. The old owner did nothing to repair this place.

"They might have been staying away after I told them you fired me."

"That's interesting." He shoots a stern look at Arielle, but she returns it even harder.

He lifts one foot with a quick jerking motion, plopping it on the chair in front of him as he folds his pizza in half like a true New

Yorker, even though he's from Massachusetts. A cheese tail dangles in front of him as he breaks off his first bite. Drool puddles in my mouth, and I dig into my own slice.

After chewing, he dabs the corner of his mouth with a napkin and resumes conversation. "How did you contact them?"

I swallow my pizza and lick the dot of sauce that leaked onto my lip. "The old owner never had a system in place for ordering online. He's old school. I give my customers my number to text an order for pickup, and I *might* have replied back to all their messages letting them know I was fired."

"Hmm." His gaze zeroes in on me, while still shoveling pizza in the side of his mouth. Even in the dimly lit room, the silverish gray inflections in his eyes sparkle with honest interest. "You don't say." Christian finishes his last bite of pizza, picks up his second slice, and holds it in the air in pause while he talks. "So, do you think you can ask them to return?"

"I didn't tell them to leave. They just did that on their own."

With no change of expression, Christian drops his tone. "I'll be honest I assumed you did something to run them all off."

"That was all on them." I wanted so badly to bat my eyelashes the way I normally do when conversations get hard, but he is holding my gaze so steadily, I didn't dare flinch. "I'm really good at this job and they were being loyal."

Christian blinks a couple of times before his gaze slides to Arielle, who hasn't touched her pizza. She is typing on her phone. "El," he verbally pokes her. "You're the one who wanted the pizza, and you're not eating."

"What did you say?" Her top row of even teeth pinches her bottom lip. "I forgot we had food."

"That's my point exactly." Christian and I chuckle in unison as he jerks his thumb toward the door. "We'd better get out of here. It's getting late." He digs in his pocket, retrieving his key ring with a rental car tag still on it.

"Thanks for helping today!" Arielle smiles sweetly at me while grabbing the dishes we used and sliding them into the sink. She takes her untouched pizza off her plate, folding it in half, and biting it as she moves toward the door. "We'll see you again tomorrow. You are still going to open for me, right?"

"Sure." My phone vibrates, and I raise an eyebrow toward the screen.

**Dad: They closed the interstate, but we pulled off in time to get one of the last hotel rooms. We are fine. Hope you are, too.**

Rolling my bottom lip, I ponder. If Dad heard I went back to work here, he'd be concerned. They already have enough stress on their plate, and I didn't want to give them more stress. I text,

**Me: That's too bad. Don't worry about me. Everything is fine.**

I drop my phone in my pocket and look up, expecting to see the door shutting as they left in front of me. Instead, Christian is lingering behind with his eyes fixed on me. "Everything okay?"

"Yeah." My brows furrow together briefly. "Just my parents. They're supposed to drive home, but there's a weather delay. Nothing serious."

"That's too bad." He props the door open with his foot, not letting it close. "I noticed you walk here. Did you need a ride home?"

Normally, I'd say no because I like to hand out QR cards on my way home, but I'm anxious to get home fast to reply to all my messages. A ride would save me twenty minutes. "Yeah, I'll take one, if you're going that way."

"Come with us," Arielle waves me forward, and I pass through the door, falling in step with them.

"Thanks for dinner, by the way," I say to make conversation before adding, "That was nice of you." Alarmed, I check behind me. Where did that come from? Christian isn't nice. Those two words can never be in the same sentence. He's not capable of being nice. He's an incorrigible jerk I can't stand. I'm only here so Oliver doesn't get in trouble.

My brow bends slightly, not into a full furrow as I'm cautious about how my face flexes now that I'm almost thirty. I recall Arielle explaining Christian's mood is a guard.

*Or is he nice?*

# Seventeen

## Christian

I take the tiniest step, about to make a joke about my granny speed when my lips cringe into a pained wince. Everything about my situation is horrendous. I hate being in pain. I hate being weak. I hate relying on people to help me. "Sorry, I'm slow," I grumble. "This happens to my back sometimes."

Portia lingers behind me. "I'm sure you'll be okay."

I use all my strength to stand up straight as I have no desire to be vulnerable in front of her. This morning, she was doing everything she could to destroy my livelihood. She isn't my ally. I'm only being nice to her because I need her to train El.

I pace to my side of the car, climb in, crank the engine while El jumps in shotgun, and Portia crawls in back. El reaches forward, rapidly switching the radio station, giving each station only a second to test before pressing the button again. It's something she's always done while I drive. It used to drive me into mocha madness, the way she pretended she owned my car. After not having spent

much time with her this last year, it brings a wave of nostalgia. I
miss spending time with her. She is quirky, doing things to bring
me out of my need for control.

My nostalgia is short lived, lasting until she parks the setting on
the latest hip-hop station and blasting back beats pound out of my
speakers. Immediately, her duck lips glue to her face, and she bobs
her head as if she is unsuccessfully trying to stretch a kink out of
her neck. I shift the gear, pulling forward as the pressure in the back
of my head swells. "Not happening." I push the "off" button and
tighten my grip on the steering wheel. "I've had this headache for
days, and that doesn't help."

She whistles, imitating a bomb being dropped.

"You have no idea the stress I'm under. I need some peace and
quiet."

"You get enough quiet sitting at the Coffee Loft all day."

That stings, but I choose to ignore it. "Portia, what's your address?" I don't even glance in the rearview mirror as I wait for a
reply from the backseat.

"I'm on Yellowstone Boulevard. Right around the corner from
the Coffee Loft."

"Nice." I purse my lips in thought. I know the exact location.
It's prime real estate next to the Long Island Railroad with plenty
of commercial amenities, and a perfect view of Manhattan to the
west. "Do you own?"

"Rent."

I glance at El. She's texting on her phone. Her chest rises gradually, falling even slower. Something's clearly up with her, but I'm
not in the mood to talk. I drive forward.

"Right here." Portia points to a driveway after a few minutes, and I pull in, and jerk to a stop in the spot closest to the door.

I stare forward at the multilevel building and gamble with a guess. "Are you on the bottom floor?"

"Nope." She pops the P. "Tenth floor."

"Elevator?" My back twitches just thinking about all those steps.

"It's under construction." She props her door open and drops one foot on the pavement. "Thanks for the ride." Her voice softens, and she adds, "I hope you feel better."

I rub my eye. That's not what I expected to hear. Contrary to what Portia may think, I'm not a jerk, but I didn't think we were being that nice to each other. While dropping a heavy sigh, I force a smile. "Thank you."

# Eighteen

## Christian

I walk El inside the hotel, both hands stuffed in my pockets as I'm concerned about her. She's typing on her phone, and I see that dumb dating site open. "Chatting with random people on the internet is dangerous. You never know who you are talking to, especially since that site doesn't verify personal info. You'd better not be pretending to be me."

"It's fun." Her breezy laugh brushes away any concern. "I'm vetting the women for you. There really isn't much on there, but there's this one who has the same sense of humor as you."

"I didn't ask you to do that. It's dumb. Make your own profile if you love it so much."

Her voice dips off as her gaze focuses on the ground ahead of her feet. "I'm not ready for that."

Being nearly ten years apart in age, El and I never had the classic sibling rivalry of closely spaced siblings. When she was growing up, I always protected her. We talk honestly about everything. However, things had changed this last year with her at university. I get it. At some point you want to find your own way. I'm conservative, and she considers me, "too serious." I'm not going to pry. Instead, I offer encouragement. "So, you said before I don't need to beat anybody up. How about blackmail?"

She doesn't even twitch a smile. "Trust me, I've thought about it, but I don't think it will help."

"That's good you're keeping perspective. Do you think it'll help to give up on school?"

She emits a disgruntled sigh, but it doesn't shut down the conversation. "It seems like I quit school because of *him*, but it's really two separate things."

I'm still not sure what *him* she's talking about, but I don't interrupt. She continues, "If school had been right for me, I wouldn't have willingly ditched it so much. I don't see what the point of the expense is. At least for right now, I'd be happy working with you. If you need help at the Coffee Loft." She draws one side of her lips into an unconvincing smile.

A knot scratches at the back of my throat while I mentally inventory my bank account. It's easy to do because it's etched into my brain. A big fat zero balance. I'm starting to consider this Coffee Loft endeavor to be a mistake. I don't bother her with my concern. I reverse the focus back to her. "I finished college before I started this business. No matter what happens with my Coffee Loft, I can always fall back on my MBA. You need to have something to fall back on."

"See, that's where we're different." She holds up an index finger, injecting a point. "Unlike you, I have my good looks to fall back on."

Her dead-serious expression pins on her face, but I instantly crack into laughter. "You may have a point. Beauty over brains." I shake my head at this conversation. "I'm glad you learned the most important stuff while you were at school."

"It's important to explore all of your options, which is why I think you need to try this app—"

I clear my throat, and a sequence of tiny explosions ripples out. "Are you trying to upset me?"

"No, I'm trying to get you to lighten up, but apparently you hate fun."

"I don't hate fun. I don't have time for it." Sneering, I avoid looking at her. "I have responsibilities I can't run away from."

"I see." Her lips purse out while she quietly nods. "Now, we are passive-aggressively insulting."

"Was that passive aggressive?" I cocked my head toward her. "I'm sorry. I meant it to be direct."

"Woah!" She flashes her palm in my face in a stop motion. "Where is this coming from? All this built-up rage. Clearly, you need to do some sugar detoxing. Too much mocha in the mornings."

Determined not to let this conversation turn into a full-fledged argument, I raise my gaze to the heavens and release it. "I'm not arguing about this, El. We are two different people. I don't pressure you to live your life the way I think you should. I would appreciate the same respect."

"I get it," her voice treads softly. "You don't want to be told what to do."

"No, I don't," I affirm as strongly as I can, while we pass through the hotel lobby together. "Thanks for understanding."

"Okay, so what if instead of telling you what to do, I *suggest* something?" There's a distrustful hint of strange blue in her eyes, which I'd only ever seen when she was trying to frame me to get in trouble for something she did.

I narrow my gaze, proceeding with caution. "And what is it that you want to *suggest* I do?"

"For starters, I think you need to offer Portia her job back."

"What?" My eyebrow spikes, and my tone crescendos in annoyance.

"Don't make that face at me," El rushes. "You know I'm right."

"First, I'm not responsible for what my face does when I speak." I steel my face, trying to control it even though I know it's pointless. "And second, no. Why would I do that?"

"Well, to put it bluntly, you were a jerk to fire her at all, let alone at Christmas time, and you're barely managing to walk on two feet. You're really struggling. I don't mind helping, but she's a pro."

"El, it wasn't about me being nice, or a jerk, or whatever. You said it yourself: the Coffee Loft is dead quiet. Even if she was a lovely peach of a person, I don't have the business to keep her there. It was a business decision."

She points a finger gun at me. "Still a jerk, and didn't you notice your customers were her customers first. They will gladly line up to get coffee from her if they knew she's back."

"Who's to say she'd even come back?"

"She'll come back because you're going to beg her to."

I cough out a series of O's, tacking on at the end, "Oh, no, I won't."

"Look." She flicks her hand out in a gesture toward me as we walk into the elevator. "The way I see it, you don't have a choice."

"I fired her to get rid of her—"

"It's the only way." El touches my forearm, giving it a more than endearing squeeze. It was a sibling twist, that reverberated into my gut. "I think she's good for the store, and you need her."

"I thought that's why I had you." I wince as she continues to playfully twist my arm.

"Well, but you can't walk. Now I have the power, and I refuse to help until you make that relationship amiable." Dropping her arm back to her side, she now holds me in an eye lock, that hint of untrustable blue blazes at me. "Plus, she's not that bad. She has the same sarcastic sense of humor you have. If you'd give her a chance, and let that guard down a little, you'd like her."

"Like her? Now you've gone too far!" I snort, raising my chin as the elevator door opens, and I storm out, making a point. There's a bit of a raised ledge where the elevator floor meets the hotel floor, and I miss it, tripping hard. As I struggle to catch my fall, I twist into an expert contortionist move. It mostly works as I don't land on the floor. Except for the jolting pain shooting down my lower back into my tailbone, I'm fine.

"So, you agree." El tracks me like a bloodhound down the hall. "You'll make amends first thing tomorrow."

"I never said that."

"You didn't *not* say that."

"Right. I never *not* said that, but I also never said that, so please don't manipulate my words."

"Good. It's settled."

"Not settled."

"You should bring a gift, too." She taps her chin with her finger. "Something thoughtful."

I make it to our room and flash the keycard in front of the door. I wait for it to open, but the light doesn't shine. I swipe it two more times. "You need to go back to school to be a lawyer."

"We already talked about school. Remember, I'm helping you here."

"You're not being helpful." Finally, the green light flashes, and I'm in my room. It's been a grueling day, and I pace forward until my feet hit the edge of the bed.

She gives me *the* glare. Her secret sauce to get me to do things she wants me to do. Since she has the same almond-shaped eyes our mother had, it infuses my soul with enough guilt to work. She whispers, "Please."

Always a softy for her, I'm done. "Fine." I crash face first onto the pile of unmade blankets, and while El is still rambling on about that person I can't stand, I close my eyes. I'm so ready for this day to be over.

"Oh, Christian." El slides in next to me, pushing the phone close. "You must talk to this one. She's so funny."

"I'm not talking to anyone on that dumb site."

"Just this once, or I won't work in your store tomorrow."

"Is that blackmail?" I open one eye and confirm she's serious. "Fine." I hold out my palm, and she drops my phone in it.

**Me: Heyyyyyy Profile 421! How are you? Fun fact. The more Ys people have in their greeting, the more interesting they are.**

**Profile 421: He**

My head jerks back, and I snicker. That's so cheesy, it's funny.

"What do you want to reply back with?" El's leaning over me, reading the screen.

I push her away as I roll over and sit up. "I'm not showing you."
I hover my thumbs over the screen and think. Something witty.

**Me: Is there an airport nearby, or was that just my heart
taking off?**

**Profile 421: That was an airplane. JFK. I heard it, too.**

**Me: So, you are on Long Island?**

**Profile 421: -es**

I chuckle at the fact she's continuing to leave the Y out. She's
clearly playful. I vow to make her slip up.

**Me: Would you rather ride in a yacht, or camp on the yard?**

**Profile 421: camp**

I bleep out a chuckle, as that was too easy.

**Me: Yogurt or Yams**

**Profile 421: Chocolate**

**Me: That isn't an option.**

**Profile 421: Chocolate is always an option.**

**Me: I got you to slip!!!! There's a y in always!!!!!**

The screen flashes, and a message pops up.

**You have successfully completed your chat. Do you vote to
continue with this person?**

Blinking, I come out of my trance. Somehow, I advanced a level.
It's like a video game. I press, yes, and wait. It appears she's gone
offline. Surprisingly a sting drops into my stomach as I feel a touch
of disappointment. It's okay, though. I'm overtired, and I roll over
on my stomach to sleep. *Only I don't sleep.* Oddly, I smile and
ponder all the Y words I should have used.

The next day, I'm feeling a little better. Yet, I know from experience to take it easy and not jump back into activity. After resting all day, I'm going stir crazy and decide to drive over to pick El up from her closing shift at the Coffee Loft. Pretending I need to grab a deposit bag, I go inside. I don't have a deposit to make, unless we're talking about a bag to put my pride in. Even the bank bag is too big for the minuscule amount of pride I have left.

El walks behind the counter to shut off the espresso machines. I stroll through the lobby, turning off the lights. When I reach the front of the store, I lock the door and inspect the street outside. People are everywhere, driving and walking to all the surrounding stores. Nobody is headed my way.

This place must be invisible.

Rubbing my eyes, hoping to bring some much-needed clarity, I turn back to find El handing me a coffee in a to-go cup. "What's this?" I take the cup while keeping my elbow straight, eyeing the cup from a full arm's length away.

"It's the almond milk, decaf, latte, but I swapped out your usual mocha for the sugar-free cinnamon dolce latte with an extra pump."

"Why would you swap out the sugar?" My voice screeches in horror. *Sugar is the best part!*

"Your mood, Christian. It's out of control." She wags her finger at my cup. "Less judgment. Just try it."

"There's nothing wrong with my mood. It's how I am. Coffee goes in, sarcasm comes out."

"The sarcasm is fine." Tilting her head toward me, she drops her voice as if someone might accidentally overhear, even though the place is empty. "It's that thing you do with your face."

I steel my jaw, resisting the urge to fight. My fingers are aflutter, but I raise my cup to my mouth and tip it back. Smooth. Surprisingly it's the perfect blend of sweet and cinnamon spice on the tip of my tongue, with a rich coffee aftertaste. *So good.* I take an extra swallow because I don't want the taste to stop. When I come up for air, El has her sus glint in her eye again. "What?"

"Somebody was here on behalf of the Chamber of Commerce, selling tickets to a fundraising dinner. I bought us tickets."

"Why?"

"What do you mean why?" Her blinks fire off in rapid succession. "You have no customers, and you are invited to a business social event. You're desperate. So, you go."

"That sounds like the kind of thing you like to attend." I swipe my hand through my hair, not caring that it didn't even tame my front spike. "You can go."

"I can go." She affirmed with a curt nod. "But so can you. It's your business that's failing."

"Thanks for the encouragement." When she doesn't defend her stupid dinner again, I know the glint was about *that other thing*. It's clearly the glint of doom, confirmed by her flashing a look at her smart watch. "We need to run along. It's getting late, and Portia might be going to bed soon." She retrieves another cup from the counter, one with a to-go sticker over the drink hole. "For Portia."

"I'm not giving her free coffee," I mutter, staring at the cup as if it will bite me. "Perhaps I need to explain what running a business is about. You SELL things to make money. If you give away more than you sell, you go broke."

She pushes the cup closer until almost touching my stomach. I take a step of rejection back. "I need to go to the bank."

"You *need* to bring her a gift, too." She floats the drink closer to me, brushing it against my arm, like a giant delicious fly. "Remember, she gets her job back, too."

I narrow my gaze. "You're such a traitor, El."

"It's the only way out of this mess." She dramatically scans the room. "You have no customers until she returns, because they are clearly following her. When she was here, it was busy. Now that she is gone, it's dead." She slowly waves the cup in front of my face like a pendulum she's using to hypnotize me.

I disgruntledly accept the cup from her hand, and spin on my heel. I didn't want to say El made me take it because that makes me look weak—like my little sister controls me—which she clearly doesn't. "Fine. I'll bring her a present, but she's not getting her job back. I'll get her to call off this war *my way*."

Fifteen minutes later, I'm holding Portia's coffee and a plastic grocery sack of almost stale Oreos I'm about to throw out from the Coffee Loft. I brace my lower back with my free hand as I hobble up the cement stairs to Portia's apartment. This isn't even my apartment, but I'm about to call the building manager to complain about the broken elevator. It's a real inconvenience.

About the Oreos. They aren't exactly a "present," as El had tried to force me to bring to Portia. It's me hating to see my money go in the trash, and I can't stand Oreos enough to eat them myself.

My aversion is due to the fact when I was little my grandma forced me to eat the last stale one after getting over the flu. I was barely even able to keep anything down. She gave me one, threatening me not to waste the cookies I forced her to buy me, all while standing over me until I ate the whole thing. Gagging, I stop myself from dry-heaving at the memory, and force my brain to the present. *El is out of her mind to think I'll bring Portia a real present. As if I owe her anything after she stole all my customers.*

"So, ten flights of stairs, huh?"

"Yep," El quips as she bounces joyfully up each stair.

"What is she, Rapunzel?" I grunt and dig deep into my core as I put one foot in front of the other, making it up the first flight with *ease.* The uneasy part came on the next flight, where I sucked in so much air I should have floated up. Turns out, it doesn't work like that. All that air inhaled, and I'm not any lighter.

This is absurd.

Did we get invited?

Nope.

Do I feel super weird?

Yes.

"I'm sure she's resting," I argue, completely annoyed El convinced me to come here.

"I told her we'll stop over." She pulls her ash blonde hair back over her shoulder and looks back at me. "I think you two need to talk things out."

"Almost there," I grunt out, rounding the last corner of the final set of stairs. I clearly need to work out more. In times like this, my lack of athleticism is a tad embarrassing. In my defense, I wasn't warned. I struggle between holding my breath and pulling in so much air, that I sound like a plugged vacuum. "Here!" I pant out as soon as my foot crests the top step. "We made it." I brace my hands above my knees and breathe. *Oh man. Life is so good when you are on flat land.* I trudge forward, leading the way to Portia's apartment door, lifting my fist to knock. I plan to knock so lightly that there's no way she hears us. I'll confirm she's sleeping, and we can leave.

It's a genius plan.

I reach her door and lightly scratch on the surface while holding my breath. *Well, looks like no one is home, or she's resting.* I hook the bag of Oreos on the doorknob, and set the cup in front of the door, careful not to make even the slightest peep. Snickering about how lucky I am that she didn't hear me, I tiptoe toward the steps. This is too easy. Now, to make it down the stairs. I slide my toes down the first stair, a sly smile growing on my face while I brace my back again.

I made the mistake of not checking my blind spot and out of the corner of my eye I see El is not following me, but rather, she's loudly pounding on the door. "Portia! Are you still awake!"

"Shh!" My hands curl into fists, and they shake as I pivot and scowl at her. "You're going to wake her with all that noise!"

As soon as the door cracks, I'm greeted by someone. Well, let's call it a some*beast*. A giant dog heaves across the hall, knocking over the coffee, only to pop off the lid, spilling it. He doesn't slow until he jumps on me and licks my cheek. He's friendly. That's amazing. "Ah, you have a dog." Struggling to hold him off me, I pinch my lips together as it won't take long for my allergies to kick in. As I push him off, I recognize him to be the same beast who broke my back, and I tense up.

"Oh, shoot, Oliver!" Portia lunges forward, grabbing his collar, but he barks rapidly trying to free himself from her grasp. I barely hear her explain over the barking, "I walked him, and his owner isn't home again. I'm holding him here until she gets back. This is so unlike him. He normally doesn't approach anyone unless I direct him too."

"Shreeeeeek!" A horrendous squealing noise wails from inside her apartment, and we all pivot to look inside. Portia leans in, quirking an eyebrow, quickly scanning inside. Panic reflects in her eyes. "Mr. Noodles is gone!" She spins in a circle, but when that doesn't bring her relief, she runs to the window. It's cracked at the bottom; the linen curtain blows slightly from the light breeze. "Oliver!" She calls as her head whips in all directions, scanning the street. "Your barking scared Mr. Noodles into jumping out of the window! He's running down the fire escape, and he's headed into traffic! We have to get him."

I don't even know who Mr. Noodles is. Apparently, Oliver does, because as soon as Portia accuses him, he turns his gaze, refusing to engage Portia. "Look at that." She aims her finger toward him as he cowers against the wall. "He knows he's guilty."

"He sure does look guilty." I fight the urge to slide my foot back. This is turning into a bit of a circus. I don't have time to look for Mr. Noodles. I don't even know what that is. Oh boy, she has tears in her eyes. "It's f-fine." I stutter out. "He'll fly back."

"He's not a bird," she sniffs out. "It's my cat. He's been with me ever since I moved out on my own. He's not an outside cat. He can't survive out there." Her shoulders tremble, resembling dainty hiccups.

"Oh, no!" El's mouth drops open. "He could die! We have to find him." She's staring at me with our mother's eyes, and it makes my gut wrench. Before I talk some sense into myself, I open my big, fat mouth. "Let's all split up, and everybody search."

What did I just say?

It echoes in my head, taunting me like a dare I gave myself.

*How am I going to find a cat?*

*I don't even know what he looks like. It's dark out.*

*This woman makes my blood boil.*

*Now I'm going to waste my time looking for a dumb cat?*

*How about I tape my mouth shut instead?*

*That would be better than this!*

"Are you sure?" Portia's gaze cements on mine—hope buds in her irises. "I feel bad. Are you even feeling better?"

"Suuuure." My voice pitches higher at the end as I mentally prepare for what I'm about to do. "It's not a problem. Let's keep the dog here so he doesn't scare it away again." I motion inside, and glare at the beast and catch sight of something on the nightstand. A 5x7 framed photo of a gray cat and her. *Oh, adorbs. A cat selfie, I sarcastically say in my head. And she framed it.* I study the creature. Gray. Cat. Whiskers. Like every gray cat with whiskers. "This should be . . . be really easy." I can't get whole sentences out, as I'm so furious with myself for volunteering, but it's late and she's crying. I can't handle when a woman cries. I glare at El. "You coming?"

"I'll head west, you go east."

"I'll go south." Portia pulls the door closed behind her as she's already heading down the stairs.

"*Sweeeell.*" I force my lips into a toothy grin. "I better get going too. It *is* rather late." I screech, the highest octave my voice has ever hit. I'm a bit amazed I even have that range. *It's clearly a hidden talent I didn't even know I had. I could totally take on one of those singing competition shows and win the whole thing. Then I can give up my failed Coffee Loft, living the dream on a yacht in the Caribbean—*

"Christian," her soft voice cuts my daydream spiral off, pulling me back to her.

I was afraid to ask, but against my better judgment I whispered out in fear. "What do you need?"

"Thank you." The tiniest smile curls on her lips. It is the first genuine smile I've seen on her face, and I can't stop staring at it. Her lips are cotton candy pink. A dimple sits right above her chin. A perfect little button of happiness— *What is wrong with me?* I jolt my head back, shaking myself out of this insanity. It's already been a loooong day.

"Yeah, whatever," I grumble as I wave goodbye and struggle to keep pace with her while descending the steps. "Don't worry about anything. One of us must find him."

Portia takes off way ahead of me, but leaves me with a burning image in my brain of her smiling. Her soft blonde waves frame her face. *She is stunning.*

*When did that happen?*

Feeling a tad feverish, I fan my face and cross the hall. "Great. Now, I'm coming down with something." *Clearly, my stress is making me ill.*

Or is it . . .

# Nineteen

## Portia

I received a text from Christian saying he had found Mr. Noodles, and I ran home at record speed to meet him. He's seriously slow because both Arielle and I beat him to my apartment and made hot chocolate by the time he hobbled up. A single knock sounds on the door, and I whip it open.

"I got your cat," he grumbles. "Now, give me Arielle, and we can leave."

My jaw plummets. He has deep rows of scratches etched into both sides of his face, mimicking sideburns. I size them to match the exact width of Mr. Noodles' claws. Mud cakes his pants all the way up to his knees. I can't even tell what color his shoes are. Mr. Noodles is wrapped in his jacket, and tucked in a ball under his arm with a scowl, clearly unhappy.

"That's not my cat, by the way." Blinking, I tease him. "You can put him back from wherever you got him."

"Not your cat!" he screeches as his face grows scarlet. "I don't care if it's not your cat. He is now. He's gray. He has whiskers. He was in a tree right across the street. I climbed the tree, but he fled before I could grab him. Then I chased him down a muddy alley, all while slipping and sliding to my death. I finally cornered him between a building and a trash can. I had to use my good jacket to restrain him but not before he ripped my face off. I'm not putting him back. I didn't want to agree to any of this." He reaches his hands out, dangling the cat out in front of him. "I'm done!"

Clumsily catching Mr. Noodles, I cradle him next to my chest, and he curls right in. I'm not mean. Christian went through the hassle of finding Mr. Noodles, and I can tell he doesn't think this is funny. "It's my cat. I was joking. Sorry, if that stressed you out more."

"Good!" He bobbles his head while parking both hands on his hips. "I'll leave you two alone then."

"Thank you for everything." My words rush out a little garbled up, and I hope they aren't lost.

He sticks his head into my door, calling out, "El, it's time to leave."

She glides across the room and smiles at me. "Christian needs to talk to you before we leave." She glares at him. "Right?"

Christian clamps down on his bottom lip, pausing for an insanely long time. I actually toss a look back to Arielle to make sure I understood her, but she only nods back to Christian. Finally, when I'm assuming, Christian lost his voice, he burps out, "Do you want your job back?"

Arielle elbows him on the arm. He snorts, pinching his lips together tightly, but sputters out, "*Please.*"

I bat my eyes. "I'd love that."

"Great, have a nice night with Mr. Murder Claws." He turns on his heel and heads straight for the stairs.

"Night." Arielle flashes a wave at me as she pinches back a smile and follows him.

Snuggling Mr. Noodles in my chest tighter, I press a kiss to the top of his head as I shut the door, and head back to my futon, chuckling.

# TWENTY

## Christian

With my hands shoved in my coat, I march up the sidewalk to my store, slowing right before I reach the door. *There are people inside!* I can see them through the window. Not just a couple of people, either. I jerk open the door and plow in, scanning the rows of tables, all filled with customers already served.

It's the very next day after I struck that truce with Portia. I struggle to open my eyes wider, taking long strides to the bar where Portia's steaming milk, a row of six to-go cups lined up ready to fill. Her hair is up in a messy bun on top of her head. She also has a funky wrap headband thing tied around her head. Festive snowflake earrings dangle from each ear, and she has a full smile on her face as she greets me. "Good morning, Christian."

My eyes scan the messy counter dotted with drips of milk in random places and a small pile of spilled coffee grounds underneath the grinder. In the corner, the trash is nearly overflowing with empty milk containers, all evidence she hasn't had even a small break in traffic. Normally, I loathe mess, and hate clutter. After days of everything being nothing but shiny clean, this mess is the most beautiful thing I've ever seen.

*Mess means money! Portia standing in the middle of the mess makes her the most beautiful woman I've ever seen.* "What did you do?"

"I sent a text to all my clients, inviting them back." Portia reaches forward, grabs the mocha sauce and pumps it into a cup. "I explained everything was a mix-up."

I'm at a loss for words. These really are my customers. El was right about bringing Portia back. She brought all my people back with her. A man in a business suit walks up to the counter, his face beaming at Portia. "Glad to see you back," he greets her.

"Good to see you, too, Trey." She beams at him, while adding lids to all the cups, and setting them on the bar for customers waiting off to the side. "Do you want your usual?" she asks over her shoulder, while she grabs the last two cups and places them on the counter for pickup.

"Yeah, please."

I stand back as she goes to the tablet, punching in his order without confirming what it is. He opens his wallet, pulls out a ten-dollar bill, and doesn't wait for change. It's the most beautiful thing I've seen since I arrived.

The door opens and more people file in, lining up. My eyes well with happy tears as I honestly was doubting there were people in this town who drank coffee. What I didn't see was their loyalty to Portia. They hadn't had time to get to know me, or my Coffee Loft.

I thought I had to do this all on my own, building up my dream store. I almost missed out on the best gift of all. Portia is a customer service ninja, taking orders with one hand while waving goodbye to happy customers with the other, calling them all by their first names. I stumble behind her, inserting myself into the happy chaos, ready to fill her orders.

We say nothing about the past awkwardness as we fall into an orderly rhythm of her taking orders, and me making the coffees, all while the traffic pours through the door all morning. It's after eleven before we get our first lull, and I'm able to take two full bags of trash outside. Hugging the bags close to my chest as if they are loving pets, I've never been so happy to haul trash out in my life. I'm humming gleefully on my way back inside, right as Portia unties her apron and stuffs it in the laundry bin.

Dirty aprons and rags! Another delightful sight I want to cry out to heaven in gratitude. It all means I'm finally making money. "That's it for my shift." She grabs the stuffed tip jar and dumps it on the counter, quickly counting the money into two piles.

"Take it all." I place my hand on the pile closest to me and scoot it all into the other pile. "I don't deserve any of this."

She hikes a brow while her hand hovers over the uncounted money. "Are you sure?"

"Yeah, I am." Usually I'm stubborn to admit my mistakes, but I'm so ecstatic to finally see customers that I don't hold back. "I'm truly sorry about everything, and I'm grateful you gave me a second chance."

She scoots all the money off the counter, stacking the bills neatly into a pile. I'm a little jealous as I see a few twenties flash, and by the height of that pile, it looks like it could pay a few bills. Clearly, her customers came out in droves to support her. Humbled, I stay mute as she finishes stowing her money and returns the empty jar to its spot on the bar.

"Arielle gave me part of her morning shift tomorrow, too. Apparently, she's not a morning person, so I'll see you then." She pivots, aiming for the door.

Before I know what I'm doing, I call out, "Wait a minute."

She does the look back. The one you see on hair commercials. With her hair piled high on her head, a few fallen strands framing her face, and she perks a feather bold eyebrow. "What do you need?"

"Ah, just to thank you."

Her lips curl into a brilliant, sassy grin, laced with the perfect balance of joy and attitude. "The pleasure is all mine." When she spins on her heel, I'm left with the impact of her smile, sending aftershocks right to my heart. I grab my chest and press my hand over my heart to steady it's pounding beats. What is going on?

*Maybe El is right about needing to switch to sugar-free lattes? Clearly, this is medical and has nothing to do with Portia.*

# Twenty-One

## Portia

It's nice to have cash in my pocket again, and a work schedule to secure even more. I love the idea of being self-employed with my own match-making business. After this last test run, I'm positive I'm not ready to pull the trigger all the way yet. The website needs more organic growth to sustain steady traffic, and not require full-time recruiting. Until I get to that point, I will proudly wear my Coffee Loft apron.

It's my second opening shift after returning to work. Today is as crazy as yesterday, bringing a steady, enjoyable, fleet of customers. I had also switched the Coffee Shop satellite station back to Christmas music, and that is putting me in the best mood. I'm one of those people who can listen to Christmas music all year round. Since it is still December, with New Year's Eve being tomorrow, I'm going to enjoy all my favorites while I can get away with it.

Humming away, I shine the counters as Christian walks through the front door, an urgency in his stride. His gaze paces the room with a few scattered customers sitting in their booths. A pleased grin grows on his face as he continues to saunter to the back. "Good morning."

"Good morning." I exude a cheery tone after yesterday went off without a hitch, and I consider friendship *possible*. "I thought Arielle was coming in this morning."

"She was supposed to, but she woke up in the middle of the night with some stomach bug. I told her to rest." He scans over my workspace, everything a whole lot tidier than it was yesterday. "Is everything okay?"

"Yeah, it's been great. Steady but not too much that I can't keep up." I jerk my thumb over my shoulder to the back freezer. "I pulled milks already, and everything up here is ready for your shift. Oh!" I hold my hand up, interrupting myself. "Before I forget, you need to add Oreos to your grocery list. I searched all over the last two days, and the pantry is bare."

"Duly noted." His expression is neutral but his gaze slides to my overflowing tip jar on the counter. "Boy, Portia, I'd say you win the tip contest. I've never seen a more crammed jar after a morning rush. How do you do it? Money sure loves you."

I lift my shoulders into a modest shrug. "My dad always says you get what you give. I consider the tips a gauge in how much care I give others."

"You are amazing with people." He walks to the handwashing station and starts pumping soap out of the wall dispenser onto his hand. "So anyway, I have a small issue with El being sick. There's this business after-hours thing on the last Friday of every month. El signed us up and bought two tickets. I guess it's a lot of walking around, and sipping wine while handing out business cards. Since it's between the holidays this month, the chamber organized a charity fundraiser dinner thing instead of the usual business promotion. Honestly, I hate these kinds of things. They are too peoply. But since I'm new to the area, I think she might be right that I need to meet people in town, especially other business owners. Uh, so I'm, uh, thinking."

He stops talking but is still pumping soap. A whole pile of foam engulfs his hand as he evidently isn't paying attention to what he's doing. I giggle as the tower wavers. It's the leaning tower of Palmolive. Likely it's Soft Soap but I was going for the P word. Leaning tower of Soft Soap doesn't have the same ring. Or worse yet, knowing Christian's cheap self, it's a store brand and that would sound even worse.

"So, I hate those people things. I guess, I already said that, but, uh, would you want to go to it, too? You seem like you'll enjoy that sort of thing." Instead of looking at me, he startles as he finally notices the mountain of soap on his hand and quickly turns on the water to rinse it down. It's extra foamy soap, bubbling into a swollen mass that looks as if it's coming alive. He pretends not to notice the bubble plume rise as he shakes the water off his hands. "Of course, you'll get paid. It's a work thing."

"A people event, huh?" Pinching my lips together to stifle my giggles, I force my gaze from the still rising soapsuds, and take my tip jar to sort through my money into a neat pile. Out of the corner of my eye, I see he's splashing water on the bubbles, hopelessly trying to wash them down the drain, but they continue to swell. "Do I get overtime pay?"

"Ah, sure." He clicks his heels together, standing up straight next to the soap pile, his eyes not acknowledging anything amiss.

I can't hold it back anymore and I burst out laughing. "What are you doing?"

Nervous laughter trickles from his lips, and he squawks, "These bubbles have a mind of their own!"

"Only because you pumped the whole bottle! You were completely zoned out." I chuckle again, enjoying how easy it is to joke with him today. "You almost need a mop bucket." I reset my tip jar, stuffing my money into my purse, keeping my gaze low. "What time is the dinner?"

"Ah, the social is at five. I'll shut the doors a little early here."

I strap my purse on my shoulder and take a few strides toward the door. As I push the door open, I flash back a smile. "You know where to pick me up." I catch his expression right as he absorbs my words and his lips bend into a winning smile.

I proceed to stroll through the door, and enter the rare winter sunshine, analyzing what happened. I get that Christian is wanting help for his event, but he wouldn't ask me to go if he still hated me, right? And if he didn't want to hang out with me, he'd probably pay me to go *without* him. Maybe I'm reading into this a little too much, but when I think about how awkward he was when he asked, he was nervous. A quibble bubbles in my gut. Why would he be nervous unless he cared how I'd reply?

My phone vibrates in my coat pocket, and I pull it out. "Hey, Dad."

"Sweetheart, how are you?"

"Good, actually." I walk briskly at a New Yorker's pace down the sidewalk toward my apartment. "I got my job back at the Coffee Loft, and finished a shift."

"See?" He chuckles his good-natured laugh. "I knew that loser would come to his senses."

"Tell me you guys are finally home safe?"

"We are home and ready to report for duty. Do you want to go to the Home Hardware tonight?"

"I would, but I can't. Christian asked me to do this charity fundraiser dinner for work."

"Interesting. Boy, it seems that Christian fellow changed his tune, giving you your job back, and having you do this. What do you think changed?"

I trap my bottom lip with my teeth, weighing the option to confess what happened. Now that Dad is home safe, I don't see a reason to hide the truth anymore. "Well, it is sort of weird, but Oliver jumped on him the other day, and made him fall down the subway. I didn't want to bother you with the stress while you were trapped out of town. Christian spent a couple of days laid up, and I didn't want Oliver to get in trouble, so I helped. I think we both realized we got off to a bad start. So, yeah, and so far, it's . . . "

I pause giving Dad time to chime in, but he is quiet, so I say, "Dad, you still there?"

"I'm here." He huffs into the phone. "Sounds suspicious."

"It's not sus. His business is failing since I took all his customers, and like I said, we're starting over."

"That's not how things usually work."

"What do you mean?"

"He's up to something. Playing a game, or he likes you. I'm going to have to meet him. Do you work tomorrow?"

"Dad," I rush to cut him off. "You're always welcome to visit me, but there's no reason you need to meet him, other than he's my boss." My cheeks heat, despite my denial.

"You didn't answer my question. Do you work tomorrow?"

"I close, so I'll be there until seven."

"Then I will, too."

"Dad—"

"Love you."

I flash my eyes heavenward and blow out a breath. "Love you, too." He'd already ended the call. I stuff my phone back into my coat pocket, focusing on my walk with a new smile on my face. What if Dad is right?

# TWENTY-TWO

## Christian

I hike the stairs to Portia's apartment with frustration over her broken elevator simmering up. I don't even live in this building, and I'm about to start looking for a new apartment. This is getting ridiculous. I brace my still-tender lower back and slay another flight.

Something is going on with my chest. It started on the drive over here. Adrenaline surged and it's been hours since my last coffee. Despite my attempts to practice measured breathing, my heart rate won't slow. Evidently, the stress of the last few days has now given me a heart condition.

I stop on the top landing, supporting my hands above my knees, panting. This must be the *last time* I climb those stairs to Portia's Rapunzel tower. I adjust my jacket collar to let in some air. It's supposed to be a nice night for December, staying way above freezing. I hadn't packed much other than work clothes when I arrived on Long Island. I knew I wouldn't have space to store anything, nor did I have plans to do anything but work. Something told me a Coffee Loft apron isn't appropriate for this event. I managed to find a red-collared shirt at a clothing store down the street, and it only set me back forty-five bucks. I hate spending money on clothes, or rather anything other than my bills, but I did it. I smooth down the front, before resuming my route to Portia's apartment, knocking firmly on the wood door.

Portia appears, wearing a smokey blue dress that sets off a fire of blue sparkles in her eyes. Now that she is not glaring at me about a missing French press, I find her eyes enjoyable to look into. No words are needed from me. I'm fine, just standing here.

"Hey, you." Portia's lips are accentuated by a rosy lip shade, a color she doesn't wear to the Coffee Loft. She pins on a grin. This isn't her malicious smile, the one that despises me, or her forced one. This one lingers, setting off another series of sparkles in her eyes, making it feel extra special—like a *date* smile.

"Hey." I prop one hand on the door frame, leaning in. I hadn't asked her to come for any other reason than to help me network, but with the way she's looking at me . . . "How's it going?" I wince as I should say something more charming than that!

"Good." She passes through the door, locking it behind her, and we set off together back down the stairs.

"I'm getting in great shape from running up and down these stairs," I say, easing into conversation.

"It's been an adjustment." One of her hands slides down the rail while the other secures a petite clutch in front of her. "But actually, I did see guys working on the elevator today. Maybe if everything goes well, I'll have a functioning elevator before I need a walker."

"I'm ready to complain for you. I'll keep my fingers crossed that it's completed soon." We round the first landing of stairs and start on the next flight. I'm trying hard not to support my back as I don't want to look weak in front of her. Actually, it's a lot better than it was a few days ago. Things are looking up.

Now, if I can meet the right people tonight, maybe even some event coordinators, who can become regular clients for large catering, I can start to get my name out there. That will be perfect.

"You seem to be feeling much better." She keeps the conversation rolling.

"Yes." I give a nod. "The first day was the absolute worst, but each day has been better, and now I barely even notice it except for a few random spasms."

We settle into a comfortable silence as I descend the stairs one stair above her, counting off each flight in my head. When we reach my car, she rushes to open the door for herself. It's a tad awkward as this isn't a date, but my mother raised me right, and I prefer to do that for her. I stand back, waiting for her to lift her feet inside the car, and close the door. Then I hop in my side of the car, crank the engine, and pull onto the road.

"Was it busy after I left the shop?" Portia leans on the door armrest, taking an angled look back at me.

"Not too bad. I had a few larger tables, and they kept me busy. Since you had everything stocked, there wasn't much to do. I locked up early and called to check on El. She's okay, for having the flu."

"I love how you call her El." She gestures toward me casually. "I sort of want to do that, too, but she hasn't said it's okay. Is it an exclusive nickname?"

"I don't think exclusive nicknames are a thing. It's what she's always been to me."

"Interesting." She purses her lips, but I can tell she's not done with the questions. Women never are. "You two seem close," she adds.

"We can be." I grip the steering wheel tighter, pondering how much of my personal life I want to tell her. The thing is, El is chatty, the kind of person who has never met a stranger. I assume El had already told Portia my entire life story. That's the one thing I hate about El. There're always two sides to every pancake, and she only ever shares her side. Sometimes she doesn't paint me in the best light. "I don't know how much El's told you, but we mostly had our dad and grandmother to raise us. Dad worked in our family construction business with my grandparents, so we all were together a lot."

"I don't recall the family business mentioned. That almost sounds like an ideal childhood, in some ways."

"Don't get me wrong, I'm glad I had that experience, but I always knew it wasn't something I wanted to do with my life. There's been a lot of drama since I chose Coffee Loft as a career. But then again," I shrug, new tension pooling in the back of my neck from the mere thought of my family, "Isn't there always drama with family?"

"Not for me." Portia's eyes light up. "My parents are my rock, especially my dad. He is overly supportive of me." She giggles, covering her mouth with her hand before finally leaking out, "There's no secret that I'm his princess. He'll do anything for me. It was his idea for me to come back and hang out in front of your Coffee Loft after I got fired."

"I do have to hand it to you." I hold up a finger. "As much as I hated you at that moment, looking back, it is quite funny."

She chuckles deviously, her chin lowering. "I only wish I could have gotten your facial expression on video."

"I'm sure it was masterful." I smash my lips together, forcing a serious expression, but it is useless. Inside, I'm dying to share a cathartic laugh after the week I had. I allow a short, sarcastic scoff. I pull into a parking space behind the venue and kill the engine.

Normally, I'd hop out and be all business, but something about the laughter in the car makes me pause. I focus directly on her. "Look at us laughing together. Can you believe we rode in a car together and nobody died?"

"Don't celebrate yet." She laughs an airy flutter before pulling her door handle. "The night is still young."

I swallow, a mixture of anticipation, dread and, oddly, excitement all swirling together in my chest. One thing is for sure, I have no idea what tonight will bring.

# TWENTY-THREE

## Portia

My fingers nervously touch my collarbone as if I'm clutching an invisible string of pearls, while Christian leads me inside the convention room. A winter wonderland greets us, lining a red-carpet walkway with Christmas trees—dotted with sparkling gold lights. A couple dressed in high-society designer labels, with magazine-ready smiles, stand by the entrance, greeting everyone and scanning tickets.

I'm not usually a self-conscious person. Dad had always insisted nobody was better than anybody, drilling that into my head from the time I was young, but I stiffen and instantly feel underdressed. Dragging my feet, I linger back as Christian pulls out his phone, presenting his tickets to the man to be scanned.

When Christian pauses to stow his phone in his pocket, he notices I'm not standing beside him. His brow hikes north. "What's wrong?"

I had assumed this was nothing more than some casual spaghetti dinner thing, and I don't want to be disrespectful. Concealing my mouth with my palm, I whisper, "I should have guessed by the rows of BMWs in the parking lot but I'm feeling a little under-dressed for this."

"Don't." His brows lower into a stern expression, and his voice deepens. "You look perfect."

Blinking, I absorb his compliment, feeling it deep in my gut. We inch forward, my trepidation simmers, and I case the room filled with people. All the women are adorned with full ball gowns, in either a festive red or black satin. I'm glowing in a bad way in my blue day dress. "Relax," Christian whispers to me.

I plaster on a smile and edge further into the room. "What am I doing wrong?"

"You're not doing anything wrong, except you look terrified."

*I feel terrified.*

But I can't admit that.

"I prefer to blend in better."

Nodding toward the doorway, he whispers, "Do you want to leave?"

I'm painfully pining for the exit, but I somehow manage to stutter out, "N-No. We can't do that. You bought those crazy expensive fundraising priced tickets, and we just got here. You need to meet some people."

He takes a step closer, nearly brushing my side as he speaks softly. "If you're uncomfortable here, I don't want to stay."

"It's weird," I speak slowly, surprised I'm confessing my true feelings instead of pretending to be brave. "I'm an expert with people when I'm in my element. Give me a hardware store, or the park, and I never even crack a nerve, but this feels . . ." I blow out a breath, unable to finish my thought as my gaze fixes on a row of model-tall women, all lined up in dresses that were more than likely worth more than all my earthly possessions combined. I search for something to soothe me. Opera music plays in the background, and everybody is eating and drinking with their pinky fingers jutting out. It's so proper—not at all my scene. "Phew. I've never been socially anxious before."

"It stinks. Trust me. It's why I hate these things."

"Here, I thought I was going to be helpful to you." I cringe into an "I'm-sorry smile" and shift my weight from one heel to the other. "Can I tell you the truth?"

"Sure."

"I sort of hate it here already."

Christian's lips spread into a genuine grin. "Did we actually find something we agree on?"

"I think so." I rush to agree, still clutching my imaginary pearls. "Let's bail fast before someone sees us."

Christian scans the room once more, not looking at all disappointed before holding out his arm for me to latch onto. "Let's bust out of this place."

I tuck my arm into his, allowing him to properly escort me out. "Where are we going?" I whisper out of the side of my mouth. Being this close to him brings a whiff of his aftershave that hints of a sea crusted breeze, making me feel lighter on my toes.

"I feel bad I dragged you out, and you didn't even get anything to eat." He tugs on my arm, pulling me faster the closer we get to the door. "I already paid for two hours of parking. What do you say we walk around the block? I saw an Irish pub on the way."

"Sounds good to me." We round the corner in the hall, taking a wrong turn. Instead of finding the hotel exit, we stumble across another event room. A cheery arch of gold and burgundy balloons frames the doorway and laughter wafts from inside the vibrantly lit room. Slowing as we pass in front of the door, I peek inside, and spot a three-tiered cake on a head table with a 'Happy Birthday, Pappi!' gold banner above it.

"That looks cute." I nod toward the room as a lady walks out. She's dressed in her Sunday best, a modest dress, and heels to match. Her hair is piled high into a Marge Simpson bun, and her shining eyes round when they find me. "Alisa! We've been waiting for you."

"Ah." I startle into a stillness. "I'm sorry, you have the wrong person."

She places a hand on my arm, leaning into my ear, and whispers, "I know you aren't Alisa. But please, please, please, if you have any spec of a human heart and ten minutes, can you go along with it? It's my grandpa's birthday, and he's sitting here waiting for his favorite granddaughter. He has dementia and doesn't remember she ran off with her boyfriend. She hasn't spoken to anyone in the family for a year. Please, just give us ten minutes." She folds her hands in prayer, pleading. "I'm afraid he's about to cry. He has terminal cancer, with only months to live, and we want so badly for him to enjoy his party. He refuses until he sees Alisa."

"Ah." I part my lips, feeling how dry they are in the stale air while I glance at Christian.

He offers an encouraging shrug. Talk about shoulders. I love it when he does that. "We don't have anything else to do."

"Okaaay." I take a few steps forward while smoothing my hair. "Do I look all right? What should I say?"

"He's nearly blind. It doesn't really matter what you look like." She extends her arm, ushering me inside the room. "By the way, my name's Ashley and we're best friends and sisters only a year apart. Just be sure to call him Pappi, and maybe joke about how he eats too much ice cream."

"Pappi? Like the pizzeria?"

"Yes, that's him. He's retired but now I run it."

"I work directly across the street from you. What a small world." As this feels a lot like my recruiting skit, I place my recruiting smile on my face and toss a glance at Christian, all the while my heart breaks as I think about this poor man not understanding why his favorite grandchild isn't there on his special day.

"Oh, he can come." Ashley waves him forward. "He's too cute to leave in the hall. Help yourself to some food. Please, make yourself comfortable. This means so much to me."

The three of us enter, simultaneously skirting along the edge of the room until we make it to the head table. A little man with a silver beard and a few long strands of a matching combover, partially concealing a shiny head, hunches over in his chair. His dull gray eyes, devoid of any sparks, stare forward with a forlorn expression.

"Pappi, look who I found outside," Ashley calls out, sparking the man to look our way. As soon as he sees me, his eyes fire a spark of light.

"Alisa!" He reaches forward, waiting for a hug. All the eyes in the room are on me, but nobody moves to act as if I'm out of place. I lean in, giving Pappi a big squeeze. His scent, a mixture of black licorice and oregano, wafts up my nose while I lightly pat his back until I pull away.

A tear buds in the corner of his eyes, and even though I've just met this man, my smile is genuine. "Happy birthday, Pappi!"

"My Alisa." He adds a sweet Italian accent to the s, making it sound utterly adorable. His whole expression has been ignited with life, which warms my heart. "I've been waiting for you all night. How have you been?"

"Better now that I'm here." I'm so touched by the tears forming in his eyes, I grab his hand and squeeze. This feels like a real reunion. "Sorry, I'm late. I had ah . . . a fundraiser for work."

Ashley stands back a few feet, her eyes beaming back at me. Tears are budding in her eyes, too. Most of the people in the room wear hopeful expressions, and all focus this way.

"You sound a little different." His gray eyes continue to sparkle back at me, but they don't look suspicious, rather seeped in joy.

"I'm getting over a cold." I squeeze his hand again. "Tell me, have you had any good ice cream lately?"

"Have I?" He raises both hands, exclaiming gleefully, "They have so many tubs of it here tonight, I could swim in it. Did you get any?"

"Ah, not yet." I blink, clearing my eyes. I'm not expecting to feel this emotion from something so random, but the love in Pappi's eyes radiates out.

His gaze shifts behind me, falling on Christian. "Who's this man with you?"

"Oh, that's just my boss—"

Pappi speaks over me, "—Your boyfriend?"

My gaze locks on Christian's before looking at Ashley, who jerks her head to Christian, waving him forward. "Yes, this is him. It's—"

"*Jack*," Ashley coughs out, adding an extra cough for good measure.

"Jack," I pause, afraid to offer anything more. I wasn't sure what he already knew of Jack.

"Come here, son." Pappi steels his gaze on Christian. "Let me get a good look at you."

Christian steps forward, extending a hand, which Pappi promptly takes and holds on to. "It's an honor to meet you, sir. Alisa talks about you often."

"I can't say it's nice to meet you!" Pappi angles his gaze up at Christian, his brows lowering into a scowl. "You took my grand-daughter away from me and never even asked my permission."

"Woo." Christian's head startles back, but I almost bubble out a giggle. This little man is so cute, and if anyone can handle some pushback, it's Christian. "I, ah, was *scared*. Now, I'm sorry." His voice squeaks at the end, but he pushes through it. "I would love your permission now."

"I don't know if I can give it to you." Pappi shakes his head regretfully. "What do you plan to offer her?"

"Um." Christian blinks twice but holds his gaze steady, not flinching again as he goes on. "Well, I ah, have my own business, and I hope to grow it into an empire someday."

"Ah, hogwash." Pappi's lips pool in the center, as if he's getting ready to spit. "Another lady's man, ladder climber looking for a trophy wife. You want my Alisa because she's beautiful."

"No, sir. I'm not a lady's man. I hardly date at all." Christian rushes out, "And, yes, Por—, *Alisa* is stunning, but I know she's also very caring."

"Of course she's caring. I raised her. Are you a cheater?"

"No, sir. I'm very loyal. Once I commit to something, or someone, I'm all in."

My smile fades because at first, I was giggling over the pressure Pappi put on Christian, but the way Christian is being genuine with him is actually so touching, it's alarming. I cover my heart with my palm and watch.

"This feels rehearsed." Pappi turns his head away from Christian, swapping his joyful-reunion smile to one that's stone cold.

"Trust me." Christian rakes a hand through his hair, his hairline glimmering with perspiration under the fluorescent lighting. "I had no time to rehearse."

"Well, if you can pass the final question, I'll give you my blessing." Pappi rubs his wrinkled hands together, preparing to trick Christian. "Tell me, in your own words, what is love?"

Christian clears his throat. "Love is . . . love is special."

"Ah, I knew it." Pappi raises a hand, shooing him away. "You're full of bologna."

"I am not!" Christian spits back, his voice getting deeper. "I'm not a phony. Let me speak. I said it's special, but it's more than that." His gaze scans the room as if searching for a clue to tell him what to say.

I take a step forward, my heart pounding away in my chest. This is an awkward position for us both to be in. We don't even know this man. I place a hand on his arm and whisper, "It's okay, we can sneak out the fire exit."

"No." He places his hand over mine. "It's a good question. One every man should have an answer for. For me, it's like." He lets out a loud breath, and when he speaks again his voice is even lower. "W-When I was little, my mom got sick. She had asthma. Every winter, she'd get pneumonia, and her recovery was worse every year. Her doctors did what they could to prevent it, but with her weakened immune system, it was inevitable she'd spend every Christmas in bed, which broke her heart because nobody loved Christmas more than her. She always made sure to take pictures of our faces right when we opened our gifts, and she referenced them all year round." Christian's forehead beads with sweat, as if a spotlight is shining directly on it, and he shuffles his feet.

Nobody dares to make a sound, and he continues, "My dad has winters off work, since he works in construction. He had plenty of time on his hands to care for her when she fell ill. One year, she got sick right after Thanksgiving, and she couldn't get out of bed to shop for our Christmas presents, or decorate the house the way she loved it. That was the thing she enjoyed the most, and looked forward to all year. She'd look online at these décor websites and save pictures." His gaze drops to his feet, and he clears his throat again. This time, the rumbles came out hoarse.

"Dad got all of us presents, and wrapped them, writing "From Mom" on them. We all knew she didn't have anything to do with the gifts, because she was gravely ill, but Dad wanted my mom to get all of our smiles and hugs." Christian pauses again and chews on his lip. I hold my breath, as the seriousness in his tone is making my heart pound hard against my ribs.

"Dad hated decorating because it was extra work and a waste of money. That year, he bought a real Christmas tree. While she was sleeping, he set it up in her bedroom and added white lights around her bed posts. It seemed like every day he'd bring home another little elf to hide in her line of sight while she slept, or a poinsettia to set on her dresser. I even started to look forward to what new Christmas surprise we'd have each day. He used the pictures she'd saved from her websites as guidance and by the end of the season, we had a winter wonderland right in her bedroom."

I'm not fighting anymore. Tears fill my eyes, and I blink them down. From the sniffles and swiping of cheeks around the room, I know I'm not the only one. I'm completely mesmerized by what Christian is saying.

"My mom actually passed quietly in her sleep the day after Christmas. Nobody knew it was going to happen. Sometimes it still feels like a dream. In a way it was a gift. I didn't have to say a final goodbye. My last memory of her is her last Christmas night as she was watching me while I opened my expected Lego set. I looked up at my dad, eager to thank him. He had done all the work to provide for us that magical Christmas, and he definitely deserved the credit. *He wasn't even watching me.* His eyes were locked on *Mom* watching me. I was only thirteen, but I was not offended that I wasn't getting his attention. My dad couldn't take his eyes off my mom as she glowed with joy." Christian blinks as if remembering he wasn't alone. "To answer your question, I don't know much about love, but I'd never settle for anything less than that."

Tears flood down my face, and my heart pounds in my chest, melting all the previous bad thoughts I'd ever had for Christian. My dad always told me that hurt people *hurt* people. He is exactly as Arielle had said. He has a shield, and after hearing that display of his parents' love, and then losing his mom at such a young age. How could he not?

The room is dead silent, except for almost everyone sniffing behind me. "That's what I want for us," Christian tacks on with his gaze locked on me. It's so intense a sonic boom explodes in my heart as he places a hand on my hip. This is all going on in front of everyone! All these strangers don't have a clue that Christian *isn't* my real boyfriend. They assume we're dating. Christian flashes me a heart-stopping smile that is totally not a typical gaze for us. Shoot, that gaze isn't my usual gaze for anyone. My heart constricts, thumping hard against my ribcage. My chest becomes an echo chamber, expanding each thump to echo in my ears.

*I'm swooning!*

Flattening my palm against my chest in a feeble attempt to calm the thumping, I'm about to start fanning myself as my cheeks glow so warm I feel like I'm tanning. All eyes are on me, and everyone is waiting.

This feels like one of those cheesy movies where the couple is caught declaring their love, only we're not even a couple. I open my mouth to say something, but I'm stuck. I'm not an actress! I can't improvise this stuff. Plus, my heart is still motoring away, and it's all I can do to stare back at Christian as he fawns back at me.

"That settles it!" Pappi declares, raising his hand. My eyes pull back to him, and even Pappi has tears streaming down his face. "You have my blessing."

Christian and I crack a smile at the same time. Not a humorous one, but a secret one. I turn back to Pappi. "Thank you, Pappi. I wasn't sure when I first met him, but now I know he's one of the good ones."

"Time for you to take this girl dancing," Pappi asserts in a celebratory way. His facial expression has morphed from that sullen and dull gaze I had first seen to one that exudes life. "Cue the music. Everybody polka!"

A niggling in the back of my mind says what we're doing isn't right. Is it too much to want to add a little joy to his life? Even if it is, I'm not going to take that from him now.

I check back at Christian, hiking an inquiring brow. "Do you want to dance?"

"I wouldn't miss it," he chimes back, his eyes steel on me, as if I'm his whole world. He's clearly still acting like my boyfriend for Pappi's sake.

I swallow as a lump buds in my throat, but it's nothing I can't ignore. What are we getting into? I don't have time to ponder as a polka blasts through the ceiling speakers. Christian wraps an arm around my shoulders and whisks me to the dance floor. The cozy little floor fills with couples who are mostly at least double, if not triple, our age. We follow their lead, holding our hands, extending them out. "Ah, problem." I'm smiling because the music has already lightened the somber mood of the room. "I have no idea what a polka is."

"It's basically a hopping two-step. I go to the left, it's your right." Christian starts slow, as he waits for me to catch on.

"And you know this how?" I hop twice and stop, forgetting to come back on the return, but Christian adjusts, waiting for me.

"Lots of Saturday nights with my grandma." He lifts his arm above his head, pulling me. "Let me guide you."

Chuckling, I traipse over his feet as I complete what I think is supposed to be a twirl. "You better not dip me," I joke. "Anything that takes me off both feet will cause you great suffering."

"Trust me, after the fall down the subway, I've been babying my back all week." He pulls my arms up, and I spin again. We repeat this pattern until the music is over, with me stomping on at least one of his feet at least every other spin.

"Sorry." I giggle through a wince as the music transitions to another song, and we break apart, heading off the dance floor. "I should have warned you that I don't polka."

"Clearly, you should have disclosed that on your job application."

Enjoying the sarcasm, I run my mouth. "I'm sorry to say, but I had every intention of deceiving you."

"I knew it all along." Playfully pointing an accusing finger at me, his voice turns serious. "What else have you been deceiving me about?"

"Oh." I rack my brain, digging for something witty, as I recall our rough start. Not wanting to lose my comedic timing, I rush to banter back, "Maybe I was only pretending to hate you, because I actually like you."

*What did I just spew out!*

Halting my feet, my eyes swell as my words ring back through my ears. My insides ice over, and I beg my mouth to take back my words—or spout off something funny—but nothing comes up my vocal cords.

*It was a joke! I beg my mouth to say, but it won't listen.*

In a rush to be funny, I didn't think how that would sound. Christian tilts his head toward me with an intense gaze that *melts my feet to the floor!* It's that look couples have at the moment everything changes, and I feel it reverberate all the way to my toes.

Bringing his chin down, he hovers his gaze intensely on mine. "Portia, did you mean that?"

"No," I spit out, tacking on, "Yes. I mean, maybe. Do you?"

*He does not take his eyes off me.*

All the love songs that have ever been sung about this moment seem to play in my head, and they've all been rewritten just for us. For the second time tonight my heart motors at top speed, and it's all I can do not to fall over dead.

He lowers his chin, aligning his face with mine, and as he starts to bring his lips down, a giant, extra pokey elbow from a child running behind me jabs me in my side. I stumble and blurt, "Ouch!"

Rubbing my side, I take a deep breath and prepare to return my gaze to Christian. Christian's smirking now. The moment clearly passed, but I hold my breath anyway.

*Things are about to change.*

# TWENTY-FOUR

## Christian

"That turned out to be a fun evening." I chuckle as I pull my car slowly into her parking lot and creep to a stop. "And again, we didn't kill each other."

"We've both gone crazy." Her eyes sparkle but neither of us move to exit the vehicle. We've been sharing these lingering moments all night.

She doesn't move.

I don't move.

We stare at each other as if meeting each other for the first time, yet it feels so familiar.

Familiar *and* exciting.

More exciting than familiar.

There's an airy feeling in my chest, making me lighter, and I feel as if I could laugh myself silly for days.

If anyone had asked me even two days ago if I would ever be able to stand Portia, I would have had a hard time believing it is possible. Now, I can't take my eyes off of her. She is stunning. Which I had always known...even though I would never admit it. She didn't have the type of beauty you see in magazines: nothing is overly made up about her, unlike all the women I saw tonight at the fundraiser. She's a true natural beauty, exactly like my mother had been.

*Only in a slightly different font.*

"Do you need me to walk you up the stairs?" I know the answer is no but I can't say goodnight. I also don't want to come off as some creep who is only walking her upstairs to try to get an invitation inside her apartment. That's not the kind of guy I am.

"Well, the elevator's still broken, and it's late." Her voice drops to a whisper at the end, and I barely hear her pronounce the T. Her eyes round even more, pulling me into her endless spirals of beryl-blue hues. "I'm sure you're tired."

It sounds like a goodbye, but she doesn't even move her pinky to graze the door handle. Once again, we gaze at each other, frozen. Don't get me wrong, I don't mind it. I feel so alive, and I don't ever want this feeling to end. I'm hesitating because I don't want to push anything. "Thanks for ah, coming out tonight."

"You're welcome." Her upper teeth clamp down on her lower lip, flushing the pink tissue into white. My heart jerks out a massive flutter as if it's having a seizure.

She is clearly waiting for me to kiss her!

As much as I want to, it doesn't feel right.

I'm her boss.

We work together.

We don't date.

We clearly don't kiss.

The thing is . . . I want to kiss her.

We had an amazing time tonight.

But I'm not the guy who goes around kissing girls because we had one night of fun. When I fall, I plummet heart first. I'm not sure what this flirtation even is. Are we riding on the coattails of Pappi's party where we pretended to like each other? I don't want to suffer in the long run for this. I break our gaze, rake my fingers through my hair, and toss a look forward over the steering wheel. "I'll see ya tomorrow at work, right?"

She startles, sitting up straighter. "Yeah, I come in at three to close."

"I'll be opening for El if she's not feeling better."

"I'll see you then." She pauses, sways forward as if testing a leanin, but I keep my eyes fixed ahead.

"Bye." My word is extra choppy, and I don't steal even a tiny glance as she climbs out of the car. I'm such a jerk to not walk her to her door. The thing is, I can't ward off another one of those moments while standing next to her. I open my window, letting in cold air, and inhale it deeply.

I should be better in the morning. This is a weird fluke. We clearly got caught up in the dancing and acting like a couple stuff. I wait in the car until she's safely in the building. Then I wait longer—nine more minutes to be exact—until I see a light flash on in her apartment window. No, that's not creepy at all. It's one hundred percent gentleman. Now that I know she's safe, I can go home.

As I drive, my mind wanders to Pappi. The whole skit we had pulled on him had started off as a friendly gesture we didn't think would last more than a minute or two. We ended up spending the evening joking, eating and laughing with his family, as if we were family. Everyone in that room was supporting him in his final days, and I don't regret what we did for him. Ashley had said privately he'd spent the last year in a bit of a homesick stupor, since he couldn't understand why his Alisa didn't call. Maybe someday God will punish us for what we did tonight. I can't help that at this moment I am honored to have met him. He will leave a lasting impression on me.

I shake my head as I turn the corner, returning to my hotel. "Life's so short. Who's to say you're owed any time?"

Thinking of my own grandma and how she ignored my call, a sour taste coats in my throat. We used to be so close. I'd assumed she'd eventually come around to understanding why I didn't want to run a construction company. It seems silly now. In the big picture, does the job you have really matter?

I park in my hotel parking lot, but don't shut off my car right away. Instead, I pull out my phone and construct the perfect text for my grandma. One to explain to her everything I was feeling and everything I had felt all these weeks we weren't talking. This isn't about me not having money to pay my loan. I need her to know how much I miss her. I type and delete so many words because I have so much to say to her. In the end, after nearly thirty minutes of analyzing every word combo, I settle on the perfect text.

**Me: I love you, Grandma.**

I reread it, a reminiscent grin lacing my lips as I press send. I don't stow my phone away just yet. I had a hunch about something. I quickly construct another text.

**Me: Portia, thank you for tonight.**

I press send as fast as I can before losing my nerve and go inside.

# TWENTY-FIVE

## Portia

"Dad?" I answer my phone before my eyes are even open the following morning.

"Did Oliver catch anything this morning?"

"What?" Pressing on my forehead, I force my mind to focus on the present. "What time is it?"

"Almost noon."

"No way." I pull myself to a seated position and squint at my alarm clock—11:47. Yep, almost noon. I can't believe I slept that long. I don't remember waking up once or even dreaming. It was the most restful sleep I'd had in a while. "Ah, I'm still in bed. I overslept."

"Are you feeling okay?"

"I think so." Curious myself, I swipe my forehead with the back of my hand and run my hand down my cheek. Nothing feels warm. "I was out late last night at a fundraiser thing for work." Scooting to the edge of the bed, I slip my feet into my slippers and stand. "Are you heading to Home Hardware?"

"No, not today since it's New Year's Eve. I want to invite you over for a bowl of my famous chili later. We could watch the ball drop on TV."

"Well, you do have the best chili, but I close tonight. It will be after eight by the time I get everything cleaned up." Rubbing my chin, I did the time math. "Can I call you when I'm almost done with my shift? Depending on how busy we are, I may be too tired to come over."

"I'll keep it in the crockpot, and it will be ready whenever."

"Sounds good." Mr. Noodles flies out from under the sink, where apparently he'd been sleeping. He loves resting in there, especially when it's extra warm inside, and I haven't been leaving the window cracked anymore. His eyes are on me as he slinks next to his bowl and nudges it forward. "I better go, Dad. Someone needs breakfast."

When I end my call, a text message flashes on my screen.

**Christian: Portia, Thank you for tonight.**

A zap slams into my gut, bringing back all the tingles from last night, and I'm instantly giddy inside. I had vowed to try to be friends with him. What I never expected was to see him so vulnerable. When he explained what love was to him, I literally melted like lava in an active volcano. I'd never heard any man speak about something so swoony in my life.

Everything feels different after last night. Christian isn't that stone-faced person he'd been. Truthfully, he felt different for the last couple of days. But this was even more different, different. It's more than trying to be friends. Like when I look at him, my breath gets trapped in my lungs.

I can't even remember what it was like not to hate him anymore.

I get to see him in a few hours, but I still need to walk Oliver. I rise to my feet and hurry to the cupboard, grabbing Mr. Noodles' sack of dry food. It's not the stuff he wants. I've been out of canned food for a couple of days as my temporary lack of employment had put a halt to my shopping. I'll have to stop at the store on my way home from work or he'll start to get moody.

"Alright, Mr. Noodles," I sing out, as I roll up the top of his food bag, sealing off the air. "You are all set. Now I need to get some more recruits."

As if it has ears, my phone bleeps. It's my app, sending me messages. I can't keep up. I've been casually messaging a few guys, most of them are boring. When I open my app, I'm greeted with a "Level Up" message, stating I'm eligible to share my name with this one guy.

He's the one who makes me smile with his sarcasm, and he's spent the last two days trying to get me to type the letter Y. We haven't chatted a ton. In a way, that makes me like him more. Like he has a life outside of cruising for hotties online. I clamp down on my lips and pause. I knew this request was coming. I'm the one who designed the app, but was I ready to tell someone online my name?

But what could it hurt? Just a first name.

Then we can chat for another week before I am forced to decide if I want to share a pic. Before I overthink it, I accept the request, type in my name and press send. He'll also have to accept the request before I can hear back. My stomach twists thinking about it.

I breathe out a cleansing breath, and throw my coat on, while slipping my feet into my sneakers. I've got a dog to walk, and recruits to find.

I can't say I've ever been excited to work on New Year's Eve before. Other years, it felt like a bad omen. Since I don't have exciting plans—other than eating chili with my parents—I look forward to getting out of the house.

Who am I kidding?

My blood is ripping through my veins with adrenaline because I can't stop thinking about Christian. Had I imagined all that chemistry last night? I'm dying to see if he'd act any differently today. What if, by some amazing miracle, we end up working so super late, and one thing *leads to another and we share a midnight kiss?*

*I blush so hard my toenails rouge.*

I pace my tiny apartment, smoothing my hair several times as Mr. Noodles' head swings back and forth as if he is watching a giant pendulum. What will I say to Christian? Do I pretend everything's professional? Well, everything technically is still professional on the outside.

Inside, my heart won't stop belting out rapid beats. I tilt my head to the side, remembering how he rakes his hand through his hair when nervous. He has great hair. And he takes care of his sister. That feels honorable. And we both love coffee. Still, who doesn't?

That one doesn't count.

He did save my life when I was choking.

Gotta give him that much.

Yep, that solves it.

Saving my life means he's a keeper.

I am clearly smitten.

I don't want to wait another minute to see him, and I rush out of the door. The air is brisk, but the sun is shining exceptionally brightly. The kind of brightness you see in all your best memories.

Strolling through the crowds of people on the sidewalk, I can't break the smile on my face, and my toes curl. I make it to work in record time, and my phone bleeps. It's my app, but I ignore it. Inhaling a final breath of fresh air, I open the door and immediately search for Christian. My heart stops pumping without notice, and I freeze.

He's standing by the window. As his gaze meets mine, I can't pretend I don't feel chemistry. "Hey." I throw my hand up in a soft wave. "How are you?"

"So much is going on right now." He tilts his head to the side, as if he's weighing a decision. "So much is happening, and the room is spinning."

"What's wrong?"

"Well, two things. First." He flashes his phone at me with an unreadable text message on the screen. "I have been trying to reach my grandmother for a few days without hearing anything back. I thought she was ignoring me. I finally got a reply from my dad on her behalf. She's not doing well."

"Oh." My heart immediately aches for him, and I so badly want to give him a hug, but instead I wring my hands together. "I'm sorry."

"El is feeling mostly better, and we're planning to go see her. The only flights available are tomorrow night. We don't want to wait that long and are considering driving." Flecks of sorrow flash in his eyes. "I just need someone to cover the store."

"I can do it." I drop my purse on the nearby table, as it suddenly feels heavy.

"We shouldn't be gone long, and you can close early when it's slow."

"It's no problem." I wave my hand dismissively. "My dad can always stop by and give me a break. Maybe Jade can cover a shift or two. I don't think she's found work since you fired her. I'm guessing you won't care."

"No, I don't mind, and I would actually love that because I don't want you to overextend yourself."

I roll my lips in, holding them in pause, feeling how heavy this conversation is. "You don't have to worry about a thing. I ran this place by myself before you got here. Go now if you need to."

"Thanks." He runs his fingers through his hair, not doing anything to smooth it down as it becomes more disheveled. "I, ah, this is weird." He balls his hand into a fist, holding it near his core. "I know this is not the right time, but I don't know when I'll be back, but something just happened."

"What?" My heart's skipping along, waiting for the punchline.

He doesn't speak. Instead, he turns back to his phone, clicks on something and flashes it back at me. I squint, ready for another cryptic message from his grandma, but it's something I recognize.

My eyes spring open, and I literally scream. "What!"

It's my website.

My dating website on his phone, and a Match Name Reveal is on his phone:

**Portia Grant from Long Island.**

*What?*

I yank my phone out from my pocket. My fingers flutter as I trace my password, and sure enough on my phone, there's a Match Name Reveal:

**Christian Hanson from Long Island.**

I'm dead. How did that happen?

"I, ah," he stutters while staring down on my phone. "El found a free match card outside and made me use it."

"It's my website," I blurt out. "I own it, and I, ah, dropped all those cards."

"Matchmaking?" He plants his feet an arm's reach away from me. Not my arm. My arms are quite petite, but his arms. His arms are long and muscular, and all of the sudden I can't stop looking at them.

"Yeah, it's a small, inclusive matchmaking app I run with my dad. It was initially my idea. He helped me research and paid to have it developed. It's one of the most fine-tuned matching algorithms in existence."

"So, this is real?" He motions back to his phone, my name still flashing in the middle.

"I think so." I feel the smile he gives me all the way to my toes. Relieved we are on the same page, I wish I could take another step closer, but now isn't the time. I can't leave him hanging, but what do I say? I'm stunned, and shocked, and stunned again. "Ah, I'm so glad you said something, because I hadn't checked my phone yet. That might have been weird if we'd never brought it up."

"Not going to be weird at all." He chuckles, dropping his hand back to his side as his face lights up in a glowing rouge. "I mean, I'm always a little weird, but I can't change that. I've honestly tried."

"Good, because I don't want things to be *weird*."

"So right. It's not going to be *weird*." He flashes a glance at his wristwatch and then back at me. "I hate to leave like this."

"Go." I wave him out the door. "I'm fine."

His feet cement to the floor, and he gives me that look again. The one that borders between flirting and pining, and I do everything possible to stay in control of my legs. All I want to do is lean in for a kiss. Thankfully, he steels his gaze to the exit. "I'll text you when I get there."

*Ah, yes!* I scream in my head, while excitement pulses through my veins and I force myself to remain calm, despite my insides scrambling in a tangled knot. "Sure, I'd like that." I hold my hand up, as he pivots and heads out the door. "Drive safe."

My heart instantly plummets. I'm spending New Year's Eve alone, working. It has such a different ring to it after planning to spend the shift with Christian. I pick up my phone to text.

**Me: Dad, chili sounds great. I'll be over to watch the ball.**

Sighing, I drag my feet toward the coffee bar and grab my French press. Might as well have some coffee because it's going to be a long, boring, and lonely night.

I arrive at my parents' house with a grocery sack of cat food I grabbed on the way over. Without knocking, I let myself into their townhouse. "I'm here."

Slipping off my shoes, I flex my feet as they start to relax after standing on them all day. After setting my sack by the entrance, I meander into the kitchen, where Dad sits at the table with his tablet. Motor noises waft from the screen.

"Happy New Year, Dad." I plop into the chair next to him. "Where's Mom?"

"Happy New Year to you." He doesn't take his eyes off his race. I peek over his shoulder. He's driving a red car, and it has number one for first place on the leaderboard on top of his screen. "She's taking a bath. She put her curlers in, so it might be a while."

I smile at how such a mundane detail of putting curlers in serves as a flag to Dad, letting him know she needs more time. Sinking lower into the chair, I rest my elbow on the table and plop my chin into my palm.

"What's his name?" Dad asks without taking his eyes from his tablet.

I tsk. "There's nobody—"

Dad hikes a brow, and that's all it takes to make me cave. "It's my boss, Christian. I thought he was a jerk, but something happened yesterday." My words spew out, like I'm that crazy lady who over shares at a bar. Only I'm not at a bar, I'm with my dad. He's the one person I trust more than anything, so I keep talking. "We went to this fundraiser thing for work, and it ended up being a weird night, but it was sort of the best night. We were supposed to work together today, but he left town for a family emergency. I'm bummed because I wanted to see him, but it's selfish since he's having family issues."

Dad lays his tablet on the table without pausing his race. Cars fly by him, and his number slips to 2, 3, 4, 5. He's losing, or as he prefers to call it, "He's getting smoked." He doesn't take a second look back when he gets up. "What are you doing?" I ask.

"Getting pie." He opens the fridge, his head disappearing inside, and I hear rummaging.

"I thought you had chili."

He reappears with a pan of half-eaten blueberry pie, grabs two forks from the sink drying rack, and plops it on the table in front of me. "Eat." He hands me a fork, as if it's a weapon that can tackle my heartsickness.

Dad takes his fork and scrapes off the edge of the pie. I peel away at the opposite end. After several bites of silence, oddly, I'm feeling better. Dad says, "Did you know that desserts is stressed spelled backwards?"

"You always know the best conspiracies?" I lick the blueberry sauce from the handle of my fork, as this is so much messier than it should be.

"Who said anything about conspiracies." He lays down his fork. "That's a fact."

My dad had an uncanny way of saying all the right things by saying nothing at all and just eating pie. I still want his advice, though. Admitting I have a crush is a big step. I've been running from love for a long time. Not that this is love but I avoid even considering dating. "What do you think I should do, Dad?"

He scratches his cheek while studying my face. "You say this boy's coming back after his emergency?"

"Yeah, his business is here. So, he has to come back."

"You call that boy and tell him that your dad knows his way around a hardware store. If I need to make a body disappear, I won't have any problem doing it."

"Dad," I rush to interrupt him. "You don't have to worry about that."

"I don't have to worry if you do what I say." He raises two fingers, making a V and points to his eyes. "I'll watch him like a dad so you don't have to worry about a thing."

"I'm done talking about this, because you're starting to get weird." I push my chair back and crane my neck to peer down the hall. "It is getting late. Should I go say hi to Mom? I don't know if I want to stay until midnight. I might try to catch the last train to Forest Hills."

"Nah, let her rest. She puts up with me all day." His grin sprouts slowly and grows until it fills his whole face. Their relationship always feels cute to me. It's not one from the fairytales, but there's a steadiness, and companionship that's lasted decades.

"Okay." I move toward the door. "I have canned food for Mr. Noodles. I'd better get home before he jumps out the window again."

"Sounds good. Happy New Year." He picks up his tablet, re-suming his racing game as if I'd already left.

"Yeah, Happy New Year." I jerk my thumb toward the counter. "Can I grab some chili to go? I never had dinner."

"I don't have any chili." He pulls the tablet closer to his face as he steers his car around the track.

I blink, dumbfounded. "You asked me to come over for chili."

"That's what I said to get you to come over here to tell me about this boy."

My mouth falls open. "How did you—"

He taps rapidly on his tablet with his gaze down. "I have my ways."

"I didn't know there was a boy until now." Placing a hand on my hip, recalling what I'd said that would have tipped him off, but there was nothing. "How could you know?"

"I could hear it in your voice this morning when I called. You were frazzled—"

"Dad," I cut him off, but he stops me by standing and dropping his tablet back to the table. "It's okay, honey. This is exactly what you need." Extending his arms out, he invites me for a hug.

I smash my lips together, holding in all my quivers, and walk forward. It's an embrace that always comforts me, even when I'm being stubborn. I'm smiling again by the time I pull back. "Okay." I point down the hall. "Tell Mom Happy New Year. Wait a second." I tap my finger to my chin. "Is Mom even in the tub?"

"Nope. Went to bed two hours ago. That's what I said to get you to stay. If you knew she was in bed, you'd have felt guilty for staying." He winks at me, nodding toward the door. "Better get home."

"Deal." I slip on my shoes while speaking over my shoulder. "I'm working extra for a while, so I won't have time for Home Hardware for a few days. I'll call you as soon as I have a break."

"It's okay." Dad shakes his head. "I don't want to go to Home Hardware. I'm sick of that place."

"What are you talking about?" I blink, rewinding his words. "You love going there."

"Nah, reminds me of work. I only went there to find you a man, but it seems you might have actually found one. So, no, I don't need to go."

"You're making this up."

"Believe what you want." He walks to the front window, pulls back the curtain, and takes a protective stance.

"Are you going to watch me walk down the street?" I retrieve my grocery sack and open the door, already knowing the answer to my question.

"Yep, and text me when you get home."

"Love you, Dad."

"Love you, too."

Now that I know Mom is sleeping, I close the door as softly as I can. My dad is a turkey. There's no way he can be telling the truth. We've gone to Home Hardware together for a year. He wouldn't have done it if he hated it. Plus, he hasn't even met Christian.

There's no way he would know.

He can't know.

I shake my head, heading down the street at a brisk walking pace.

Could he know? Wait. What's there to know?

Now I want to know.

# Twenty-Six
## Christian

I tap lightly on my grandmother's bedroom door, not moving even a toe inside. The pit of my stomach feels heavy and sour as dread consumes me. "Grandma," I whisper. "You awake?"

"Christian, is that you?" Her voice sounds more tired than usual, but not weak.

"Yeah." Accepting that as an invitation, I walk forward until she can see me. She looks like her same old self, with straight dark hair ratted in the back from laying down. Her skin is relatively warm toned for someone who is ill. Wheel of Fortune plays on the wall TV, and she has a tray with several glasses of fluids next to her. If I didn't know better, I would say it was an ordinary day for her. But I do know better, and I step forward respectfully. "How are you?"

"Well, I've heard it might be my time to go, but I'm not going to listen to that." She looks at me straight, her eyelids fluttering closed before she pulls them open again. "Plus, you and I have some business to talk about."

I lower my eyes to the floor. The heaviness consumes me. "Grandma, you don't have to talk about anything."

"Nope." She adjusts the linen blanket, pulling it tighter around her. "I've been unfair to you. We both know that."

As much as I want to agree with her, I don't. I also want to ask what made her change her mind, but it didn't matter now. "It's all right."

"Well, here's the deal." Her tone sounds a tad exploratory, as if she's not quite sure what the deal actually is. "I always knew you weren't right for Total Trucks."

"How so?"

"You're the only boy I'd ever seen beg for a seatbelt when given the chance to drive a dump truck." Her lips pull into a sweet grin, but her eyelids droop so low, I can barely see her pupils. "I didn't think it was fair that your mom got sick. I had made up my mind that all the rest of my dreams would come true if I held on to them. I was being stubborn, but I have never been prouder of you. You followed your own path despite the pressure I put on you. You are always my sweet Christian."

A dam of tears wells in my eyes. My mom used to call me her sweet Christian. I hadn't heard that in years. The nickname echoes in my heart, melting the barrier I'd built up to keep it from being hurt. An instant release of the pressure I'd felt for years opens my chest, and I'm able to breathe so much deeper. I don't fight the release, as I would have done in the past. I allow my stress to erase with each new breath, the knots untangling even more. "Thank you."

Her eyes seal all the way tight. "Your mom would have been so proud of you, too."

I breathe into that compliment as it hits my gut like a stone. It isn't something I'd ever let myself consider. I flash my gaze to heaven. Not in the annoying way I usually roll my eyes, but instead I check for signs of Mom. Despite the many years of searching, I've never gotten a clear sign. "I hope so," I murmur while I silently pray it's loud enough for her to hear.

A pleasant grin sweeps over her lips as her chest rises further now, and settles into deep, restful breaths. I tiptoe to the edge of the bed, drop a kiss on her cheek, and turn to leave.

In the hallway, I catch the end of El's ponytail sneaking out the back door, and I whisper-holler her way. "Hey, where are you going?" She doesn't hear me as the door latches behind her.

I approach the door, and my gaze follows her to a truck parked a couple of houses down the street. I don't recognize it, but that doesn't surprise me. She climbs into the cab, and two seconds later they are driving down the road. "What are you up to, El?" I ask out loud, knowing full well this has to do with the mystery dude she's been wallowing about. Maybe they can straighten things out? Maybe that would mean she couldn't stay in New York? There's an awful lot of maybes. I haven't even gotten to the one that's strongest in the back of my mind. Maybe I should text Portia?

I walk back down the hall to the living room and drop onto the couch. It's hours past dark, after an exhaustingly long day. This is as good a place as any to sleep, and I stretch my legs out while pulling a throw blanket over me. I unlock my phone, and it flashes 12:01. I smile as I type a text.

**Me: Happy New Year.**

Flicking my thumb off the edge of my phone, I weigh the decision of whether to send it so late. I told Portia I'd text. She won't expect something this late. I don't want to wake her since she has to get up at five to work. But what if she's awake? What if she went out? We never talked about our plans for the holiday. What if she met some dude on her website, and they're toasting right now? I tug my fingers through my front spike and wince. I'm making myself go crazy. It's just a text.

I press send, staring at my phone, holding my breath as it gets marked "Read." Then, the screen changes to texting dots, and my heart motors rapidly.

**Portia: Happy New Year to you, too!**

"Phew." I blew out a breath. Not sure why this is so hard. Oh wait, she is typing more. I suck in a hard breath and wait.

**Portia: Did you make it to Massachusetts okay?**

**Me: Yeah, we got in about an hour ago. Grandma's resting. El snuck out the backdoor to meet some hick in a truck, and I'm getting ready to go to sleep.**

**Portia: Was it blue and white?**

Squinting as if it can help me see into my memory better, I think back.

**Me: Yeah, I think so. Why?**

**Portia: That's Tom's.**

**Me: Who's Tom?**

I type rapidly now, shooting off a stream of steady texts.

**Me: How do you know about Tom?**

**Me: Do you know where they went?**

**Portia: They dated, but she suspected he might be married because all their dates were always secret.**

**Me: Yeah, why was he hiding on the street?**

**Portia: I mean, your guess is as good as mine.**

**Me: He better not play her or he's going to get it.**

**Portia: Speaking of such things, my dad told me to tell you he knows his way around a hardware store and he's an expert at disposing of dead bodies.**

I chuckle. Of course she can't be serious.

**Me: Why were you talking to your dad about me?**

**Portia: ?**

**Me: What does ? mean?**

**Portia: I might have said we went to a fundraiser last night.**

**Me: Is that all?**

**Portia: You tell me. Is that all?**

**Me: It didn't feel like it.**

**Me: I wish I could see you tonight.**

**Portia: Yeah, me too.**

**Me: I'd better let you sleep since you have to run my store for me.**

**Portia: K.**

**Me: Are you tired?**

**Portia: Maybe**

**Me: What are you thinking about?**

**Portia: You.**

An arrow splices through my heart, and I drop my phone to rest on my chest. Something about late night texting doesn't feel real. Is she playing with me? I wish I could see her expression. I grapple for my phone and reply before she thinks I ghosted her.

**Me: Good.**

**Me: I'm thinking about you, too.**

**Me: But you need to go to sleep.**

**Portia: Night.**

**Me: Night.**

I set my phone down, keeping the text open, rereading the part where she says she's thinking about me over and over. Smiling so big, like I haven't done in years. There's not a doubt I care about this girl. Man, I wish I would have kissed her when I had the chance.

If I get a chance again, I won't hold back.

# TWENTY-SEVEN

## Portia

I lean over the counter at the Coffee Loft as my phone lights up.

**Christian: How's the store?**

**Me: A little rush this morning. Now it's slow.**

Biting my lip, I press send and wait. It's only a mere moment later, and my screen lights up again.

**Christian: Does ur boss know you text at work?**

My smile is instant.

**Me: He does now. But I don't think it will matter. He's already fired me once. Then he found out he can't live without me, and begged me to come back.**

**Christian: He sounds like a jerk.**

**Me: I used to think so.**

Hovering my thumb over my phone, I figure now is as good of a time as any to be honest.

**Me: Now, I think I might like him a little.**

**Christian: So, you forgave him for firing you?**

**Me:** I think so.

**Christian:** That's good.

**Me:** How's your grandma?

I press send, and then scan the store to make sure none of the remaining customers need anything. Everybody looks fine. I return my gaze to my phone as another text comes in.

**Christian:** Waking for shorter periods.

**Me:** I'm sorry to hear that. R U OK?

**Christian:** Yeah, we had a nice chat right when I got here. That helps.

**Me:** Well, if it helps, everything is fine here. Take as much time as you need.

**Me:** Is it weird that we are texting, and we barely know each other?

**Christian:** No, because I know a lot about you.

**Me:** Oh really?

**Christian:** Yeah, I know you steal Oreos, have an awesome boss, live in a Rapunzel tower, have a cat with a murderous spirit. You are daddy's princess, you can't dance, and have an awful preference for French press coffee. You have a handsome boss, and stunning blue eyes, and did I mention your boss is a stud?

I giggle as I read through his description of me, and my heart nearly skips a beat each time he mentions how cool he is.

**Me:** Wow. You know a lot.

**Christian:** What do you know about me?

**Me:** I know you

My thumb slips and I accidentally press send when I meant to delete it.

Christian: You know me what?

Me: Never mind.

Christian: No, tell me.

Me: I know you love your sister, your grandma, and your business. I know you loved your mom. I know your definition of love, and I love it.

Christian: You know you're at work and have been texting for twenty minutes. Your boss is going to be so mad at you.

Chuckling, my mind flashes to when Christian was furious with me for standing outside his store. I swore I saw steam come out of his ears. I can't believe we are even talking, but somehow it worked out.

Me: I don't care.

Christian: That's a bold statement.

Me: Something tells me he'd approve.

Christian: I better let you go, or he's going to fire you again.

Me: Ok. 1 more question.

Christian: No, you can't have a raise.

Me: Really?! You wouldn't give me a raise after seeing how amazing I am?

Christian: Okay, change that. I'll adjust your pay for the next check.

Me: Mean that?

Christian: I do. I appreciate you putting up with me.

Me: Are you trying to buy my affection?

Christian: No, but would it work?

Me: No.

**Christian: Clock's ticking and boss man is going to be livid. What's your question?**

**Me: Ah, a customer just walked in. Text me later. I'll see if you're worthy of it.**

I rest my phone on the counter and stare out into the empty Coffee Loft lobby. Nobody is here. I didn't even accidentally hear something that sounded like a customer. I made that last part up when I lost my nerve.

And it's good to play a little hard to get.

# TWENTY-EIGHT
## Christian

Finally lifting myself out of Grandma's bedroom armchair, where I had sat with her all night, I stretch with my arms high over my head. Since I don't have to work, I volunteered for the overnight shift. Now it's after seven in the morning, and the sun is fully up.

"How is she?" El peeks her head into the open door. Grandma refuses to go to the hospital, and we are all rotating shifts, not leaving her alone. It's hard to believe she's so ill, as she appears peaceful. "She's resting. Hasn't complained, or made a peep."

"Well, I'll be here all day. Why don't you get some sleep?" She pads into the room and sinks down into the armchair. "You don't want to get run down."

"I'll rest later. I'm going for a quick walk to loosen up. I'm super stiff. Is there anything you need from the store?"

"No, I'm okay, and Dad will be here in an hour or so." She jerks her head forcefully toward the door now, shooing me away. "I promise. I'll call if anything changes, but you need to take a break. You look like a zombie."

"Grandma," I whisper, before I lean in and drop a kiss on her cheek. "I love you." Her eyelashes flutter but don't open, and I know she feels me here.

I back out of the room, heading outside, and allow my breaths to deepen in the fresh air. Fresh frost has blanketed the city, making the trees sparkle in the early light. With no plan, I walk toward downtown, where a small diner used to be. I'm not hungry, but coffee sounds good. It's not Coffee Loft coffee, but it'll work. Speaking of Coffee Loft, I pull out my phone to check in.

**Me: Are you at work?**

**Portia: Depends. Are you asking as my boss, or as that guy I've been texting?**

I've heard the expression that your heart can skip a beat, but I always assumed it was an expression. Now I know that to be the truth. My heart literally skips a beat.

**Me: I'll go with option B.**

**Portia: Oh, that's not an option right now because I'm at work.**

**Me: OK. As your boss, how is work?**

**Portia: Everything is fine.**

**Me: I'll take my question now please?**

**Portia: What question?**

**Me: Don't do that.**

I flash my gaze to the sky. This woman really does know how to drive me crazy.

**Portia: Do what?**

Me: Pretend you don't know what I'm talking about. I have a whole string of text messages that leaves a solid paper trail clearly showing you have a question to ask me.

Portia: Oh, that question. How's the weather there?

Me: It's about to get crazy if someone doesn't tell me what they are up to.

Portia: Who said I was up to anything?

Me: You seriously don't have a question for me?

I pause on the corner and wait for the crossing sign to change to 'walk.' People are out, and the city Christmas tree is still up in the town square. All that time in Grandma's house had left me feeling in a trance, like nothing was real anymore. It's weird to think how life goes on, despite what anybody's going through. I cross the street and then check my phone.

Portia: Not right now.

Me: What if I guess?

Portia: You can try.

Me: Okay, you were going to ask me if I like long walks on the beach?

Portia: No.

Me: Oh, well, the answer is yes.

Portia. Ok

Me: Do you like long walks on the beach?

Portia: I don't really think I've ever taken a long walk on the beach. Just a short one across it. Who do you take long walks on the beach with?

Me: Nobody.

Portia: You walk by yourself?

Me: Sometimes when I'm back here, I like to walk along the harbor.

Portia: Interesting.

Me: Next guess. Were you going to ask me what my hobbies are?

Portia: No. You seem like a pretty boring guy who doesn't have a life outside of work.

Me: That's almost right. Except, I do have some hobbies. I'll list them in alphabetical order so you can jot them down. Expert at Uno, the card game, not counting. Reading. Amateur at playing guitar (five-string bass), and dancing the polka with you.

I walk right to the center of Townsquare and pause at the city gazebo, taking a seat on the steps. It's chilly out, but the fresh air feels so good, and I'm able to breathe so much more deeply than I have in weeks, and it's invigorating.

Portia: That's not in alphabetical order.

Me: Yeah, I saved the best for last.

Portia: I hate to break it to you, but I don't think I'll ever dance the polka again.

Me: You really shouldn't. You were terrible.

Me: Next question. Were you going to ask me what my favorite childhood memory is?

Portia: Nope, that wasn't even on my radar, but why don't you go ahead and tell.

Me: Don't mind if I do. You know how Christmas mornings were a big deal at my house, right?

Portia: Yeah

Me: That.

Portia: What about that?

Me: All of that. All of the mornings. Can't pick one.

Me: Same question to you.

Portia: Well, I played a lot of Barbies when I was little, so anytime Barbie got married was fun, which was like every other day. I don't know if I can pick just one.

Me: Right, those memories are clearly overshadowed by that stupendous day you first met me.

Chuckling, I consider laying off the silly bragging, but I'm waiting to see if I can get her to agree to anything. Just once I want to hear her say she likes me.

Portia. You seem fairly confident.

Me: Oh, were you going to ask me about my ideal date night?

Portia: No. I wasn't going to ask you that.

Me: I wasn't going to answer you about that.

Me: Okay, you want to know my favorite movie? I'll tell you. The Sandlot.

Portia: I love that movie too!

Me: I have fond memories of it. What's yours?

Portia: It's hard to pick just one.

Me: Give me five.

Portia: I'll say I love romcom, and all those cheesy Christmas movies.

Me: Gah! I just went blind.

Portia: How's your grandma?

Me: Resting. Peaceful. El is with her.

Portia: That's good.

Me: Can I have my question now?

**Portia: Ask me tomorrow. I'm too tired now.**

**Me: Tomorrow is Wednesday.**

**Portia: Oops. Coffee Loft is on fire. Gotta go!**

Chuckling, I picture Portia's face when we locked gazes at the fundraiser. A lot has changed since that night. Clearly our opinions of each other have improved. It's weird how we didn't know it then, but a spry old man named Pappi was exactly what we both needed to get past our giant egos. We really aren't that different when it comes to our stubbornness.

I can't wait to see her again. Maybe it's all in my head, but she's texting like she likes me, too.

Sighing, I stand back up and head toward the diner.

Now, if only I can get her to admit she likes me.

# TWENTY-NINE

## Portia

Three days have passed since I've heard from Christian, and it feels much longer. It's funny how you think you know what you want in life, and then something simple like someone coming into your life changes everything. I haven't been obsessing over my female to male ratio on my website at all the last few days. Sure, I hand out QR codes, but then I leave it up to fate. So far, the website hasn't crashed. I take that as a good sign. It actually feels healthy for me to take a small step back from my website now. I check it but only once a day, as opposed to at least once every hour.

I'm completely whipped when I crawl into bed. I've been hoping Christian texts me, harassing me to tell him my question. I toy with the idea of texting him with a random clue to my question, but since he is the one spending time with family, I keep my space.

I tap my phone, not engaging any letters to actually type. It's too early in this situationship for me to justify bothering him at his grandma's, but I can't help but wish my phone would light up with a text. I have no idea how long I stare at my phone but without noticing, I nod off.

Sometime in the early morning, I wake up to my phone chiming.

**Christian: I'm headed out for a morning walk. Want to talk with me?**

**Me: Ok.**

**Christian: Tell me your ideal match.**

**Me: Excuse me?**

**Christian: You're a matchmaker. Was that your question for me? Were you going to try to match me again?**

**Me: No. I wasn't going to match you!**

**Christian: Ok. Good. I'm happy with my first match.**

**Me: Oh, really? What's she like?**

**Christian: Big attitude, and is very sarcastic.**

**Christian: But she's gorgeous.**

**Christian: Have you heard of Rapunzel?**

**Me: I don't live in a Rapunzel tower!**

**Christian: Until they fix your elevator, you'd be better off growing your hair out.**

**Me: Funny.**

**Christian: What's your ideal match?**

I think back to when I randomly filled out my own match questionnaire a few days earlier. It wasn't hard for me to select things. I want all of the things most women want.

**Me: Family centered.**

I barely press send, and it hits me that I don't think I've ever met a man more family centered than Christian. Other than my dad. Christian has his sister's back a hundred percent, and now he's clearly put his own business on hold for his grandma.

**Me: Good sense of humor.**

When I press send, I check another box. I've laughed so much with Christian over these cute text messages.

**Me: Has a good heart, doesn't take love for granted.**

A tear pops into the corner of my eye, and I can't help but get emotional. He hasn't replied while I sent off all these texts, but he must know he meets all the specs, and I'm setting him up.

**Me: What about you? What's your perfect match?**

I watch my phone screen, now fully awake and I hold my breath waiting for him to flirt. He doesn't reply, and after ten minutes, I risk another text.

**Me: Let me guess, needs a working elevator.**

I bite my lip, holding back a giggle, and press send. Within seconds, I see he receives my messages and is typing back.

Then he stops typing, and I wait.

I decide to tease him.

**Me: I'm ready to ask my question.**

He doesn't reply.

# THIRTY

## Christian

# Three days later

"Do you need help with those boxes?" I ask El as she retrieves another large box from the stack of boxes pressed against grandma's bedroom wall.

"Sure. Help me load them in Tom's truck. He left it parked outside. We're donating all this stuff she won't need at the nursing home to Goodwill."

"Tom," I echo, while I grab two boxes and lead the way down the hall. "Do we finally have a name for the mystery man you've been seeing every night?"

"I guess so."

"I confess I already had a name but it's good you've finally told me about him." I push the back door open with my shoulder, holding it while waiting for her to pass through it. "Why all the secret meetups?"

"I was wondering the same thing." She walks in front of me, heading to the curb where the now familiar blue pickup is parked. "I had suspected he was married, but he always denied it. It turns out that he's a first-year lawyer at the same office handling Grandma's estate, and he was assigned to her team. I didn't even know he is a lawyer. When I met him, he was driving an Uber, and he didn't tell me right away. Uber is a side hustle he works to help pay off his school loans.

He didn't realize the conflict of interest until after we already had a couple of dates, and by then he was catching feelings for me. He didn't want me to think he was dating me to get access to grandma's inheritance, nor did he want to get in trouble at work for a conflict of interest. He broke up with me right when he found out, but he never told me why because of client confidentiality. That was when I left school." Reaching the truck, she drops her box into the back and brushes her hands off by rubbing them together.

"Interesting." I plop my box next to hers and push them both back to make room for more.

"We spent the last week talking." Her eyes sparkle back at me, giving away her true feelings about him. "He asked to be transferred to another work team. His boss didn't even care because he understood the accident, and we both want to try to work things out."

I stuff my hands in my pockets and rock back on my heels, enjoying the confession. "You know, I'm going to have to meet his guy before I approve."

"I know. But hey," she pivots and starts walking toward the house, "at least you don't have to worry about supporting me in New York anymore."

"I don't know if that's a huge bonus or not. I'm used to you being there. Now that Portia's back, I have the funds to start looking for an apartment. I envisioned you tagging along."

"I'll still come to visit." She reaches the door first, pulls it open, and we both go inside, grabbing the last of the boxes.

We loop back down the hall and out the backdoor again in silence. I can't think of something to say worthy of the gift that I've been given. I'm so immensely grateful for the chat I had with grandma, and the time I got to spend with her this week. Then miraculously she sprang back to life, even getting to her feet on her own. That is the biggest gift.

Everyone, including Grandma, agreed she'd be safer in a retirement home. We found one not that far away, and it is perfect. Each resident gets their own suite, and they have plenty of activities. When El requested they add Candy Crush tournaments to their rotation of fun, and they agreed, we knew it to be the perfect one. So here we are, loading the last boxes in the truck, and I slam the dented tailgate shut.

It's funny how things are the same for days, and sometimes years, and then one single moment makes your whole world change.

Having my grandma's forgiveness is one of those moments. It seemed to heal the part of my heart that was damaged after my mom died. Everything feels different now. Like I can do anything or go anywhere, and everything will work out.

And there is only one place I want to go.

# Thirty-One

## Portia

It's been a whole day of working from open to close, and I'm exhausted as I drag my feet up the final staircase to my apartment. I bend over to catch my breath while fumbling for my keys from my purse. I'm about to start watching YouTube videos on how to fix an elevator to handyman ours back to working order. I cannot do ten flights of stairs after working all day on my feet.

My phone vibrates and I pull it out of my pocket as I head down the hall to my apartment. I haven't heard from Christian in days, and my smile can't be contained when I see his name.

**Christian: Sorry I've been MIA. My grandma recovered. It's seriously a miracle. We've been busy cleaning her house because she's moving to a retirement home.**

My heart fills with joy for him in all the ways I didn't know it was even attached to him.

**Me: That's great news!**

**Christian: It is. How are you?**

Me: OK. The store is good.

Christian: That's good.

Christian: I found out who the mystery man is.

Me: I told you, he's Tom.

Chirstian: I know, but El finally told me.

Christian: He's not married BTW.

Me: Why was he being so secretive?

Christian: I guess he was worried because he is working for grandma's lawyer.

Me: Interesting.

Christian: It is. But not as interesting as something else.

Me: What?

Christian: Whatever your question is.

I sputter out a laugh, as I don't think my original question is worth this much hype. Now that we are a week into this, the pressure's on not to disappoint.

Me: I forgot it.

Christian. Funny.

Christian: Can I ask you a question?

Me: Yeah.

I unlock my door. My shoulders literally decompress the stress of the day as soon as I enter my apartment. It's so good to be home. I shut the door behind me, toss my purse on the chair, and throw my whole body on my bed and read my text.

Christian: Do you want to go somewhere with me tonight?

Me: Tonight? Are you back in town?

Christian: I will be there in about an hour. I'll open the store tomorrow, so you can have the day off and not have to worry about being tired.

**Me: Where?**

**Christian: Secret.**

**Me: Sure. Just text me when you get here, and I'll come down.**

I pin my lips together, suppressing a squeal. Bubbles of excitement rush to my gut, and I feel the jitters all the way to my fingers. One more text bleeps on my phone.

**Christian: BTW – I never replied to your question about my perfect match.**

**Christian: It's you.**

# THIRTY-TWO

## Christian

"You're taking me to work?" Portia's brows rocket north as she stares forward while I park. "I worked sixty hours last week, pulling all the shifts myself. There's no way I'm going back in there." She grabs the dashboard with one hand and secures the door handle in her other, ready to fight an exit from my car.

"Relax." I shut off the engine and open my door, calling back while I meander to my trunk and yank out a heavy duffle bag. "You aren't working. Since it's too late to go anywhere, and El's currently sacked out snoring in our hotel room, I thought we could hang out here."

*I honestly don't care where we go. I'd camp in this parking lot in the freezing cold if it meant I got to see her. Her presence offers a balance I desperately need.*

"As long as I don't have to make our drinks, I'll come." She drags her feet out of the car, but I have a hunch she's pretending. It's her sarcastic sense of humor I enjoy so much. I'm already fighting back a laugh as I unlock the door and turn on only one set of lights, keeping the place dim.

I set my bag on a nearby table and unzip it. "We don't even need to have coffee. I thought we could make popcorn and watch a movie."

"For real?"

I lift out a projector I'd confiscated from my grandma's basement. It's old and clunky, but it comes with an air of nostalgia. I stack several old black and white film strips next to it. "This should work well if we set it here and aim it at that wall." I position it perfectly, sliding it almost to the edge of a table. "We can either sit in one of these back booths, or I can move them out of the way to sit on the floor." I pause, checking her expression, praying she'll accept this offering. "Unless you hate this idea, we can go back on the dating app to chat."

"Stop it." She playfully punches my arm. "No more dating apps." Her gaze drifts to the row of tables and back to the floor. "This is perfect. I love this idea." She plops down on the floor, stretching her legs out in front of her.

"I hoped you would." I plug in the projector and place a reel on. It's been years since I had a peek at any of these movies. "It's not a romcom," I warn, as I feed the strip through the projector. "It's romance without words. These were my grandma's favorite." I thread the film, flip the switch on the projector, and light flashes on the wall. "And really, the dialogue in romance movies is too cheesy, anyway. They are better without words."

She tips her head back and laughs, showing me her best smile. I pause, watching her. It's funny how this seems so normal. Even though this is technically a first date for us, neither of us seems nervous. "Okay." I clamp my hands together. "I'm going to throw some popcorn in the microwave. What would you like to drink? If you say French press coffee, you die."

She chuckles another full laugh. "I'm telling you; you need to try it. It's superior."

"I have no intention of ever betraying my franchise like that."

"Water is fine."

"Deal." I run back behind the bar to make our snacks all the while I can't stop smiling. "Can I have my question now?" I ask on my return.

"I forgot it." She locks her gaze forward, avoiding me.

"You seriously are a bad liar." I hand her a bowl of fresh popcorn and her drink and then plop down beside her.

"It's lame, and not worth all this hype." She grabs a few kernels out of her bowl and drops them into her mouth one by one.

"Tell me. It can't be worse than any of the other embarrassing stuff you've done in front of me."

"Okay." She sighs, shaking her head. "But don't laugh." Drawing in her legs, she crosses them in front of her and turns toward me. "I must put it into context that I asked you right after we went to the fundraiser. That was before the last week of texting constantly."

"Right." I dig into my bowl and shovel a handful of popcorn into my mouth. I'm famished as I drove straight through all night without stopping because I couldn't wait to see her.

"I was going to ask if you had felt the chemistry I did." Her cheeks blush. She doesn't take her eyes off of me. "I assume since we're both sitting in the Coffee Loft hours after close, getting ready to watch a movie, you felt something."

*If she only knew. She's all I've thought about, and I couldn't wait for a chance to tell her this. I haven't stopped thinking about how she felt in my arms when we danced, and how stupid I was that I didn't kiss her.*

I can't tell her that though!

I'm determined to make her like me, I put on my best flirty smile. "I would say your assumption is correct."

"Good." Her smile colors my heart neon pink, as it feels as if it's glowing in my chest.

"Shall we watch our movie?" Getting back up on one knee I reach behind me and switch on the projector. The film begins when a lady flashes on the screen. Once I'm happy with the picture alignment, I sit back down and take her hand in mine. We both freeze, sharing a look, before we return our gazes to the screen and watch the movie sitting shoulder to shoulder like this is the most normal thing in the world for us.

My eyes are heavy as tanks when the movie ends. I can barely stay awake. It's been many dreadfully long days in a row, and as much as I want to stay and talk to Portia for hours, my heavy eyelids have another plan. "I'm really sorry to bail on you, but can I take you home now?" I already got off the floor, doing whatever I could not to pass out. "I can barely stay awake, and I have to come back to this place in like four hours."

"Sure." She rises to her feet, standing so close to me, I can smell her. She smells like every summer sunset I've ever watched, and it warms my skin to be near her.

I take a few minutes to pack away the projector, so I don't have to mess with it in the morning. When I return from stowing it in my office, I take her hand in mine again, and we walk together to my car in silence. It's the most comfortable silence I've ever had. Even though we aren't speaking, it's a moment that feels we are creating a bond.

I drive home, the music plays quietly on the radio, and my mind drifts over all the events of the week. Everything from my grandma, to El, to my money issues, and back to land on Portia. It's been one giant roller coaster.

I don't doubt I'm exactly where I need to be.

I park and drop a giant sigh. "I'll walk you up the stairs."

"No, you look exhausted." She waves her hand dismissively at me. "You don't have to. Trust me, I don't even want to walk up them again."

"No, I insist. This is our first date, and I'm all about doing things properly." I open my car door, running to open hers before she can, and we link hands while strolling toward her building.

"I feel like this is boot camp," I joke as we embark on the first set of stairs. I know if I want to do any talking, it's best to get it out now, because I'm going to be out of breath in the next couple of minutes.

She laughs but doesn't reply and we take our time ascending the stairs together. We reach the last landing, and I'm breathing heavily as I walk her straight to her door. She places the key inside, unlocks the door, and pauses, turning back to me. "Thanks for the sweet movie. I'm glad you asked me to go out."

"Ah. You're welcome." This is it. This is where we share our first kiss. Her eyes lock on me, and she doesn't even try to go inside her apartment. I'm so ready for this moment. I've been ready for this moment since the fundraiser.

*Something doesn't feel right!*

It's not that I'm exhausted. At this moment adrenaline is pumping through my veins, and I'm fully alive. It's that I know in my heart Portia is special. She will be that girl who consumes me, and suddenly I don't feel enough.

What do I really have to offer her?

I'm practically homeless and barely have a functional business. The customers I do have are all thanks to her. I honestly have not even kissed a woman in well over a year.

*Man, I want this to be so special because she's amazing, but I really don't think this is good enough for her.*

Instead of leaning in, I chicken out, stuff my hands in my pocket, and smile. "Can I take you to lunch tomorrow?"

"Can you get away from work?"

"Yeah, El came back with me to help out until I get people hired. She said she would come in at noon."

"Sure." Her lashes lower, and she stares at my lips. I can't do this anymore. The look she is giving me is making me weak, and I hold my hand up and wave. "Alright, night!"

"Oh." She straightens her posture, turning toward her door. "Okay. Night."

I spin on my heel and turn before I change my mind. My adrenaline's pumping so hard that I make it down all ten flights of steps in record time. I'm all the way in my car before my phone pings with a text.

**Portia: You should have kissed me.**

"I know!" I yell loudly inside my car, resisting the urge to chuck my phone. *I'm so mad at myself!* I've been ready for days to kiss her. That's all I think about, but I choked. Clenching my teeth, I slowly inhale the biggest breath of my life and pull my shoulders back.

I will *not* be that guy who chokes in the last inning.

I must go back up there!

Ten flights of stairs or a thousand—it doesn't matter.

That's my girl, and there's no way I'm going to leave this place with her being disappointed in me!

I yank on my car door handle and set off. My feet fly forward, adrenaline moves them swiftly up the stairs and I practically fly up each new flight. I'm on a mission, and nothing will stop me now.

Sure, I'm breathing heavily, but I've never felt more alive as I charge up the last flight and practically dive the last steps to land with both palms on her door.

This is it.

Pulling out my phone, I construct a text and press send.

**Christian: I forgot something. I'm outside your door.**

It's eerily quiet as I wait in silence. The long fluorescent hall light flickers behind me.

Portia's door opens slowly. The cute tip of her nose peeks through the crack, but it doesn't take more than a moment for her to open the door wider. She's wearing fuzzy cloud pajamas. She's got a faint trace of mascara smudges under her eyes, but she's never looked more beautiful with the rosy glow on her cheeks. Her brow furrows into concern, and her lips part.

Before she can ask why I'm here, I swoop in, placing one hand on her hip and pull her close to me. My knees buckle, but I don't wimp out as I take her chin in my other hand and guide her mouth toward mine.

Her eyes are wide, but she is not hesitant. I lean closer, inhaling her breath into mine. Her sweet as honey essence wafts under my nose as I inch closer.

I can't bear to close my eyes.

*She's so irrationally beautiful.*

All I want to do is absorb everything about this moment with all my senses.

Her eyelids close before our lips meet into a sweet, pillowy kiss that leaves the softest tickle under my nose. I seal our kiss with a softer kiss and pull back.

Blinking several times to be sure this was real, my smile only grows larger when she doesn't dither. She stays in my arms, her cheeks glowing. I drop my forehead to touch hers, enjoying having her in my arms. "I've been waiting to do that for so long."

"Me too," she whispers. "You do realize you have to wake up in three hours, don't you?"

Sighing, I know she's right. "Yeah, I need to go, but we're still on for lunch tomorrow, right?"

"Absolutely." Her smile grows, and I take that as an invitation to lean in, stealing another quick smooch.

As I back away, I wave, and softly call, "Good night."

Then I practically float down the stairs, knowing full well there is no way I'm getting any sleep tonight.

*But it is worth it.*

# THIRTY-THREE

## Portia

It's noon, and I finally venture out of my apartment after sleeping in all morning. Christian had called when Arielle arrived to relieve him for her shift. He asked me to meet him for lunch. I lock my door, and I'm about to pivot on my heel when my phone dings in my hand.

**Christian: Pizza okay, or do you want tacos?**

**Me: How about we meet at the park and find a food truck? I've been inside all day.**

**Christian: That sounds amazing.**

**Christian: Do you want to know something else amazing?**

I bat my eyelashes, a blush heating my cheeks as I get ready for him to flirt.

A ping I hadn't heard in months sounds from across the hall at the same time my phone lights up with a text.

**Christian: They fixed your elevator.**

My insides freeze and I look up as the elevator door opens again. Christian's standing in the middle, phone in one hand, and a sideways grin on his face. "Isn't it amazing that it works?"

"What are you doing here?" I rush inside the elevator, excitement budding in my chest.

He pretends to scoff. "Did you think I could climb those tower stairs again?"

"I thought we were meeting at the park."

"We have a lunch date, and." He takes a step closer to me. "I still need to make up for the other time I didn't kiss you." His hand drops to my hip, and his eyes pace between my eyes and lips. I know this look. I've memorized it by now, and I am so ready to kiss him.

As if on cue, the elevator door closes, and music plays out of the speakers, a light jazz that couldn't set the mood better if I had tried. As he leans in, he doesn't close his eyes. My eyelids drift down as our lips meet in the sweetest smooch. My heartrate skyrockets all the while I struggle to prevent my knees from knocking together. I can't help but wonder how I got so lucky.

We ride the elevator down with our lips locked until the door dings, and rapidly opens. Startling us to take a step back, we both stare wide-eyed. My jaw drops. Mrs. Nelson is walking Oliver, and they are waiting for the elevator on the bottom floor. "Who let you guys out?"

She waddles inside, taking her time, but Oliver's a good companion not pulling her faster than she can manage. "We walked to the mailbox because it's such a lovely day out."

"I see that." A smile spreads across my face as Oliver greets me by licking my hands. "Hey, boy. I'm sorry I didn't walk you today."

"He's fine." She pats his head and takes a step toward the door. "I'd better hurry back upstairs before the elevator breaks again and traps me down here."

I nervously chuckle, not at all doubting that could happen. Mrs. Nelson looks back at me. "Well, I'm afraid I do have bad news, and I hope it doesn't upset you. I do think now that I don't have to take the stairs, I'll be able to walk Oliver all the time. I enjoy getting outside."

I bite back a smile, not wanting her to see that I consider this good news. "I will miss our walks, but I totally understand. I'm getting regular shifts at the Coffee Loft again, and my website will be just fine." I bravely reach out, grab Christian's hand, and lace my fingers through his. We step out of the elevator together as I call back, "Besides, I don't need to look for hunks anymore. *I just had my last first date.* "

# Epilogue

## Six months later

"Well." Christian brushes his hands together and swipes the newly signed contract off the desk. "That settles it." Slipping the contract into a manilla envelope, he seals it all the while his eyes are on me. "A business partner is the last thing I ever wanted, as I had dreams of building this empire by myself, but I can't afford not to keep you around."

"It's hard to believe we ended up as partners after the rocky start we had." I chuckle reminiscently as I stand, and we both exit Christian's Coffee Loft office together. It's Friday night, after closing and we're the only ones in the store.

"I guess you're no longer my boss." My lips curl into a dubious grin. "We are now equals, which means I get to make decisions, too."

"Oh, man." Christian playfully rolls his eyes. "What did I get myself into?"

Tapping my chin, I pretend to assess the store. "It looks like we might need to do a little remodeling." I walk to the coffee bar and motion to the empty counter space. "We need a long row of French presses here—"

My voice drops off because I find a random French press with a giant gold bow on it, sitting exactly where I had motioned. *How'd that happen?* "What's this doing here?" I motion to it, as it's clearly out of place. I had just cleaned this counter. It must be part of one of his jokes.

"Pardon my French press." Christian swoops in front of me, and slides the press off the counter, removing the lid with his other hand while tipping the canister toward me. "That's because I have a question for you."

"You do?" I run my tongue over my lips, hydrating them. "What is it?"

A glimmer of light reflects off something inside as my heart slams against my chest, pounding so loudly it echoes in my ears. Everything's playing in slow motion, and I want to scream in all caps that I can't believe this is happening!

"Oh, wait a second. I thought I had a question." Christian mumbles with a taunting grin on his face. "I forgot what it is."

"No, you didn't." I squawk out with a high-pitched laugh.

"Maybe I didn't forget, but it's really late." His gaze slides to the door, and he takes a step back. "I need to get to bed."

"That's pure torture." My stomach tanks, yanking my heart with it. I can't believe he's playing me like this.

"Oh, look." He points to the backroom as his sarcastic grin appears. "The store's on fire."

"I don't like you anymore." Pushing my pouting lip out, I cross both arms in front of my chest and take a giant step toward the door.

"Stop." He holds his hand up. "It's just a joke." He slides in front of me with the ring in his hand. A perfect princess cut on a white gold band. We never talked about rings, but it's exactly what I would have wanted. "After I had the contract drawn up this week, I was thinking about partnerships a lot. It wasn't enough for us to be business partners. I can't imagine my *life* without you. When you know, you know. I want that for us—to be life partners."

His eyes sparkle, and I'm back to screaming in all caps inside as he takes a knee and holds the ring out. "Will you marry me?"

"Yes." I squeeze my toes together as he slides the ring on. I eagerly pucker my lips, but he doesn't kiss me. Instead, he smiles one of his secret smiles at me, signaling my interest to pique. "What's going on?"

"Just one thing?"

Ice runs through my veins, as I can't believe he's placing a condition on our engagement. It's such odd timing, and my brows angle down. "What is it?"

"You have to agree from now and until *forever* the only French presses we are going to have in this store is your lips on mine."

"Deal." I smile sweetly and press my lips on his. While our lips are pressed together, I reach back and grab the French press off the counter. When I pull back from our kiss, I slip on a sly smile and hug my French press to my chest. "This is coming home with me."

# Welcome to the Coffee Loft,

## where the romance is always brewing.

Grab your favorite table over in the corner and be prepared to be swept off your feet. This multi-author collection features some of your favorite sweet romance authors that you already know and love as well as a few new names you'll be rushing to check out. From cold brews to cappuccinos and frothy frappes, there's something on the menu for every romantic comedy reader. Fake dates, meddling matchmakers, friends-to-lovers and so much more, each stand-alone story is the right blend of sweetness, guaranteed to warm your heart.

Happily-ever-afters coming right up!

**Series link** →https://books.bookfunnel.com/thecoffeeloftseries
Guess what else?

I have another release planned for this series and it's up for pre-order now.

**No More Mr. Chai Guy** → https://www.amazon.com/dp/B0C
QDQCF8F

No More Mr. Chai Guy  - Part of Coffee Loft Fall
Collection and coming in to kindle 9/04/24

"I'm open!" My throat burns with hot breath as I emit a scream that formed from the bottom of my gut. I weave to dodge defensive player #22. Our star running back, Rocco Bella, hurls a long pass at me. I lunge forward, grappling for the football, barely staying upright, if not for the tips of my toes. Once I regain my footing, I'm gone.

Destination: endzone.

"Ladies and gentlemen," the announcer's voice ticks up in tension, running back #47, North Newson, has the ball, and he's heading to the endzone!" The crowd rushes to their feet with fanatical screaming. I pump my legs faster while the announcer echoes over the speakers. "Forty yards, he's going for it!"

I'm lightning, but my immediate goal is to be even faster. I dig in and pull as much speed as I can. This touchdown is all we need to take the lead, and we are down to two minutes on the clock. I don't even want to think about the scout in the stands tonight who made it clear he was watching both Rocco and me. It's both of our goals to play in the NFL, and winning this game could make both our dreams come true. "Thirty yards!" the announcer counts down, his voice on edge. The crowd becomes unhinged.

A linebacker's behind me now. He's so close, his breath puffs out in audible waves, which make the hairs on the back of my neck stand up. My chest drums out explosions, as my heart crawls into my throat and I top out my speed. I'm almost there. Twenty more yards.

Cramps snake up my calves, begging me to slow down, but my mind is a tank, and I refuse to cave to any pain.

The linebacker finds a burst of speed, rushing my side, but I'm slick and weave to the side, dodging him. The crowd rumbles with so much noise, it's as if the bleachers are about to collapse, and the ground is going to split open. The linebacker isn't done, and he is back on my side again. There's nowhere for me to go! I'm blazing forward and being run out of bounds.

*There's someone here!*

A cheerleader in mid-cheer.

I frantically swipe my hand to push her out of the way, but she's not paying attention and *wham*! We collide. I tumble over her, taking her with me, and we roll together off the field all the while the crowd is roaring.

When we finally stop turning, I steal my gaze forward. I'm laying smack on top of Gia Bella.

Head cheerleader.

Prettiest girl in school.

Rocco's little sister.

She also just happens to be the woman I've been secretly in love with for *years*.

Her gaze hooks mine, and our breaths heave out, blending as we freeze together by instant magnetism.

"North! Nice job throwing the game for us," Rocco sarcastically screams as he jogs to the sidelines, anger oozing out of his eyes. "And get off my sister!"

Ice pumps through my veins as my body awakens to the fact that *I'm lying on top of Gia Bella*! I quickly roll off her, face fiery with embarrassment, and I pray we can laugh this whole thing off. As I rush to my feet, I reach back to offer Gia a hand up, but her face pinches and she grabs her knee.

The crowd quickly hushes, and it's so quiet you can hear a fly fart. "Are you okay?" I whisper as if the sound will cause her more pain.

Her silky ponytail cascades over her shoulder, shielding her face from me, but it doesn't fully conceal her clenching eyes with a single tear drop below the left one.

I suck in a hard breath.

She's hurt.

*I did this to her.*

I blink, and Rocco slides in next to her, pushing me to fade to the background before I have a chance to plead sorry. She's quickly surrounded by medics. Her dad flies out of the bleachers, huddling in, and then she's whisked off the field. My team's lining up again, but I'm frozen.

"North!" Coach yells at me. "You're benched."

*Of course, I am!*

At this point I hardly care about the game, as my heart's slamming against my ribcage, panting Gia's name. I want to run after her, but there's nothing I can do for her.

The game must go on.

I regretfully take my seat on the edge of the bench, while my teammates pound my back. "Wrong kind of touchdown, Bruh," someone snickers.

Rocco returns, glaring at me through narrowed eyes, smeared with his eye black, and he grumbles, "You know, you just ruined everything. We were supposed to win tonight."

"How is she?" I rise to my feet, searching his face for clues.

"Stay away from my sister," he growls while piercing his eyes into mine, sending a chill spiraling through them all the way down to my toes.

"It was clearly an accident," My voice is resolute, and I take a solid step back from Rocco. A switch has been flipped, and Rocco's grin widens as he steps closer, closing the gap I had just created, while invading my personal space.

"You better watch your back," he sneers, his breath hot on my face. But as he raises his fist to strike, coach comes out from behind us, freezing us both in place.

"To the bench, boys. *Now!*"

*She's fine*, I reassure myself, as I pivot, and plop down on the bench, hanging my head. I've taken way worse hits than that and walked them off. She'll be right back out in a few moments. I stare down the path that leads to the locker rooms, waiting.

*Please come out and be okay.*

But she never returns to the field.

# Also By J.P. Sterling

### *Bosses and Billionaires Series* (**All Standalones**)
Maid for my Billionaire Boss
Upcycling My Rig-Pig Boss
Marooned with My Celebrity Boss
Kissed by My Billionaire Boss

### *A Heart that Dances Series (New Adult)*
Dancing on Broken Ankles
The Stars We see
A Heart that Dances
A Heart that Loves

### *Water and Stone Duet (Young Adult)*
Ruby in the Water
Lily in the Stone

# About J.P. Sterling

**Hey you! Thanks for being here.**

Let me introduce myself.

I write wholesome stories and adore all things slapstick humor and heart strings.

Growing up, I binged on classic comedy like Lucille Ball, and Carol Burnette. It was a great escape from reality, even when the plots were farfetched. I discovered my love for writing slapstick comedy after motherhood, and I haven't looked back.

Aside from writing, I'm also a wife and homeschooling mom, a holistic nutritionist, a jewelry designer, a professional archivist, former college instructor and lover of all things dark chocolate.

**Author Clean Code: I like to make my stories about the story and not about a bunch of profanity, mature content, or graphic violence that are only there to shock you. I write my stories to be family friendly.**

**Let's get social!**

I just launched a private reader group on Facebook. I can't wait to welcome you there. This is where we share all the things humor and heartstrings.

Hop in my reader group here: →**https://www.facebook.co m/groups/1500850764081965**

FREE AUDIO BOOKS: → **https://www.youtube.com/c/J pSterling**

INSTAGRAM: →*https://www.instagram.com/authorjps terling/*

FREE NEWSLETTER: →**https://landing.mailerlite.com /webforms/landing/q9c0v3**

FACEBOOK PAGE: → **https://www.facebook.com/jpster lingauthor/**

# NO MORE
# MR. CHAI GUY

# Contents

# Blurb

*An All-Star football player. A popular cheerleader. Can they finally move from the friend zone to the end zone?*

### Gia Bella

I've been working this low-wage-going-nowhere job for ten years. Don't even ask about my dating life. Yes, sir, life is pretty...uneventful. That is until my hoarding dad accidentally burrito-wraps himself in his collection of fly paper.

I'll pause so you can visualize that.

Who should answer his bellowing cries for help, but none other than the boy next door—A.K.A. North Newson, the single man I've loved since I was six years old. Only now, he's all grown up, and still oh so handsome. With decades of unrequited love steeping, I can't fight the attraction anymore.

*However, there's one small issue.*

Just when we make progress, he pulls away as he did last time, leaving me to wonder if he's falling for me too, or if he's just simply being a nice guy.

### *North Newson*

Highschool was football and Gia, but life brought about one giant fumble for both.

I moved on from football, going to college for coaching instead. I lucked out and scored the head coaching job at the very same school I had attended. But I never moved on from Gia no matter how hard I tried. When a second chance with Gia shows up, the instant magnetism returns, and I try my hardest to win her heart.

*However, there's one small issue.*

*Someone is trying to keep us apart . . . but I won't be defeated again.*

*No More Mr. Chai Guy is a 2nd chance, Brother's rival, sweet romcom with a HEA.*

# ONE

## Gia Bella

# Homecoming Game

A rush of adrenaline fuels my heart to thump out like thunder-claps as I weave in between the support beams of the old rickety bleachers. It's junior year Homecoming, and I'm finally an upper classman. I'm determined to make this year the best year—and one to remember forever. Our mediocre-and-a-tad-squeaky marching band has begun to practice the school's fight song for the half-time performance, and the disjointed melodies fill the crisp autumn air. The anticipation of the year's most exciting event already hangs thick as fans trickle in.

Here I am squinting—I lost a contact lens in cheerleading prac-tice—until my eyes land on him.

North Newson.

The single soul I've been enamored with since I first laid eyes on him. With a deep breath, I pool all my courage, and continue towards him, heart pounding against my rib cage.

North is so handsome he makes people around him halt in their tracks. Being humble, he returns my gaze with a nonchalant smile and shy wave, but I can't imagine he doesn't know what his presence does to all the girls. The flush of his cheeks gives away his true feelings as more than modesty. He is one thousand percent shy, but that only makes all the girls fawn over him more. Despite his many options—any girl he'd want—he remains single, adding to the mystery.

Oh, and he's in the senior class with my older brother, Rocco, and happens to live right next door, so I see an awful lot of North.

Not that I'm complaining.

Nope, nothing but positive vibes from me.

Maybe a little blushing.

I was six years old when we moved into our little rambler next door to him. The drive from east Long Island wasn't long, but I had packed all my stuffed animals in the backseat in between Rocco and me. Of course, Rocco grumbled about them, but I tuned him out by sticking a Hello Kitty earbud into each ear. When Dad pulled our Dodge minivan into our desperately-needing-some ce-ment-patches driveway, I had loaded as many stuffies as I could carry in my arms—with no help from Rocco.

Being independent for a grade schooler, I had planned for a second trip. When I returned for them, North stood with the rest of my stuffies. He had watched us pull in from his picture window and had run over to help. With his wild dark mop of hair that curled by his ears, and the perfect shade of naturally-sun-kissed olive skin, I had decided then and there that he was the most beautiful boy I'd ever seen.

Ever since football season started, we've been secretly meeting under the bleachers before the games. It began as a cheerleading thing, as my squad had put together treat bags for each player, filled with a sports drink, protein bars, and cards we all signed. I begged my squad to let me personally give North his bag, and then he started asking to meet in the same spot each week. He claims I'm good luck. Last week he even brought me a blue carnation.

What in the world of flower language does blue mean?

He said it was Bulldog blue. Our school colors are red, white, and blue, but I'm not going to lie, I hope it means he loves me. I don't want to be that pick-me girl that people complain about but when it comes to North, yes, I'm her.

Being so shy, he didn't say much about the flower other than, "It's for good luck." I didn't care if it was for horrible luck, I accepted that flower, and when it started to die, I pressed it in my chemistry book.

My heart pumps against my ribcage. The mystery of this meet-up and the excitement of my crush swirl together. "Hey Gia." The light wind rustles the lush curls by his ears. He's already wearing his #47 Bulldog jersey, complete with eye black, while he cradles his helmet under his arm. My heart could literally skip an entire chorus of beats just to hear him say my name.

"Hey." I do my best to act chill, and flash him my cool smile. "How are you?"

"I can't believe it's my last Homecoming game." He shifts the helmet from one arm to the other. "I guess I got the warmup time wrong, and I only have a few minutes." Pausing, he scratches an itch on the back of his head and speaks even slower, "Ah, earlier I overheard Rocco mention you didn't have a date for the dance tonight." His gaze dips to his feet before raising back up to lock on me, and his words rush out, "Would you save me a dance later?"

A ping slams into my heart, almost breaking my balance. I grab onto the bleacher support beam and pray this isn't the day these ancient poles decide to disintegrate into the ground.

I nervously twirl the end of my long ponytail with my free hand and pause, desperate not to look too eager. Then a weird thought enters my mind.

*Why only one dance?*

Is he asking me because he feels bad that I don't have a date? Why would he not ask me to be his date? The mere thought of me being his date, dancing in his arms, makes my blood pressure skyrocket.

His deep, espresso eyes dig into mine as he waits for an answer. Those eyes do nothing to lower my blood pressure, and my breathing ticks up another notch as I fight the steady slams of my heart headbutting my ribs. If he keeps staring at me like that, I'm going to need a paper bag to breathe in. There's nobody else I'd rather dance with. "I'd like that," I say softly, before lowering my lashes and smiling sweetly.

"Cool," he quips, and jerks his head toward the locker room. "I better go. I'll look for you later."

"Same." Suppressing a squeal, I nibble on my bottom lip and wave as he turns to leave. This night is going to be magical, just like I knew this whole year would be.

# Two
## North Newson

"I'm open!" My throat burns with hot breath as I emit a scream that formed from the bottom of my gut. I weave to dodge defensive player #22. Our star running back, Rocco Bella, hurls a long pass at me. I lunge forward, grappling for the football, barely staying upright, if not for the tips of my toes. Once I regain my footing, I'm gone.

Destination: endzone.

"Ladies and gentlemen," the announcer's voice ticks up in tension. "#47, North Newson, has the ball, and he's heading to the endzone!" The crowd rushes to their feet with fanatical screaming. I pump my legs faster while the announcer echoes over the speakers. "Forty yards, he's going for it!"

I'm lightning, but my immediate goal is to be even faster. I dig in and pull as much speed as I can. This touchdown is all we need to take the lead, and we are down to two minutes on the clock. I don't even want to think about the scout in the stands tonight who made it clear he was watching both Rocco and me. It's both of our goals to play in the NFL, and winning this game could make both our dreams come true. "Thirty yards!" the announcer counts down, his voice on edge. The crowd becomes unhinged.

A linebacker's behind me now. He's so close, his breath puffs out in audible waves, which make the hairs on the back of my neck stand up. My chest drums out explosions, as my heart crawls into my throat and I top out my speed. I'm almost there. Twenty more yards.

Cramps snake up my calves, begging me to slow down, but my mind is a tank, and I refuse to cave to any pain.

The linebacker finds a burst of speed, rushing my side, but I'm slick and weave to the side, dodging him. The crowd rumbles with so much noise, it's as if the bleachers are about to collapse, and the ground is going to split open. The linebacker isn't done, and he is back on my side again. There's nowhere for me to go! I'm blazing forward and being run out of bounds.

*There's someone here!*

A cheerleader in mid-cheer.

I frantically swipe my hand to push her out of the way, but she's not paying attention and *wham*! We collide. I tumble over her, taking her with me, and we roll together off the field all the while the crowd is roaring.

When we finally stop turning, I steal my gaze forward. I'm laying smack on top of Gia Bella.

Head cheerleader.

Prettiest girl in school.

Rocco's little sister.

She also just happens to be the woman I've been secretly in love with for *years.*

Her gaze hooks mine, and our breaths heave out, blending as we freeze together by instant magnetism.

"North! Nice job throwing the game for us," Rocco sarcastically screams as he jogs to the sidelines, anger oozing out of his eyes. "And get off my sister!"

Ice pumps through my veins as my body awakens to the fact that *I'm lying on top of Gia Bella*! I quickly roll off her, face fiery with embarrassment, and I pray we can laugh this whole thing off. As I rush to my feet, I reach back to offer Gia a hand up, but her face pinches and she grabs her knee.

The crowd quickly hushes, and it's so quiet you can hear a fly fart. "Are you okay?" I whisper as if the sound will cause her more pain.

Her silky ponytail cascades over her shoulder, shielding her face from me, but it doesn't fully conceal her clenching eyes with a single tear drop below the left one.

I suck in a hard breath.

She's hurt.

*I did this to her.*

I blink, and Rocco slides in next to her, pushing me to fade to the background before I have a chance to plead sorry. She's quickly surrounded by medics. Her dad flies out of the bleachers, huddling in, and then she's whisked off the field. My team's lining up again, but I'm frozen.

"North!" Coach yells at me. "You're benched."

*Of course, I am!*

At this point I hardly care about the game, as my heart's slamming against my ribcage, panting Gia's name. I want to run after her, but there's nothing I can do for her.

The game must go on.

I regretfully take my seat on the edge of the bench, while my teammates pound my back. "Wrong kind of touchdown, Bruh," someone snickers.

Rocco returns, glaring at me through narrowed eyes, smeared with his eye black, and he grumbles, "You know, you just ruined everything. We were supposed to win tonight."

"How is she?" I rise to my feet, searching his face for clues.

"Stay away from my sister," he growls while piercing his eyes into mine, sending a chill spiraling through them all the way down to my toes.

"It was clearly an accident," My voice is resolute, and I take a solid step back from Rocco. A switch has been flipped, and Rocco's grin widens as he steps closer, closing the gap I had just created, while invading my personal space.

"You better watch your back," he sneers, his breath hot on my face. But as he raises his fist to strike, coach comes out from behind us, freezing us both in place.

"To the bench, boys. *Now!*"

*She's fine*, I reassure myself, as I pivot, and plop down on the bench, hanging my head. I've taken way worse hits than that and walked them off. She'll be right back out in a few moments. I stare down the path that leads to the locker rooms, waiting.

*Please come out and be okay.*

But she never returns to the field.

# THREE

## Gia

I sprawl out in the center of my queen bed, my back propped up on a pile of goose-down pillows with a bag of frozen peas strapped to my puffed knee. *She's All That* plays on the TV again for what seems like the hundredth time. I turn the volume all the way down until the only sound that echoes in my room is the rain outside my window. I flick the remote next to me and wince.

My knee pulses with a heartbeat of its own.

The x-rays showed nothing broken. Thankfully. However, I was mid-cheer with my raised leg bent when the blunt force met my knee, and it dislocated my pelvis. Now I'm stuck home on the night of the biggest dance of the year with a giant stabilizing belt strapped around my hips. My cheer squad all called to express their concern, but they sure didn't slow down their plans on my account. I can't believe I'm missing the Homecoming dance. Not to mention, I didn't get to take North up on that dance I promised him.

That one hurt the most.

For two weeks, I had washed dishes at my dad's pizzeria to earn money for the perfect mermaid-silhouette dress. The stylish garment hangs from the back of my closet door as a taunting reminder—tonight is not going how I had envisioned it. My friends are all at the dance, wearing their dresses. I can almost see them with their hair and makeup done, and dancing with the biggest smiles on their faces. I want to be happy for them, but it stings to think I'm missing out.

Major FOMO.

Worst of all is the nagging thought in the back of my mind that North's dancing with someone else. Clenching my eyes, I gulp another lungful of air and hold it as I struggle through the tears. Junior year is supposed to be one of my best years, but so far this year has been hellacious. One month in and I'm nearly disabled. So much for the cheer team.

What else can go wrong?

A soft knock comes from my bedroom door.

Really? I arch a suspicious brow. I wasn't inviting something else to go wrong. How's this happening?

"What?" My voice drips in nasal-ly inflections, but I don't reach for a tissue. I'm so over everything.

The door pushes open, and I'm expecting my dad, or my brother, but it's neither.

*It's North.*

My eyes immediately skirt over the dirty cheerleading uniform I'd lazily dropped when I changed. My soggy shower towel still lays mid-center on the floor, as I was too disgruntled to bother to hang it up. It's all so cringe, but I can't even move to try to nonchalantly kick those things under my bed. My eyes bug out of my head as an inventory of all the childish stuffed animals I still had lined up on my dresser runs through my head. Can't a girl get a warning? I force a calm smile and lock my gaze back to him.

That did absolutely nothing to calm my nerves, because while I'm laid up, looking like a spicy disaster, he is killing all the looks categories. He's so tall and fit, he looks like a football model in his letterman jacket, and his tousled hair only makes him look more smoldering, drawing me in like a magnet. My palms are pouring out sweat, my hands growing sticky, as I try to casually wipe them on my blanket all the while my cheeks flush with anticipation.

North is here.

In my room.

To see me.

Of course, this is about what happened. More than likely it's a welfare check, but my heart is already making wedding plans. I can't for a second be mad at him for running into me because it was an accident. His brow lowers as his gaze glides from my pea-encapsulated knee back up to my face. "I'm sorry, Gia. I honestly didn't see you there until it was too late."

"It's okay." I sigh, hoping I will be okay.

"Rocco said nothing is broken." His athletic-build shoulders fall, as if he is giving himself permission to let go of his own anxiety. I find myself staring at them. If things had been different tonight, I would be at the dance with my arms wrapped around those brawny shoulders, spinning around the dance floor...

Heat creeps over my cheeks and I blink my way back into this conversation. "Nope. Nothing is broken. I get to rest a lot and start some physical therapy." It's never hard to form a sweet smile for him. His eyes are so wide with concern, molten honey hues sparkle out of the center like the deepest espresso. They are more decadent than a morsel of the most desired candy, and all I want to do is study them until I have a Ph.D. in his eyes. I struggle not to blurt out how handsome he is. "I'm going to be fine."

He stuffs his hands in his letterman jacket pockets and rocks back on his heels. Need I comment on how doing something as simple as that makes him that much hotter? Anything he does adds another layer of handsomeness to him. He's clearly won the gene pool lottery for every feature of his face, but the fact that he's humble about it magnifies his handsomeness by a billion. "I, ah, brought you something."

My head springs back, and I give him another quick once over. He's not holding anything. "You did?"

"Yeah, I left it in the hall because I wanted to check on you first." He sticks one of his Nike sneakers back out the door, before softly calling back, "I wanted to make sure you were awake first." When he pops his head back in, he's got a half-crooked smile on his face—the one all the girls talk about—and he's carrying a *toddler-sized*, reptilian, stuffed animal. It's bubblegum pink with three horns sticking out on each side of its head. He has an open mouth grin on his face, he's literally the cutest lizard I've ever seen. "I hope you still like stuffed animals."

The memory of our first meeting slams into my brain, and my cheeks rage with fire. I can't believe he still remembers. And yes, I'm still obsessed with stuffed animals, even though I'm supposed to be past that age. I'm stunned into silence, rapidly blinking to see if I'd somehow opened my eyes to an alternate reality. One where this isn't happening, because this doesn't happen to me. I take the stuffie into my arms and squeeze him tightly as if this alone has the power to heal me. He takes up my whole lap, but I don't set him next to me. I can't stop holding him. It's comforting to have something weighty on me.

"It's an axolotl," North is now standing so close to my bed, I can smell his deodorant. It's like miles of evergreen forest doused in rainwater, mixed with the embers from a recent campfire. I've never yearned to be a Girl Scout more in my life. I blink, forcing myself out of my distraction, *again*, North is still talking, "—a special type of salamander who's endangered. They make the best pets because they always look happy, and my goal is to get a real one someday."

I cling to my stuffie, peering at North over his adorable head, the kindness of his gift sweeping into my heart with the speed of a desert windstorm. I really didn't hear more than a few words about his weird amphibian hobby, but I had never been more ecstatic to pretend to care about something boring. "That's awfully sweet of you, and so fascinating." I bat my lashes, and I continue to gush. "I saw you skip lunch a few times for the science Olympiad, but I didn't know you were such a fan of lizards."

"What's not to love?" He gives me a masculine one-shoulder shrug before tacking on, "I was hoping he'd make you smile."

"Thank you." Despite my knee pulsating like a strobe light, my lips are about to crack down the center as I'm beaming brighter than a spotlight. After a pause, I force a change of subject, "How was the dance?"

"Ah, I never made it there. I was worried about you."

"Oh." A magnified ping—that was more like a clang of cymbals—vibrates in my gut. I hadn't considered North's visit to be anything more than an obligation to clear the air. The dance is the biggest event in school and everybody and their dog goes. My voice is tiny, as if afraid to mingle with the air when I echo, "You didn't want to go to the dance?"

"Nah." He passes his hand through his hair, ruffling it even more. "The only reason I wanted to go in the first place was to get a chance to dance with you, but since I ruined that, there was no reason for me to go."

My eyes skirt my room. He really is here to see *me*. He could easily have sent the stuffed animal home with Rocco if he had wanted to go out, but he didn't.

He came here.

The hottest guy skipped the biggest dance of the year to see me. That means something, right? If I had known that blowing my knee would summon the hottest boy in school over to my bedroom, I'd have hired my own hitman.

My heart motors against my ribcage as I take a risk and motion to my desk chair. "Did you want to hang out? I can put something better on the TV."

"Yeah, I would." He glances down at his Nikes for a split second, before bringing his gaze back up, his beautiful eyes trapping mine. "I ah, actually, am, wondering if maybe sometime, you'd—"

"Gia!" My dad manifests in my doorway behind North, holding a plate up near his ear like the perfect waiter. I love my dad, but I want to shoot daggers out my eyes at him as he has the worst timing. Could he not have eavesdropped first to find out we were about to have a moment! "Pizza's here." Dad gestures to the plate he's holding, as if nobody on the planet has ever seen one of those.

Of course it's pizza. It's clearly not a chicken. Add to the fact that dad *always* has a pizza.

He's owned a pizzeria called Bella's—named after our last name—since he was fresh out of school. He always jokes that since my mom died, pizza is his one true love, and the only thing he knows how to cook. He's not a man of many words, but he loves to use food as a point of connection, and this is clearly his way of cheering me up.

"Hi, Mr. Bella," North bleeps as he straightens his posture and darts his hand through his hair again.

"It was a good game." Dad obviously ignores the bigger issue as he pats North on the back with his free hand. "We almost had them." Another one of Dad's loves is football. North is clearly a third. He has a heart for many things, and he's never been one to hold a grudge. He also isn't one of those overbearing dads. He's the dad who effortlessly smooths everything out. "Did you see they patched Gia back together?"

"Yeah." North's dimpled chin moves up and down, fire on his cheeks. "I'm so sorry for all the trouble I caused."

"Not your fault. Accidents happen." Dad gently waves off North's apology. "There's plenty more pizza in the kitchen. Go back and help yourself. I brought extra home so the kids can stop over to eat after the dance."

North's gaze bounces back to me, and then on Dad. "Ah, I—"

"Grab a slice and bring it back." Dad jerks a thumb over his shoulder toward the kitchen. "Gia's not going anywhere." Dad advances to the chair I had moments earlier offered North, and plops down. "I'm here, too. We can all hang out."

"Th-thank you." North stammers before scurrying down the hall. Dad slides my plate over to me, his gaze snagging on the axolotl. "Did North bring you that?"

I nod, as I blot the top layer of grease off my pizza with a napkin Dad had tucked under my slice. I've never kept any secrets from dad as we had a very open and chatty relationship.

While scratching his neck, Dad stares back to the empty hall. "That boy has always had a serious case of puppy love for you."

"—Dad!" My cheeks glow warm as I rush to cut him off in a hushed voice. "He can *hear* you."

"Nothing wrong with what I'm saying. He's a nice guy. Just too shy. He needs to get over it and just come out and tell everyone how he feels about you."

My gaze slides to my knee. "He said he feels awful."

"I wasn't talking about your knee." Dad scoffs as North's footsteps return in the hall, but he doesn't shut up. "We all know there's more going on in that boy's head than feeling awful."

Dad's words drop off right as North returns, and an echo reverberates in the room. I fight the urge to crawl under my blanket. I love my dad dearly, but some days he's so cringe. "Come on in." Dad's boisterous voice fills in the pulsating silence, and I suffer through the next twenty minutes of listening to him tell North all about the new mixer he got at the pizzeria. North's a good sport and doesn't let a stray eye linger my way as he stays glued to dad's every word, leaving me to wonder if it will ever be my turn to talk to North.

Truthfully, it's very unlikely as he just seems so shy about some things. The fact that he came here at all is really a miracle.

# Four

## North

My lower back is a bay of sweat by the time I finally find a long enough pause in Mr. Bella's pizzeria stories to excuse myself for the night. He's alright for a dad, and all, but I get the impression that he's suspicious of me, like he can tell how much I care about Gia.

Maybe I'm overreacting.

I hope I'm overreacting.

With a cringe on my face, I tiptoe down the hall at record speeds, ready to make a clean break. It's apparently not my night as I nearly smack into Rocco, who is coming through the kitchen side door. His eyes immediately narrow, skipping over me to bounce on Gia's open bedroom door then dart back to me. "Sup, Bruh?"

"Nothing." I rub the back of my neck, forcing myself to appear casual. "Just stopped over to see how Gia is doing."

"It's almost midnight."

"Right." Standing my ground, I jerk a thumb over my shoulder back toward her room. "Dude, your dad's been here the whole time, feeding us pizza. He had all these stories, and I thought it was rude to leave."

"Are you for real?" He steps forward, his nostrils flaring out like he's sniffing me. Even though he plays running back, the dude's built like a linebacker. But it doesn't matter if he's built like a ballerina, he's not a dude you want in your face. "What do you have going on with my sister?"

"Nothing." I clamp my mouth shut and wag my head, totally confused he'd care this much. Before I know it, his fist finds my jacket collar, and he slams me against the wall. "I'm only going to tell you one more time. You stay away from her, or else."

"—Ah, or else." I scramble to find my footing, and slide against the wall, inching toward the door. I know giving into his taunts will only make it worse, but I really have no intentions of fighting him. I'd rather just walk away.

"Just stay away from her," he hisses right as Mr. Bella appears in the hall.

*Finally,* one time Mr. Bella's magical manifesting power helps me out. "I thought I heard someone out here. How was the dance, Rocco?"

"Fine." Rocco's dark eyes never leave my face, and he takes another step, crowding me toward the door. "Just seeing North out."

"R-right," I stammer, as the doorknob is finally in reach, and I toss a wave over my shoulder. "Bye, Mr. Bella. See you later, Rocco."

I'm out the door in the next second, slamming it behind me to race across the yard. I have no idea what got into Rocco. He's never been that way with me before, but apparently, he's protective of his sister.

I don't ever want to see that side of him again.

# Five

## Gia

The next Friday night, dad picks me up from school, but since he has to close the pizzeria, he takes me back with him. We sit in my favorite booth, the one with the red stained-glass tiffany lamp hanging above it, and a black and white photo of the Brooklyn Bridge next to the large window. Rocco—along with all my cheerleading squad—had gone on the bus with the football team to their travel game. As much as I try to be optimistic, it's hard to be left out. Everyone is gone.

I rest my elbow on the table and plop my chin in my palm to sulk. This is going to be a long football season if I must sit out the entire time. Dad goes behind the counter to grab our pizza, leaving me to stare out the window. The weather even matches my mood, overcast, with thick clouds threatening rain. With the temperature hovering right around that thirty-three-degree mark, rain will easily turn into freezing rain, creating the worst-case scenario for travel. I really hope the bus makes it back tonight, or I might be spending the whole weekend without my friends. I sigh heavily as everyone is experiencing junior year without me.

"I'm glad we have this time together," Dad starts when he returns with a small pizza, taking a moment to center it in the middle of the table, and we both dish up a piece of my favorite pepperoni and jalapeño. While dad stuffs the end of his napkin into his shirt collar, he adds, "I was hoping we could talk."

My expression may have been a bit guarded. Dad and I have always been close, but with everything going way wrong this year, I'm scared of what's next. "Talk about what?"

"What's up with Rocco?" Dad's dark eyes soften, but he doesn't hold back from taking a bite of his slice before he speaks again, "The coach called me and said he's been having a lot of issues with his temper, even more than usual."

"I don't know." I pick at the cheese strand that never ends as I try to politely nibble it off my slice. "You know how he is. He has a chip on his shoulder, and he doesn't let anyone talk to him."

"I know." Dad lowers his lashes, hooding his eyes, being hard on himself. The truth is, Dad has done about everything he can think of to help both Rocco and me succeed in life, but he's only one person. It was certainly easier when Mom was around, but she passed unexpectedly last year after a very short battle with breast cancer, and Rocco has had anger issues ever since. "I sure wish he'd talk to me."

"Maybe someday he will." I dab the corner of my mouth, ignoring the knot in my stomach that always buds when we talk about any of the changes our family has gone through this last year. I change the subject, "Hey, I have a question for you."

"What's that?" One of his bushy brows spikes over the other.

"Something happened to Rosie, my axolotl. I had her when I fell asleep last night, but when I woke up, she was missing. I looked all over for her, but with my knee throbbing to its own tune, I had to give up. Have you seen her?"

"I have not." Dad tilts his head, thoughtfully. "Not aside from the fact that every time I've seen you this week, you've had her on your lap."

"Right," I exclaim, as I love her so much. "I never let her out of my sight, and now she's gone."

"I'm sure she'll show up." Dad pats his hand on top of mine, just as a crowd of teens walk up outside the window. It takes a moment for me to recognize the Bulldog blue, red and white. "Oh, look at that. The team must be home early. It looks as if they are all headed to the coffee shop."

I recognize my whole cheer squad and several of the players. My heart skips a beat when North passes in front of the window, with Rocco behind him. The crowd rushes across the street, and I feel a pang of envy as they all file into the coffee shop. *Just another thing I'm missing out on.*

"You should go." Dad coaxes softly. "I'll help you across the street."

Pulling one side of my mouth up into a lazy smile, I hate to leave him, but he understands. "Do you think I'll be crashing?"

"Not at all. You may not be able to cheer anymore, but you can sit at the coffee shop to hang out. You need to at least be able to do that much." Dad jumps to his feet and holds his hand out to help me up. "Besides, then you can keep an eye on that brother of yours."

"Thanks Dad." I take his hand, and limp forward, favoring my swollen knee as a bubble of excitement fills my chest. Finally, after a solid week of being left out, there's something I can do, too.

# Six

## North

Due to the forecasted sleet, our game got called after the third quarter, giving the win to us, and we make it home before eight. We're all hyped up, and head to our favorite spot, the old coffee shop by the school, for a celebration. It's nothing fancy, and the old guy who works here gives us a side eye more than a smile, but it's big enough we can all go, and it fits a teenager's budget.

Although, one thing about me is, I despise coffee. I love the smell, especially if it's freshly roasted, but I will gag on even the lightest coffee flavor. Blah, no thank you!

I order my chai tea, and head to the back booth, sliding in next to Rocco, who's trying to flirt with one of the cheerleaders. I forget her name, or maybe I never knew it, but she's the red-headed girl who's always next to Gia on the bottom of the pyramid.

"I think we lucked out tonight getting the game called," I say, trying to get in on the conversation.

"We wouldn't have to rely on luck if you could catch the ball." Rocco teases a smug smirk with both corners of his mouth. Sometimes, he doesn't know when to shut up. I had dropped two passes this game, and I admit I can play better, but it's not like it's on purpose. Swallowing, I bite back a rebuttal as every day it gets harder to be on a team with Rocco. I know he's been through a lot this last year, losing his mom, but that didn't slow him down on the football field, or with the ladies. If anything, he's gotten more popular, and it often seems like my presence is annoying to him, and he uses me as a verbal punching bag to inflate his own ego. Don't get me started on the weird threats to stay away from Gia. As if I'm some predator. I've known them both for over a decade.

I don't care to sit here with Rocco and be insulted. My gaze slides back to the counter, and I see my drink waiting for me. I slide out of the booth and stroll back through the narrow row of tables. Out of the corner of my eye, I recognize Gia standing next to her dad, both waiting at the counter as well. I quickly scan her body and let out a giant sigh of relief that she's standing. Engrossed in conversation, neither one of them notices me.

I slip my tea off the counter, raising it up and pause for a quick temperature check against my lip. It's perfect—not too hot or too cold—the Goldilocks of temps, and I take a giant sip before my taste buds register the bitter afternotes and a tornado of a dry heave spirals up from the bottom of my gut. I gag so hard, all while trying to avoid vomiting. "Blah," I choke out. "This is *super strong* espresso."

"Oh no!" Gia's gaze perks back at me as she registers what's happening. "You must have gotten mine. It was called, but I was letting it set for a while to cool."

It's too late, the espresso is making me feel ill, and I grab my stomach and gag again. "That has to be the most disgusting thing I ever drank."

"I'm so sorry." She reaches out, placing her hand on my back, giving it a sort of motherly pat, but the chemicals her touch ignite in my body sends a whirlwind of sparks to rapid fire in my heart. Add that to my near-vomiting and I'm about to lose my balance.

"Here's some water." Mr. Bella presents a glass, and I eagerly accept it, swallowing all of it while closing my eyes. The water cools my gut and resets my tase buds.

"You guys got back early tonight?" Gia's look of concern is still pinned between her brows. She's so unbelievably beautiful, but my gaze drifts to the back booth, and sure enough Rocco's glaring at me with narrowed eyes. He's never going to let up about this. I can't even have a simple conversation with Gia without him hovering.

"The game got called due to the weather forecast," I say with a concise grin as I slip my foot back away from her. "Let me pay for a new drink for you since I ruined yours."

"Don't mention it," Mr. Bella cuts in. "I took care of it."

The barista places another cup on the counter calling out, "Spiced chai."

"That's me." I nervously chuckle, as I feel so torn. I want so badly to talk to Gia, but also don't want Rocco to slam me against the wall again. Choosing the latter of the two options, I flash my palm up in a wave, and turn away from Gia, dragging my feet back to the booth.

Some days I can't wait to get out of this town. Not to put any distance between Gia and me, but you know when you've outgrown some people, and maybe even a place. That's clearly Rocco and me. Eight more months until graduation, and it can't come fast enough.

# SEVEN

## North

## About a decade later . . .

Finally, it's the NFL season kickoff. I've been waiting for months, excited to try out my new, mounted 72-inch flatscreen. Of course, I've been using it for months, watching animal and nature documentaries, but that's not nearly the same as football. On my back porch, I've got Cajun seasoned chicken wings perfecting in my wood chip meat smoker. They'll be done by halftime.

Sunday excellence.

I ease down onto my soft leather La-Z-Boy recliner, kick up the footrest, and crack open a frosty Dr. Pepper. The carbonation bubbles burst out and fizzle against my palm. I'm almost salivating as I slowly raise the can to my mouth.

*"Heeeeeelp!"*

One of my brows hikes as I follow the sound, and I sit up straight, arching my neck to see out the window. Nothing out of the ordinary. Mr. Bella's old red Ford is running in his driveaway, but he's nowhere around. Maybe that's a little odd, but I'm sure he ran back in the house to get something.

It's not worth missing the first kickoff for.

*"Heeelp me, please!"*

I advance toward the door, bracing it open, but still, I see nothing. I scratch the back of my head as my gaze draws back to the TV. I missed the first kickoff. I glance at the clock counting down the minutes until the end of the first quarter. There is nothing I want to do more today than watch my Giants win, but I can't ignore someone screaming for help. I sigh, tucking my phone into my pocket as I rush out the front door.

My concern growing with each passing second, I follow the bellowing around the back of Mr. Bella's house to the detached double garage off the back alley. The overhead door is open, but I can't see inside of it. Stacks of boxes—every size and shape—overflow out the front. It's like it's moving day, or something. "Mr. Bella," I holler. "Are you there?"

"North?" His voice staggers from somewhere deep inside the caves of boxes.

"Yeah, it's me. You okay?" I inch closer, but there's no path to go between the boxes. "Where are you? What's all the hollering about?"

"Don't laugh," his voice is stern, echoing off the unfinished walls and cement slab floor. "I seem to have gotten trapped back here when I stepped on some of my fly trap paper, lost my balance, and knocked over a stack of boxes on top of myself."

My gaze scans the boxes, and again, I'm amazed how he got past the first row. I'm going to need a crane to get him out. "Um, hold on a second!" I pull out my phone, still assessing the stacks of boxes.

If they are heavy, it could take an hour, or more, to get back to him. I couldn't help but feel an intense pang of regret. *I'm going to miss the game.* But deep down, I understand Mr. Bella needs me. "I'm calling for backup. We'll get you out."

I scroll through my contacts, looking for a number to call. I sure don't want to call Rocco. Even though he lives in town, he turned into one of those dudes I never care to see again. I scroll through my small list of names, landing on my group list for the football team I coach. They'd muscle these boxes out of here in a hurry, but if he's hurt, his family needs to know. Since I already established I'm not calling Rocco, that leaves me with *Gia.*

A ping sparks in my gut at the sight of her name in my phone. Gia and I hadn't spoken to each other since high school. I had all my dreams come true, getting drafted to the NFL right after high school. Actually, Rocco and I both got drafted, and it was such an exciting thing for our school and town.

My dream was short lived when I blew out my ACL during training, before I even played in a game. I returned home to attend college for coaching. It was around that time, I quickly discovered Rocco was illegally betting and cheating, and he got kicked out of the NFL. I was not the one to turn him in, but since I was the only person he knew that fully understood his secret, he blamed me for getting caught. I tried to tell him so many ways, it wasn't me who turned him in, but he always seemed to blame it on me.

After that, we drifted apart, as my life was heading in a different direction. I got a job teaching and coaching at my old high school. The housing crunch was in full steam, and I couldn't find a place to live. When my parents decided to retire, move to Mexico, and sell their house, I jumped at the chance to buy them out. Their house is in my district, and close to work. It was an afterthought when I remembered that Rocco and Gia's dad still lived next door.

Rocco hardly came home, so that isn't an issue. Gia moved further west, to the Hamptons, working in some fancy resort. When she does come home, I avoid going outside, or I stay late at work. We never had a falling out.

It's the opposite.

Gia and I never had much of anything, thanks to Rocco making sure I never got near her. Staying away didn't do anything to cure my affection for her, because even after all these years, the sound of her name makes my heart slam against my ribcage, reminding me of all the risks I didn't take in life. Not to mention, all the ways Rocco bullied me, and larger than anything else—all the love I've stored for Gia.

I rake my hand through my hair and cringe.

I can't believe I never asked her out.

I almost did, once.

I chickened out, instead asking her to save me one dance.

*Ha! Not sure what I was going to do with one dance, but the thought of holding her in my arms for even a few minutes made my heart quake at a magnitude 9.0.*

Later that night when I visited her, I tried to ask her out again. There was a moment where she looked at me as if she could think of me as more than a friend. My mouth went dry, and I couldn't get the words out fast enough before Mr. Bella showed up.

I take a deep breath, my memories telling too much truth. Rocco threatened to destroy me if I ever touched her. At first, I thought he was joking, but his pupils got all dilated, and he never dropped it.

I tried to pretend that I didn't love her.

I'd look the other way when we'd cross paths in the hall at school.

My feelings just continued to grow.

It was as if Rocco could smell them, because he was always there, too. He refused to get out of my way, and now after so many years have passed, I've still never had the chance to tell her how I feel.

"Hey, are you still there?" Mr. Bella hollers back through the boxes, inserting himself into my memories.

"Yeah." I blink, and remember he's still trapped. "Give me one moment, I'm calling Gia."

I swallow, coating my throat as this is going to take every ounce of strength I have.

# EIGHT

## Gia

As the sous chef of the resort's five-star restaurant, I take my desserts very seriously. I had my perfect round cakes cooling in the pans, and I'm starting work on my famous chocolate ganache to coat the layers. I drop the vat of butter in the pan and turn on the stove, taking a moment to adjust the temperature just right.

"Wow, Gia!" Grace exclaims as she returns to the kitchen with a matte black folder in her hands. Even with her blonde ponytail tussled under her hairnet, and one single wispy strand of hair dangling next to her face, she still looks like a model. "Someone is blackmailing you. They dropped off all these photos, and there's no note." She yanks a glossy 8 by 10 out of the packet, flashing it at me. "It's scathing."

Churning my stomach into knots, I advance towards her while frantically wiping my fingers on my apron. "Give me those." I tug the packet out of her hands, but my stomach loop easily relaxes. "These aren't embarrassing photos. These are my new headshots.

I paid a lot of money to have them done." I flip through the pile of 8 by 10s. Sure, my glasses are bigger than average, and I've sprouted more than a freckle or two since moving near the beach, but there's nothing *scathing* about these.

She perks a feather brow at me. "Headshots?"

Half embarrassed, I lower my gaze. "I'm thinking of going on this new dating app called, *Your Last First Date*. My dad got a free match card the other day while he was standing outside his shop. He clearly isn't going to use it, so he gave it to me. I looked it up, and it has really good reviews, and frankly, I must be doing something wrong." I shake, the hopelessness of being forever single seeping in. "I'm not having any luck with the available dating pool."

"What?" Grace's perfectly pink-stained lips part into a gasp. "When were you going to tell me this secret?"

"It's not a secret." I drop my voice, remembering we're still at work. "I didn't think I needed to advertise it everywhere."

"I totally understand." She asserts with a giant supportive nod, and whispers, "Did your date last weekend not go well?"

"There wasn't anything *wrong* with him, but there wasn't anything right either," I continue in a hushed voice, hoping our manager, Marcie, doesn't overhear my personal life saga. "He was so distracted by everything. If he wasn't looking at his phone, he was ogling the table of women next to us. It's my pattern that I get men who don't care to spend quality time with me."

"I had no idea you were feeling so overwhelmed you were looking online." Grace's lips grow into a full smile. "Online dating is going to be so much fun. What else do you have up your sleeve?"

A chuckle falls from my lips. "Well, this morning it was a sock left over from the dryer." Before I can crack another joke about my lackluster life, my phone vibrates in my pocket. I pull it out, and my breath hitches in my throat.

*North Newson.*

His name sears a trail right to my heart. I hadn't spoken to him in years. Not that I ever forgot about him. He seems to be that one "what if" in my life that never resolved itself. If I'm honest, he's one of the main reasons I don't care to go home much. It's torture to my heart to see him over the fence. I'm instantly transported back to high school when I was head over heels for him.

Or maybe I'm not remembering the past feelings as much as I'm unable to push down current ones.

Either way, it's immobilizing.

"I'm going to step out back and take this," my voice floats out, while my eyes hang onto North's name.

"Oh, more secret dates." Her voice drops into a sweet giggle.

I wave her off as I step out the kitchen backdoor and into the private loading dock. The phone's ringing, and I dig deep and suck back a chestful of fresh air before I press the phone to my ear. "North Newson. What a surprise."

"Gia Bella. Your voice sounds exactly the same."

"I would hope so. Last I checked, I'm still me."

Expecting him to chuckle at my witty banter, his silence tips me off that this call is serious. I clear my throat. "How have you been?"

"I'm well, but that's not why I'm calling. I'm calling about your father."

Ice frosts my veins, stilling me. "Is he okay?"

"Oh, yeah," He rushes in a calming tone that soothes my nerves. "He's fine. Not in any trouble at all. Except, he's stuck in his garage."

"Oh." I nod even though no one is here to see me. This news isn't anything shocking, as my dad's hoarding situation has slowly gotten out of hand. I joked it would only be a matter of time before his stuff would swallow him up. "How bad is it?"

"His garage is a sea of boxes. I can hear him bellowing back there, but can't see him. I'm going to call some of my football players to help, or it will take me all night."

"I'm a couple hours away at work." I let out a sigh as I add the hours on the clock. "It'll take me a while to get there, but let me make some calls. I'll get a hold of someone who can help you. I'm so sorry he's bothering you."

"Oh, he's no bother. No need to send more help. I have it under control. I just felt like his family should know."

"Well, thank you. I appreciate it." Blinking my eyes, I push back the smallest tear as his thoughtfulness is so touching. North always was the most kind-hearted man. "I, ah, I'll figure something out with work and get back to you."

"No problem. I'll be busy digging him out."

His voice ticks up at the end as he is ready to sign off, but in a freak moment of bravery I cut him off. "It's great to hear your voice again." He immediately hushes, and the silence drags on for the longest beat before I tack on, "Anyway."

"Same," he softly quips.

A moment later and the line goes dead, and I'm running my hand through my needing-some-fresh-highlights hair.

*Who am I going to call?*

It's Friday night. Not that it would matter if it was Monday morning, I still wouldn't have more friends. I'm sure not calling Rocco. We'd had a falling out last year after his NFL career imploded amidst a cheating scandal, and he cut me out of his life.

North said not to bother sending help, but this is my dad. Someone needs to talk to him about the bigger issue. He got lucky this time, but what happens when he gets hurt? I can't put this off any longer.

I turn back toward the hotel, knowing I don't have anyone to call. This was a me problem. "Grace!" I call out, as I tiptoe back inside, ready to bargain with my future first born child. "Can you cover for me? I need to leave."

"Dad!" I call into the open overhead garage door, peering through the narrow pass in between the stacked-to-the-ceiling boxes. An echo ricochets back, but no answer from him. He's only lived here a couple of decades, but his garage is so jam-packed, it looks as if he's lived here a hundred years. Being a collector of all things, he hates to toss anything out if they might be useful. His thriftiness has gotten out of hand. My brows pin together as I turn back toward the house and continue up the broken steppingstones leading to the side door.

I forgo a traditional knock and open the side door. It creaks with the exact same squeal it did when I lived here. It's not that Dad is lazy, because he's not. He still works nearly every day at the pizzeria, but it's becoming clearer he's in some sort of funk, letting things go. "Dad!" I call out, "you alive in here?"

"Umph." His old man sigh wafts from the living room and I pad forward to find him sitting on his favorite recliner, watching ESPN, with an open jar of honey roasted peanuts on his lap. "You didn't have to come over," he grumbles.

"Yes, I did. I was worried. Are you okay?" Scanning his physique for any signs of physical damage, I find nothing out of place except for his unibrow pinned together in a lowered position, hinting at a bruised ego.

"It was nothing. I slipped on my vintage fly paper. I think it is defective because it really didn't need to be so sticky. You should have seen it, stuck on me like cement and tangled me up until I knocked over some boxes, and they trapped me."

Resisting the urge to roll my eyes at his lack of accountability, I instead scan the lone box in the corner of the room. "Did you get a recent delivery?"

Dad's gaze follows mine to the box. "Oh, that." He shakes his head, tacking on, "That's some of your brother's old high school football trophies. After he got kicked off the team, he wanted to throw them out. I'm saving them in case he ever wants to look at them some day."

I roll my bottom lip in and survey the rest of the house. Except for the box of stuff, it's actually pretty neat. There are no dishes in the sink, and his throw blankets are neatly folded. *Maybe the hoarding is not really that bad if everything is in the garage.* I mean, he can always close the door and not look at all his junk. "Well." I tsk, and stride toward the box, scooping it up. "Do you think we should tuck it away in Rocco's old room, so we don't have to look at it?" I'm already walking down the hall to Rocco's door. Dad's reply muffles as I turn the knob and immediately startle, taking a giant step back.

*A mountain of stuff is about to crash into me!*

"Aaggh!" I scream, and slam the door shut, ducking against it as crashing noises sound like a fireworks finale. *Who was I kidding?* It isn't just in the garage. I'm pretty sure every room, drawer, nook and cranny is stuffed, and dangerous! My eyes grow wide as I frantically search for my dad. "Dad, this is serious. You need help cleaning your house out."

"Nah, it's not an issue." He waves his hand dismissively. "It doesn't bother me."

"Dad, you almost died today because you have an insurmountable amount of clutter. It's a life-threatening issue. We're cleaning this out, starting now, with this room." I press my ear against the closed door, all the crashing noises have died off.

It should be fine. I swallow, and twist the knob slowly, pushing the door open.

Piles!

The stacks are not even neat like in the garage. There are mounds of clothes, and most don't even look worn. On Rocco's old desk, there're stacks of opened bills that I assume are paid, and for no reason I can think of—other than Dad hates to throw things away—they've been allowed to accumulate. There are boxes of old Christmas decorations I don't remember ever seeing in the house, and so many collections! He must have a collection of everything! Old books, model cars, footballs with every team logo on them, and so much sports memorabilia he could start a museum.

I inhale a deep breath and slowly let it out. "I'm going to need some coffee for this."

It's Saturday night, and I spent all day cleaning out Rocco's old room. Dad and I only had one minor argument about a stack of 1970's newspapers. Dad insisted we needed to save them. I offered to clip out the articles he wanted to save and make him a scrapbook, but he couldn't tell me which articles were even in there. At that point, I girl bossed those papers into the recycling. You'd think that would be the end of that, but no. Later when I was using the restroom and went on a hunt for some toilet paper, I found the newspapers had somehow escaped from the recycling bin and stuffed themselves underneath the bathroom sink. I can't fathom what's so special about them.

We ended up bargaining. He keeps the papers, and I get one single box with some of Rocco's football memorabilia: trophies, medals, photos, even old jerseys. It seems like everything football he'd ever owned from the time he was a little kid is in his old room, and I promised that I wasn't going to throw it away.

I wanted to. I certainly had to chew the inside of my cheek, to get through that conversation. I might have fibbed that first time I sternly said I wasn't throwing it out, but then there was a tiny tear in the corner of his eye, and I had to come up with a better plan.

He suggested donating the junk to the high school where Rocco played. Rocco is still a local legend. They will surely love to put this stuff in their glass display cases in the hall. Or at least that's what I need dad to think they are doing with it. It's just too painful in so many ways for us to keep this stuff around. Besides the fact that Rocco created one of the biggest NFL scandals and cut out his entire family, there isn't any room for it.

As I drive over to the school, my mind races with all the signs I overlooked about this hoarding issue. Clearly, I looked the other way when I shouldn't have, but I'm doing my best to right the situation now.

I smile nostalgically as I see the school. Some things never change. A sigh falls from my lips as Dad's old Ford putters forward over the rocky-road parking lot. Even after all these years, there's still the giant pothole near the entrance, and thankfully, I remember to slow for it. There must be something going on tonight as I can hardly find a parking spot. I jump out of the truck and grab the box. It would be better if I waited until Monday to call the principal and drop by, but I have to work next week. Surely there are some teachers here I can talk to, and they can pass my stuff to the right person.

I tuck my face down to keep warm and out of the chilly fall breeze. I should have grabbed a thicker jacket, as I had dressed to clean in old knee-ripped jeans and a faded sweatshirt, not considering I'd be making deliveries. Racing to the entrance, I'm easily able to enter the unlocked door.

I scan the lobby. It had been almost ten years since I was here, but boy am I instantly transported back, feeling as if it is my first day of school. The same blue carpet and white lockers. A ticket table is set up near the auditorium entrance next to a sign that announces a band concert. Even the not-quite-desirable smell is still the same. Like old buildings mixed with teenage drama.

I never thought much about high school after I left. I wasn't one of those kids who pined for those years. I had fun. I did the things and attended the events, but I was glad to move on. I slow my steps as I near the office. The lights are off, but this is the hall where all the cheerleading memorabilia is hung, and I have to see my old photo.

All the varsity squads for the last twenty years have a 5 by 7 framed photo. I quickly find my squad, cringing when I see my bangs. At the time, I remember quite clearly my plan was to hide my giant forehead, but this photo is evidence of the fact that it did quite the opposite. I turn on my heel, as my cheeks burn, and I'm glad I'm alone. Down the hall, the band door is open. I heard everything in their room is updated, and they finally got some fancy tiered seating. I stroll down the hall, curious to peek inside.

"Ahem!" A stern, deep phlegmy throat clears from behind me, startling me to stand up straight and pivot toward it. A stout man wearing a dark button-down shirt with a badge on it glares at me with lowered eyebrows. "Excuse me, ma'am. What are you doing here?"

I eye his badge, concluding he must be some sort of rental cop for the concert. "Sorry." I pull up one side of my lips into a half smile. "I don't have my hall pass."

Rent-a-cop has no sense of humor and doesn't even twitch a lip. "I'm going to have to ask you to come with me."

"Now, is that any way to ask a girl out on a date?" I'm not trying to be annoying, but this guy is too serious about his rented badge.

I'm clearly not doing anything wrong. I'm standing in the hallway with a box of antiques.

"I see you have confiscated school jerseys in that box." Shortie rises to his toes, peering down into the box.

"I didn't steal this!" My jaw dramatically flops open. "I brought it here to donate. These are my brother's, Rocco Bella's, jerseys." As much as I didn't care to talk to Rocco anymore, it felt good to name drop him because he is famous. "He played quarterback here and holds all the school records—"

"Ma'am, I'm going to ask you one more time to come with me, or I will be calling the cops—"

"Gia! There you are." A familiar voice wafts from behind me as an adjacent classroom door sweeps open. As I pivot, the voice carries on, "Glen, she's fine. You can let her go. I asked her to come visit and bring that stuff."

I know that voice!

My heart thumps against my ribcage as I raise my gaze.

North Newson.

He hasn't aged at all, with his dark-chocolate-espresso-brown eyes, still as dreamy as ever, in addition to his full mop of hair that falls to frame his eyes, drawing all the more attention to them. He looks better than a walking deep fried donut, and he's coming this way.

# Nine

## North

"Gia," my voice hangs on to every letter in her name, and it feels so right. I had heard Glen harassing someone in the hallway, the voice teasing familiarity, but when I heard her say her brother was Rocco Bella, my heart puttered to a screeching halt, and I knew I had to rescue her from creepy Glen.

I step into the hall, making up a story as I speak, "Sorry if you got lost. I should have given you better directions." I look back at Glen, my irritation with him growing with each passing second. "She's my guest. You can leave us alone now. I'll make sure she's properly escorted out when she's ready to leave."

Glen stutters out tsks, like an old engine that won't turn over but can't quite form a word. Obviously, his ego got deflated, and he takes a minute to regain his composure before he finally hmphs and heads out.

Gia places a perfect hand over her mouth, suppressing airy giggles. Not wanting to risk Glen circling back to find us laughing at him, I wave her inside my classroom. "Come on in here." She flashes me a sweet smile, sending a shiver down my spine. I couldn't help but follow her every step with my eyes, captivated by her graceful movements as she disappeared inside. I might have let out a giant sigh of relief that she didn't have a permanent limp. I dart inside right behind her, and we burst out laughing once the door closes.

"Thanks for saving me from whoever that was." She dramatically stares in the direction Glen went.

"It's Glen. He does the nightshift and gets a little carried away. I'm sorry you had to deal with that." My smile lingers, but I pause and remind myself to breathe. Even though I had just spoken to her the other day, it's the first time I've seen her in years, and she's stunning. A rush of excitement and nervousness spirals together. Her intense eyes lock onto mine. With the chalkboard as her backdrop, I can't help but feel like I'm sixteen again, staring at her. "I, ah, saw your car in your dad's driveway. How's he doing?"

"He's good." A single lock of dark hair falls in front of her shoulder as she thoughtfully shakes her head. "And thank you for rescuing him. I'm sorry I didn't make it back in time to help you. I had no idea things had gotten that bad, but I'm cleaning stuff out today. That's actually why I'm here." She peers down at the cardboard box she's holding. "I'm trying to donate some of Rocco's football trophies. I don't care to ever see them again, but I promised Dad I wouldn't throw them out. I know Rocco and you had a falling out, but he does still hold the school records. I thought the kids might want to see them. Do you think there's room somewhere for them?"

A deep heartburn sizzles in my chest, and I twitch at Rocco's name. Having lived in his shadow the entirety of my football career, I thought after I left the NFL, I'd finally break free from it.

That didn't happen.

Even now that I'm coaching a winning football team, I still get asked almost daily about Rocco.

I'm never going to get away from him.

But yet, this is *Gia* asking for a favor.

I'll do anything for her.

"Sure. You came to the right person." I tilt my head thoughtfully and reach forward. "I'm the head football coach now. I can put it up in the locker room."

*Not that I really want to have to look at Rocco's dumb stuff, but if it makes her happy, I'm doing it.*

A relieved sigh falls from her throat. "Thank you. I was getting nervous for a minute, thinking I might end up hauling it back to the house." A smile blooms on her lips, lighting up the whole room with her radiance, and reminding me how she always had that ability to spread joy just from the expression on her face. People just felt welcome around her. "One box down, at least a hundred to go."

Pulling my gaze from her smile, I force myself to walk the box over to my desk, pushing a mountain of still-needed-to-be-graded papers over. Doing my best to sound relaxed. I call back over my shoulder, "So, how long will you be in town?"

"Through tomorrow." She scratches at her earlobe, appearing a little extra fidgety than I remember her being. "I'll have to head back in the evening because I work Monday, but I'm hoping to be able to get through the garage before I leave."

I throw my head back, forcing a sarcastic laugh. "Good luck with that."

"Right." Her smile is still growing, which makes mine larger, too. It's been years since I've seen her, but this feels so different than previous times I've chatted with her. In the past, Rocco was always loitering near, with his nostrils flaring.

Rocco isn't here now.

This may be my only chance to spend some time with her.

I cocked my eyebrow. "Do you have time for me to show you something?"

"Ah, yeah." She nods, her eyes widening, becoming even more captivating. "Please do."

With my index finger, I point behind her where a fish tank lines the back wall, and it is home to one of the coolest creatures on the planet.

"You finally got a real axolotl?" She steps forward, all the features on her face are etched in anticipation. "It's exactly like the one you gave me but waaay smaller."

*She remembers the gift.*

My heart rockets into my ribcage.

Swiping my tongue over my bottom lip, I force my lips to keep moving. "I'm impressed you still remember what they're called. Most people have no idea they exist."

She's standing in front of the fish tank now; her button nose almost presses the glass. "I wouldn't either if it weren't for you. That stuffed animal is one of my favorite gifts I've ever gotten."

I turn my head, doing my best to hide the heat on my cheeks.

"Oh, look how cute he is!" She gushes as she pushes her finger on the glass, and he swims right to her. "I can't believe he's in school."

"The kids love him too, and since I teach biology, the school actually gives me a little stipend for projects, so it was a no brainer."

"I love that you got one finally." She rotates back to me, and I wouldn't have believed it is possible with her previous smile already radiant, but now her whole face is beaming, emitting so much exuberance, it's hard not to think it's genuine. I'm vastly aware this is one of the few times I've been alone with her. Except for the stolen moments we used to have under the bleachers, and that night at her house, there aren't any other times I can think of. That night is a haunting reminder of the time I failed at asking her out. I still think about what might have happened if her dad hadn't barged in.

Shoot, that was years ago, and who knows when I'll see her next.

I might not ever get another chance to ask her out again.

My palms are awash with sweat. It really is now or never. We aren't going to be able to small talk for much longer. "Gia." I clear my throat, my heart fluttering with nerves and uncertainty. I've never wanted anything more than for her to say yes.

"What?"

"Ah. I know it's late, but I'm done here, and headed out. I'm, ah, wondering if you want to grab a coffee with me?"

Her eyes flick side to side before replanting on me. "You mean right now?"

"Yeah, if you don't have anything else going on, I'd love to catch up."

She doesn't pause for even a beat. "I'd love to."

I swallow a larger than average swallow. Okay, it's a gulp. It took me years to do this. An immediate surge of relief washes over me, until I realize asking her out is the easy part. That was one sentence. Now, I have to remain calm for the next hour.

My heart constricts, begging me not to blow this.

# Ten

## Gia

North and I stroll down a quaint street to the coffee shop that, to my surprise, has recently been bought out by a new franchise called The Coffee Loft. For an early Saturday evening, the shop is extremely bustling. We pass through the heavy door and are instantly met with the aroma of the deepest roasted coffee and cinnamon, making saliva swell in my mouth. "This place is adorable," I coo, taking in the new remodel and the rows of unique coffee cups hung on the wall, and finally latching my gaze on the chalkboard menu on the back wall.

With every possible flavor anyone could dream up, I have no idea how to pick just one. We shuffle our feet until we get to the front of the line, where we are greeted by a blonde woman with a ponytail pinned on the top of her head. "Chai guy, how are you?"

"Good evening, Portia, I'm good." He slowly pulls out his wallet while keeping his attention forward, "And you."

"I'm still brewing." They both laugh at the pun, and I smile, already feeling welcome.

North extends a hand toward me. "You can go ahead and order."

Without having had much of a chance to read the rather extensive menu, I eeny-meeny-moe the fall flavors in my head until I land on the last one. "Ah, I'll try the frosted maple latte."

"Great choice." The barista, who I now know is named Portia, punches some digits into her tablet and shifts her gaze to North. "And your usual spiced chai?"

"Yes, ma'am." He taps his debit card to the scanner before I have a chance to offer to pay.

"You guys can grab a seat, and I'll bring them right out." Portia grins at us before she turns her back to pour our milk.

"She has a nickname for you." I turn and whisper under my breath. "You must come here often."

"Yeah, it's the closest place to the school." We shimmy down the narrow aisle of tables until we get to the only open booth in the back. We both slide in, and North continues the conversation, "They're swamped in the mornings, and I usually don't have time to wait. Somehow, I made this a daily habit on my way home from work. Portia is one of the owners, and she's always so nice."

"And you are addicted to the spiced chai?"

"Addicted makes it sound so negative. Let's just say I have a high chai absorption rate, and I'm not much of a coffee drinker. I love the smell but can't stand the taste."

"Don't like coffee. I'm not sure if we can be friends." I bite back a fit of laughter as I recall when I almost made him vomit so many years ago. "I remember when you grabbed my straight espresso by mistake."

"Yes," he quips, his cheeks growing pink. "That was the second time I tried it, and it was not successful. Ever since then I've stuck to the chai."

"What?" I tilt my head closer, pretending to have a hard time hearing. I couldn't help but notice the way North's eyes light up when I tease him, so I keep going. "That menu is packed with amazing flavors, and you haven't tried anything else?"

"That's sort of how I am." His easy smile falls into place, and it does everything to make me feel comfortable, while pulling me to him. He looks exactly how he used to, still the most handsome man I've ever seen. He tacks on, "If you haven't noticed, I like my routines."

"How would I know that?" I tease, as so many sparks of connection fire between our gazes. It feels amazing to banter with North. "I haven't seen you in years."

"I guess we have Rocco's junk to thank for bringing us together again."

"I guess." My gaze falls to my lap, where I had started to pick at my fingernail. I still my hands and ask softly, "Do you talk to him much?"

"More than I'd like." He blows out a hard breath right as Portia arrives and quietly slides our drinks onto the edge of our table. We both take our cups, and I eagerly take a sip of mine, while he places a palm over the top of his lid. "At first, I didn't really believe he did all that bad stuff, and that's what made it hard for me to see his life fall apart."

"Same," I quip. "At first, I couldn't fathom he was that person, either."

"When he moved back to town and bought that car dealership, I was surprised because I had assumed he went broke paying for the lawyers. I tried to come around as a friend, but there were an awful lot of closed-door deals going on. Then out of nowhere he became the town mayor by that landslide write-in vote, and I was blown away. How can anyone with a criminal record be in his position? He must be paying everyone off, and I still don't have a clue where he gets his funding. I don't want anything to do with that."

North shifts his jaw side to side, as if he's grinding his teeth. "The kicker is that he is practically my boss because his dealership is the biggest sponsor to my football team. As much as I'd like never to see him again, a couple times a year I have to take a photo with him, or sit by him at some booster dinner."

"Yeah, I've seen his name in the paper a few times for his support of the football team." It doesn't sting to hear that North doesn't talk to Rocco anymore. I'd mostly gone numb to any news about Rocco. He was the golden child growing up, and that would have been enough of a shadow to live in, but when he made it to the NFL, his whole personality changed. "We don't have to talk about him anymore. I think we've both tried to move out of his shadow long enough."

"What would you like to talk about?" His lips curl up, higher on one side. "What have you been finding at your dad's?"

"Well, aside from the sports junk I found at the house, I also found a collection of bird houses. Say, you like biology. Do you think your students would maybe like twenty-seven bird houses? It could be a class project. Adopt a bird forest," I ramble, hoping I'm persuading him. "Extra credit if you get a bird to move in. Think of the options."

His laugh is instant. "Sure, I can take them off your hands if that makes you happy." My gaze locks with his. He's so dialed in to me right now, sitting across from me. Not at all like the last few dates I'd been on where the guy had been distracted.

Not that this is a date.

It's just coffee.

He takes a slow drink of his chai and lowers the cup back to the table. "Okay, so we have football trophies and bird houses. Anything else?"

"The better question is what didn't I find. He has a collection of everything from rocks and seashells to teapots and towels. It never ends."

"And he's fine with you giving away all his stuff?"

"No." I fight back a small tear as this is the first time I've been able to let out any stress over this predicament. Hearing my dad had been trapped by his stuff had been overwhelming, and I have so much guilt over not helping sooner. "He's not fine with it, but I'm doing it anyway. I booked a therapy appointment for him to try to get to the bigger issue, and he is so upset with me for doing that, but I have to put my foot down. I love him. I don't need to have a Lifeline Alert about him being swallowed up."

"It's okay, you had no idea it was that bad." His hand slides across the table, and he gently places his palm on mine. "You're doing a good job." He says it so convincingly I actually believe him. "If you want," he goes on, "I can stop over tomorrow and help take out a load. I mean, that is if your dad doesn't mind me helping."

"Dad doesn't mind you helping at all. He's always had a soft spot for you." *Not as big as the soft spot I have.* "We'd both love it if you can help."

"It's settled. I'll come over in the morning after Sunday service." He sneaks a look at his watch, the sparkle in his eyes dimming a little. "It's almost closing time. I hate to get kicked out." His words are slow and measured, like he's torn.

I flash a look at the clock on my phone. A half hour had gone by, but it felt like five minutes. "Oh, I didn't realize it was getting so late." I shimmy out of the booth. "I didn't mean to keep you so long. I truly was just dropping off a box, but I enjoyed your company."

"Don't apologize. The pleasure is all mine." He gives me a crooked smile. My toes curl as we stroll together toward the door, extending our goodbye way longer than it needs to be. "Thank you for the coffee."

"You're welcome. Thank you for having coffee," he replies.

I can't help but feel a sense of contentment wash over me. We follow the streetlamps back to the school. The lamps cast a warm glow on the sidewalks, and something about the moment feels a little magical. We walk side by side, but I catch myself staring at his strong arms, wondering what it would be like to link an arm into his. Before my cheeks warm, I let a sigh out, figuring it's best to wait for him to make his move. "Thank you for showing me the Coffee Loft. I'll have to try them again. Next time I think I'll try the cherry mocha." I stop in front of dad's truck, and turn toward him, enjoying how easy it is to be with him.

"I'm sure the next time I go, I'll have the spiced chai." A glimmer sparks from the corner of his eyes, and it almost melts me.

"Thanks for walking me back to my car." My gaze paces to the truck and then back to North. I don't want to get in the truck. Behind him, the streetlamp glows, setting the ambiance as the light wind tousles the tips of his hair, doing everything to make this moment feel romantic.

"You're welcome. It was easy since you parked next to mine." His eyes bounce off his car, and land back on mine. "Well, I'm leaving now. Tell your dad, hi."

"I will." I place one hand on my door, still not wanting to get in the truck, despite my cheeks starting to sting in the chilly air. North's standing so close, our breaths waft together as his gaze bounces around my face.

"Night." His feet are cemented, and he's not moving.

"See you tomorrow." I slide only one foot close to the truck, hoping he'll maybe try to kiss me, or shoot, ask me to hang out longer. It's really not that late for Saturday night.

"Yeah, I'll call before I come over."

"Sounds good." I slowly open my door, and I climb inside, my heart sinking a little. "Bye."

"Yeah. Nice seeing you again." His feet still don't move, and it's not my imagination that he's wanting to ask me something else, but it's just not working. It's beyond awkward now.

"Nice seeing you, too." I put my hand on my door, closing it a bit.

"Okay. Bye." He turns toward his car, and I quickly shut the door before we invent another fifteen ways to say goodbye. I never remember him being that uneasy before, but at least he wasn't as shy as he used to be.

He definitely is still thoughtful, and as good looking as ever. I turn the truck on and steer forward, seeing that North's in his car, politely waiting for me to pull out. He waves. I wave back. I move in front of him, and wave again. In the rear view mirror his reflection waves back at me.

# Eleven

## North

Somehow, I make it to bed, but now I'm lying here flat on my back, hands locked behind my head, staring at the ceiling. I don't settle as I replay everything I said to Gia over and over in my head. It is so easy to converse with her. She was so attuned, and acted like she had nothing better to do than spend time with me, though she has a literal mountain of work to get back to at her dad's house.

My eyes drift to my alarm clock. 2:14, and I'm still wide awake with a cheesy grin on my face. I can't help but wonder if things would have been different for us had I not been so shy. I had fallen in love with her literally the first time I saw her, but being shy, I made friends with Rocco first. I thought he could be the bridge to bring us together, but it had turned out to be the opposite. All he ever did was warn me to stay away from her. I tried for years to forget about her, but it was useless. There's always a gigantic pull when she is near, like my soul recognizes her presence, and I don't want to deny that anymore.

Even if I wanted to, I don't think I can. It's been escalating so much. Now that I've finally had a chance to sit down with her, I feel like if I don't let her know how I feel soon, I'm going to explode.

I get up early, head over to the church, where I sit in the same pew I've sat in every week for the last decade. After the service, I stop at the Coffee Loft for my daily spiced chai and that cherry mocha Gia had mused about. While I wait for our drinks, I tap my leg and stare at the menu. I should get something for Mr. Bella, too. I have no idea how he likes his coffee. Wanting it to be a surprise, I don't text to ask. "How about an extra mocha," I add to my order after Portia made my other two drinks.

"Absolutely, chai guy." She smiles at me coyly. "Are you seeing your lady friend again today?" The mere mention of Gia makes my heart stutter like a manual car that can't find its gear. "Who said she is my lady friend?"

"She's a lady, and I assumed she's a friend. Most people don't have coffee with their enemies." She holds on to a teasing smirk as she hands over a drink carrier with three cups.

I grab the drink carrier and simply say, "Thanks for the drinks."

"See you tomorrow." She waves at me until I turn my back. As I walk out the door, I text Gia.

**Me: Are you ready for backup?**

**Gia: Yes! I found his stored canned food collection. Some of these pickles are older than me and have horns growing out of them!**

The anticipation of seeing her sets my gut in fire knots. There've been so many times I've wanted to spend time with her that I can't believe it's finally happening. Though, I chuckle that it's not the romantic picnic or walk on the beach, I would have wished for. Nope. I'm literally going over there to clean out her dad's junk.

Yet, I couldn't be more excited, and I grin all the way to her house.

After parking in my driveway, I kill the engine, grab the drinks, and cross the front yard to her dad's. I've taken this path so many times under the pretense of seeing Rocco, when I was actually doing all I could to get a glimpse of Gia. Even after all these years, the grass never regrew fully. I make it to the front step. It's barely forty degrees out, but my palms gloss with sweat.

I'm sure it's the coffees.

It couldn't be anything else.

It's definitely not my stomach flutters.

I shuffle my feet a few times before I decide on the perfect stance to take. I need one that doesn't make me look too eager, yet excited to see her. I hold the drink carrier by the handle and knock quickly before casually leaning against the house with my free hand. All the effort to look relaxed is wasted when Mr. Bella promptly swings open the door.

"North, what a neighborly thing to do." He stands back, and I pass over the threshold. "Gia was telling me you're helping today." He leans in close, dropping his voice to a whisper, "Between you and me, I don't need any help. I'm allowing her to do this because I think she's miserable and misses—" Gia rounds the corner, and Mr. Bella interrupts himself mid-sentence shouting out, "It looks like you brought refreshments. What a saint!"

Gia's gaze catches mine, and a ping blasts to my heart. "Hey," she says softly, the sweetest smile curling on her lips. "I was half-expecting you to have a late awakening about what you agreed to do, and bail."

"No." Shaking my head, I struggle for the right words. Words to tell her there isn't anywhere else I'd rather be. I'm more than willing to throw out moldy food if it means I can see her. "I'm a man of my word. I'm here as I said I would be." I retrieve her drink from the carrier and offer it to her. "And, I picked up the cherry mocha you wanted to try."

"That's very sweet of you." Her lashes lower to the cup, and she doesn't wait to sip out of it. "Thank you."

I pivot and turn back to Mr. Bella. "I couldn't remember how you take your coffee, so I grabbed you one of Gia's mochas too. I hope that's acceptable."

"It's much appreciated." He takes the cup from my hand, and with his free hand pats my back the way he's always done. "Thanks, son."

"So." Gia's voice ticks up a notch, taking on an adventurous tone. "Shall I show you to the pantry and the mystery pickles? I don't have the stomach to dump them out myself. I'd love to stand back on that one."

"I got it." I step toward the kitchen, ready to banter. "My stomach's as strong as steel. If you've got petrified pickles, I can handle it."

Gia opens the large walk-in pantry and motions to the bottom shelf. There're rows of mason jars with dark murky water with barely visible shadows of items inside. "Have at it." Her shoulders bounce as if she's suppressing a dry heave. She's clearly in agony, but I find her animation quite adorable.

"I'll be across the kitchen, sorting through his shot glass collection."

"Hey!" Mr. Bella pipes up with his nose toward the cupboard. "You'd better not get rid of any of those. They're souvenirs from our travels."

"Dad, you don't even drink." She whips open the cupboard to display stacks of shot glasses, one from every state, and every sports logo ever.

"They might be worth money someday." Mr. Bella advances toward the cupboard, but Gia maintains her position, blocking him from getting nearer.

"They'll be worth money now, because I'm selling them on eBay." She's stern in her stance, revealing how feisty she is, and it makes my heart pitter even faster. I don't think there's anything about Gia I don't admire. Even though she can be a little sassy, it's not in a loose cannon kind of way. She always retains her softness. She just has that ability to make the people around her fold.

He rocks back on his heels, glaring at her. "Now I didn't say you can do that."

"*Dad*," She says his name so gently, it's as if she's talking to a baby bird. "If you let me clean these out, I promise I won't touch your hat collection."

He sucks in a hard breath before quickly spitting out, "Deal."

I try not to show my immediate glee as Gia and I share a victory eye lock. It's random, but yet so normal, it throws my heart into a whirlwind spin. One side of her lips curls up. If there is ever a smile to set off sparks, it's hers.

"This needs to be the last box." Gia covers her yawn with a flattened palm as I skim another giant box off the stack of doom in the back of the garage. We've cleaned all day, and now we're burning the midnight oil under the single 60-watt bulb light fixture. It sounds like drudgery but it's not. We've been laughing like kids, talking about the lost years, and sharing stolen smiles as if we're teenagers. My heart is fluttering so hard, it feels like it's in spring training camp. "I can't believe I kept you this long," Gia speaks through another yawn, this one making her eyes water.

"I'm not a prisoner. I want to be here." Each time I smile at her, we hold our gazes a little longer. At first, I thought it may be wishful thinking. She's being nice to me because I'm helping her with this never-ending junk pile. As the looks got longer, smiles turned flirtier, and I can't deny the chemistry at this point. "But I'll agree. Last box, and then we call it a night. We both work in the morning, and you still need to drive home."

"What do you think it is?" Rubbing her hands together in front of the box, she builds anticipation before digging in. "Another bug collection?"

"Judging from how heavy this one is, I'm going with more tools." I lean over and flip open the box flaps one by one.

"I hope it's not another box of clothes. That last one had way too many clothing moths in it for my comfort."

"Nah, it's too heavy to be clothes." I peer inside until I make out stacks of flat, black, and vinyl. "Records!" I gleefully report.

"Another box of records." She scoots closer, and we both take turns pulling them out to read off the funny names, "*Yummy, Yummy, Yummy.*"

"That sounds yummy," I tease.

"I actually remember playing this one when I was a kid." Her smile is so big, it shows all her perfectly even teeth. "Oh, The Everly Brothers," she coos and holds up the next one. "They were my mom's favorite when she was younger."

"1963." I read the date of release on the record. "It's crazy to think that wasn't that long ago, and look how music has changed. Everything is digital now."

"Sixty years." Her eyes widen as they snag on the next record still in the box. "*My Girl*! I wish we had a record player because I loooove this song."

"I'm sure if we keep digging, we'll find one or two." We both chuckle lightheartedly, but I sneak my phone out of my pocket, tap on the YouTube app, and type. "I might have something better than a record player."

Her eyes shift to me when I tap on the Temptations video, and the first few chords of the song ring through my phone. I set my phone on the box as her gaze goes to watch the video, but that's not what I have in mind. Instead, I hold out my hand, gesturing for her to stand. "I think I still owe you a dance."

"Are you for real?" Her brows raise, but she slips her hand into mine, and suddenly time slows way down.

"I hope I'm not too late." Of course I'm asking about the dance, but everything in my expression wants to make it about the possibility of *us*. My breath is even as soon as I wrap my other hand around her back and lead her into a twostep. Holding her is everything I dreamed it would be, and worth the wait times one thousand. The song is an interesting choice for a first dance as it's a bit of an up-tempo beat that causes us to sway together more than embrace tightly, and it's impossible not to sing the lyrics. We both drown out the singer through our off-key belting, but we are giggling nonstop by the time the song ends.

"It's been too much fun today, North." When the song is over, she sighs dreamily and slips out of my arms, heading back to the box of records, staring down at them. "Should we keep the records, or sell them?"

"Vinyl can be worth a lot of money, and you can't replace it easily. I'd say, this is one thing he can hold onto."

"Deal." She closes the box and pushes it back against the wall. "He can keep them." Standing up straight, she brushes off her jeans. "As promised, that is the last box. Thank you for helping."

"The pleasure is all mine. I really enjoyed spending time with you." Her smile lingers in what I have come to recognize as her flirting smile. "So, you are heading back home tonight. Are you going to return any time soon?"

"Oh yeah." She dramatically scans the rest of the boxes. "I haven't made a dent, and I'm not a quitter. I'll be back up next weekend."

"I look forward to it. Give me a holler, and I'll come help."

"I hate to bother you again. This is an awful lot of work, but I do look forward to seeing you again. Maybe we can do something else, too?"

"Yeah…I'd like that, too." I'm not a genius, she's fishing for me to ask her out, but something feels off. It's not for lack of flirting, but there's a knot in my gut, begging me to play it safe. "Ah, my boys actually have a game on Friday night. If you make it back early, you're more than welcome to come watch."

"A football game?" Her gaze angles away, as if floating back to her memories. "Boy, I don't think I've been to that field since you blew out my knee."

"You'll be safe." I hold both my hands up as if I'm under arrest. "I promise, I'll watch my big clown feet, and nothing bad will happen. You might have some fun."

"Maybe I'll make a point to get off work a little earlier so I can come."

"Yeah, I'd love to see you again."

"Me too." I zip my lips, vowing not to go into the longest good-bye again. This time I gaze into her eyes, enjoying how they seem to change colors as they sparkle under the faint garage light. Part of me craves to wrap my arms around her and pull her close. From the look she is giving me, I know she'd kiss me. We've known each other twenty years, it's not like it's too soon, but another part of me wants to savor the sweetness we have between us right now. I don't need to rush anything.

I pull the string on the garage light, and we walk together out of the open overhead door. We are quiet as we walk side by side to her door. I wait on the grass as she hops up the steps and I call to her, "Night, Gia."

"Night, North." She flashes a wave at me and her soft smile beams before she ducks inside.

Sighing, contentedly, I head across the yard to my house, humming the tune to *My Girl,* when something catches my eye. A box is sitting outside of the garage on the driveway. I don't remember putting it there. Maybe Gia dragged it out to make more room? It should be fine there until morning, but you never know...it might be something valuable. Just to be safe, I circle back, grab the box, and take it inside my house. I can run it over to Mr. Bella tomorrow when I see him outside.

Once inside, I place the box on the kitchen table. The top flaps aren't taped shut, looking as if we already went through this box. I don't remember it though. Curiosity piques, and I lift the corner of one flap. Bulldog red, blue and white meets my gaze, and a poster of our old high school football team comes into focus. Now that I know it's nothing personal, I flip open the flap and take the poster out. It's a game schedule with our old team roster.

*Boy, Mr. Bella didn't get rid of anything.*

Near the top of the photo, Rocco and I stand next to each other, arms around each other's shoulders, being the best friends we were back then. Shaking my head, I now know loyalty was only one way. I tried my hardest to be his best friend, even staying away from Gia after he asked me to, but that loyalty didn't get me anywhere. When news of his cheating scandal broke, I tried to give him the benefit of the doubt. He made up lies about his teammates to frame them. I defended him publicly, which almost ruined my career as a coach.

I wish I believed he'd learned his lesson, but I've noticed a pattern where he always gets what he wants. His life has taken him on such a different path, and he's known for hanging out with some of the shadiest business owners, and even politicians. I know one thing...he's not a man you want to cross.

A spiral of shivers trickles down my spine.

Rocco doesn't even talk to Gia anymore.

She said so herself.

Rocco can't possibly still be obsessed with keeping us apart. That was high school. Kid stuff. Gia's a grown woman now

Could he still care?

# TWELVE

## Gia

"You sure are cleaning fast." Grace stands back as I shuffle my empty dessert pans through the dish area, blast spraying each one before pushing them into the automatic dishwasher. Normally, I wait for the hired dish boy to do this. However, he's been on his break for longer than usual, and I'm anxious to get on the road. "I have plans to go to a football game." Hot water steam fogs the little wispy hairs that frame my face, and I brush them to the side.

"I thought you swore off football after Rocco...you know." Grace is always the curious type, poking her nose into my business, but she does it in the most loving way, I can't even pause.

"Not NFL. High school. Actually, my old high school where I used to cheer. However, I'm going to watch the *coach*, not the players." I can't resist a lofty smile as I do one final inspection over the kitchen, not wanting to leave any messes. I've restored it to predinner status with gleaming countertops, and every pot and pan is hung neatly in its place. The only thing left to do now is pull meat from the back freezer for tomorrow, but Grace always insists on doing that on her own, since she's the head chef.

When I finally draw my focus back to her, her feathered brows waggle at me. "Oh, is that so?"

"I think it is so..." I chuckle airily, as this whole week I've been extremely giddy, lighthearted, and nothing can put me in a bad mood.

She smirks knowingly. "So that's the real reason you spent all weekend at home?"

"No." I shake my head, as the stacks of boxes still cloud my brain. "I went there to clean, but I reconnected with someone, and well, we are *connecting.*" My voice trails off into another giggle. "I'm excited to see him again. And, then tomorrow, I'll clean out all the junk."

She sighs, as if she's holding back hordes of advice, but heads back to her prep area, where pans of chicken breast are already prepped, but because she's a perfectionist, she grabs a ramekin of olive oil and a brush and dabs a little on each one. "What are you doing with all the purged junk?"

"Ah, it depends on what it is. If it's worth the money, I'll sell it online. If it's usable, but not worth any money, I'll donate it." The dish boy still isn't back, but I turn to Grace anyway. "If it's okay, I'm going to head out early. All my brownies are cut, plated, and chilling. I even did all the dishes, which clearly isn't the job of a sous chef."

Her grin is instant, teasing yet supportive. "I'm going to need a full report on Monday, but have a great weekend."

"Thanks." My cheeks heat, as I head to the back door, and grab my coat off the hook. Despite being in a hurry, I still pause to peer at the ocean, my daily unwinding, and the sole reason I moved here. I'd dreamed my whole life of living near the ocean. With the meager wages of a cook, I never got close, but I get to work on beachfront property every day, which is close enough for me.

The sun is setting off a kaleidoscope of colors in the sky that reflects off the low tide. There's a soft wave teasing the shore, bringing in random strings of algae as sea treasure. I inhale the salty air and can't help but feel blessed. It's a tad interesting how I had been in a hurry to leave my hometown, but now I rush back home with butterflies in my gut. I'm left wondering if maybe my being in a huge hurry to move away made me miss out on something—or someone—better?

It's first and ten when I scramble through the already-filled bleachers to find a seat near the team. Friday night football is like a holiday in our town, and I quickly determine I'm going to the nosebleed seats. As I pivot to climb the stairs, a husky voice bellows out above the cheers of the crowd, "Gia! I saved you a spot."

A couple of women near me give me a sly smile, and suddenly I'm sixteen again with my first crush, all the butterflies spiral into my gut. I practically float down the steps. True to his word, North saved me one of the best spots, right behind the guys. Across the steps, the band toots out the school song, and it's all I can do not to make a cheerleader high V, as I practiced this song so much, I could dance to it in my sleep.

"I hope this is okay." North quickly leans in, putting a Nike on the bleacher below me. "I had to bribe a lady with a bucket of popcorn to give it up."

"It's perfect." The air is crisp, and stings to inhale. I pull my canary-yellow knit mittens out of my coat pocket and slip my hands into them.

"I'm glad you made it. I'll find you after the game." He strolls backwards onto the field, waving at me. One side of his lips is higher than the other, and a single dimple drops below it like a little exclamation point to his smile.

"Good luck!" I tug my beanie lower to cover the bottoms of my ears. It's been years since I sat outside on metal bleachers in the frigid air. I clearly forgot I should have brought something to sit on. My teeth chatter through each quarter, but there's no way I'm leaving because there's nothing I'd rather do than support North.

North has been amazing for the team—and the whole town knows it—bringing the Bulldogs to the state championship the last two years. It ignited a plethora of school spirit that has taken over the town. Every seat in the stadium is colored white, red, or blue, and flags and posters dot the rows of fans.

A tinge of sadness buds in my chest as I recall how the crowd used to cheer like this for Rocco when he was the town hero. I never assumed he'd always stay in the limelight, but I sure didn't expect him to become such a disgrace.

"Excuse me, ma'am." A young kid taps me on the shoulder, and I turn to find him holding a hot chocolate out. "This is for you."

"I'm sorry, I didn't order that." I tap my coat pocket, feeling for my wallet to pay because it sounds like the perfect thing to warm me up.

"It's yours, and it's paid for." He pushes it further toward me. "Coach Newson put it on his tab."

"Oh." My lips form a perfect O, as a ping spirals right to my heart, and I eagerly accept it. "Well, isn't that thoughtful." The hot chocolate is the secret sauce to keep my teeth from chattering, and I didn't realize how thirsty I was as I quickly finish it.

Before I know it, the guys line up for their final defensive play, and the ball is quickly intercepted. The crowd jumps to their feet, and everyone screams their hearts out while the ball is carried all the way to the endzone. It's a play for the movies as time runs out right when the winning touchdown is scored. I'm back in cheerleader mode, standing on the bleachers, screaming with everyone else. "Bulldog Victory!"

I pump my fist in the air, and the crowd around me cascades down the bleachers, rushing the field. I get caught up in the excitement and run right to North. His open-mouth grin displays all his joy as he effortlessly scoops me up, swinging me around, and we scream out in excitement all the while I'm acutely aware that *I'm in his arms.*

Like his strong masculine arms that have never looked better. Yep, those are the ones. They're wrapped all the way around me, and he's holding me right next to his chest.

Yep, that's strong and masculine, too, and I would have definitely remembered if I'd felt that before. The musky scent of his aftershave permeates off of him, and I'm being consumed by it in the best way.

*This is better than winning the football game.*

After twirling me for more than a few complete circles, North sets me down...but he doesn't let go, his eyes lock on mine. A bolt of electricity slams into my heart, completely disabling me. Being this close to him is all I ever wanted, and it's better than I could have imagined. He's tall, but so am I, and we fit together perfectly. As I tilt my head back just a little, I can see directly into his eyes, and they capture me, drawing me further into his joy. He drops his chin next to my ear, and whispers, "Meet me under the bleachers," before he pulls away, while motioning with his head toward the team huddle. "Wait for me."

My lips curl up, all the while my heart pounds against my rib cage, and I step back, waving until he runs to meet up with his team. His dark wavy hair ruffles under the congratulatory pats on the head. Seeing him so happy makes my heart swell with even more joy.

Taking the long way back to our little spot under the bleachers, I absorb the aroma of the field. Popcorn and fresh air—it all comes rushing back at once. All the nights I watched Rocco play, many years as a cheerleader. After he got kicked out of the NFL, I was embarrassed to show my face anywhere that had anything to do with football, not realizing I lost one of my passions too. I loved watching the games with dad. Even with all those memories of watching Rocco, I can't find one single memory where I wasn't also secretly watching North. He was always in my peripheral vision, but in the center of my heart.

"Hey!" North jogs my way, his voice hoarse from all the screaming. By now the wind is in full force, and light flurries are swirling, causing the tall trees behind the stadium to sway.

"That was fast," I call back to him, while rubbing my mittens together and shuffling my feet. As the sun had gone down below the horizon, it had gotten so much colder out.

"Yeah, it's just nasty out." He slides in beside me as if it's natural for him to reach a protective arm out, wrapping me in his warmth. "You're shaking."

"I'll be okay." I still under the warmth of his arm. "Great game."

His espresso eyes lock on me. "I couldn't be happier."

"I would say," I blurt out over my chattering teeth.

"Not about the game though." His eyes sparkle with so many hues of gold and copper, it's as if they are putting on a tiny fireworks show. "I couldn't be any happier because you are here."

My throat dries, and I swallow as my chatters are stopped with warmth pooling in my chest. I've dreamed of him saying that to me for so long.

That's what this is. A dream.

The best dream.

One I never want to wake from.

I swallow again, gaze into his eyes, and swoon. "I'm happy I'm here too."

Both sides of his lips raise, and I ponder if this is my favorite smile yet. It's hard to decide as all his smiles are his best smiles. "Did you know I had the biggest crush on you in high school?"

"Ah, no. I couldn't tell." The breath rings out of my chest. "You never said anything, other than that time you asked me to save a dance for you."

"Right." He nodded, his movement so smooth, and easy. "I was shy. That obviously didn't do anything but waste a lot of time."

He raised his hand, touching my chin lightly with the pads of his fingers.

*So much time! I scream in my head. It's been years!*

"I assumed you thought I was Rocco's annoying little sister."

His fingers graze my chin as he lowers his lips closer, parting them in the slowest speed setting.

I'm unable to make a sound but my lips part. Drawing his chin even closer to me, the warmth wafts off his skin.

It's surreal.

It's serendipity.

It's our most romantic moment, and I don't ever want it to end. I start to close my eyes and lean in, but he tips his head up and softly presses a smile on my forehead.

Is this right?

Time literally stills as we hold each other – *not kissing.*

*Why aren't we kissing?*

After so many several long moments, I wonder if we are frozen before he reaches for my hand, lacing his fingers into mine. Yes that part is amazing, but *it's not kissing!*

"How about that coffee?" he asks like this is the most casual encounter ever.

"Coffee is always a yes." I force a grin with my un-kissed lips. I don't even have to ask where we're going because he's a man of routines, and his routine is the Coffee Loft.

# THIRTEEN

## North

Sitting across from each other at the same Coffee Loft booth—me drinking my ol' reliable spiced chai, and Gia risking a blueberry mocha—our free hands slide across the table until they meet, and we playfully hold hands like two giddy teenagers.

Gia dips her drink straw into the mountain of whip cream, scoops a glop up, and then brings it to her mouth. I fight the urge to hang my jaw as this might be the most entertaining thing I've seen all year, and I coach football for a living, so I see an awful lot of entertaining things. Need I say more?

"I'm still in so much disbelief over this last week." Her voice is relaxed and smokey, as if we've finally broken all the nervous jitters we've had between us for the last...well forever.

"I've enjoyed this week so much." I make sure to close my jaw, securely fastening it into place, but find myself biting my lower lip.

As she sips from her straw, I slide to the edge of my seat, my gaze glued to her lips. My own lips tingle as if they feel hers on them.

"Let me ask you something." She shifts in her seat, leaning back, relaxing even more. "If you liked me in high school, why didn't you ever say anything?

One word—or rather one big aerodynamic face—flashes through my mind.

Rocco.

I don't dare tell her that her brother had threatened me to stay away, because it will upset her. She already has such an emotional time talking about Rocco. She doesn't need to know another way he potentially destroyed her happiness. I shrug a shoulder, but it does nothing to ease the tension that Rocco's name instills in my body. "Ah, I've always been shy, especially when it comes to you."

"Right, back then." She drags an index finger in the air, as if to motion to the past. "But this week you haven't been shy at all. What changed?"

"I guess the fact that I saw how fast time goes. I figured if you rejected me, I could just avoid you. It's not like you live next door anymore." I reach across the table and grab her other hand. Even holding both hands, I still don't feel close enough. "And because it had to be for something. Someone doesn't hold onto that kind of chemistry for so long if it doesn't matter."

"I know you like your routines." Her eyebrow spikes to challenge me. "Hanging out with me may *mess* all those up."

"To be honest," I slap on my mischievous smile. "all I ever wanted was you to mess up my life."

Her lashes flutter, and I bring her hand to my lips, dropping a chaste kiss on her hand.

It's the most amazing feeling to be able to do that.

Better than winning *any* football game.

Well, maybe not the super bowl, but let's be realistic in our comparisons.

Better than winning any *high school* football game.

Her cheeks flush, and she looks down at her phone. "I think they're going to close soon, but I'm at my dad's all weekend. You're welcome to come on over."

We rise to our feet at the same time, meandering to the door like we've been in sync for years. I walk her all the way to her car and give her my most natural smile. "My car is in staff parking, so I'll say goodnight here." I don't think it's too soon to risk a kiss, but I'm just savoring the sweetness we have right now. I lean in, wrap my arms around her for a long hug. It already feels like we've belonged together forever. When I pull away, I open her car door and say, "Night."

She plops down onto the driver's seat, smiling in a way that brightens her already glowing face. "Night, North."

I close the door and stand with both hands in my jacket pockets as she drives out of the parking lot, and then I stroll back to my car, whistling *My Girl* the whole way.

I round the corner, and notice my car is the only one left in the employee lot, but I'm not alone. A dark figure paces around my car, causing me to squint, and bring him into clearer focus. I understand the presence is no accident, nor coincidence.

Ice floods my veins, and I slow my steps until we're standing face to face. "Rocco."

He stops in front of my driver's door, blocking my car. His shaved head glimmers under the streetlight, and he's dressed like he's in the mob or something in his ominous monotone black.

He's always had a flare for the dramatic. "Well, look at you. Hometown football coach hero, winning the game at the last second."

"What do you want?" My fingers dig into my palms. I'm not afraid of him. I can hold my own. Rocco has never been about physical violence. He always aims deeper than that—the pocketbook.

"Who says I want anything?"

"Well, it's almost ten o'clock." I struggle not to put my fist in his fat smug lip. "You're out here pacing an empty parking lot."

"I thought we could chat." His nostrils flare, tipping me off that he's lying. "With it being near the end of the year, and everything, I was looking through some tax stuff, and we need to talk about my sponsorship check for next year—"

"Cut to the chase," I speak over him. "It's Friday night. This isn't about your check. What do you want?"

He pulls out his phone, flashing something at me on his screen. "Want to explain what this is." He snarls.

My gaze centers on his phone.

*A photo of Gia and me holding each other under the bleachers.*

"I told you to leave my sister alone. Did I not?"

I scoff. *He can't be serious!* "We were kids, Rocco." I shake my head at how preposterous this is. "She's an adult now, and so am I. This is crazy. Can you please step aside so I can get in my car?"

Shoving his phone in his pocket, he narrows his gaze, resentment etching the tips of his lips. "You seem to forget; I never *asked*. You will stay away from her, or you will pay."

*Pay.*

That's exactly what he's after. Blackmail of some sort, but joke's on him, I'm a teacher. I don't have any money. The only thing he can possibly take from me is that sponsorship check, but the whole town counts on that. He'd only be hurting himself.

The thing with Rocco is he is too stupid to see that. He'd be the guy who would destroy his own livelihood if it meant he could take down someone he hates. Every fiber of my being knows he isn't bluffing, but I've spent my life afraid of Rocco.

*I'm so done having him bully me. My entire life I've cowered from his threats. It's gotten me nowhere.*

*I'm done being that guy.*

Anger buds from my gut, burning a spiral of adrenaline through all my extremities. My fingers tighten one by one into a tight fist, and I slowly pull my hand back, winding up. The sequence plays out in slow motion, and it's everything I've wanted to do to Rocco for years. With the deepest breath I can suck in, I dream of slugging him in his gut. Instead, I take the higher road, push past him, bumping my shoulder into his. "Get lost," I murmur and I steal the opportunity to slide into my car. I don't even check the rearview mirror as I squeal the tires and speed off.

I've never felt better.

# Fourteen

## Gia

"Dad." My palm frantically finds the dash while my other hand secures the door handle. "You need to let me drive."

He putters forward in his old red Ford. It's not his speed that is making my heart screech in my chest, but his lack of sense of space. We're on our way to Bella's for lunch and to grab the daily deposit. That part is dandy and sounds like a nice little Saturday. The part that's aging me faster than a banana in an oven is he's *nearly* clipped every car parked on the side of the road.

"There's nothing wrong with my driving." He slams on the old, squeaky, disc brakes. With only the lap belts holding us down, we both swing forward at the waist.

*This is worse than Space Mountain Roller Coaster!*

Cars stack up behind us, serial honking.

*This is where it all ends! I'm clearly going to die!*

"You're lucky you don't have GPS in this old thing, because instead of giving directions, it would be rattling off prayers!" I scream out as I frantically swipe my hand through my hair, pulling it behind my ears, resisting the urge to yank it all out.

"Ah, those GPSLMNOPs robots these days are overrated." He puts his blinker on to turn left but then proceeds to take a *right* on red.

"Dad!" I grab his wheel, yanking it hard to the right to dodge oncoming traffic. "You had the wrong blinker on!" He slams on the brake, halting us in the middle of the road. Again.

*Beeeeep!* A double-decker tour bus nearly sideswipes as it wails past, and icy sweat frosts my forehead.

"We are in the middle of the road." Tossing a look behind me, traffic is lined up down the next block, and mortification washes my face with a warm flush. "Move, Dad!" I hastily wave for him to pull forward.

"Hold on." He guns us out into traffic. Sweat pours down my brow, and my shoulders hug my ears as tension pulls them together. When he rounds the final corner, he finds a metered spot in front of the pizzeria, I let out the biggest sigh of relief.

A series of chuckles radiates from Dad's lips.

"How can you laugh?" I give him a stoney glare.

"I long since learned not to cry in times of stress."

"It wouldn't have been stressful if you'd let me drive in the first place."

"True." He tips his head toward me. "But then we'd have nothing to laugh about."

"It's not funny." I let out a huff as I tug on the door handle to let myself out. "Plus, now I need to ruin my diet, because the only thing that's going to help me is a giant cup of diabetes."

"You should try that new Coffee shop." He winks at me as he hops out of the truck onto the busy sidewalk.

My gaze skirts to the other side of the street where I see the Coffee Loft. It's the breath of fresh air I need. I tap my chin only one time before I give into the temptation. "I think I want to do that. Do you mind if I run over and grab a coffee and meet you back here for pizza? You can order, and I'll be right in."

"I don't have a problem with that." Dad wobbles forward to the pizzeria.

Dodging traffic, I dart out as soon as it's clear, and I make it across the street in a few seconds flat. As always, I slow my steps right as I pass through the front door, and deep roasted cinnamon wafts under my nose. It's impossible to not feel rejuvenated when I'm in this place. The lady working behind the counter smiles in full recognition and waves. "Welcome to the Coffee Loft. What can I grab you today?"

With so many options, it's impossible to choose. "What flavor pairs well with three hours of sleep and a near-death driving situation?"

"May I suggest the French Press?" Her lashes bat as she looks back at the man behind her who rolls his eyes at her. I suspect some serious flirtation and it puts a smile on my face.

"That sounds perfect. Lofty size, please."

While she gets busy scooping coffee into the French press, she starts small talk. "Is the sun still shining out there?"

"A little bit." I nod, adding, "Starting to get windy though, but considering it's fall, I'm happy."

"Right? We never have this much sunshine in November." She pours hot water in the French press, and sets it aside on the counter before returning to the tablet. "Is that everything, or do you need a spiced chai for North?" She grins slyly at me, winking.

"I ah, don't know. I suppose I can grab one, and he can heat it up later. I haven't talked to him yet today." My cheeks burn as I ramble. I hadn't expected people to assume we were together, but after recalling how we sat practically cuddling in the booth last night, I can understand why she thought that. "Was he here yet?"

"No." She shakes her head back and forth. "Normally, he stops in after his morning run on Saturdays, but no sign of him today. That's why I thought you were grabbing for both of you."

"Well." I open my purse, and dig for my debit card, excitement budding in my gut. I can't wait to be able to surprise him with his 'coffee' order. "You better add a spiced chai to my order, please."

"You bet." She punches in the second order. "Spiced chai coming right up!"

I swipe, and quickly stow my card, and while she's working on North's drink, I scroll my phone. No text messages from him. He'd been texting me almost every morning since we cleaned the garage. But not today.

*For a guy who clings to his routines, it seems odd he's so off schedule.*

The barista slides a drink carrier with the two drinks across the bar. "I put stoppers in them, so they stay warm."

"Thank you." I take the carrier by the handle and head out, noting it's only been about ten minutes. Dad usually spends at least thirty minutes talking before he remembers he's actually there to eat, he likely hasn't even ordered yet.

I push open the heavy door, taking a big stride out, hoping to rush back across the street in record time, when I nearly run smack into someone. "Pardon me." I startle, trying to steady my drink carrier. Thanks to the stoppers every drop is spared. I smile and raise my gaze.

My stomach instantly knots, and I squeak out, "Rocco. Hi."

"Hey, lil sis." His face is stilled, not wavering into even the tiniest smile. It's been months, if not even a year or two since I've seen him, but he has his shaved head, which highlights his oversized nose. It's identical to dad's nose, but oddly while it makes Dad look endearing, it gives Rocco's face a disproportionate effect. Cloaked in a long trench coat that stops above his shiny black shoes, he's definitely dressed for business.

*I just can't tell if it's legal business or not.*

"H-how are you?"

"I'm fantastic." With precisely measured words, he doesn't break direct eye contact. "I actually just completed the final steps to run for Senate."

*Senate? Boy, that really is where all the crooks go.*

Biting my lips, I offer nothing. But running for Senate doesn't surprise me. He's always doing everything to gain more power and control.

"I didn't realize you were in town." He offers after the silence drags out. "It's been a while."

"It's been a looong time." I nod, feeling as if I'm shrinking in size right in the middle of the sidewalk.

"How have you been?" Pulling his hands out of his pockets, he extends his arms wide, and waves me forward for a hug.

*It feels off.*

Rocco and I never had a close relationship even before fame and money ruined him, but I don't have an excuse not to hug him. I shuffle the drink carrier into one hand and lean in sideways for the world's fastest hug. "I'm well. Just back for the weekend. Helping Dad clean out his house."

Angling his head toward me, he echoes, "Cleaning it out? Where's he going?"

"Nowhere. His clutter has gotten out of hand." I gesture with an open palm forward. "You know how he is with his collections."

"Right." His lips thin into a straight line.

"Well." I jerk my thumb over my shoulder toward the pizzeria, careful with my words not to accidentally invite him to lunch. "I need to go."

"Oh." He nods, planting a smirk on his face. "Sorry to bother you."

"It's no bother. Just have plans." I wave as politely as I can, my skin crawling with the creeps, and I can't rush across the street fast enough.

My mind is a whirlwind as I stare down at my coffees.

North, the man with the world's most routines is off routine.

And Rocco's running for the senate.

What next?

# Fifteen

## North

The next morning, I'm in my kitchen, staring at Mr. Bella's junk box still sitting neatly in the corner of my kitchen table. Not wanting to snoop, I had left it untouched after seeing Rocco's football poster. Now I want to grab the whole box and chuck it out the front door in hopes that something valuable of Rocco's smashes into a million pieces.

Anger fires in my chest. I can't believe Rocco had the *audacity* to threaten my football team, which is my livelihood over me spending time with Gia.

I'm not fourteen.

I have no ill intentions toward Gia.

I've literally loved her my entire life.

All I want to do is love and protect her in the way she deserves.

He's the monster who needs to be taught a lesson.

If he thinks I'm giving up this easily, after all the years I've pined over Gia, well, he has another thing to learn. I may be a little slow to make my move, but when I put my mind to something, I'm in one thousand percent.

Gia's always been in my head.

She's always consumed my heart.

But now, she's in my life and I'm not giving that up.

*Knock, knock.*

My gaze skirts to the front door. I had been so wrapped up in my head, I missed Gia crossing the yard. She stands on my front porch, looking more amazing than ever. Her hair is up in one of the homeless messy buns she wears that looks hot. She's wearing an oversized, washed-out Bulldogs sweater. I know for a fact she's had it since high school, because she used to wear it to cheerleading practice. I'd always fight it, but many days they'd practice on the edge of the football field when we were running scrimmages. There was no way I could ever keep my eyes off her. Seeing her wear that sweatshirt after all these years sets an explosion of sparks right to my heart. It's like a symbol that it's finally our time to be together, and all those years wasted in unrequited love are about to pay off.

I push open the door, and her cute button nose wrinkles from the smile on her face. "Hey, you." I step aside, motioning for her to come inside. "What a nice surprise."

She offers me one of two cups in her hands. "Coffee Loft spiced chai, just the way you like it."

"I could get used to this service." I take the drink and immediately enjoy a sip. It's lukewarm, but still delicious.

"I was downtown with Dad for lunch, so I stopped in. Portia mentioned you broke your routine and hadn't come in for your morning coffee. I know how you are with routines, and it made me a little concerned." Her gorgeous green eyes travel over my face. "Is everything okay?

"Yeah." I pause, not wanting to lie to her. I'm an overly honest person, but I don't want to cause her to worry. I certainly don't want to give her a reason to pause *us*. I nonchalantly pat my abs. "My stomach is having sort of an off day. I hadn't left the house yet."

"That's no good."

I wave, dismissing her concern. "If I had to diagnose this, I'd say it was mostly related to butterflies." That earns me a raised feathered eyebrow and a flirty smile, and I tack on, "I have no idea what species they are, but they moved in last weekend, and it's clear they're taking over."

My heart swells from her joyful giggles, and we lock our gazes and stand frozen. The corners of her eyes crinkle in the cutest way as she retorts back, "I'm afraid they aren't butterflies."

"They aren't?"

"Nope, not for you. You're more special. You have little baby axolotls in there, hopping around."

"I do?" Our laughter mingles together perfectly in sync. "I think you're right. That's exactly what I have."

She takes a step further into my kitchen, glancing around. "It's been years since I've been here. Not much has changed, huh?"

"Nope. When my parents moved, I left everything exactly as it was. You know me." I wink and shoot a playful finger gun at her. "I like routines."

As she continues to look around, she tosses me a smile that transforms her face. It's flirty, but yet it has the sort of expression that says she's testing me.

I step behind her. "Are you looking for something specific?"

"Nah, just seeing what your life is like."

I casually extend my arm, ushering her further in. "You're welcome to take a tour. Mi casa es su casa."

"Oh." Her eyes round, glinting with bright green specs. "Are we at that stage already?"

"Baby," I tease, my voice lower than normal. "I'll meet you at any stage you want. You tell me. What stage are we at?"

She holds my gaze, and I don't waver as I'm ready to see this through.

She's all I ever wanted.

Her teeth dig into her plush bottom lip, flushing it to a darker pink, and I can literally see the wheels turning in her pretty little head. The anticipation of her next words makes those stomach axolotls come alive. They're gearing up to swim a marathon. She can say anything, and I will agree.

Does she want to be my girlfriend?

Yeah, I'm there.

Heck, does she want to get engaged?

I will *run* to the jewelry store with bare feet.

Would she prefer to skip the engagement and get married?

Vegas, here we come!

I don't want to close my eyes, but if I do, all I will ever see is her beautiful face etched into my brain.

Because it's already been there forever.

She's etched into my soul.

"Gia," I whisper, my voice growing with concern because she hasn't answered me yet. "What do you think this is?"

"I didn't think we were allowed to put a label on it yet." Her cadence is slow, as if she is weighing each word carefully before allowing it to make a sound.

My heart deflates. That doesn't sound like someone who's all in. Maybe she's not ready?

"*We* don't need a label," I rush to downplay everything. My inflections mirror her cautionary ones. "But I want you to know I've enjoyed spending time with you."

Her lashes flutter, the way they always do when she's trying to avoid blushing. "Me, too."

"Good," I assert, pulling my lips in, and biting hard, as it's a struggle. Her hesitation to put a label on us makes me think she might not be ready yet.

A horrible thought enters my brain. What if she's just being nice to me so I'll help her clean out all that junk? Even if that is the case, I offered to help, and I'm a man of my word. I jerk my thumb over my shoulder at the door. "What do you say, I help you clean another stack of boxes?"

"Well, I'm hoping to take a load of boxes to the dump. Would you want to help with that?"

"Yeah." I slip on my tennis shoes and grab my keys. "Let's go throw out some trash." Loving how the least desirable chore in the world can feel like I won the lottery when I get to be next to Gia, I'm unable to stop grinning as we stroll through the door together, and head back across the yard toward Mr. Bella's loaded-down-with-junk truck.

It only takes about an hour to drop everything off, and when we return, we spend the rest of the day cleaning more boxes. This time we find a stamp collection, and something a little odd, an assortment of dog toys—even though Gia swears they never owned a pet. That discovery made us both burst into fits of laughter, and just like all the other days we'd worked, time got away from us, and it's time for me to go home.

With Mr. Bella lingering in the kitchen, we say a quick good-night, and I head across the yard to my house.

What do you know, I'm not alone.

Rocco's wringing his hands together, blocking my front door. "Well, well, well . . ." His sinister grin cements on his face. "Tell me this isn't what it looks like."

Grinding my back teeth together, I fight back every urge I have to flatten his smug expression. As good as it would feel to hit him, that's not going to solve anything. He clearly didn't get the hint that I'm not giving up Gia.

My hands shake, but I squeeze my fist into a ball and stuff it in my jacket—for now.

I'm not going to let him control me—or Gia anymore.

"Look," I growl. "If Gia doesn't want me around, she's perfectly capable of letting me know that herself. She doesn't need you butting in. I'm sorry if that hurts your tiny feelings."

Rocco's head rolls back, and a haughty laugh pipes out for an egregious amount of time before he finally forms actual words. "We will see who's sorry." His eyes narrow into slits before he spins on his heel and strides to his black car, parked at an angle in my driveway, blocking me in.

If this were a movie, the only thing that would have been missing is the evil mustache twirl before he stormed off. I have no idea how he got this way, but that man is delusional. I'm not above calling the cops if it gets to that level, but I just hate to do anything rash that will upset Gia. He may not be able to keep me away, but there's burning in the back of my brain telling me he will do something.

# Sixteen

## North

I clear my throat and steel my shoulders back in the doorway. "You want to see me, Principal Lane?"

"Yes. Come on in." Principal Lane swivels on his computer chair to face me while gesturing to the chair in front of his desk. It's Monday morning, and first period is just about to begin, but I had an urgent message to come here. "Have a seat, please."

Principal Lane leans back in his chair and adjusts his beige sport coat collar to lay flat against the high-back leather chair. His suit is practically the same color as his hair, his mustache, and his skin tone. It's so monotone, it makes it hard for me to find his face, but he's always worn this color. "I'm afraid I've had some bad news about the football budget. Our biggest sponsor, Rocco's Motors Company, has not renewed their sponsorship for next year."

"Wh-what?" I stammer and jump to my feet, searching for something—anything—on this desk or computer screen that has evidence this isn't some practical joke. Rocco mentioned pulling support, but I didn't think that he actually meant it. His ego was making the threats. Swallowing down my shock, I look Principal Lane in the eye. "What was his reasoning?"

"He's had a change of priorities. He said he's running for Senate and wants to use his philanthropy funds towards more humanitarian missions, such as feeding and clothing the homeless. He did say he feels terrible because the town's gotten used to his hefty donation, but he said it was God's calling."

Nearly choking on my own tongue, I fight every urge to explode with the truth.

This is no spiritual awakening.

This is revenge.

Principal Lane didn't need to know about my personal life, and how I might have caused this, but there must be some more details. "So, um," I stretch my neck forward, already feeling the strain of this financial burden move into my body. "What are we looking at for cuts? Do the boosters have a plan, or fundraiser?"

"The boosters haven't been doing a whole lot other than the Homecoming auction and raffle. Rocco's made their job easy, but I'm not going to abandon you, and it's early. I'm sure we can plan something. A good car wash fundraiser, and perhaps the guys could sell those pizzas the cheerleaders always sell?"

"Right." My mouth dries up. Selling frozen pizzas is not going to come close to replacing the money that Rocco donated.

"Effective immediately, we'll have to eliminate assistant coach, Rod, from the payroll, and we'll do our best to keep your hours as is. However, we're in need of some major fundraising and possibly cold calling businesses for donations."

I nod, and then nod again, because I know if I open my mouth, I'll have some choice words to say about Rocco. I zip my lips as I don't want to say anything I'll regret. "I'm sorry to hear this, but hopefully it's only a minor setback. We'll figure something out." I rise and offer a handshake. "Thanks for keeping me in the loop and let me know when more news arises."

"Will do." Principal Lane finally grips my hand, shaking it extra *firmly*. "We'll see your boys out on the field again Friday night. This won't faze them."

"Sure thing." I fake a toothy smile and pivot to exit his office. I know one thing. As much as I hate this, I'm going to need to tell Gia. It's way beyond a coincidence, and I need to warn her to watch her back. My cell vibrates in my pocket. I never get calls during the day. Everyone knows I'm at school. My gut clenches before I even look.

I duck into my classroom, as I have ten minutes before the first period starts, and I close the door.

**Rocco: I warned you. Stay away or you'll *both* be sorry.** Both.

That has to be a typo. He can't mean us both. Would he really hurt his own sister?

Stunned, I stare at the wall as if the air is too poisoned for it to be stirred. It definitely is blackmail. Rocco and his dirty friends are behind all of this, and I must find a way to stop him, and warn Gia.

*Gia*, my heart slams against my chest. I can't have him going after her. I must protect her at all costs until I can find a way to stop him for good.

It's like he has some super GPS on us, and spies everywhere. He just knows when we are together. I rub my chin, hating that I have to tell Gia this bad news, but it must be done. I've held off telling her long enough. She needs to know everything.

# SEVENTEEN

## Gia

"Sorry I'm late!" I yank my heavy coat off, and neatly toss it on the coat hook as I breeze by it. The aroma of thyme and fresh basil tickles my nose, awakening me. Grace is already aproned up and spacing cinnamon roll dough on the pans, something I usually do. I grab an apron, quickly tie it around my waist, and scoot in front of the handwashing sink to scrub. "Let me do the rolls."

"It's fine." She plops the last of the dough on the pan and whisks the bowl into the soaking sink. "I already have all my roasts in the convection oven."

"That's what smells so hearty." I stick my nose high in the air, inhaling one more time.

"Yes, I used all the leftover onions." She pauses and her eyebrows clamp together, tipping me off to her confusion. "So, get this. An administrative meeting is going on in the brunch room."

"An admin meeting on a Monday morning?" I echo, my Spidey sense alerting. "As long as I've been here, they've always stuck to Thursday lunches."

"Right? It felt off to me, too. It was deathly quiet when I walked in this morning, and the curtain dividing those two dining rooms had been rolled back. I thought maybe the weekend staff never closed it. I went in there to tidy up, and that's when I saw Gerry, and Marcie. It's both of their mornings off, but they had gotten emails last night, announcing an emergency meeting this morning."

"That doesn't sound good." I swallow, bustling to the kitchen door to peek out the window into the dining room, all the seats at the round center table are filled with management. All their faces are devoid of expression. "Are we supposed to go to this meeting?"

"Nobody said." She slides her pans into the oven and joins me, standing on her toes to look inside. "It doesn't look like we're getting huge bonuses, does it?"

"Nope."

"I don't know." She drops to her flat feet, brushing off her apron. "I can't imagine it's anything *bad*. The holidays are right around the corner, and it's our busiest season."

"Do you know what? I bet that's what it's actually all about." I breathe out, hoping to convince myself that this isn't going to negatively affect my position, or my pay. "Maybe we are going to be so busy, they need to implement some new schedule?"

I back away from the window as Marcie rises from her seat and heads our way. I push open the swinging door for her, and a look of dread consumes her face.

"What's the meeting about?" I ask so softly I can barely hear my own voice.

"We got shut down." Marcie exhales, disbelief in all her facial features. Even her perfect perky-Karen haircut seems to be deflated today.

"What?" My T ticks hard and I stammer, "Wh-what do you mean?"

Her gaze waffles between Grace and me. "They pulled our hospitality license, citing health and safety concerns. The guests are all being asked to check out this morning, and as soon as they have vacated, we lock up."

"I don't believe it." My jaw hangs low, and I rack my brain for clues. "Did something happen over the weekend? I don't even remember any inspectors coming around."

"We were never notified about anything." Marcie shrugs hard, her whole face falls with her shoulders. "It almost seems like sabotage. This is a high-demand beachfront property. Some businessman is probably trying to get this place to foreclose so they can buy it on the cheap."

"That's crazy." My voice pitches higher, anger filling my chest. "Who would do that?" Goosebumps rip over my arms, and the hair on my arms stands straight up. I gulp, scanning the kitchen with tears stinging my eyes. This has been my entire life since high school. It's not a perfect job, and I'm not getting rich, but Grace is like a sister to me, and food service is really all I know.

"Ah, it's going to be okay." Grace rushes over and wraps her arms around me. I hadn't realized Grace was also tearing up. Speaking through her sniffles, she tacks on, "We'll figure something out together."

"Yeah," I assure us both. "We'll find something else much better than this."

A niggling in the back of my head haunts me.

*Who would want to sabotage this hotel?*

# Eighteen

## North

I stop by the Coffee Loft on my way home from practice, my brain still abuzz with Rocco's threats. While I wait for my spiced chai, my phone vibrates with a text.

**Gia: How was work?**

My fingers itch to type back but my heart knows this must pause. Not forever, but until I can find a way to stop Rocco, or she'll get hurt. I'm not worth losing anything for. After several moments of staring at my phone and not texting back, she sends another text.

**Gia: So crazy thing … I guess I'm staying at my dad's house tonight. The hotel got shut down unexpectedly. I'm going to finish cleaning the house. If you're around, come over. You don't have to clean. LOL**

Anger boils in my gut and I fire off a text.

**Me: What? Was it foreclosed?**

**Gia: No. The health inspector shut us down, but I don't even remember being inspected. It's really odd. My boss thought it was sabotage to buy up the prime real estate.**

Sabotage or revenge?

Did Rocco pull something to shut it down? It wouldn't surprise me, and he has the means to do it with all his buddies on political favor payroll. Which means he already got to her. I can literally hear her sweet voice. I want to protect her. It feels like a knife is stabbing my gut to even think about someone hurting her. Now I'm torn. Do I stay away and hope he backs down? Hope isn't a plan, and it's clearly not working.

I'm not sure how I'm going to stay away. I certainly don't want to alarm her before I have the proof of harassment, I need in order to call the cops. Until I get that proof, I need to have her stay away.

**Me: I'm really sorry about your job. I'm sure something amazing will come along. I'll see if I can get my work done and get ahold of you later.**

I fight the urge to tell her I know exactly how she's feeling as I had my job nearly threatened today too. All I want to do is see her. The fact that she's going to be next door tonight is going to kill me, but I can't waste time. I need to gather my proof. There's something shady going on at the school. I have no idea how Rocco got to Principal Lane so fast. I stuff my phone in my pocket, grab my chai and head back to school. I have work to do.

The hairs on my arm stand up straight when I park in the employee parking lot, hours after dark. It's not unusual for teachers to return to their classroom to work, as we are all trying to get ahead, but tonight, it looks as if I'm the only one taking a second shift. As I exit my car and walk to the door, I jingle my keys in my hand, my senses alerted.

No sign of Rocco or Principal Lane.

Or at least no sign that I can see.

After unlocking the door, I slip inside and quickly lock it behind me, before flipping on several sets of lights. To deal with the silence, I whistle down the hall to my classroom. I'm not a musician and barely know any tunes, but automatically default to *My Girl*. A smile teases at the corner of my lips as I recall how it felt to hold Gia while we danced.

It will not be the last time I hold her.

I grind my molars while I unlock my classroom door. Maxlotle's aquarium is already glowing fluorescent, lighting up the back of the room. Still, I flip on another set of lights. "Hey, Buddy." I only speak out loud to him when I know we are alone. It's good for him to hear my voice, but I always feel looney doing it in front of people. "What are you up to tonight?"

He swims to the front, his perma-smile pressing up against the glass. I don't think anyone could ever be grumpy around an ax-olotl. "Well," I continue as if he can fully understand me—because

I know he can. "I'm in a bit of a pickle. There's this woman, you met her the other day, Gia. I'm heartsick over her, because I really thought we could finally be together, but her brother is doing everything he can to keep us apart." I rub my forehead, as my tension automatically pools there. This all seems so ridiculous. The part about Rocco keeping us apart. Not me talking to a salamander. That's completely sane. "What do you think I should do?"

He stares at me through the glass with his beady eyes, not blinking. He's looking past me now, back to my desk.

"That's what I thought. I need to get into Principal Lane's office. I'm sure there's something on his computer to prove things aren't right." I get up, pooling my bravery as I trudge my way to my desk to look for a file, or something I can use to get into his office, when my gaze snags on something.

Gia's box of Rocco's stuff.

It's still sitting on the corner of my desk. I haven't really wanted to look at his trophies and jerseys as anything of Rocco's makes me ill. I only took the box to make her happy, but now seeing it there infuriates me. After all these years of doing everything I could to cut him out of my life, he has managed to creep back in, and now has more control than ever before. It's not just Gia he wants to keep me from, now he's after my career and her job.

What next? Is he going to get my teaching license taken away? It's never going to end!

My fingers wrap into a tight fist, and I plot what to do with his trophies. I could smash them all up. It will feel amazing, but make a mess that I will have to clean. I really don't want to give him any more of my time. Dropping it in the trash would be the easiest way to get rid of it. It's dark out. Nobody would even see the box inside, and the garbage truck will take it away.

But what if Gia wants to see them someday?

What will I tell her?

I can't lie to her.

I also know I can't sit at my desk and look at this dumb box. The mere thought of him being in my life makes my frustration soar through my entire body, and I rip open the flaps, ready to deal with what's inside. I can stash this stuff in the corner of the locker room and just never go there. I'll keep my promise to Gia and get rid of it all at the same time.

"Alright." I sigh again, summoning the strength to deal with this. "What do I have here?"

I yank out the first trophy. A 12-inch plastic pedestal with a football on top. The plaque reads: Rookie of the year.

Cute, I mock and grab the next one.

Most valuable player.

Gag me.

Maybe I don't need to read them? Just grab them and go. I close one eye, as I go in for another, but my fingers brush up against a manila envelope.

Oh, what is this? Fancy certificates? Shaking my head, pushing them off, I vow to pretend I never saw them. I'm sure not framing anything.

A panic niggling in the back of my head screams at me, *You better check this.*

Really? I sigh again and impatiently grab the envelope, rip it open, and my eyes immediately swell round.

This isn't an award.

Mr. Bella clearly had *everything*.

Including these original loan papers for Rocco's car lot.

I would think Rocco would want these in his office, because it has all his personal information, and because he's shady as an oak tree, my interest is full throttle. I flip through the papers, and the hair on my arms rises again.

Something is immediately off.

Principal Lane's signature is next to Rocco's as a co-owner, alongside Tom Schank, president of the school board, and one of the shadiest businessmen in the town. He used to work in education but now he sits on several of the most influencial boards in town and owns a string of hotels.

Hotels.

Might he own Gia's hotel?

Ice frosts my back, spiraling chills to creep up my spine as I scan loan papers. Underneath the bank papers is another letter, a printed email from Rocco to Principal Lane. I speed read it with my heart nearly pumping out of my heart. I can't believe what I'm reading but *everything* becomes unveiled. Tom bought Rocco and Principal's vote for all these boards he's on. Tom basically owns them both as Tom is the one who gave Rocco money for his car lot, and in exchange for that, Rocco had to agree to sponsor the football team, which apparently was a condition Principal Lane made.

They are in on this together.

I smash my lips together and keep reading, as it all makes so much sense. That's how Rocco got to Principal Lane so fast. He's blackmailable. Swallowing hard, I stuff the papers back in the envelope and scan my room.

Still eerily quiet, but I have what I need to out Rocco now. That these papers landed in my hands at the exact time I need them is a miracle, but I'm not going to bury them. I protected Rocco when I found out about his cheating, but it got me nowhere. I'm done with him. Rocco's going to jail, and I'll be able to see Gia. Adrenaline surges, as I slide the envelope in a book bag, wanting to conceal it. To think, I almost threw it in the trash.

I stride out of my classroom, shut off the lights, and lock my door. I must get to Gia and tell Mr. Bella before it's too late, and Rocco does something else.

Oddly, Mr. Bella had the smoking gun to take down Rocco this whole time. It's weird it would end up in this box, without him knowing it.

Or did he know?

# Nineteen

## Gia

Peering out Dad's window for the third time in the last five minutes, I crane my neck.

Still no car in the driveway.

I wonder what North is doing. Going out on a Monday night is against his normal routine, but it's a little too soon in our situationship for me to demand he tell me what he's up to.

He was awfully vague.

What if he's on a date?

Nah—I cut my thoughts off, and then immediately remember he was the one who rushed to say we don't need a label for our relationship. At the time, I assumed he was being shy, but maybe that was to cover up something else?

Would he really date someone else?

He also didn't kiss me when he had the chance.

Again, I thought he was being shy.

What if he really isn't interested, and I've been misreading him the whole time? He said he went out of his way to be a friend to Rocco when he got in trouble. What if he's just a nice guy, trying to be a friend to me, because he saw my dad get stuck.

To be honest, he hasn't ever asked me out on a proper date. We've only grabbed coffee and tea from the Coffee Loft and cleaned. If he is truly interested, he'd take me to dinner or a movie. Right?

"Gia!" Dad calls as he walks through the front door, pizza in his arms. "I'm so sorry to hear about your day."

"It's okay. Just a job. It's probably time I move on anyway. I was at a bit of standstill with my career." Closing the window curtain, I hang my head, sulk into the kitchen, and pull up a chair at the table while I wait for dad to bring over the pizza.

He drops the box in the center of the table and flips open the lid. Pepperoni and jalapeño—my favorite. Not waiting for a plate, I dig right in, help myself to a nice cheesy slice and take a giant bite.

Dad mirrors me, plopping in the chair across from me, and grabs a slice. "I was thinking," he says while he chews down his food. "You can help me in the pizzeria."

"Dad." I sigh, as I really don't need him to offer me a pity job.

"No, hear me out." He places his hand on mine. "I've been enjoying my house being so clean. It's so freeing, and in a way it feels like I've gotten a new chance at life." His voice cracks, and I stop mid-chew. I knew he was dealing with heavy emotions, but he hasn't opened up to me about it yet, other than the arguments we've had about not throwing out his stuff. "After your mom died, and Rocco got in all that trouble, I just sort of wanted to hide."

"I know, Dad." I match my gaze with his. "I've never faulted you for any of this mess. We were all doing the best we could."

"Well, but I do think I'm better now." His eyes are bright and clear, clueing me in to his honesty. "But, I'm tired, and I want a break. When North's parents sold that house to him, they retired to Mexico City. They invited me to visit, and you know, I think it sounds nice."

"Oh." Tipping my head to the side, I let that sink in. "I had no idea you needed a break. Of course, I can cover for you. How long are we talking about?" I take another bite, and chew.

"I'm awfully sick of the cold. My bones don't handle it like they used to. I've been thinking about it for a while, but never had a way to swing it. If you think you can cover for me, I'd like to leave soon. Maybe give you a week to train you back in as it's been years since you covered a shift, and I'll make the arrangements. I'd love to stay until spring." He jerks a thumb over his shoulder, pointing down the hall. "You can stay here in your old bedroom. I know you have a couple of months left on your lease, but by all means, if you want to let it go at the end of the year, you're more than welcome to crash until you get settled into a new job."

I swallow the last of my pizza, but really, I'm swallowing more than that. I'm so overly touched that Dad thought this all out before I had a chance to get worried about my bills.

"And," Dad cuts into my thoughts. "If you find a job you want to take before spring, just holler and I'll be right back."

"I love you, Dad," I say, the words spilling out as tears fall. Tears that I hadn't even realized were hiding back here, but these last two weeks have been such a whirlwind. Swiping my eyes with the back of my hand, I lean over and wrap my arms around his neck.

He hugs me back, and I inhale the scent of fresh oregano and pepper—the scent he's always worn since he works at the pizza shop. I bite back a smile, knowing this is going to be my new scent.

"Say," Dad says while finishing his pizza and brushing off the last of the crusts into the open box. "I want to show you something." He stands and starts walking down the hall. "You'll never guess what I found . . ." His voice trickles off as he enters into Rocco's room. When he pops back out with a toddler sized, pink stuffed amphibian, I jump to my feet.

"Rosie!" I hold my arms out, waiting to receive my axolotl. "I looked everywhere for her. I swore I lost it. Where did you find her?"

"It was in Rocco's room. I was cleaning up the last of everything and wanted to pull the bed back so I could shampoo the carpets. She was stuffed between the wall and his headboard. It looks like it was intentionally hidden." His voice lowers, but I still make out the last of his mutter, "stupid kid was always so jealous of you."

"Wow." I hug Rosie, remembering how it felt the first time North gave her to me, and I could have sworn that night he was going to ask me out.

He didn't.

Yet another example of how I thought he was shy, but he was merely being a nice guy. You'd think after all the chances that boy has had to ask me out, and he never has, he's just not interested.

Nobody is that shy.

I half smile, not feeling light enough for a full smile. I'm happy to have Rosie back, but in a way, it feels bittersweet. Part of me had hoped this gift had been more than a get-well gift, but I'm finally seeing that North never wanted to be with me. He was always just being a nice guy.

If he wanted to be with me, he would have said something by now.

*Knock, knock, knock.*

I jump to my feet and fly across the room because nobody uses the side door but North. As soon as I open the door, he exclaims, "You'll never guess what I just found!" He bursts over the threshold while waving papers in the air. "Oh, hi Mr. Bella." He tips his head toward Dad. "How are you?"

"I'm fine, son. What's all the commotion about?"

"You're not going to like this." His words take a cautionary tone as he plants his gaze on Dad. "Gia dropped off a box of Rocco's trophies at the school, and I got to putting them away tonight, and look." North slides papers in front of Dad. I peer over Dad's shoulder and gasp.

"What is this?" Clearly, I can read, but I don't believe it! "Is Rocco getting funding for his car lot in exchange for political favors?"

"It looks that way." North shifts his feet, as he keeps his gaze glued to Dad. "Did you know about this?"

"How could he know about that?" I scoff, but Dad blurts over the top of me.

"—I did." His eyelids lower, hooding his eyes, and his skin grows ashen. "Forgive me, but I found that box the other day, and that's why I had it sitting in the living room. I didn't have the heart to turn in my own son, but I know it needs to happen. I was hoping you'd come over, look in the box, and find it. Well, things didn't really go that way. When you offered to donate it to the school, I figured this would work out."

"Were you ever going to say anything?" Anger sizzles in my chest, not for Dad, because I oddly understand his plight, but at Rocco, who is about to drag our family through another scandal.

"I planned to send anonymous copies to the local press if you didn't find it. I also knew my heart can't handle the constant news and gossip, and that's the real reason I planned to go to Mexico." His head's still down, and I can't see his expression, but his voice is strong with conviction. "Rocco's a grown man who's made his own bed."

"If you'd like to avoid a mess with your own son, I can take this to the police myself," North offers. "He won't ever need to know you were going to turn him in. I know he's estranged now, but maybe some time in jail will help him to see things differently, and he won't blame you."

"I really don't think it will make a difference who turns him in but be my guest." Dad scratches at the back of his head, thinking through his words. "All I know is going through another one of these scandals with him is not on my Bingo card this year."

"It's not on my Bingo card either." A disgusted snort bleeps out of my mouth.

"You're welcome to come too." One corner of Dad's mouth curls at the tip as his gaze cuts to North. "But something tells me you have a reason to stay."

"I don't know if I do." With emotionally exhausted eyes, I turn to North. He seems to avoid my gaze, looking at the floor.

"I think that's my cue to leave you two." A gleam sparkles out of the corner of Dad's eye as he passes me on his way out of the kitchen, calling back, "I'm going to start packing my bags."

The silence that Dad's absence creates pulsates as I fix my gaze on North. *This has to be it.* We've been dancing around our connection for a decade. If North doesn't say something, then I'm going to. I can't wait another decade, wasting years we can be together.

And if I'm wrong about this?

Well, at least I will find out now.

"North." My voice cracks and I pause to swallow. "Dad asked if I have a reason to stay." I squawk out, so afraid of another disappointment. "Do I?"

"Do you?" North's dreamy eyes lock on me the same time his feet propel him across the room, closing the gap between us. He's so tall, he dips his head down to align our gazes, all his attention on me. "Gia, I've been in love with you from the first moment I saw you, but I couldn't tell you because Rocco threatened to destroy us both. I never wanted to cause any trouble for you. I held in my feelings all these years, wishing them away, but they only grew stronger." His eyes fill with tears, and his words float out like poetry, each word swelling my heart even more. "I know you said it was too soon to decide what we are, but it's killing me. I need you to know that you're the only woman I've ever wanted."

His eyes bounce between my lips and my eyes, all the while his gaze becoming more heated, and the strongest magnetic pull of gravity I ever felt, draws me directly to his lips. We lean closer and closer, with each second ticking until our lips finally crash, instantly tangling as if we've been training to do this our whole lives. There isn't anything shy about the way he kisses me, or even polite. The chemistry is beyond anything I could have dreamed. We are perfectly matched to each other, and before I can take a deep breath, he pulls away, a boisterous smile covering his face.

"Mama Mia," I whisper, and fight back all the happy tears pricking the backs of my eyes.

"Mama Mia is right," Dad's voice echoes from the edge of the kitchen. Apparently, he used his snoopy manifesting power to sneak back down the hall and overhear our confessions. My laugh mingles with North's husky chuckle. I don't even care that Dad overheard us. It's not like any of this is a secret to him. He's the one who had called it all those years ago.

As the laughter dies, I gaze back at North. Talk about a truth bomb. It all makes so much sense now. I thought he was too shy, but he was protecting me from my own brother. After all this time, we can finally be honest with each other and be the couple we've always wanted to be.

"This calls for a celebration." Dad whoops from the corner.

"What's on your mind?" I turn back to Dad, enjoying how he's taking part in this whole thing. It's not the romantic declaration of love I dreamed about, with my dad in the corner, but in an odd way, it doesn't feel uncomfortable either.

"How about we go for one of those coffees you've been bringing over? My treat."

Pushing out my lower lip, I only need to muse for a second before I know I'm game. "Sounds good. North, what do you think?"

"Let's go."

"I'll drive." I lunge to steal my keys off the hook, before Dad can grab them, and race out in front of him.

Dad bursts out next, calling out, "Shotgun."

North laughs, as he pulls up the rear, shaking his head. "Maybe I should have been more careful about what I'm getting into," he teases while he climbs in the backseat of my car.

"It's fine. We aren't that scary. Just Dad's driving is awful. I couldn't let you experience that on top of everything else we've put you through." Nothing can erase the smile on my lips, as I gaze at him in the rearview mirror. On the drive over, Dad jokes about all the times he caught North looking at me over the years, and North's ears grow a healthy shade of crimson. Before he starts revealing my secrets—because I know he caught me looking back at North—I pull over in front of the Coffee Loft and rush to get out.

North and I link hands, weaving our fingers together, and stroll through the Coffee Loft door with Dad in tow. Dad smack talks North from behind us "Tell me you're going to try something other than that stinky chai."

"What?" North jolts, turning back to fake scowl at Dad. "You did not just insult my drink order."

"I did. After all these years, you finally brewed up the courage to kiss Gia. It's time for you to turn a new leaf all together and try a new drink."

"What's going on here, chai guy?" Portia butts in, leaning over the counter with her gaze directly on North. "Are we seriously talking about not having chai?"

"I guess, I'm breaking my habits." North shrugs, and looks at me, his eyes glittering back with all the shades of dreamy, rich espresso. "I'll have whatever she's having."

"You got it." Portia's curious smile curves on her lips as she punches our order in, and we pay. Then we link arms, heading back to our booth, and slide in to sit shoulder to shoulder with Dad across from us. We aren't the couple of kids we were in high school. I can't say we're better off, just different. Our lives are actually fairly uneventful, which will leave us plenty of time for long dates at the Coffee Loft where we laugh, bond, and fall in love, one sloooow sip at a time.

# TWENTY

## A month later

As we survey the piles of remaining items in my dad's garage, North and I can't help but chuckle at the absurdity of some of them. First, there is a broken pizza oven that Dad swears still works. Before we packed it up to donate, he added a note saying, "Works, but cooks unevenly. It doesn't make the best tasting pizza, but it makes a fun conversation piece." I really just want to chuck that oven into the garbage, but getting rid of this stuff has been an emotional journey for Dad, and the only way he's made it through it is by believing his stuff will find a better home where people who need it, can use it.

My favorite item is the whole box of flamingo yard ornaments. I can't fathom why someone would ever need that many, but my childish brain wants to prank North by putting them in his yard one night.

Such innocent fun, but I resist.

Oh, and don't get me started on the hideous plastic garden gnomes. There are eleven of them. Who in their right mind needs that many lawn creatures? I would think if you had eleven, you'd actually want a full dozen, which leads me to think one is missing. Frankly, that's a little terrifying. I've learned to tiptoe around, hoping it doesn't pop out at me sometime. Their facial expressions are just too creepy.

I know it's silly.

But really, its creepy.

Now, we are down to the last load of stuff, and I couldn't help but rub my hand along the base of the old palm tree shaped lamp adorned in Christmas lights.

"Quite the assortment of stuff, eh?" North chuckles, his eyes wafting to the lamp, and I couldn't help but join in.

It is definitely a relief, after the last few weeks, to finally be able to laugh about this stuff. "Yeah, I think we can honestly say we have something for everyone."

"Too bad this violin doesn't have a bow. I'd definitely give you ten bucks for it." He picks up a small stringed instrument. Dad is always more eccentric, even in his collections, and I doubt that he had any classical instruments. I squint my eyes at North, and I burst out laughing.

"That's not a violin. It's a Ukulele, and it's definitely worth at least twenty bucks," I tease, pretending to be offended.

"Sorry." He put it back in the box with his fingers exaggeratedly spaced, as if he is now afraid to touch it. His expression takes on a bit of a conspiratorial gleam. "I have a surprise."

One of my brows rises higher than the other in a skeptical glare. "After reading the news article this morning about Rocco and his buddies and how detectives were able to bring to light even more closed-door embezzlement and fraud, I don't know if I can handle any more surprises."

"This has nothing to do with them. I actually think they are the only ones who are surprised they didn't get away with their scams for good. They will be in jail for a long time." He shakes his head, but continues with excitement inflections in his voice, "This is a good surprise. I was talking to your dad about Mexico. It turns out my parents aren't that far from Lake Xochimilco, the most popular place in North America for finding wild axolotls."

"Oh, I see where this is going." I pretend to be alarmed, but inside I'm already excited. "That's enticing, and you want to visit, right?"

"What do you think?" His head takes an inquisitive angle. "Both our parents are there, and maybe we could visit for Christmas? It would be our first vacation together, cementing another milestone in our still new relationship."

My heart patters over several beats as I love how thoughtful North is, and how willing he is to include me in his life, making plans for Christmas, which is a month away. It feels normal though. Like how it's supposed to be. "You're asking me if I want to go to Mexico in cold December? Of course, I would love to go."

"One more thing." His easy smile graces his face, but I freeze as a serious gleam sparkles out of the corner of his eye. "In the spirit of letting go, I cleaned out a few of my closets, too. I was going to toss this, but part of me always had this weird fantasy and I wanted to give it to you." He lifts up a box and pushes it toward me. "You'll like this one."

"Promise?" I hesitate, but lean over, peering inside the box. When I make out the contents, a full smile bursts on my lips. "Are you kidding me?" I yank it out, and eagerly slip it on. "You brought me your high school football letterman jacket?"

"I know we aren't in high school." He shifts his weight from one foot to the other, "But seeing you walk through the halls in my jacket was one of those things I always fantasized about. If only I would have been a little braver back then, we'd have a lot more memories." He pulls up one side of his mouth into a flirty grin. "So, what do you say, Gia Bella...I'm a little late but will you wear my lettermen jacket?

"Gosh, North." I playfully bat my lashes and tug on the collar hugging it closer around me, already loving everything about this jacket. The worn leather still smells amazing, and it's soft and so easy to mold against my skin. "If you want me to wear your jacket, that must mean I really am your girl?"

"That's exactly what you are to me." He leans in, stealing a chaste kiss from my lips, before tacking on, "*My Girl.*"

That kiss isn't enough for either of us. Our gaze lingers over each other, and he dips his chin again, pressing his lips against mine. This kiss is sweet and filled with the promise of something more. As we pull away, I see the same wonder in his eyes that I feel in my heart.

I tug the jacket even tighter around me, a warmth seeps into my chest, and I take one more look around the garage. I can't help but smile. It had been an overwhelming several weeks, but now that we'd gotten through all that junk, I know we have better things ahead.

# *Epilogue*

## Christmas in Mexico

The waves cascade gently on top of the water, creating a ripple that goes on as far as I can see. We're staying at North's parents' house, but I decided to take the day to visit the ocean as it's always been where I felt the calmest. For a moment, I'm sad as I reminisce about how I used to look out at the beach almost every day when I worked at the resort. Though I love working at Dad's pizzeria, it's not the same as having a career that's solely mine.

"What are you thinking about?" North walks barefoot beside me on our sunrise walk. His face is already sun-kissed even though we've only been here two days.

"Just how peaceful the ocean is, and how I miss working at the resort."

"Have you thought about what direction you want to go with your career after your dad returns to Bella's?"

"No." My mind is calm, and it doesn't pull me in any direction except to whatever direction is closest to North. "I know it wasn't in my plan to have a career change now, but I do think it's been the best thing that could have happened because these past few weeks of getting to spend so much time with you have been everything to me."

"I feel the same way." North takes my hand in his, and my heart melts how our fingers lace together so perfectly. "I hate to say I'm grateful you got laid off, but I've been selfishly enjoying all the late-night left-over pizza dinners together."

"Those are amazing, but my favorite is the daily Coffee Loft visits." I hold up a teasing finger. "Maybe, when we return, I'll try to get a job there?"

"That's actually not a bad idea." North's voice ticks up in excitement. "I saw a Help Wanted sign in the window before we left. It's right across the street from the Pizzeria. You can see your dad all the time, but still have your own space, and room for upward advancement. I know Portia and Christian so well, I'm sure they'd hire you."

"Maybe." I purse my lips out, mulling over the idea. The sun is rising higher over the horizon, casting a warm glow over the water, making everything tranquil. "I do have my Food Manager's License already, and I enjoy that type of work."

"It would be perfect." North gushes, and everything suddenly feels perfect. North is the man of my dreams, the one I've been hoping for my whole life. Now that we're together, he's not only the sweetest guy ever, but so supportive in every way. Getting laid off could have been stressful, but it just seems like things work out better and better now that he's by my side.

"I really appreciate how supportive you've been with me." I halt and look deeply into his eyes. North never had one those piercing gazes you read about in romance novels. His is the kind of warm intensity that brings so much familiarity, I'm always left feeling like I had known North not just since my youth, but for a thousand lifetimes.

North reaches for my other hand, pulling both of my hands to his heart. This is honestly my favorite thing he does, and it makes my heart skip a beat every time. His chest rises and lowers in the deepest breath as I stand before him, my eyes searching his face for what feels like an eternity. And then, with a rasp in his voice, he finally says, "I don't know if this is too soon or not, but I can't hold it in anymore. I love you, Gia."

His declaration echoes in the air between us, as if suspended by the salty wind. A gentle smile tugs at the corners of my lips, and I squeeze his hands back. "I love you too," I whisper, my voice surprisingly cracking as I felt the weight of these words I'd never said to any man wash over me like the waves lapping at my bare feet. And in that moment, we stand on the sandy shore with nothing but the sound of the ocean. I have no clue where I'm going in life but I don't care. I just want to grow closer to North as I finally found someone special – My *one true North*.

# *Bonus Epilogue*

"Welcome to the Coffee Loft." I adjust my apron, clear my throat, and bat my lashes over the counter at the handsome man waiting to be served. It's my first day on the job, working as a new assistant manager, and I already know I'm going to love everything about working for Coffee Loft. "How can I help you?"

"I'm not sure yet." North leans over on the counter, resting both elbows. "Whatever I get I'm going to need a Lofty size as the car wash is just beginning, and I have a feeling it's going to be a long day."

"That's right." I slowly press the buttons on the tablet to punch in a Lofty size drink, making sure I don't miss anything. "How many players do you think will show up to help out?"

"I made it a required practice, so it better be the whole team. We have to earn money some way."

"Oh, before I forget." I grab his coffee cup but rest it in my palm as I have so many thoughts racing through my brain. "Did my dad get ahold of you for the final count of pizzas you need donated? I think he was going to do about thirty. Is that okay?"

"That should be phenomenal. I hate fundraising, but every little bit helps."

Portia walks forward, smiling sweetly toward North. "Why don't you put Coffee Loft down for donating some gift cards for the auction."

"That's awfully sweet of you." North nods, pulling his phone out to make a note. "I'm messaging our secretary now before I forget to add it to the roster." After a moment of typing, he looks back up from his phone. "Boy, there's so much to remember with these things, but it's coming together. We'll have football for at least another year."

"That's the goal, right?" Another customer passes through the front door, and I hate to rush North, but I'm super slow at making drinks, and I hate to get behind. "Did you want your chai?"

"What do you think?" North beams at me as his gaze paces from me to Portia, who quietly stands behind me to assist with my training. "Should I go back to my usual chai, or find something new?"

"You know what I think." I playfully hold off to wait for that sparkle in his eye that always appears when I tease him.

"What's that?" He leans one arm on the counter, and I marvel how his arms get better looking every day.

My heart blooms full of so much love as I know I finally found my place. I love my new life, working at the Coffee Loft. I get to see Dad most days as he's only across the street, and I love that I'm finally living my days with North. Nothing else matters. "I don't care if you order pumpkin spice, vanilla or chai. The only thing I care about is that you are *my guy*."

*Thank you for reading No More Mr. Chai Guy.*

*Just a note to say, if you enjoyed Rocco being a villain, he returns in The Pucker-Up Pact.*

The Pucker-Up Pact is a grumpy sunshine, revenge fake-dating, sweet romantic comedy with a HEA.

Instant Chemistry

Revenge Fake Dating

Forced Proximity

She's Mine Vibes

If you haven't read it yet, it's available in KU.

# Welcome back to The Coffee Loft,

## where a new round of stories has been brewed especially for you.

**COFFEE LOFT SERIES**

Those of you stopping by to visit again, we've missed you. The feeling of home is the same that you loved before. If it's your first time, prepare to be swept off your feet.

While our menu hasn't changed, we think you'll be pleased with the fall favorites we've added. Fans of pumpkin spiced lattes, peppermint mochas, and rich, chocolaty cocoas will not be disappointed. This multi-author collection of stand-alone sweet rom-coms is filled to the brim with the swoons you love and adore.

From sweet kisses to grand gestures and matchmaking surprises, each mug and story will be filled with everything you crave. So come on in and let us
serve you with that happy ever after you've come to expect.

Find the entire collection here: https://www.amazon.com/dp/B 0CXQBFPHK

While you are at it, visit the first collection here: https://www.amazon.com/dp/B0CG2MQP2J

# *Sneak Peek*

## Let's Not and Sleigh We Did - Coming October 2024.

Oh, oh, the mistletoe, hung where I did NOT see.

My brother's friend waits for me and gets down on one knee— *What is happening?*

*Somebody stop it, please!*

Oh, those dreamy blue eyes batting at me, and all the words he dares to say

This is bad

Like really, really bad

We're now planning a wedding day

But it's all for a good reason, *not love*

Oh, cough, cough, let's not bust out the L-word

It's purely business

It is a solid plan until it isn't

So maybe I love him, but we agreed not to do that . . . whoops

*Let's Not and Sleigh We Did* is a fake marriage of convenience, brother's best friend, *just-kisses-but-all-the-swoons* Romcom

It's up for preorder now at an introductory price. https://www.amazon.com/dp/B0DF1PB7DY

# Also by J.P. Sterling

**_Christmas Shenanigans_ (All Standalones)**
Mingle All the Way
Tis the Season to Get Married
Let's Not and Sleigh We Did (Coming Oct 2024)
**_The Coffee Loft Series (_All Standalones)**
Pardon My French Press
No More Mr. Chia Guy
**_Sweet Hockey RomCom (_All Standalones)**
The Pucker-Up Pact
Shot Through the Heart (Coming 2025)
**_A Modern Fairy Tale Series (_All Standalones)**
Royally Rugged
Royally Guarded (Coming Spring 2025)
**_Bosses and Billionaires Series_ (All Standalones)**
Maid for my Billionaire Boss
Upcycling My Rig-Pig Boss
Kissed by My Billionaire Boss

Marooned with My Celebrity Boss

### *A Heart that Dances Series*

Dancing on Broken Ankles

The Stars We See

A Heart that Dances

A Heart that Loves

### *Water and Stone Duet*

Ruby in the Water

Lily in the Stone

# About J.P. Sterling

J.P. Sterling grew up watching old reruns of Lucille Ball and Mary Tyler Moore and fell in love with wholesome entertainment and slapstick comedy. She loves leaning into the over-the-top humor and full circle moments, especially if it means the underdog gets to shine.

Aside from writing, she's also a wife and homeschooling mom, a holistic dietitian, a former college professor and lover of all-things dark chocolate.

*No swears. Just kisses. No Blasphemies. *

Let's get social!

Hey you amazing reader! You are invited to join my private reader group for all-things clean books and friends. Enter the group here: https://www.facebook.com/groups/1500850764081965

Other places to follow me:

Instagram: https://www.instagram.com/stories/authorjpsterling/

Facebook: https://www.facebook.com/jpsterlingauthor/

Amazon: https://www.amazon.com/stores/author/B01N9TJXJN/about

# Acknowledgements

With every book I write, my list of people who have found their way into my path just keeps growing, and it's impossible to thank everyone. It's truly the best problem to have.

I first thank God, who gave me this mission to write clean books. I never in a million years thought I'd have these many books (20!). I seriously was going to write only one as a bucket list thing.

Always, I thank you, amazing readers and everyone in the book world. It's an honor to have a corner in this space.

Brooks is always on top on the list because he helps me plot everything out, and I really couldn't do this writing thing without him.

My team of editors and proofreaders. I have so many amazing readers who don't hesitate to send me screenshots of all the little missed words or extra spaces. It seriously takes a whole village for me to write a book, and I'm so thankful for mine. A special shout to Natalie this round.

For Amy, my Coffee Loft copilot, and all my fellow Coffee Loft authors! This set was never on my radar. It started as a serendipitous event of accidentally designing the cover concept with Amy. We took that concept and started playing with titles, and we just knew we had to bring it life. It has been the most fun labor of love I've done in my writing career, and I'm grateful everyone is plugging along with us.

My family – *hearts to infinity.*

# TRULY, MADLY, STEEPLY, BREW

Truly, Madly, Steeply Brew

Editors: Rebecca Carpenter, Barren Acres Editing

# Contents

# Introduction

Welcome to the Autumn-perfect, Christmas-perfect, and falling-in-love-perfect town of Mapleton, Vermont. If this is your first trip to town, sit back and prepare for fun banter and shenanigans to bring you all the feels. If you are returning to Mapleton, welcome home.

Welcome to Mapleton, Vermont

# ONE

## Arielle Hanson

Yanking on the wrought iron door handle of the Long Island Coffee Loft, I storm through the entry with so much anger bubbling in my gut, my gaze has morphed into tunnel vision. I barely pause to scan the lobby, making sure it's clear of customers before I zero my gaze on my brother, Christian, and shriek, "Tom *is* lying. He has another girlfriend!"

Portia, Christian's fiancée, pops up from where she was restocking supplies behind the counter. Her snow-blond hair is pinned in a messy bun, making her look like she hasn't combed it for the day, but that doesn't slow her down. She immediately paces toward me, hands outstretched. "That dirty scumbag."

I stand with my feet shoulder width apart, but still feel increasing weakness in my knees. Portia wraps her arms around me, and I drop my head on her shoulder and sob, unleashing a flood of tears.

Christian strides forward, determination in his straight path to us. "Are you *sure* this time?"

I raise my head enough to catch his gaze. He's the one person I'm totally honest with, and I desperately need consoling on this. "Yeah. You know how I had suspected it, but he assured me so many times that was not the case? He always had perfectly reasonable excuses why we had to sneak around. Remember when he said he was a lawyer, who worked at the same law firm handling Grandma's estate, and he was worried about the conflict of interest?"

Christian's eyes narrow, red hues flaming on his cheeks. "Tell me he's at least a lawyer."

"He's a lawyer." I nod, sniffing back tears. "Yet, still a liar."

Christian's hands roll into fists and his lips snarl and twist to the side. "I'll show him what a loser he really is."

"No, I don't want him to know how much this bothers me." I place my hand on his shoulder, attempting to take his fury down a notch. "I'm ready to never hear his voice or see his face again."

"How did you get him to confess?" Portia stares at me, her eyes wide with piqued interest.

"He never confessed but nothing ever added up. Today is his birthday, and he said he didn't have time to get together. I offered to meet him for lunch at his work, but he didn't want me to come to the office. I thought that was weird, but he assured me he was concerned over the conflict of interest. I showed up anyway—"

"You did not!" Portia's jaw practically drops to the floor.

"I did." I swipe my eyes with the back of my hands, doing everything I can to restore my vision as Portia's sweet face blurs in front of me. "That's what you do when you love someone and it's their birthday. I understood he was busy, but I thought I could still drop off a birthday lunch and give him a hug and kiss. But when I got there, he was having lunch in his office *with his other girlfriend!*"

Portia gasps, covering her mouth with her palm. "She was there?"

"It was a good thing too." I don't conceal the exasperation layering in my tone. I've been holding it in the entire drive here. If I don't let it out, my emotional tank is going to explode. "Tom would have never fessed up. At least since his other girlfriend was literally right there in front of my face, there was no way to lie his way out of it."

"I'm so sorry." Portia squeezes me tighter and pats my back in a motherly way. "He really doesn't deserve you. I know this hurts, but it's better you find out now. You should be with someone who treats you the way you deserve."

My bottom lip rolls under until I trap it between my teeth. I want to believe she's right, and there is someone better out there for me, but I'm honestly so tired of dating. I stopped looking for the perfect guy years ago. He just doesn't exist, and if I had to be honest with myself, I know I was settling with Tom. It's part of my personality though, which I have an impossible time giving up. I don't like to admit defeat at anything, including relationships. I had desperately wanted to make this relationship work, because I'm ready to move on to the next stage of my life—to get married and have a family.

Growing up without a mom taught me a lot, but the loudest lesson it imparted to me is there are no guarantees. Life is short. My heart hollows fractionally more with each depressing thought until it lands on this last one. *I don't want to start all over again.* I'm gutted. I gave everything I had to Tom.

I can't do this again.

"I'll tell you what he deserves," Christian cuts in, wringing his fists together. The sight of him puffing up his chest, acting so tough should make me giggle, because Christian is the last guy to ever be physically aggressive, but I don't have even a snicker inside me.

"Violence is not the answer." Portia raises her gaze to lock with Christian's, but it's not scolding. She has a way of making him *even*. He immediately comes down another notch, unrolling his clenched fists.

"I agree." I sniff, finally straightening up with the bitter after-taste of my dream of getting that Instagram-perfect wedding to disintegrate right before me. I take an urgent step back from Portia to look at Christian. "Violence will not help anything, but I can't go back there anytime soon. I was hoping I could stay with you for a little while."

"Stay here. Isn't that what you did the last time Tom hurt you?" Christian rubs his clean-shaven chin; a challenging gleam sparks in his eye. "I'm detecting a pattern where you always run away from your problems."

"It will not be a pattern once I get Tom out of my life for good. I'm humiliated. I can't imagine running into anyone I know right now, while I'm still so emotional." I sniff, and my shoulders shake from the internal pressure of holding back more tears. This isn't one of those problems I can solve by eating too many pints of ice cream and blaring Taylor Swift while I drive aimlessly around town.

This is my heart squeezed so tightly, it's impossible to breathe.

I've never been betrayed this badly before. I close my eyes, wishing the pain to go away, but Tom's face floods my mind, making my stomach lurch. I can't fathom ever feeling normal again.

I know one thing. If I do ever heal this pain, I'm not ever dating again.

*This will not be my pattern.*

I'm going to heal, but never date again. Problem solved.

"Don't you have a job to get back to?" Christian's protective-older-brother tone turns on. "I thought you had started cleaning for Dad's offices."

"I did, but it's just cleaning. It will not be the end of the world if I skip a week." I drop my voice into an indistinct murmur, adding under my breath, "Or a month." I can't afford to miss work with my dad, who's not exactly the understanding type. He'll more than likely "teach me a lesson" and fire me for not coming in. I'm willing to risk it, because as of right now, I can't imagine ever going back there. People are going to find out what I did—dating a guy with another girlfriend—and they'll talk. That's not my personality at all, but are they really going to believe that it wasn't my fault? I can't imagine the rumors going around about me. Nerves quake out of the depths of my gut, and I desperately motion to the counter. "I promise I'll earn my keep. I can take as many shifts as you want to help here."

"I actually just hired an assistant manager, Gia. She's not here right now, but she's working full time. With her new position, I really don't need any help, and I honestly can't afford it." Christian shrugs. His gaze bounces to Portia then back to me, all the while my heart sinks lower.

Is he really going to tell me I can't stay?

I get he has a life, but he's my older brother, who is *always* there for me.

"Christian." My voice is soft, cracking. "I don't have anyone back home but Dad, and I'm not ready to face him yet. He's going to throw it back into my face that I quit college to be with Tom and tell me all the ways I ruined my life. I know I messed up, but I can't hear that right now. Please—"

"I wasn't going to say no." He peers down at me, his words rushing out faster. "You didn't give me a chance. I was going to say I don't need help here, but I'm leaving on a business trip to acquire a new location. I'll only be gone for a couple of days to get the paperwork done. You're welcome to come with me."

"You're leaving?" I blink, and then blink again. Enough with my whining, this is great news! "I had no idea you were looking to expand. I would love to go anywhere as long as it's not back home." I jerk my thumb over my shoulder toward the parking lot. "My bag is already packed. We can take my car."

"That's fine." He nods, and his gaze trails back to Portia, who beams an approving smile.

"That's a wonderful idea, to have El come with you." She winks, and tacks on, "She'll keep you out of trouble."

"Yeah, it'll be good to have company for the drive, especially since I'm running late." He takes a step back, rubbing his chin. "I do need to request a loan pre-approval form from the bank before we head out, so if you'll excuse me a moment, I'll be ready to leave shortly."

"That's fine." I pace toward the nearest booth and plop down, staring at both my hands on the table. It's as if my body prefers to stay frozen.

"Can I get you something to drink?" Portia asks softly, her kind-hearted smile aimed at me. "I'm partial to the French press."

I can't even fake a warm smile to repay her generosity. My heart is ripped open, but coffee sounds soothing. "Sure," I whimper as she turns on her heel to make my drink. I'm left to myself and it's overwhelming. I lay my head down and weep.

"Oh, honey." Portia comes from behind me and wraps both hands around me into another hug. "Please don't cry. He's not worth it. Trust me, I have a slew of men on my website who would love to meet you."

"Please don't even mention dating again." I shudder at her suggestion.

"I hate seeing you so upset over someone who clearly isn't worth it." Her kind eyes never leave my face as she rolls her bottom lip under her top teeth for a beat. Then she breaks the silence she created by rushing out, "If I let you in on a secret, do you promise not to say anything?"

"A secret about Tom?" My brows spring up, and my heart slams against my chest. "How do you have a secret?"

"No!" She pats my back, soothing me. "Not about Tom. This is something to cheer you up."

"No offense, Portia, but I just found out the love of my life was living a whole secret life. I really want to be miserable right now—"

"Stop!" She grabs both of my hands and squeezes them in a motherly way. "This isn't your fault and trust me," —she tosses a look over her shoulder before whispering— "This secret is so much fun, you can't be sad."

I slope my gaze up to her. "So, Christian doesn't even know?"

"He knows." She nods, dismissing my concern. "It's something I'm working on, and I haven't told many people because it's in beta."

"I don't know," I start slowly. After the worst day of my life having secrets being unveiled, I don't know if I can handle another secret. "You know what they say. Secrets are lies."

"This isn't a lie." She whips her phone out of her apron pocket and taps on the screen, and I immediately roll my eyes.

"I'm not going on your dating site—"

"It's not my matchmaking app." She slides her phone screen in front of me, and a bright blue screen flashes. "Karaoke Cash-oke," I read out loud, confusion bunching my brows together. "What is this?"

Her index finger taps her lips as she breathes out a quiet, "Shhh."

My eyes case side to side, confirming we're still alone. Unsure of why I need to be quiet. Unless that's just the presentation she does to drum up excitement for this thing. I give in and whisper, "What is this?"

"It's my new app." She taps the screen, and the app loads another screen where a personalized avatar with blond hair like hers pops up. A scoreboard floats above the avatar's head. "Like I said, it's still in beta," she explains. "I'm mostly just letting my paying clients from my other app get a free account here, but you pay to join these karaoke battles. I actually went out of my way to get a lottery license so I could upgrade the prizes, and now you can win real cash." She taps on the screen again, and a countdown starts on the top. "Here, try it."

"I didn't know you liked music." I take the phone from her, and stare at the brightly colored numbers, counting down from thirty seconds.

"Sure, everybody likes music, and it's just karaoke." Pointing to the screen again, her expression pulls into a serious one. "When that gets to zero, it's going to throw you into a round where you are randomly matched with another contestant. You battle it out, singing the same song."

"What?" My arm automatically stretches, thrusting the phone farther away from me. "I'm not in the mood to sing."

"It's so much fun." She pushes the phone closer to my face again. "Trust me, you will forget about what's his name."

The timer runs out, and the screen goes dark. My heart ticks up a notch. I have no idea what I'm doing. Bright red letters flash a song name, "I Will Survive," and I resist rolling my eyes on Portia. I know she's trying, but I just got done crying. I'm all nasally. "I'm not singing," I assert, crossing my arms across my chest.

"It's starting." Portia wags her index finger at the screen. "Please just try it this one time, and if you hate it, I won't even ask again." She's seriously the sweetest person ever, and I hate that she wants this so much. I roll my bottom lip in and glare at the screen. The lyrics scroll across the screen. I swallow and open my mouth to sing very softly and annoyingly monotone but on time. A gauge on the side of that screen turns green, marking the notes I hit, and it keeps glowing, seeding my confidence.

Portia bobs her head along, mouthing the words with me. I can't carry a tune, but the app doesn't seem to care about my pitch. It has some technology that senses the timing of the words.

I don't know how, but the gauge is overflowing by the time I am done with the first chorus. Maybe it's rigged or Portia has it on an easy setting to make me feel better, but since I'm doing well, I start the second verse. It's clearly the song choice that's helping, and I start to replace my shallow breaths with deep ones. When it's over, there's a pause on the screen. For a moment, I think it's jammed, but Portia leans over. "The app has to wait for your opponent to finish and compare scores."

Digital confetti falls over my screen and a giant "Congratulations!" flashes.

"I won?" My tired and rubbed-red eyes grow wide as a little bit of pride puffs up my chest. Christian always teases me there is no one on the planet who loves winning more than me, and I sort of agree. Even when I'm completely shattered, I still love winning.

The screen does some tally thing, and it flashes. "You've won a thousand diamonds."

"Look how many diamonds I won." I tap on the screen, watching them all pile up. "What do I do with them?"

"Since you start in the amateur level, nobody spends or wins money. So, this was just a way to make it fun. You can use the diamonds to level up your avatar and advance in levels, which will change the contestants you may challenge. If you make it to the pro level, you can win real prize money."

"Really?" My eyes are glued to the screen as these shiny diamonds just keep coming.

"Told you it was fun." Portia reaches over, taking her phone back from me, giving me the side-eye. "I'll text you a promo code for a free download."

I take a deep breath, about to tell her no thanks.

It's a silly game.

I don't have time for games.

However, upon second thought it was a mere three minutes of distraction that allowed my tears to dry. I'm not by any means healed, but I will take a distraction. "Thank you." I breathe a little easier as the flood of tears I was holding back earlier has seemed to lessen.

Christian pops his head out of his office. His front hair spike looking extra disgruntled. "Are you ready to get this show on the road?"

"Yeah." I stand, ready to walk out with him. "I'm ready to move on . . ."

# Two

## Arielle

We arrive in the heart of downtown Mapleton right around dinnertime and pull into the historic Harbor Inn and Lodge parking lot. I've visited plenty of small towns, but unlike most, where it's clear their better days are behind them with old infrastructure and deserted downtowns, Mapleton appears to be quite the opposite. People of all ages bustle in and out of downtown businesses from street corner to street corner, and everyone has a cheery smile on their face. I step out of the car and do a double take when I see I'm walking on an actual cobblestone covered street.

"This way." Christian motions toward a robin's-egg blue, two-story building. It's perfectly colored to match the pattern of all the other buildings surrounding it, resembling something out of a storybook.

Finding the bookstore sign right where it should be—above the door—I read it out loud, "The Bookshelf. Isn't that adorable!"

"You say adorable, but I say it looks like money." Christian rubs his hands together, the smirk on his face growing even wider. "I've been talking to the owner for weeks, and he's looking to expand coffee sales. He thinks franchising would be a great option—which I agree. I've pretty much got him sold on partnering with me for a Coffee Loft franchise."

We slow our steps, and I take in the large street window display full of paperback books. I can't help but think I've been here before, even though I know I haven't been. After pondering for a moment, I conclude the reason it looks familiar is it resembles the quaint little bookstores you see in Christmas movies.

Christian opens the wooden door, and we are hit with the scent of paper mixed with hints of vanilla and deep espresso. My nose perks at the scent cocktail. I'm not a huge reader, so the scent of new books doesn't excite me, but the coffee notes feel like home. My attention lands on an impossible-to-miss mahogany staircase that lines the wall, leading to an overhead loft filled with more books. We meander past it, like two lost people, toward the familiar sound of a milk steamer.

"Morning," a gentleman from behind the coffee bar calls as he snaps a plastic lid on the hot drink in front of him. He's tall, and with his head bent over the drink, his dark wavy hair flops almost over his eyes.

"You must be Graham." Christian steps forward, offering his steady hand over the bar. "I'm Christian Hanson."

"Oh, yes." Graham lifts his head, shaking his hair back and finding a hand towel, wiping his hands before he takes Christian's. "How do you do?"

"Excellent." Christian leaves on his business-neutral expression as he drops Graham's hand and turns to me. "This is my sister, Arielle."

Graham's gaze plants on me, and he extends his hand again. "Nice to meet you, Arielle." I shake his hand, and Graham nods to the barstools at the bar. "Welcome to my office. Have a seat. Can I make you a drink?"

"Thank you, but I've had plenty already." Christian waves off his gesture.

"No, thank you." I smile politely, and then stare past him to survey his bar. He has all his syrups on a bookshelf on the wall, which is cute since it's a bookstore. It wouldn't be my first choice to put the coffee bar way in the back of the store, but he has it decorated well, with lots of coffee pun signs and colored mugs hanging on the wall.

"I'm glad you made it over here." Graham takes the coffee he had just prepared and lifts the cup to his mouth, sipping out of it. "I've been reading about Coffee Loft for months, and I'm a huge fan of what they're doing."

"Same. Once I started looking into their franchise, I knew it was perfect for me. I'm certain you'll love it too. The buy-in is lower than most other coffee franchises." Christian holds up a finger to make his point and continues to add a finger with each point he counts off. "Their yearly fees are lower. They have better quality products, and the opportunity is endless, as there is no saturation."

"It sounds perfect for my situation. My wife and I are about to have a baby." Graham's happy life slams me back inside my head, where I can't help but feel a sting of sadness. Not that he's married—well, he is handsome with dark-blue eyes set behind thick lashes—but I had been doing okay. It had been at least an hour since I thought about my heartbreak. Hearing him achieve a milestone reminds me I recently got sent all the way back to the bench and am starting all over again. Again, the tears bud in the backs of my eyes, and I struggle to hold them back. I hate that it makes me sad to hear someone else is happy, but I desperately want that to be me.

"Weekends are our busiest days," Graham continues. "My wife and teenage daughter usually come to help. That way, there's always someone at the bookstore checkout and the coffee bar. With Elinora having the baby, she needs to be home more, and Hadley's going to be hopefully off to college after this year. It's made me consider my options, where I don't have to rely on them so much. I'm so busy with the bookstore, I would love to bring in a partner to manage the coffee bar. I think if it's done well, I'd make the same money, but with half the hassle."

"I hear what you're saying." Christian rubs his chin, and I can literally see dollar signs bling in his eyes. "That's right up my alley. I have one shop on Long Island, and I've done a lot to turn it around. I would love another location, but I can't be in two places at once. I love the idea that we'd be partners. You could be here to monitor it, but essentially, I'd manage it, train, and hire the staff. I think it would work well." Christian turns on his heel, scanning the store again. It's quaint compared to his huge Long Island location, but that dollar-sign gleam in the corner of his eye tells me he's already sold. "I love your store. It's so cozy in here, and Mapleton seems like a great little town," he adds, buttering up Graham even more.

"It's great. I moved here in my early twenties. Later, I moved away for what I thought were better career opportunities, but this always felt like home. So, after I got married, we came back, and we love it." Graham nods to the door, not unwelcoming, but excitement shines through his smile. "Why don't you spend some time downtown and get to know the area? I've already signed the contracts you sent over, but I don't want you to have any buyer's remorse. Even though I'm certain you won't. If everything checks out, I think tomorrow morning we can officially make this transition."

"That sounds like an excellent idea." Christian rocks back on his heels, surveying the place one more time. I've seen that glazed over expression before. I bet he's already envisioning himself carrying loads of money to the bank. I shake my head, rather amused. Christian is good for a distraction from my miserable life. It has been at least another minute since the last time I thought about Tom . . .

I'm getting better.

I think.

Except for this rock that I have in my gut that's so heavy, it makes it hard to pretend I'm normal. I try my best to ignore it and continue forward out the door with Christian into the crisp winter air. We amble back down the block to the lodge.

As soon as we pass through the sliding front doors, we are met with the most gorgeous mountain lodge décor. An enormous stone fireplace fills the far wall, and a roaring fire crackles, bringing warmth to the entire room. Knotty pine beams frame out the high angled ceiling, and I instantly feel welcome. My shoulders fall, releasing tension, and I'm suddenly ready to relax.

We check into our room and walk down the hall, both of us checking our phones for messages. Christian's busy texting Portia—those two are so cute—they never stop talking. The rock in my gut swells when I see I have no messages.

*Not that I want to hear from Tom.*

However, there's an obvious void in my life that is going to take some time to fill. It's like I have a nervous jitter now as I wonder what I should be doing with my time, now that I shouldn't be thinking about Tom.

Christian swipes his key card to unlock the door to our room and winces. "I forgot to pack underwear."

I sputter out laughing. "Don't think you're going to be sitting next to me."

He extends his arm, holding the door open for me to pass through. "Nah, I saw there was a general store right down the block. You make yourself at home. I'll run over there before it closes."

I roll my suitcase forward, finding the perfect spot to park it in the closet. "Can you pick up something to eat too?"

His unruly brows stoop down as his gaze bounces around my face, and he asks in a kind voice, "You don't want to go out for dinner?"

Tugging one side of my lips into a lopsided grin, I force a positive expression. "I don't care to go out. Takeout sounds so much better." His gaze hangs on me, and I rush out, "It's not about Tom."

After a long beat of silence, he finally replies, "Sure, I can find some burgers or something."

The way he looks at me with his eyes so full of empathy makes tears prick the backs of my eyes, and I get choked up. The only thing I can force out is, "Thank you."

"Sure thing, El." He backs out of the room, softly closing the door behind him, and I'm left alone.

The rock in my gut balloons, feeling ten times heavier, and I grab my stomach to brace it. I can't hold it in for another second. Tears rapidly fall down my face, and I swipe them away as I scurry to the bathroom for a tissue. I've never been a huge crier, but this isn't a normal breakup. I thought Tom and I were going to be married. I quit college so I could be closer to him. I was so dumb for thinking that was a good idea. Now I have no job skills, and the only job I could get was cleaning. I screwed up my life and all I got in return is a broken heart.

I ugly cry, letting my shoulders shake, and I blow my nose into a tissue. I let it all out before Christian gets back, because he won't tolerate me crying over Tom. After all my sobs are out, I blow my nose one more time and toss my tissue into the trash. I take a deep breath, clearing my head of all things Tom, and I mentally draw a line to be done crying. I need to clean up before Christian gets back. I splash water on my face, drag my feet back to the bedroom, and pick up my phone. My throat instantly dries when I see an unread text message.

No, not Tom.

It's the code for the karaoke app that Portia told me she'd send me. A frown of forlornity tugs on my lips.

*I will not sing karaoke.*

*Especially not here in a hotel room.*

Portia has the wildest ideas.

I mean, if that's what she likes to do, then more power to her. Shaking my head, I let my fingers hover over the code as I'm ready to delete it. My gaze floats back to the door.

The room is empty.

No one would hear me.

It distracted me last time.

Right on cue, the rock in my gut swells, threatening to spring more tears.

I just cleaned up from ugly crying. I can't cry like that again.

*I need a distraction.*

At least until Christian gets back.

My fingers tremble as the tears travel up from the rock in my gut, and I panic and click on the code.

*Anything is better than crying.*

# THREE

# Stallone Hart

My eyelids shoot open, darkness is all around me, the wind howling so loudly it sounds like a freight train is barreling through my front door. I glance at the alarm clock on my bedside table and groan. 3:00 a.m.

Always, I'm up at this hour, as my life seems to be stuck on autopilot.

On this unordinary day in the middle of a not-special week, the house shutters and the evergreen branches scrape at my bedroom window, but I'm not scared. I've heard worse. It does, however, prick at my mind, telling me I won't be going to work. A knot swells in my throat, and I swallow to force it down, but it stays. The knot doesn't care about the money, as I have more of that than I'd ever dreamed of.

It's a knot of avoidance.

And it's a real jerk, reminding me to keep busy so I don't remember *her*.

I swing my legs over the edge of the bed, force my tired body to my feet, on the hunt for a glass of cold water to soothe my throat. It's been ages since I slept through the night, and getting up way before the first light of dawn is my pattern. I shuffle my feet forward until my hand finds the cool stainless-steel handle on the fridge. I grab a bottle of water and down most of it before I pivot and turn on my coffeepot. It gurgles to life while I lean over the kitchen sink to peer out the window into the night sky.

The light I always leave on above my front porch for security reveals a blanket of fluffy snow has already accumulated in my yard, and all the branches on my pine trees are bowing down from the weight. Sighing, I turn away. The moisture isn't a bad thing. It's the fact the rural backcountry roads have nearly washed-out with mudslides, making it impossible for my oversized trucks to haul logs to the mill. We've been piling up everything we chop until the roads dry out. This weather is going to turn the mudslides into ice, which is so much worse.

This means another few days—at best—until I can move wood.

I run my hand through my hair, pretending it's pain in my head and not my heart that keeps me up. Right as I'm about to let out a defeated sigh, Lucky stirs awake from his spot by the front door and walks over, greeting me with his tail wagging. Lucky is a stray I found roaming these hills. He got his name after he narrowly missed getting slammed by a tree. I used to call him Lucky Nine Lives, but he has far surpassed nine lives in the two years he's been my logging partner.

He's also gotten used to my predawn rising, and he's ready to go for our walk. "Just a moment, boy." I pat his head before filling a travel mug with black coffee. I always take my coffee to go, as it keeps me warm on our walks. "Let me get dressed, and we'll be on our way."

I head to the door, where all my outer clothes are neatly hung on hooks, and I slip on my thickest lined flannel shirt and cover it with a pair of coveralls. I slide my feet into a pair of snow boots and tug a thick beanie over my head. The front door isn't even cracked before Lucky pushes his nose out, leading the way.

The frigid air slams into the inside of my lungs, pulling me out of any remnants of slumber I was holding on to. It's an odd sensation to welcome the sting of the wind, because at least for the moment, I can blame my pain on something temporal. I take a deep inhale, as there is nothing better than the fresh mountain breeze, and start off on our regular morning walking trail with Lucky running all around me in search of fresh scents.

When we coast around the bend in the road, I toss a look over at my little brother's cabin. It's only a few hundred yards from where Ryson and I grew up, in a cabin of humble beginnings. Ryson's younger by five years and completely my opposite. He's socially outgoing and can barely stay out of trouble, except for the fact that he's a smooth talker. Me, being the more introverted, reliable brother always trying to talk sense into him.

All the windows in Ryson's cabin are dark—as they should be for this time of the morning. I can't help but envy his ability to sleep. He doesn't have the stress I have running a company. He drives a truck for me, except for when he can't, like now. Then he watches TV. I sigh heavily and carry on the path as it narrows and winds around another bend—this one is my favorite one of all. The point that overlooks the entire city of Mapleton.

It's the perfect town, in my opinion. Small enough that you know everyone by name, but large enough you have the local businesses you need for a proper community. Quaint cobblestone streets are lined with old-fashioned streetlamps, and I never get tired of looking at the glow they create down below. It's like tiny stars at the bottom of a valley that watch over the people while they sleep.

A few wispy snowflakes flutter to the ground, as if they are tasked with the job of adding the finishing touches on the already blanketed streets. It all appears magical from up here, and I never tire of seeing—wait a second . . .

My brows bend together as the streetlamps pulse off and on twice in unison before finally settling into the darkness, and the little town at the bottom of the mountain almost disappears.

I slow my steps, easing closer to the edge of the trail and wait for the lamps to turn back on. Several long beats pass, but all the lamps remain dark. Clearly, the town has lost power. More than likely some power lines have fallen under the weight of this dense snow. My cabin is powered by propane, so it won't affect me, but if they don't fix the power lines soon, people will get awfully cold fast.

My gaze slides back down. I still can't see even a spark, but I know how to help them. I have so many logs piled up; it would be nothing for me to take a load to town for firewood. I slide my fingers into my mouth, whistling through them. "Come on, Lucky. Time to go."

His tongue hangs low, and his tail sweeps back and forth. He's as happy as a clam on a beach, fully unaware that people are about to freeze from this power outage. His smile is contagious, erasing at least some of my heartsickness. I stride next to him; glad I have a companion.

Lucky pushes his snout into my leg as he follows on my heels. I pat his head, chuckling to myself.

*If only a pat on my head could make me that happy.*

# Four

## Arielle

I wiggle my toes and pull the scratchy comforter tighter around my neck, but it does nothing to warm me. "Christian," I hiss over the narrow aisle between our queen beds. "Did you turn the air conditioner on?" It's pitch dark in the hotel room, but I angle my gaze toward Christian's heavy breathing.

When he doesn't reply because he's still sound asleep, I take my spare pillow and whip it toward him, the way a sister should smack her annoying big brother. "Christian," I say, raising my voice as my eyes slowly adjust to the darkness.

"Whoa, what?" He startles awake.

"Did you turn the air on?" I wrap my blanket even tighter around me, but shivers erupt from my extremities. It's absolutely freezing, and these thin hotel blankets don't hold any warmth.

"Why, yes, I keep the air on full blast in January in New England because I love to bleed money." He pauses for a beat before adding, "The clock isn't glowing. I would guess the power went out."

"Ah, great," I mumble under my breath and reach for my phone, which I had set on the nightstand. I click the power button, relieved to see a tiny flash of light and use it to guide me to my suitcase for a sweatshirt. "I didn't pack for a power outage." I shiver as I also find my winter beanie, and yank it on, covering the bottoms of my ears. I don't stop dressing until after I've slipped on my down winter coat—it's that cold in here.

"I'm sure it will be on shortly," Christian speaks through a yawn.

My phone confirms it's almost time to start the day. "It's after six. The sun should come up soon. That might help warm things up a little." I hustle back to my bed, crawl under the blankets, and stare toward the window.

"You should try having high blood pressure like me. Then you'll never be bothered by the cold." Christian's grumble is muffled by the pillow he's pulled over his head to more than likely tune me out.

"Wait a second." My head springs back from an image that flashes in my brain. "Do you remember when we checked into the lodge last night? The lobby had that huge stone fireplace. Do you think we should sit downstairs until the power comes back on?"

Christian's sleepy grumble is barely audible. "I mean, it doesn't make sense to just lie in bed to relax."

"Right." I ignore his sarcasm and spring to my feet. "It's too cold in here, even under the blankets. They had those big leather couches downstairs. It's perfect." I'm already slipping on my Uggs when I toss a glance over my shoulder. He hasn't moved from his spot in bed. "Let's hurry before someone else gets the same idea and takes our spot." I yank on the doorknob and prompt the door open with my foot. "Last one down has to buy the other person breakfast."

"No power means nobody will get breakfast." Christian drops one foot to the carpet and does a falling motion to get out of bed. It's ungraceful and seems a bit harsh, but Christian has a dramatic way of doing most things. He whisks his phone off the nightstand and shuffles his feet forward, mumbling through another yawn, "Besides, I need to get dressed." He takes a minute to swap his shorts for pants, slips on a jacket, and then loafers before he stares at me for the first time this morning. "Happy now?" he grumbles.

"Not until we get our spot." I rush him out the door. We follow the dark hall, guided only by the light on my cell phone, as it seems the rest of the hotel customers are still asleep. It might be my optimistic imagination, but I feel the temperature increase as we get closer to the lobby.

"I guess the interstate is closed." Christian reads a notification on his phone. "We won't be going home today."

I'm about to let out a groan but the lobby comes into view and the permeating warmth muffles my annoyance. The massive stone fireplace doesn't disappoint with a soft glowing fire to welcome me. I smile slyly at the desk attendant as I beeline to the couch in front of the fireplace. "Our room is so cold, I couldn't sleep," I say and plop down, scooting my body all the way to the armrest closest to the flame.

"The power has been out for several hours already," he reports in a monotone voice. "The forecast said it's just a pause in the snow, as it's supposed to dump more later this morning."

"Oh, look. That's Graham from The Bookshelf going in to work." Christian uses his index finger to point out the window while he scratches his belly with his other hand. Happy to not watch him scratch, I willingly follow his gesture.

Sure enough, Graham's unlocking the bookstore. "I guess this city never shuts down."

"I guess not." Christian jerks his head to the exit as his feet move toward it. "We might as well head over too and start our first day."

"Can you hear yourself talking right now?" I stumble to my feet, hating to leave the warm haze from the fire. "You are obsessed with money." I wave my hand over his body. "You haven't even showered for the day, nor have I."

"I'm not going to shower without hot water. Plus, nobody cares how I'm dressed." His face is stern, focused, telling me there's no use in protesting. Christian is that kind of guy who can never sit still, especially if he's anxious about something. It's his turn to lead, and out the door we go. I'm grateful the sun is starting to peek over the mountain range, but still unimpressed by the frosty air that nips at my extremities. I tug on my coat, both concealing my warmth and my nightshirt.

"Morning, Graham!" Christian calls out across the road as I struggle to keep pace with Christian's perky steps. We race right to Graham like we're stalkers. "Lovely day, isn't it?"

Graham's gaze finds us, and he immediately responds to Christian's sarcasm with a chuckle. "Right. So nice out."

"I think the whole town is out of power." I steel my face to the ground. Christian is so embarrassing sometimes as he states the most obvious things.

"We lost power at our house a few hours ago, but the store has a generator." Graham turns his key, releasing the door. He yanks it open with one smooth motion and jerks his head in an inviting nod. "Come on in. I'll see if I can make some coffee."

Graham switches the closed sign to open and heads toward the back, disappearing through a door that appears to lead to another staircase. After a few moments, the lights flicker on, and the fan of the furnace hums, bringing a promise of incoming warmth. I almost cheer. It's funny how you never think of electricity until you've lost it, but I couldn't be happier to see artificial light.

When Graham reappears, he has a full smile on his face and heads behind the coffee bar, flicking on the drip coffeepot and espresso machine. "There's a tiny apartment upstairs that I used to live in. Before I lived there, the old lady who owned this store before me lived in it, and she had to be on oxygen when she was older. They had that generator installed for emergencies, but it comes in handy."

"I bet." Christian takes long strides toward the coffee bar and straddles a barstool like he already owns the place. His flashing dollar signs return to his pupils. "I love what you've done here. I can't wait to see this place grow even more."

"Yeah, like I said before, if it wasn't for the fact my wife and I are expecting a baby, I'd keep plugging along. However, I learned the hard way with my daughter that I need to be home more, and running a bookstore is plenty enough on its own." Graham casually takes his phone out of his pocket, and starts setting it on the counter, when his gaze flicks to it momentarily, and his eyebrows practically shoot to the ceiling. "Oh, my!"

"Everything okay?" Christian arches his chin, trying to peek at the phone in the most not-nonchalant manner.

"Ah, not sure." Graham is rapidly texting, his eyes locked on his phone. "My wife's water broke, but it's too early for the baby." His gaze cuts to Christian. "I've got to go."

The front door jingles open, and a couple meanders in. "Guys, we're closed," Graham calls out while he digs in his pocket and pulls out a set of keys. He takes several steps toward the exit. "I need to leave."

"Oh, I saw the lights on, and thought it was a place we could keep warm," the man says while rubbing his bright pink hands together. "Our apartment is out of heat."

"I was going to open." Graham's words rush faster as he continues to the front and switches the open sign back to closed. "But that was before I found out my wife is in labor, and now I need to go."

"Oh, we're sorry," the woman says while the small smile she had been wearing noticeably plummets when she pivots to return outside.

I know how she feels.

The wind is howling, the snow is blowing, and I'm getting the shivers just thinking about going outside. I don't want to go back to our freezing hotel room. "Ah, maybe you don't have to leave." My voice cracks and I clear my throat, tossing a look at Graham. "I can make them a coffee and give them a place to sit until they warm up a little."

"I don't know about that." Graham's expression pulls into a wince. "It seems like a big ask to leave you guys here. I really think we need to just lock up."

"Well," Christian speaks matter-of-factly, "Today is our day to transition everything, so really the coffee bar is mine, right? It really makes sense for us to stay. We can just tell everyone the bookstore is closed but we are here."

Graham's wince deepens as his gaze bounces from me to Christian and back to the couple. The couple's smiles droop even more as they back away from the counter. "It's just coffee, and we can handle it," I say. "Christian and I both know our way around a coffee bar, and we have nothing else to do."

Graham's silent but he turns to Christian, who doesn't disappoint, piping up again, "It'll give me a chance to get to know the customers."

Graham's gaze bounces from the couple to Christian, and then his phone rings. He yanks it out of his pocket. "Hello?" His inflections are strained as he lowers his voice, but it doesn't conceal the conversation that his wife's waiting for him. Christian steps forward, waving Graham out the door. "Just go. You have my number. Call when you know she's safe. I'll help these people." Graham takes a moment to look around the shop again, before giving a deep shrug, and eventually nods an agreement with his phone still glued to his ear.

I turn on my heel and head to the coffee bar. "What can I start for you?" I ask the couple.

They step forward. The guy, who is dressed in very nice business attire, says, "Just hot coffee would be great."

"I can handle that." I easily find the cups and pivot to fill them, but the coffeepot that Graham had switched on seems to have been backed up. There's hot water in the pot, but no coffee. I open the back of the machine and check for grounds. They are there. I flip the switch off and then on, but it only makes a dying noise. Pursing my lips, I study it. I can't see any switches I'm missing.

Maybe Graham has it on a rinse cycle?

There must be a switch or something I need to use to get it out of hot water mode that I don't know. Under my breath, I hiss at Christian, who's watching me do all the labor. "Can you look at this?"

He takes long strides over and stands in front of it with his hands on his hips. "I'm looking."

Sometimes I just don't have the patience for his humor, and I sigh and turn back to the couple. Now I understand Graham's hesitation for leaving us here. Apparently, there's a trick to his coffeepot that isn't obvious. I'm not calling him while he's already so stressed out. "New plan," I say slowly, "I have hot water but no coffee. How about some tea?"

"Yeah, that sounds fine," they both quickly agree, and the woman points to the jars directly behind me. "That breakfast blend looks great."

"Deal." I ready their teas, and I check the menu for the price and turn to the tablet on the counter. Thankfully, it has full charge, and it's pretty much the same point-of-sale system Christian uses at the Coffee Loft, and I'm able to ring them up.

When they leave, Christian's beaming at me. "You just love getting us into these things, don't you?"

"Me?" I jerk my thumb to my chest defensively. "You're the one who made us come over here this morning."

"I wanted to get things swapped over to Coffee Loft. I didn't volunteer to run the place with no training. I know nothing about these machines, and they look so vintage compared to what I'm used to. I had planned to shut the place down as soon as I get the key to remodel."

"How hard can it be?" I gesture toward the espresso machine behind me. "It's not half as complicated as the Coffee Loft fancy stuff." By now the heat has returned to the room, and I'm getting used to feeling my fingers. I don't want to go outside or back to the hotel where there's no heat. "If you don't want to figure it out, then don't. I'm not going back to that hotel. If I'm going to stay here, the least I can do is give people a warm drink."

"I guess," he mutters as he joins me behind the counter. "I might as well start doing inventory." His eyes pace the bookshelf of syrups. "I need to run back to the hotel to grab my laptop—"

The door pulls open, bringing in a powerful gust of wind, and a swirl of glittering snow, followed by the biggest, burliest man I've ever seen. His shoulders are so broad they fill the doorway, and his face is covered in a thick dark beard, the very tips of his whiskers frosted with snowflakes. He seemingly knows his way around the place as he crosses the bookstore and heads straight toward me.

"Morning." His voice is gruff, but not unfriendly as he catches me staring. "Some weather we have here, huh?"

"R-Right." I stammer and close my mouth before I catch the logo on his shirt, *Hart Logging,* and I ask the most obvious question just to make small talk, "Are you a logger?"

"When I can get to work." There's a gleam in the corner of his eye that is so warm I fight the urge to stare at him. He gestures forward. "I'm also a coffee addict, and I saw the lights were on."

It's easy to return his smile, but I'm not sure why my face is suddenly feeling so much warmer. "Yeah, I'm happy to help you."

He cuts his gaze back to the menu. "I'll take a large black coffee."

I grab the cup and turn toward the coffeepot, and a frown pulls on my lips. The pot still only has water. I push the on button again.

From the noise it's making, I doubt it will work. "Ah, my coffeepot is broken today." I pull up one side of my lips into a lopsided grin. "I'm actually not really working here, as I'm just filling in. So, I hate to mess with it and break it more, but I have hot water. I can make any tea."

"Tea?" he echoes as if I've said a curse word.

"Sorry." I smile politely and quickly motion to the assortment of jars behind me, all filled with tea leaves. "I always love a good black tea, and I can add milk and some vanilla flavor."

His bushy eyebrows bend down, but he grunts. "If that's all you have, I guess."

I get busy steeping his tea leaves in hot water, but I can feel his stony stare on me, which pricks my nerves a bit. I ask another question to keep the conversation going. "So, what are you up to today in this blizzard?"

"I'm in the park with firewood. If you know anyone who needs any, send them my way."

"I'm new to town." I add the lid to his cup and place it on the bar in front of him. "I haven't met many people yet."

My gaze snags on his hands when he passes me his debit card. With raw callous scabs covering the tops of his palms, his whole hand is easily the width of two of mine. My gaze trails down his arms, and I struggle to not let my jaw hit the floor. His arms are so round, they are practically the size of Tom's whole scrawny body. My cheeks warm at the comparison, and I force my gaze back to his face. "Just two dollars," I say and swipe his card through the Square before I hand it back.

Our gazes linger on one another as we exchange goodbyes, and the lumberjack exits the building, leaving a trail of the whole evergreen forest behind. I've never seen a man like that before, and he's left me with a strong curiosity.

"Don't even think about it." Christian's warning cuts into my thoughts like nails on a chalkboard.

"What?" I cut a glance back at him, defensiveness building in my chest. "What are you talking about?"

"I saw the way you were drooling over him." He chuckles, shaking his head. "The last thing you need is a big old mountain man to break your heart while we're here."

"Who said anything about romance?" I snap back, hating how Christian jumps to conclusions. I never thought for a single moment about him breaking my heart.

I've sworn off men.

I was simply admiring his scent.

And his beard.

And his big strong hands.

And his enormous arms.

And his kind eyes.

Yeah, he has an awful lot of good qualities to think about. I pinch my lips together, holding back a secret smile. Out of my peripheral vision, I catch the lumberjack's backside in front of the big storefront window as he crosses the street.

He certainly is easy to look at.

And an excellent distraction from the fact I've sworn off dating forever.

"All right." Christian's stance straightens toward the door. "Enough stalling. I'm going to run to the hotel, grab my laptop, and see if they can extend our room for another night since the roads are closed. Is there anything you need me to grab for you?"

I survey the store, and the only people in here are the first couple. It's pretty uneventful. "I should be fine."

He throws up his palm as he marches forward. "Be back in a bit."

I watch him leave and then because I no longer have an excuse to avoid it, I pull out my phone and text my dad

**Me: Hey, Dad, I'm not going to be in for another day or two. Christian and I ended up getting snowed in.**

Dots indicating he's typing show on my screen for a long time, which is weird because my dad hates texting, and he usually only types one or two words. The amount of time it shows him typing makes me think that he's going to lecture me about something.

**Dad: Everything else okay?**

My top teeth crash down on my bottom lip, as I reread his text and wonder if he suspects something else is up. Had he heard the rumors about Tom? I can't even begin to think about how I'm going to explain that whole thing to him.

**Me: Yeah, it's fine. Just helping at the coffee shop today.**

I drop my phone onto the counter before I'm tempted to add anything else. Now determined to get my mind on other things, I turn back to the coffee bar with my eyes on the broken coffeepot. *There must be a button or something I'm missing.* Running my hand all along the base, I can't find anything that even resembles a button or a switch. I grab the plug out of the wall and plug it back into a different outlet. Still nothing. A cool breeze comes in from behind me, alerting me to the front door being open, and I toss a glance in that direction.

It's just Christian.

"Back already?" I push the coffeepot back to its original spot and step away from it.

"Yeah." He's breathing heavy, most likely from running, and he plops his backpack on the table near the front window before he takes a moment to brush the fresh powder snow off the bottoms of his pant legs. "It's really coming down."

"I figured." I slowly stride to the front of the store and peek out the large front window. There's so much frost accumulated on the glass, it's hard to see except for a few bare spots right in the center. "Did you notice if anything else is open? I'd love to see if I can find a coffeepot."

"Nah, there really isn't a point since Coffee Loft has its own brand. Just wait until we get our franchise one. That's better than anything you'll find at the store." Christian unzips his bag, pulls out a thick black binder, and sets it on the table in front of him.

I turn my gaze back out and study the town. Mounds of snow are piled up on the sidewalks, making some places nearly impossible to walk. The streets have yet to be plowed, and there's just a single lane of tracks blazed through the snow by the trucks that risked travel. Town is essentially deserted except for in the center of town where there is a park and a single truck pulled over with firewood in the back.

*That must be that man who was just here...*

"What are you looking at?" Christian holds his gaze on me, as if I'm accountable to him.

"Just the snow everywhere." I shove my hands in my pockets and move away from the window, sneaking another peek at the truck before I turn completely away. "You know, since you're back, I might step out for some fresh air."

"Did you already forget it's freezing out?" Arching his chin, his gaze slams to the window like he's inspecting the outside for something he suspects he missed. His smile grows flimsy when his eyes roam over on the lone truck. "El..."

My lips curl against my will, and I move toward the door before Christian has more time to solve this riddle. I push the door open and step out, calling back, "Just grabbing some fresh air . . ."

I turn toward the park, and add under my breath and only for me, "And a better view."

# FIVE

## Stallone

"Oh, thank you so much, Stallone," Mrs. Beasily, the old lady who owns the laundromat, clenches her patent leather coin purse in front of her and watches as I load up two bundles of firewood in the trunk of her old red Buick. I've already given out half my load of wood today. If my calculations are correct, I should be able to head home within the hour.

"It's my pleasure." Her trunk smells like dog food, and I'm grateful when I get to shut it, and turn to head into my truck. I left it running with the heater cranked, and it's comfortable.

Her frail, bony fingers find my forearm, causing me to pause on my heel. "What do I owe you?"

"Not a thing." I shake my head, adding a please-to-serve-you smile to my face. "It's my pleasure. I just hope you stay warm."

"Oh, goodness." She squeezes my arm tighter, and I fight the urge to wince as I've never been much of a person who enjoys people in my space. "How about I bake you a potato pie once the power comes on?"

"I didn't know potato had a pie." One of my brows hikes above the other into a quizzical expression. Nothing about that word combination sounds appealing. She's still got hold of my arm, and I frankly don't care to argue if it extends this encounter. "Sure, but only if you go home now, because it's too cold for you to stand out here."

Her eyes spring wide for a moment, but she bows her head a bit and says, "All right. I'll see you soon."

"Stay warm." I toss a silent wave up, as snow crunching from nearby footsteps draws my attention to turn the opposite direction and I freeze. The woman I had just spoken to earlier at the coffee shop is headed this way. Her hood is pulled up tight around her head, adding a little extra fluff of fur trim around her face, but that doesn't take away from her gorgeous icy-blue eyes. I wave at her, curious about what she's doing. She said she didn't need any wood, and it's way too cold out here to just stand around. She waves back and when she smiles, her smile is mischievous and focuses right at me. "Did you change your mind about needing some firewood?"

She shields her face from the blowing snow. "No, I don't need any. I was just going to stop over—"

"Stall*ooone!*" A shrill noise that frequents my nightmares cuts through the air, stealing both of our attentions. My eyelids crash down, and I know who it is before I ever complete my blink.

*Nora Worley.*

The single most annoying woman I've ever laid eyes on. She can never say a smooth Stallone. It was always crooning out, Stal-*loooone,* drawing it out like a game show host who's being choked.

I grunt and brush my hand over my whiskers, turning enough to see her walking this way. "Stallooone Hart," she croons out again, her hips swaying in an exaggerated way until she stops a few feet from me and the coffeehouse lady.

"Did you need some wood?" I ask with a straight face. No time is ever a good time to have to see her, but this is the worst timing, because I really was interested in talking to the coffee shop lady. I flicker my gaze back to her, hoping she doesn't walk off. She's biting her bottom lip—which in my humble analysis—doesn't look like a good thing.

"No wood." Nora's voice is unnaturally loud like she's trying to speak over a crowd that isn't here. "I need you to call me back for once."

"You called?" I blink, terrified she might have my phone number. I never gave her that, and if by chance I had given her my number, I'll change it.

"No, I didn't call. It's just proper manners to call people after *a date*." Her T is extra enunciated, making it sound even more terrifying.

"Date?" I choke out an echo, as I have no idea what she's talking about. I haven't been on a date in over a year, and I certainly would never go on a date with her.

Her lips pinch together momentarily before she says, "Remember, two nights ago, we had drinks?"

*What are you even talking about?*

Coffeehouse girl starts to slide her feet, backing away, and I feel the strained expression on my face that wants to ask her to stay, but I have no idea where this conversation is going. *Nora is clearly delusional!*

She may say something I don't want anyone to hear. Instead of calling out for her to stay, I flash my palm to her and say, "Stay warm." She gives me a mellow smile and turns to trudge back to the coffee shop. The sight of her leaving sends a ping of disappointment right to my gut. My annoyance at Nora's presence quadruples, and I blurt back, "I didn't go out with you. I grabbed a to-go dinner from The Grove and went home."

"Right." She nods as if I'm a small child not understanding instructions. "Remember we sat together at the bar and had drinks, and we laughed. It was such a nice time."

I jab my hand through my hair, resisting the urge to yell at this woman. I ordered a drink while I waited for my food, and she plopped down next to me and talked about her hair salon business the whole time.

I wasn't listening.

Maybe I'm good at pretending.

*She thought that was a date?*

I almost vomit in my mouth. "That wasn't a date, Nora. You can't go around saying it was."

She perks an over-tweezed eyebrow at me. "You hugged me extra long when we left."

"I stood up to leave, and you basically threw your arms around my neck. What was I supposed to do?" I tried to forget about it because it had to be the most cringe moment of my year, and having to flesh this out now with Nora is making my blood pressure soar. I know when to pick my arguments, and this isn't one I want. "Look, I'm done here for now." I pivot and slam the tailgate shut and don't offer another word when I climb in my truck.

By now, coffeehouse lady is all the way back to the coffee shop. I see her open the door and disappear inside. I so badly want to make Nora disappear too. I don't have the patience for pleasantries or pretending that she isn't completely nuts. She's been trying to get with me for years, and I've always been as much of a gentleman about it as I could stand, but this is too much.

*Of all the things to have happened, Nora is going around telling people we went on a date. What next?*

*This is why I stay away from town and people in general.* I rant in my head as I crank my truck and steer back to my house, feeling as if I just dodged a bullet. All the good women are taken and I'm not desperate enough to deal with a nut.

Another day on autopilot. I wake before dawn and reach across my bed, finding it cold and empty. I blink, wishing my view would change.

*It never does.*

It's a feeling of being lost in your own home, in my own bed. I'm supposed to be living through my first year of marriage right now, not in this constant state of heartache. The quicker I get out of bed, the sooner I can breathe.

Today, I walk straight to the front door—eager for all the distractions—and whip it open. My head jolts back at the chill, and my eyes are met with more snow. It's frozen hard, which means the roads will be too. It's a tad risky to take the semi out, but the news reported Mapleton had their power restored last night. I'm not needed in town today, and I can't sit around all day and let my mind wander. I power through the motions to get ready with my usual clothes and coffee.

Whistling, I summon Lucky, and he eagerly runs to my truck and jumps in, and we putter down the winding roads, stopping at Ryson's cabin and honking the horn until he manifests in his Hart Logging flannel shirt and cargo pants—coffee mug in hand. We Hart brothers are serious about our coffee.

"Did you get enough sleep there, Lazy?" I tease, and Lucky makes his way over to sit on his lap. Lucky clearly isn't a lap dog as he weighs over seventy pounds, but nobody could ever convince him otherwise. He's also so tall, he has to duck his head to fit, but he doesn't whimper a complaint.

"There wasn't much else to do but sleep." Ryson lifts his mug to his lips, sipping. "How are the roads?"

"Slick and terrible," I grumble as I shift the truck back into gear and pull out carefully to avoid spinning out.

"Perfect." His easy grin fills his face, and he lets out a sarcastic snicker. "That's exactly how I like them."

The thing about being a logger is it's the perfect job for introverted people like me. I never have to say much. I turn up the tunes on the radio and drive on. Me, thinking about the woman I should be over. Ryson, more than likely wondering what beer combo goes best with wings. And then there's Lucky, who just chills and gets his back scratched.

As I pass the lumber mill, my gaze scans over the yard filled to the brim with logs. There's not a single truck lined up to drop off logs or move any out. I simply turn my head away. Apparently, that invites Ryson to talk.

"Did you hear Nora Worley is back in town?" It's been nearly a half hour of silence, and that's how he breaks it?

The last thing I need to talk about is Nora Worley. I'd sooner drive this truck right over the edge of the mountain than ever hear her name again. "No thanks."

Ryson's head locks forward on the road. "It's time you start living again. You've grieved over Lindsey long enough. She's not worth it."

I click my tongue on the roof of my mouth, holding back all the things I dare not say. Trust me, I think about it every day. Every day I feel the same. Dating is the last thing I'd ever want to do again. It's right up there with hearing from Nora again. Maybe I'm a fool or just too fragile, but I have to believe if I'm meant to love again, the very thought of it won't feel like my heart is being ripped out of my chest.

We fall into a stony silence until I pull into our worksite and back a trailer right up to the timber crane. With logs already piled up, it's an easy switch for Ryson to jump into the semi. "You need to go to the mill in Carson County," I say, even though I'm sure he saw our mill was closed. It doesn't really make sense for him to drive the extra hundred miles, as the gas bill cuts into our profits, but I need a reason to be busy.

I'm eager to be alone and hop into the crane, which fires up easily, despite the cold temps. We settle into an easy grind, filling his trailer in no time. It's monotonous work that leaves plenty of time for thinking. Most days I wear earbuds with upbeat music to keep my mind off Lindsey but today, something odd happens.

I think about yesterday.

I had left the bookstore holding a warm cup of the sweetest smelling tea I'd ever smelled. Course, I know nothing about tea except for that horrid stuff my mom used to force down my throat when I was a young child with a chest cold.

That tea yesterday was so different. When I tipped that cup up, and the warm, creamy liquid hit my tongue, my taste buds sprang wide awake, wanting even more. I could definitely go for another one of those. More than that, I think about the woman who made the tea. She seemed so eager to help me, despite her machine being broken. She had this sweet smile that lit up the entire room, even though she was quite small and compact for a chick.

Petite—I think is the proper word.

But she didn't give off the air of being a helpless damsel. She had a gleam in her eyes that told me she prefers to be sweet, but she wasn't afraid to be sassy. Although, she is as attractive as any model you'd see in a magazine, I spared a second glance because I am not looking for anything, especially not some girl who thinks tea is an adequate substitute for coffee. The nerve.

Ryson waves at me, indicating his trailer is full. I back up, and he pulls his semi out of the yard. I'm not ready to go home, and the sun is still peeking out behind the clouds. I might as well work while I'm here. I fill up two more trailers without hardly trying. Right as I'm leaving the yard, Ryson texts me.

**Ryson: The lumber mill approved my delivery. They said they can take more tomorrow.**

Pleased with the news, a smirk spreads wide across my face.

Work is done for the day, and it looks like I'm actually getting paid.

Suddenly, I don't want to go straight home. I'm in the mood to celebrate—to the coffee shop I go.

# Six

## Arielle

"Graham's wife had a boy, and they named him Vincente," Christian reports from the high-top table he's been sitting at all morning. The power has been restored, but since Graham couldn't come in, we offered to help again. We are on day two of running this place, and we've quickly settled into a pattern, where Christian "works" on his laptop, and I help all the actual customers.

It's fine though.

Keeping my hands moving is preventing me from thinking about Tom. Whoops, I just thought of him again. He's sneaky like that. Also, the people in this little town are the sweetest. I've learned a lot about this place. Like, how they have a new AHL hockey team that is extremely bad, but the town loves them anyway. Or how they have a famous restaurant called Red Barn Kabobs that started in an actual barn. I've learned so many random facts about this place from the small-town gossip mill, but the thing I'm most curious to know about is that lumberjack who was in here yesterday.

He's so different from any of the men I see in Boston, and he had this easygoing way about him, despite how huge and scary he should have looked. It was oddly alluring. I've found myself peeking out the window every few minutes, hoping to see his truck at the park.

"You're not hoping Tom is going to show up, are you?" Christian parks a hand on his hip, his big brother tone firing in all decibels. "I know you think you love him, but I guarantee if I ever see his scrawny little body again, I'm going to make sure he knows he's not welcome."

"No." My brows furrow together. "Of course not—" I stop myself because I don't care to argue. Something about being out here in the mountains is a respite from so many things, including any desire I would normally feel to defend myself. I didn't know it when we first set out for this place, but it was exactly what I needed. "I'm watching the snow, wondering if we are going to leave tomorrow."

"We better." Christian slams his laptop shut and slips off the stool with urgency. "I need to be back on Long Island for a food vendor show. It's the largest one of the year, and I'm hoping to snag some more catering clients." Christian flashes his phone screen at me, and a swaddled-up baby stares at me.

"Aw, cute." I smile at the photo, as if the baby can see my big cheesy grin through the phone. "I'm glad mom and baby are safe."

"Graham says he'll be back to work tomorrow for part-time hours." His brows lower as he reads his phone. "What is this? I have a text message I didn't see." He taps on his phone, reading aloud, "'The Coffee Loft truck will be here in five minutes.' Oh, man." His gaze jerks to the backdoor where the loading dock is. "We might have to lock up early." He scoops up his laptop, stuffing it into the backpack he always carries. "The truck is bringing all our Coffee Loft branding. I can't wait to see it because they are transitioning to a new color scheme of blue and cream. After it's set up, I'll need to shut down for a few days. I'll have a huge grand opening in the next couple of weeks." He zips his bag and slips it onto his back. "That will happen on the next trip though. I can't be gone that long. I've put an ad in the newspaper for an assistant manager's position. It's best if I leave it open for at least a week. Then I can come down to interview and hopefully hire and train." His eyebrows wag playfully at me as he drops his voice, pretending to add an evil inflection when he says, "It's all part of my master plan."

*An assistant manager position.*

I sort of like the sound of that.

It definitely has a better ring than "my dad's cleaning lady."

I'm not sure why I never thought of working for Christian for real before, but I could easily get used to this little town. The thing is, if I say something about it now, Christian will think I'm running away from my problems. My jaw twitches, begging me to offer to take the job, but I don't take the bait. It's too soon. I need to show him I'm serious about the job, and not just about hiding out.

The door whips open, pulling my gaze with it. My heart instantly thrums against my chest to see the same imposing, bearded man who was in here yesterday. "Good morning." I bite my lip, trying to keep from smiling too large as I sneak a glance at his forearms.

"Good morning." He nods to Christian, who is hurrying to the back, and waves on his way out to meet the truck.

The man's eyes are fast to meet mine. My heart skips a beat when he doesn't look away. I swallow and move my feet until I'm behind the coffee bar. "Nice to see you again. What can I get you?"

He's slow to pull his gaze away from me and onto the menu. "I guess that depends if you have coffee today?"

"So sorry." I shake my head and stare off in the direction Christian just left. "We are transitioning to a Coffee Loft franchise. My boss decided rather than fix the equipment, he's waiting to install the new stuff." I pull my lips into a big smile, hoping to smooth everything over. I'm not sure why I care so much about making this man happy, but he's huge. I would hate to see him grumpy. Especially if he hasn't had his coffee yet. "Tomorrow," I rush out. "We'll have our new stuff and trust me." I lean in, as if I'm letting him in on a secret, "We'll have our signature Coffee Loft blends. Once you try those, the wait will all be worth it."

His lips straighten into a neutral expression. Under his thick beard, it's hard to read if he's upset. I hate to warn off customers when we haven't even officially opened. "How about this?" I blurt out, hoping he doesn't leave upset. "I'll make whatever tea you want, and it's on me today, but you have to promise to come back tomorrow to try the coffee."

"You're asking me to come back tomorrow?" His dark eyes hover over mine, tension rising between us, and my heart beats hard against my chest.

"F-For coffee," I stutter.

His broad shoulders move up and down and he stares deeply into my eyes, as if he can feel how hard my heart is beating. The silence drags on past a normal pause into something that feels like a challenge, a languid flirtation with so much deep eye contact, it affects my breathing. "I guess I'll stop back tomorrow." His words are smooth, easy.

His gaze drives my adrenaline to rapid fire through my veins, and it makes me feel attractive in a way that Tom never made me feel. He never looked at me like that. All I want to do is think of something witty to banter back, but that's not something I've ever been good at. "You'll be glad you did because you'll love it," I finish in my best professional tone, despite my heart hammering out beats. I swallow and carry on in my happy-to-serve-you voice. "How about another tea like I made you yesterday?"

"That would be great." His gaze drifts to the floor for a moment before he lifts it back to me. "I, ah, am sorry I didn't get a chance to talk to you yesterday when you came over to the park. Was there something you needed?"

I can feel a warm blush creep on my cheeks as that whole scene was so cringe. I had tried to talk to him, but clearly, I wasn't the only woman vying for his attention. I guess I'm not the only one who thinks he's handsome. Sighing, I answer with the safest answer I can, "No, I was out on a walk for some fresh air, and thought I'd say hi."

"Well, either way, I'm sorry we got interrupted," he says. I struggle not to stare at his hands when he offers me his card. I pass his cup over, and our fingertips brush together. I can't help but think that was intentional—on both our parts. Goosebumps spiral up my arm as we hold each other's gazes. They are joined by a magnetism I've never felt. We reluctantly exchange goodbyes. When he leaves the store, my heart beats so rapidly, it's like I just worked out.

"Relax," I breathe out, letting my shoulders fall as I scold myself. *This is ridiculous to be this flustered.*

I'm obviously overly emotional about Tom still and have forgotten how to have normal interactions with men. I shake my head as I reach for a towel and wipe my sweating palms off.

Get a grip, girl.

It's just a man.

A gorgeous and muscular man, whose smile has the power to stop my heart—that's all.

And besides, I've sworn off dating—forever.

My gaze makes a circular arc around the tops of my eyes as I rethink that. All I can think of is that man's smile.

Well . . . maybe not forever.

Just until I get over Tom.

# Seven

## Stallone

I wake up abruptly with sweat pouring off my chest. The sunrays peek under my window's pale shade, revealing I've slept to a normal time.

I blink.

This is a strange anomaly, but wonderful, as I can already tell I'm more rested than normal. My joints move with an ease they haven't had in a long time, and I spring up.

It's also bad because Ryson will be waiting for me.

I scurry to get dressed while Lucky hangs back in the hall, pacing between the bathroom and the kitchen. He's not quite sure what to think about our change of routine. I'm in such a hurry, I don't have time to think about it either and pull up to Ryson's cabin with a screech of my brakes.

Ryson's smile is pressing as he hops in and patiently waits for Lucky to plop on his lap. He gives me the side-eye. "Did you go out last night?"

"No." Instant irritation kills my grin, and I take a defensive tone. "I actually slept for once."

"Ah, too bad." His expression falls to a woeful one as his hand lazily pets Lucky.

"What do you mean it's too bad I slept?" I'm immediately annoyed, as Ryson does not know what I've been through this year. He's never had a relationship that lasted longer than a slow country western song, and he surely doesn't know what it's like to have your fiancée leave you right before the wedding. A wedding we took a year to plan together, and all our friends and family were already in town, ready to help us celebrate.

"Not that it's bad you slept." His eyes roll, but his voice softens. "Just that I thought maybe you went out for once."

"What does it matter?" I clench the steering wheel and peel out of his driveway. Everyone has a timeline for me. They all think I should move on, but what they don't know is I have my own timeline: one that says, I don't care if I ever move on.

"Have you even gone on one date yet?" He stares forward, as if he knows not to dare challenge that question with direct eye contact.

Tongue-tied, fire ignites in my chest, and I stomp on the brakes, bringing my truck to a screeching halt before I managed to blurt, "What do you want from me?" I glare at him like he's my nagging mother, and not the little brother who I helped raise.

"I want you to be happy." His dark eyes that match mine level with me. "You deserve it."

I swallow, as he has no idea what I deserve, and I steer the wheel straight again and press on the accelerator, grumbling, "Mind your own business."

We are silent until we get to the jobsite, and I don't hesitate to jump out of the truck to run to the timber crane. I can't wait to be alone, and I mutter, "Ryson doesn't have a clue what will make me happy."

# EIGHT

## Arielle

"My job here is done." Christian zips his black hardcover suitcase up and slides it off the hotel bed. Brushing his hands together, he plants a pleased smile on his face. "Do you have your stuff together? They opened the interstate, and I'd like to get on the road by nine."

I'm having the hardest time crawling out of bed, and I struggle to keep my eyes open. My body decided to take up permanent residence in this spot, despite the many times I've rubbed my eyes and stretched. "Yeah, I just need to grab my stuff out of the bathroom." I roll over, letting one foot hang to the floor, testing an upright position.

Ert.

Nope.

I pull it back onto the bed and sigh. "Do we have to leave so early?"

"You don't have to go back to Boston." Christian's words are measured, as if he's rehearsed this speech. "You can stay with me if you want. It might be helpful to have an extra hand in the store since I'll be returning here in a few days."

"Oh, wait a second . . ." My brows bead together as I visualize the return to Long Island today. I sit up straight as I recall inviting that man to come back today. It was a casual comment I made to prevent him from being upset. I hadn't thought that we wouldn't even be here. That was a hairbrained thing to do. I scratch the back of my head, lazily speaking through a deep yawn. "I did something dumb. I was so eager to get the new Coffee Loft equipment yesterday, I told the customers to come back to try the coffee today."

"Why would you do that?" Christian parks a hand on his hip, never disappointing when it comes to all-things dramatic.

"I wasn't thinking clearly." I rub my eyes and yawn one more time as I stand and stare at the bathroom, all the way over on the other side of the room. It feels like a lot of effort right now.

"We can stop by on the way out of town. I can put a sign on the coffee bar explaining we're closed to prepare for a grand reopening."

My gaze directs to the tiny hotel window, the tops of the distant snow-covered mountain range peeking out from behind the downtown buildings. I feel so different in Mapleton. My chest isn't as tight as it was back home, and I can take real breaths. I'm in a little bubble that's safe from real life. When I think about going back to Long Island—even though it's not Boston—I think about reality hitting. I'm not ready to hurt again. "You know," I say slowly, already positive Christian will hate my idea. "I could stay."

His head cocks to the side, and he freezes. "Why would you do that?"

I lift one shoulder into an anticlimactic shrug. "I can keep the coffee bar open, and you won't lose customers from being closed. Maybe I could even screen the job applicants for you?"

"I would be tempted to take you up on the offer if I didn't think you were using this as an excuse to hide from reality." Christian's mouth takes a downward angle as his eyes pace my face. "I don't think that's healthy."

"Just for a week." My voice cracks, as I hate explaining to Christian, of all people, how I'm a classic avoidant personality type. I would rather just deal with my heartbreak my way—by pretending it didn't happen.

He whips his head to the side. I'm sure he's about to roll it back in a hard "no" shake, but instead, his gaze finds mine and he's unusually soft in his tone. "I'm going to worry about you if I leave you here."

"I'll be fine," I say, my voice barely above a whisper. "Just let me take this time for myself."

His lips bunch to the side, into a hard thinking position, before he heaves a heavy sigh. "Call me immediately if you hear from Tom."

I nod, my lips bending as I know he's already giving in.

"If Dad finds out, tell him I had nothing to do with this. I'll be back on Sunday to take you home." He removes his keys from his coat pocket and slides one off the ring for me, handing it over. "To the bookstore. Don't lose it."

"I won't." I reach for my boho-style bag on the nightstand, retrieve my key ring, and slide it on. I don't have many keys on the ring, but one that stands out is the key to Tom's place. My lips paste into a frown. I'm not sure why he ever gave it to me because

I wasn't allowed to use it without first letting him know I was coming. My frown doesn't abate, instead my brows lower, tipping my expression into a scowl. I had overlooked another clue to his infidelity that was right in front of my face. My cheeks heat from the pure anger that's left at all the lies he told me and for taking advantage of me. My fingers move with precision to slide that key off the ring, and I cup it in my palm and walk it over to the trash.

If I wasn't trying to keep my cool in front of Christian to install confidence that I actually am fine, I might have tried to do something more dramatic with this key. Not sure what, but slamming it over and over with a hammer might have been fun.

Christian doesn't see me toss it away because he's typing on his phone. After a moment, he says, "I let Graham know you'll be staying."

"I'm not a little girl." A chuckle twitches from inside, as I had forgotten how protective Christian can be of me. It's one result of us growing up together without a mother. I playfully shoo him away. "Leave. I'll be fine. Better than fine. I'll have the coffee shop deep cleaned and running at full speed by the time you get back."

*And maybe I'll have a new friend by then too—One who has excellent taste in flannel shirts.* My heartbeat picks up the pace as I tease the idea.

"I'll stop at the front desk to request they extend the stay in this room." He grips his suitcase handle, pulling it behind him as he stops right before the door. "I don't mean to rush, but I really do need to get to my vendor show."

"And to Portia." I smile teasingly at him, as I'm so happy he has someone to rush home to.

"And to Portia." His smile matches mine, but he doesn't pause for a beat when he adds, "You'll find your happily ever after too." His eyes spring open, and he tacks on, "Just don't let Portia know you're looking, or she'll add you to her website."

"I already told her I wasn't interested in ever going on that website." I flash my hands up in a silent wave, because if I don't end this, Christian will stay all morning "making sure I'm okay." He'll miss his vendor show. "Love you."

Flashing his palm up in a wave, he says, "I'll call you later."

"Bye."

Bowing his head, he opens the door, pulling the suitcase behind him. I wait for the door to click and turn on my heel, heading to the window. I'm not sure what I'm expecting to see. People bustle in and out of the downtown shops, carrying perfect little packages filled with the treasures they found, all wearing smiles on their faces. That part is enjoyable to see, but the best part is that none of these people know me or Tom. That's exactly the kind of place I need to be right now. I cross the room to my suitcase and pull out a pair of faded jeans and a cream sweater and head to the shower.

Today is going to be a good day.

Because I said so.

And maybe, a handsome guy will come in for coffee.

It's ten minutes to six o'clock, and I shut off the brightest overhead lights as the last two customers head out. It's been a slow day with the bookstore remaining closed. I assume most of the town residents are yet to find out about the new partnership with Coffee Loft. That makes sense to me since Christian hasn't done any advertising. I open the cash drawer to count the bills. Like clockwork, as soon as I stop thinking that *maybe* he'll come in, the door swings open, and my heart skips a beat.

"Am I too late?" My lumberjack peeps inside. He's wearing a heavy blue flannel shirt and jeans, looking as casual as can be, but the way he immediately finds my gaze and holds it sparks the butterflies in my gut.

"No, not at all." I push the cash back into the drawer and close it with my hip. "I was hoping you'd stop by."

"I told you I would." He steps forward, letting the door jingle to a close behind him. "You owe me a coffee."

"I do." Heat flushes my cheeks as everything about the way this man looks at me makes my knees jelly. "Have a seat." I gesture forward, adding in a playful tone, "Let me guess how you like your coffee."

He pulls up the closest barstool, plopping down, both eyes locked on me. "Not with tea."

"How about something sweet?"

"I like my coffee so strong my ancestors can taste it." His chuckle slips out at the exact time mine does: his baritone sound perfectly balances my sweet inflections.

"Maybe just a little sweet then." I scan all the new Coffee Loft syrups displayed behind me until I catch the perfect one, or in this case two. I've never been one to initiate any kind of flirting, but since no one knows me here, I seem to have found the confidence to be a little bold. I grab the marshmallow and the raspberry and hold them up. "If I mix these together, and add a little milk, you get something called a raspberry kiss." I hold my gaze steady on him and bite back a smile as he squirms in his seat, shifting from side to side.

He doesn't disappoint, flirting right back. "It's our first coffee together, and you're already offering a kiss." He lets his direct eye contact linger.

It's suddenly apparent the heat in this place is definitely working at full steam today. I push up my sweater sleeves to my elbows, all the while wishing I could crack a window open. "Technically, this is my *third* time serving you." I set the syrups on the counter and grab a large drink cup, the one we call the Lofty size. I don't care what size he orders, but I'm giving him a free upgrade. I tip the empty cup toward him. "This one is on me for all the trouble this week." After sidestepping to the espresso machine, I push the button for the espresso before I ask, "Caffeine good or do you need decaf?"

"The only time I've ever gotten decaf coffee to work for me is the time I threw it at my brother." He holds a straight face, but as hard as I try to bite back a laugh, a snort bleeps out. He acknowledges my snort with a simple, "That's classy."

"It really wasn't." I pump the syrups into the cup, add the milk and espresso, mixing it all together. A gleam in his eye sparkles when I set the coffee in front of him, and it encourages me.

I hate for this conversation to be over.

I spent all day looking out the window for him, and now *it's over*. He's so fun to banter with, and it's been ages since I let myself do this. I point to the coffee-mug shaped clock on the wall, now one minute past six. "I have to lock up, but if you don't have anywhere to go, you're welcome to sit with me while I clean." I hold my breath, unsure where my sudden bravery came from.

"I really should be on my way." His gaze regretfully pulls to the exit, and my heart drops. How did I get this conversation so wrong?

*He was totally flirting with me.*

Maybe he is dating that lady in the park or someone else? My gaze drops to his hands. Not a ring on any of his fingers, but I dare to ask, "Are you involved with someone?"

His lashes flicker, blinking several times. The time it takes for him to answer my question makes me wish I hadn't asked. My fingers get jittery, and I reach for the bar towel for something to fidget with. I direct my gaze down and wipe the counter before I hear his down-hearted reply, "I was, and not looking for anything."

I raise my gaze up to meet his. "Me too, and me neither." I add a shoulder shrug. "Or maybe just a friend."

His Adam's apple bobs, marking his swallow. I stand back, waiting for him to get up and leave. To my surprise, he lifts his drink and takes a sip. He swallows slowly, like he's savoring the flavors, before he sets down his cup. His lips tug up gently in the corners. "Your kiss is very sweet."

"Too sweet?" I park my hand on my hip, feeling the tension rise back up between us.

"It could be perfect." He nods more to himself as his gaze is locked on his drink. "I might need to try another one tomorrow. Just to make sure."

"I'm here all week," I speak softly, as if I'm afraid to stir the air. We'd somehow built a bridge of camaraderie without even trying.

I know I could use a friend. Especially one who is as handsome as he is. "My name's Arielle, by the way, but people call me El."

"I think we are doing this backward." He rises to his feet. "You're supposed to tell me your name before you give me your kiss."

I've never met a man who can make my knees shake from just the way he looks at me, but I place my hands on the counter to steady myself. "You can give me the kiss back if you don't want it," I tease, batting my lashes as I gaze up at him.

"Nah, I never said that." He snickers, his gaze drifting from his drink to me. "My name is Stallone."

"Stallone." My smile is flirty, languid. The heat from our direct contact melts my insides. That is such an unusual name, but it suits him well. "Did your parents love *Rocky* movies?"

"My dad was a fan." He shifts his weight from one leg to another, as if he is unsure if he's coming or going. "I'd better let you lock up."

Disappointment trickles into my heart, and I lower my gaze to the bar towel again, saying, "Thanks for stopping in."

"Night." His tone is laced with confusion, and he turns and lumbers out the door. I stare after him.

How did I get that so wrong?

I thought he was coming to see me, but maybe he really did just want coffee.

# Nine

## Stallone

A battle rages between my head and my heart. My head scolds me, telling me not to go back there. I definitely don't need to get caught up in some weird flirtation.

My heart is quieter, yet somehow stronger, saying, "She's one you won't want to pass up."

I get no sleep.

I'm up even earlier than usual. I fumble through work, all because I have only one thing on my mind.

*Arielle and her sweet kiss.*

Okay, that's two things, and it's all I think about. One doesn't offer a drink named kiss to another if it doesn't have some sort of innuendo, right? There are rules about that kind of thing.

After work, I lose control over my legs and drive right to the coffee shop. Butterflies spark alive in my gut as soon as I see El is working—and better yet—it's closing time.

We are alone.

I march up to the bar and drop my palms on the counter. "I'll have one of your sweet kisses."

"You're in luck." She bats those flirty and superfluous lashes at me, not missing a beat. "I've been saving an extra sweet one for you all day."

That certainly makes my mouth water.

It's been ages since I've allowed myself to banter with a woman. The innocent smile she gives me when she moves in front of the espresso machine makes my heart putter in full throttle. It's like I've been sleeping too long. I'm finally feeling what it's like to be awake.

"How was your day?" she yells over the milk frother, giving me her sweetest smile. My knees weaken, and I match her smile.

"It was good." I nod, and then nod again. It's silly to be here flirting like a teenager, but I can't resist. "Except I was thinking about your kisses all day."

"Good. I like them to be memorable." Her demure brows rise, and she steps to the side, adding the rest of the ingredients to the cup. She pops the lid on and sets the cup in front of me. "Try this one. It's the leprechaun kiss."

"Leprechaun?" I lift the cup and snicker right over the top of it. The drink heat seeps through the thin cardboard, warming my hands, and I hold it steady and enjoy the thawing.

"They're minty." She tips her chin up, exposing her long neck momentarily before her hand curls around it in a resting position. "Let me know what you think, but I'm guessing you'll like this one even better."

Her lips pinch in anticipation as I lift the cup to my lips and sip. It's toasty, and rich with chocolate coffee notes, and it pulls me even more awake. I lower my cup and say with a straight face, "Definitely lucky."

The sweetest chuckle rolls out of her lips. Her gaze levels with mine, and my heart hammers against my chest wall as I feel this human connection I haven't felt in forever. I pull the stool out and plop down and make a dramatic eye sweep to the clock behind us. "Are you closing?"

She slowly nods, and her voice drops to a low hum. "I need to."

I could be wrong, but I've seen this look before. It's the way she looked yesterday when she asked me to stay, and it makes me weak in the knees. "I could stay if you want company while you clean."

Her perfect white teeth slide over her bottom lip, and she bites down, holding that pose for a moment. "I actually have everything cleaned already."

"Oh." I sit up straight and rotate on the stool so my legs angle toward the door. "Ah, that's fine. I got stuff to—"

She reaches over the counter and places her hand on mine. Fireworks explode right in my palm—no exaggeration. I struggle to feel my skin as she says, "I got all my cleaning done early, because I was hoping you'd want to hang out."

The heat from her hand zips all the way up my arm and doesn't stop until it makes a nice ring around my heart. "Okay," is all I can manage.

"I thought we could have coffee together." She grabs a coffee that was sitting on the back counter, waiting for her. "I made one for myself." She gestures toward the table up front next to the window. "Is that okay?"

"Sure." I rise to my feet, and we drift together as we cross the room. Now I'm wishing I'd put on my good aftershave, the one I haven't worn in a year. Too late for that. I take a deep breath as a light row of perspiration layers on my lower back.

She gingerly slides into her seat, and I plop down across from her, and when our gazes slide together, everything else fades away. My nerves instantly melt because it's the most natural feeling in the world to sit across from her. She leans over her coffee cup and blows into the drink hole before asking, "How was work?"

I blink, hardly even remembering work. It's impossible to think about anything but her gorgeous pale-blue eyes when I'm sitting this close to her. "It was work. How about you?"

"It was wonderful." She runs her hand over her hair, tucking one of her wild strands back behind her ear with a dainty twist of her wrist. It's mesmerizing to watch the way she moves with such feminine grace. "I love being here, and I'll be sad when I have to leave."

Wait. What? She's leaving?

My hand finds my chin, and I rub my beard while I rewind my memories. "I remember you said you were new to town but guess I didn't realize you weren't staying."

She slouches back in her seat, appearing to get more comfortable. "I'm from Boston but was looking to stay in Long Island with my brother for a while when he decided to open this store. My brother is my boss, and well, he's not actually my boss, because I don't officially work for Coffee Loft. It's just easier to call him that." Her words trail off into an airy laugh.

"Interesting." I can feel my brows bunch together, all while a sting digs into my chest, and I repeat, "I didn't realize you're leaving."

She nods, her head bouncing several times into the silence. "Yeah, Sunday will be my last day."

I clear my throat, wishing it was that easy to clear the sting in my chest. "Then I guess we should make use of the time we have together getting to know each other."

"Right." Her tone is flirty and even, not disappointing at all.

I bite my lip, oddly feeling a tinge of relief. I was never looking for anything more than a little flirting. It's actually quite perfect. We can hang out, but nobody gets attached. "So…" I return my cup to the table and lean forward. "Who else is enjoying your kisses?"

"Excuse me?" Her head springs back before she blinks and sputters out a laugh. "You mean the coffee, right?"

I shrug playfully, leaning forward. "Maybe."

"Well, for the coffee-flavored kisses, I've actually saved that recipe for you, and for the uh, other kind of kisses"—her gaze dips to the floor before she rushes out— "I just had a breakup a few days ago, so nobody at the moment, which is how I like it."

I stay quiet but maintain a full smile teasing my lips. She's been flirting with me, so I give it right back.

"What about you?" she quips back, her posture extra tall, and her gaze is pointed. "I know you're single, but it sounds like you had a recent breakup too."

"Ah." My breath is heavy as it crawls up my throat and forms the words. "Not real recent." Her gaze dances around my face, softening as the silence drags on, but she doesn't ask for more clarity. I suppose I could drop it, or change the subject, but as her expression continues to warm, she starts to feel like a friend—someone I could confide in. Maybe it's a mistake, but she'll be gone soon. I haven't spoken about this to anyone other than Ryson. For a reason I will never understand, I test the words I've never even dared to speak. "I was engaged."

Her lips form an O, but no sound leaks out.

"She left me suddenly a few days before our wedding." My words are steady and surprisingly easy to express. My chest literally releases the tension that's been there for months. "We never even fought. I had no idea, but I guess she had been talking to an ex-boyfriend for a while, and she wanted to be with him."

"I'm so sorry to hear that." El's eyes swell rounder and her hand slides across the table, not stopping until it's on top of mine. "I actually know exactly how you feel. My last boyfriend was cheating on me too."

"You definitely didn't deserve that." My instinct is to go off about how it's okay she left, because she showed me how evil women are, and I dodged a bullet, but El's hand is still on mine. A spiral of heat flows up my arms, melting those thoughts into nothing but air that makes it easy for me to breathe.

I don't know how, but I allow my lips to slide over my teeth into a small smile. "You're going to be okay." A thick tension in the air, and neither one of us bends a lip upward, but our gaze is held together as we both seem to study each other from across the table.

*Thud. Thud. Thud.*

A rapping on the window pulls our gaze to it, and El immediately gasps. "Look, a dog!"

Not just any dog.

My dog.

Apparently, he got bored sitting in the box of my truck. The evidence is the fact he's covered from head to tail in clinging snow.

His paws completely caked in ice clumps frozen to his fur, and paw prints marking his path from my truck to a huge snow pile at the corner—which he apparently rolled in—back to the window. Now he stares with gleeful mischief in his eyes, as if he's proud of how messy he is. His huge eyes peer directly through the window, like he can't take his eyes off El.

*I know the feeling.*

*She's that showstopping.*

Everything about the way her hair frames her perfect face makes it impossible not *to stare.* She's just so unbelievably stunning. My heart rams against my chest being near her. "Yeah." My smile grows even wider. "That's my dog. His name's Lucky. I think he's being impatient and was trying to find me. I had him in my truck. I guess he just hopped out." Shrugging, I add, "He's mesmerized by you."

Her airy laugh leaks out of her lips. "I don't know why."

My chest pinches tighter, warning me not to say the words that are about to roll out of my mouth. Not because they are mean, but quite the opposite. I swallow and say, "I know why."

There's still a hint of laughter in her voice when her gaze pulls playfully to mine. "Why's that?"

"He's never seen a woman as beautiful as you." Her mascara-clad lashes flutter but our eye lock holds steady, and I can count the beats of my heart slamming against my chest. "I clearly speak dog."

She throws her head back as her dense laugh fills the air. It's a beautiful sound that sparks a chuckle to form from deep in my chest, and I join her in her laughter. It's been a long time since I laughed like this. It's so effortless to sit here with her. Her gaze slides back to the window, where Lucky still lingers. "If you speak dog, can you tell him it's rude to stare? It's making me a little nervous."

"I can't tell him that." I slide to the edge of my seat, steeling my jaw forward. "Because I know how he feels. He's clearly stunned by your beauty. It's your fault."

A rose tint fires on her cheeks, and she shakes her head, matching my gaze. "You're too much."

"I'm too much?" My voice ticks up, adding playful inflections as I jerk my thumb back to Lucky, whose nose is still pressed against the glass. "I'm not the one drooling all over the window trying to get to you." Her giggles fill my confidence, and I playfully tap the glass and say, "Buzz off, Lucky, I saw her first."

Her laughter upticks even more, her shoulders shaking in synchronization. I sit back in my chair and marvel that I could seriously sit here and listen to her for days. When the last of her cackles die into a playful smile, it feeds my ego even more. "Now what did he say?" She raises her brows at me, challenging me.

"He's not happy. He wants to fight me for you." Before I second-guess myself, I take a huge risk and say, "I told him there is no use in fighting, because you've already decided that you're going out with me next."

"Oh, I have, have I?" Her head takes an angled position, but her smile doesn't deflate. "Where are we going?"

"It's a surprise. Tomorrow." I lower my voice, ridding it of all teasing. "After work. I'll pick you up here."

Her lips part, and her tongue slides out and runs along her bottom lip before she says in a soft voice, "You said you weren't looking to get involved with anyone."

"I'm not," I rasp, knowing this decision is about to change everything, but with the way she's looking at me—all the light firing in her eyes—I don't care. "This is us going out to have fun together without the pressure of dating."

I glance back at the window, but Lucky has walked away and is loitering by my truck, sniffing the tires.

"So, just going out to have fun?" Her heated gaze pulls mine back to her.

I swallow and reply, "Yes."

"Okay." Her bottom lip pushes out, making it incredibly hard not to notice how plush and kissable it is. "I get off work at six. You can meet me here."

"I'll be here." I tip up my cup and finish the last of my coffee, and as I'm trying not to wear out my welcome, I slide off my chair.

"Are you leaving?" Her gaze follows me as I walk to the trash to throw away my empty cup.

"It's time. I don't want my dog to get run over, and he's clearly asking for some trouble since he wants to hang out in the road." I walk to the door and pause to hit her with a direct gaze one more time, taking a moment to linger. Then I put my hand on the door handle and push it ajar. "See you tomorrow, El."

"Bye," she calls after me, and I leave the shop, all the while my heart is slamming against my chest.

What did I just do?

I didn't want to go out with anyone.

She just has this power over me. As soon as I sat next to her, I couldn't help it. I shake my head as I stride to my truck, my eyes peeled for Lucky, who's taken it upon himself to dig in the snow right by my front tire. "Get in, boy." I open the driver's door and wait for him to scurry into the passenger seat. Then I get in and say to him, "I have a date to get ready for."

# TEN

## Arielle

The coffee shop is agonizingly slow. I prop both elbows on the counter, rest my chin in my palms and sleepily stare out the window, wishing customers would come in. I honestly think everyone assumes since Graham isn't here, the place is closed. With nothing else to do, I think about my non-date tonight and now my gut wads into a ball of nerves.

It's been so long since I hung out with a new guy, especially one this handsome.

What if I say something dumb?

Really, it's not even a "what-if" for me, but more like how many times something embarrassing will slip out. I don't want to get all worked up about it though, so it ruins my chances of having fun. I let out a sharp sigh, refusing to let my nerves get the best of me, and I open my phone, ready to scroll.

The karaoke app finds my attention, which makes me smirk. I haven't needed the distraction since I met Stallone. It's crazy how things can change in just a few days. Now it just looks like something I could do to pass some time. With my free hand I drum my nails on the counter. I'm not huge into karaoke but if they are playing the right song, it might be fun.

I might as well check it out.

I tap on the screen to see what my first challenge is, and my song appears: "Fishing in the Dark."

I let out a haughty laugh. I know that song and could sing it in my sleep. Challenge accepted. Rolling my shoulders back, I do a warm up stretch as I wait for the timer to count down. The screen changes, and I'm thrown into a challenge room, and I start singing.

I'm not going to say I could be rockstar material, but I've definitely found my rhythm, and I take down the first challenger—no problem. I really hope he doesn't cry because he honestly never had a chance.

I advance to another level, and another after that. I just keep going, and my competitive side comes out without apologies. I'm taking out everyone.

All afternoon I keep advancing and leveling up. I sing so many songs, and I dominate. I don't know why I have never tried karaoke before, but this is really a hobby I could enjoy more often. One thing I figure out is I especially excel at anything Disco.

*It's my genre.*

I'm two verses into ABBA's "Dancing Queen" when Christian calls me. I literally growl at his name on my phone as it forces me to forfeit my round. I hate doing that, but I'm so far ahead of everyone else. Even if I forfeit this round, I can win the overall tournament. "I'm fine," I assert as soon as I answer the phone.

"Whoa, what's wrong with you?" His big-brother tone passes through my phone. "I wanted to make sure you had enough cash in the till, since you haven't been doing any bank runs."

"I'm fine." I quickly pop the drawer open to confirm there's plenty of change and cash, especially since no one has come in today. After a second eye sweep, I press the drawer closed. "I know how to go to the bank if I run out." I sneak a peek at the time. The app sends me an invite when it's time for my next challenge, and it could be anywhere from one minute to a half hour, depending on how everyone else sings.

*I can't miss my invitation.*

"I don't know." He sounds panicked. "I really shouldn't have left you there. I think it's best if we close the store until we get ready to do the grand opening—"

"It's fine," I mutter again as I wonder how many times I can repeat the same exact sentence in one conversation. "I'm getting to know your customers." *Well, only one of your customers, and he's quite nice.* My lips curl into an amused smile at the mere thought of Stallone.

"I know how you are when you are going through a breakup. You get unpredictable mood swings. You keep saying you're fine, but"—he stalls for a beat— "but are you, really?"

"Yes." I soften my tone, hoping he finally believes me. "And if it makes you feel better, I promise if I'm not fine, I will let you know."

"Do you really promise?"

"I do." I pace back and forth behind the counter, my fingers itching to end the call. "Trust me, it's so good for me to be here alone, because nothing here reminds me of Tom. I haven't even once thought of him. I'm pretty much over him."

A heavy sigh passes through the phone and relief fills his voice. "That's good to hear."

"It is."

"Okay, you've convinced me for now, but don't hesitate to call if you need anything."

"Of course." The edges of my lips bend into a larger smile. "Love you, bye."

"Bye, El."

I end the call and swipe my screen to see I'm still in the hold queue. "Phew," I breathe out. "I didn't miss my round." Lifting my gaze to scan the coffee shop, I'm further relieved to see there are no customers inside and no one even remotely close to the door. This place is beyond dead. I don't know what I'd do all day without this app.

Since nobody comes to the coffee shop, I keep accepting karaoke challenges. After winning my twenty-fifth challenge in a row, it's time to lock up. It's perfect timing too, because I need to refresh my makeup before Stallone arrives. Some of these choruses make me work up such a sweat; my eye makeup has been long gone.

I set my phone down and reach under the counter for my purse and pull out my sparkly pink makeup pouch. I carry little makeup with me. Just the essentials, so it's easy to find my finishing powder right on top and my favorite lipstick. I blot all the oily spots on my face with fresh powder and apply my lipstick when a message pops on my phone.

CONGRATULATIONS ON BEATING 25 CHAL-LENGES! YOU ARE CURRENTLY IN SECOND PLACE. IF YOU WIN THE LIGHTNING ROUND, YOU WILL BE THE ULTIMATE CHAMPION AND WIN $500.

DO YOU ACCEPT THIS LIGHTNING ROUND CHAL-
LENGE? YES OR NO.

My eyes round with excitement. *Five hundred dollars!* Up until
now, I've only been accumulating those fake diamonds. I somehow passed the threshold into the rounds where I can win actual
money. I'm not one to get excited about the possibility of prize
money, but since I made no tips today, and I haven't been to my
actual job in days, that money could certainly be useful. My rent
isn't going to pay for itself. I've always been a competitive person. I
love winning, but the thought of winning money now when I need
it the most is appealing. My gaze hangs on the word *champion*—so
enticing.

I can see my name next to that word, and the mere thought of it
makes saliva pool in the center of my mouth.

*I could be a karaoke champion.*

I like the sound of that.

And I'd have an extra five hundred dollars, which means I have
even more time before I need to return to work.

My gaze scans the coffee shop.

There's no one here.

I can't take too long because I have a date.

How long is the lightning round?

Lightning is fast.

That's why they call it lightning.

And then I'd be the *champion.*

Without another look around the room, I accept the lightning
round challenge. I hold my breath as I wait for my first song to pop
up, but instead, the front door swings open.

And I drop my phone to the counter like a hot potato.

Stallone passes through the door and it's like he walks in slow motion. His hair's slicked back like a movie star, and he's wearing dark trousers and a black button-up shirt. The sleeves are rolled up, showing off the corded muscles of his forearms, and he's carrying a bouquet of pink roses. Seeing this gorgeous hunk of a man dressed up and walking toward me with flowers makes my cheeks heat as my lips slide into a full smile. It's been years since I've gotten flowers. Tom always said they were a waste of money.

"I hope you like roses," he greets me with his arms outstretched, and I lean in with one arm to give him a hug. The evergreen scent of his cologne hits me, and it infuses my smile with an even bigger curve. *He smells amazing.* Like the manliest man who could pluck an entire tree from the ground—roots and all—if I asked him to.

"I love them." I lean out of our side hug, accepting his flowers at the same time. "That's so thoughtful of you. Thank you."

"You're welcome." He passes his hand through his dark, rich hair. "I didn't know what kind of flowers you liked, but I wasn't going to let that be an excuse. I wanted to bring you something to make you feel special."

My gaze lingers on his eyes. They are dark and rich like his hair, but even better than that, they are *honest*. Of all the characteristics a person could have, that's the one thing I need the most right now. I press my nose to the center of the bouquet while I walk behind the coffee bar. "Let me put these in water before we leave."

I scan the coffee bar.

I clearly don't have a vase.

The cups are cardboard, and more than likely won't be sturdy enough.

*Coffeepot it is!*

Smirking, I yank out the empty coffeepot from the base, place it in the deep sink, and turn on the faucet.

"It works." His agreeable smile doesn't leave his face, and my cheeks warm from the magnetism I feel when he's around. "I hope it's okay, but I assumed you'd be hungry, so I reserved a table at The Grove restaurant. It's the nicest place in town."

"That sounds amazing." Shutting off the faucet with one hand, I grab the pot with my other hand and shimmy it over to the back counter, where I remove the plastic off the flowers and arrange them into the pot. They are gorgeous, huge roses that barely fit, but I squeeze them in and take another giant whiff. "They really are lovely." I stop myself from gushing, because it's not like he's my boyfriend or anything.

It just feels nice to be spoiled a little, and I stride toward the coat hook on the back wall, grab my heavy blue coat, and tug on the beanie I wear every day. Then I cross the room again, grab my purse off the counter, and shoulder it. I spot my phone setting on the counter where I had tossed it, and I slide that into my pocket. "I have everything I need."

He's so handsome, dressed all in black, and my gut quibbles as I walk forward and synchronize my steps with his as we stride to the door. "The restaurant is just down the block, so we can walk if you're comfortable," he says.

"That works for me." I tug at my coat and pull the top two buttons through the holes to close it. "I'm getting used to this little town. It seems like everything is mostly within walking distance."

"Downtown has everything you need." He holds the door open, and we pass through it, and then pause on the other side so I can lock it. I stuff my keys back into my purse and look up at him. His hand is outstretched to me. It's a sweet gesture that feels natural, and I take his hand in mine. I bite my bottom lip to keep my jaw from dropping when I struggle to intertwine our fingers together. His hands are so big, it's like I'm holding a bear's paw, but I love it. It's so strong and steady, I'm overcome with the feeling of security. Nothing could ever harm me if I'm near these hands.

We cross the street, walk past a small school and bakery, and arrive at the restaurant. He opens the door for me again, and we meet the host, dressed in a formal white shirt and black pants. The host bops his head as if in a nod of recognition at Stallone as he grabs two menus and immediately says, "Right this way."

As we stroll through the dining room, people slide their gazes to look at us. Several people actually stop chewing as we pass. My cheeks heat, and I remove the beanie from my head, thinking that's the problem.

*The stares continue.*

The host leads us all the way to the corner booth in the back of the dining room. Gesturing forward, he says to me, "Ladies first."

I slide into my seat, take the menu he hands me, and I listen as he recites the specials: lobster for seventy-nine dollars and filet mignon, also for seventy-nine dollars. After he leaves, I lean over the menu and snicker. "Boy, that doesn't sound like a special for seventy-nine dollars." My gaze falls to the menu, and there isn't a thing on here for less than twenty-five bucks.

*This place is expensive.*

My gaze slopes back to Stallone reading the menu, unbothered by the prices. I don't have it in me to order anything that costs a whole day's worth of wages. Scanning the menu again, I land on the appetizers and find clam chowder soup for fifteen bucks.

*Clam chowder it is.*

And just in time. The waiter arrives to take our order. Stallone orders a steak and baked potato, and he watches me closely as I order my soup. I hand my menu back to the waiter and look around the place again.

It's dark in this little corner, with only soft candlelight on our table. I still can't shake the feeling that people are staring at us. I look around, seeing people all dressed in their finest, and decide maybe it's the fact I'm underdressed. I can't do anything about it now. I clear my throat and lock my gaze back with his. "How was work today?"

"It was good. The roads finally cleared up enough. They've been a mixture of mud or ice, and that kept us at a standstill for weeks." He takes his water glass and sips out of it before asking, "How was your day?"

"Really slow." I nod as if I'm agreeing with myself. "I don't know if people think the place is closed since Graham closed the bookstore, or if it's always this slow, but I think I only served five people all day."

"Only five people?" His eyes round with interest. "What did you do all day?"

All the song lyrics I belted out scroll through my mind like they are playing on the phone screen, and I almost giggle. "Ah, just looked at my phone all day." I tightly pinch my lips together, holding back a laugh. "Good thing for technology, right?"

"Right." He's so dialed into me, not taking his eyes off me. It feels like we've known each other for much longer than a few days. It doesn't feel like a first date. He clears his throat, and starts slowly,

"I know this is forward of me, but I'm curious about something. Can I ask you a question?"

"Sure." My interest is piqued, and I wait.

"I hope you don't take this the wrong way, but from the moment I saw you, I honestly thought you are the most stunning woman I've ever seen. But for the life of me, I can't really tell how old you are. Can I ask your age?"

"Oh." My brows pin together. I thought he had something serious to ask me. My age is nothing. "I just turned twenty-one."

He's just about to take another sip of water, but spits it back into his glass. "Twenty-one?"

"Yeah." My gaze shifts side to side, and my nerves tick up as I clearly missed the punch line. "What's wrong with that? How old did you think I was?"

"I didn't know." He wags his head back and forth and sets his glass out of reach. "I assumed you were older than that, since you worked day shifts at a coffee shop. Maybe twenty-seven or thirty."

"Nope. Not thirty." A chuckle sputters out. That is the funniest thing. "Well, how old are you?"

"Aw, not thirty." He holds my gaze for a moment, and then it dawns on me what he's concerned about.

"You're older than thirty?"

He nods but adds no words.

"How much older than thirty?" My gaze washes over his facial features. It's so hard to tell because of his thick beard. He doesn't have any wrinkles. All his hair is dark, void of any gray. He's seriously so dreamy, he could be a movie star. There's no way he'd be older than thirty-one or thirty-two.

"I'm thirty-five." His tone is even as he stares deeply into my eyes.

"Wow." My head springs back as his words echo. "You don't look that old at all."

He runs his hands over his beard, proudly smoothing his whiskers. "Yeah, I think the beard makes it hard to tell."

"I agree." I marvel at how, again, I had no idea he was *fourteen* years older than me.

One of his brows takes a northerly hike. "Does it bother you I'm that old?"

"No—" I'm interrupted by my phone vibrating in my pocket. Nobody calls me, except for Christian, and I already talked to him today. "Excuse me." I retrieve my phone out and glance at the screen: **Lightning Round Loading... You are a finalist. Your round begins in one minute.**

*Oh no!*

I had forgotten about my karaoke battle! I was in the holding room the whole time.

"Is everything okay?" Stallone asks.

"Yeah." I hover my thumb over the screen, ready to put it into sleep mode, but then another message flashes on the app.

**Your randomly selected genre is: Disco.**

My eyebrows shoot to the ceiling.

*That's my genre!*

**Another message: You're randomly selected song is: "YMCA." Your round begins in 30 seconds.**

*I know that song!*

Like not only do I know that song, my friends and I dressed up as The Village People for a talent show one year, and we performed that song. I know everything there is to know about that song.

*I could win five hundred dollars and be the ultimate karaoke champion.*

"Are you sure everything is okay?" Stallone's voice is so kind, and the look of concern he has for me melts my heart. "You look a little flushed."

"Yeah," I breathe out a heavy breath. "Now that you say it, if you don't mind, I'm feeling a little warm." I look behind me and see a back exit. It doesn't look like anyone's back there. It's more of a loading dock or something. I hate to be rude to step out for a minute, but really, I could seriously use that money. If I won that money, that means I can actually stay in Mapleton even longer, which could help me get to know Stallone even more. I jerk my thumb toward the exit. "If you don't mind, I'm going to step out for some air."

"Are you sure?" His gaze shifts to the back door, and I'm already sliding out of my booth. "I can come with you."

"Nah, I just need five minutes, and I'll be fine." Well, actually four minutes and one second to be exact, but he doesn't need to know I need to belt out a disco song. I beeline to the back and slide through the door right when my round starts. I toss a look over my shoulder as the door latches shut, and I belt out the healthiest "Youngman" anyone has ever heard.

This is my jam!

Not only do I know all the words, but I got the moves.

I hold the phone to my mouth, the lyrics flowing out in perfect timing. With my free arm, I flay out all the motions. I feel it in my soul that I'm going to win this round. It's confirmed when the meter fills all the way with green and confetti falls.

*I won the lightning round!*

*I am the champion.*

I ninja kick the air, as this victory is all mine.

*Wait.*

*What?*

A message pops up.

You've won round one of three. Your next round starts in fifteen minutes.

What? How come I have to sing again? This must be a scam.

I just won, but clearly it was an elimination round, which means I'm still in the running for the money. Money I could seriously use.

My gaze cuts back to the door. I better get inside because I would hate for Stallone to get the wrong idea and think I'm rude. Plus, I only have fifteen minutes before I have to sing again. I'm so close to winning this thing, there is no way I'm quitting now.

I can almost taste this victory.

# Eleven

## Stallone

The waiter brings our food, but El hasn't returned to her seat. Clearing my throat, I check behind me at the back door again. She had looked like she was about to be ill. I hated to let her run off alone, but she also looked embarrassed.

Should I check on her?

She was fine when I picked her up. I hope it's not something I said.

Oh wait.

She got sick right after I told her my age.

That has to be it.

She doesn't want to be here with an old man.

I grossed her out.

My gaze slides to the table, and a knot bulges in my throat. I had no idea she was *that* young. It's so hard to tell these days how old women are. Maybe I should apologize and take her home?

She flies around the corner, bringing a gush of cold air in with her, plopping back down into the booth with an enormous smile on her face. "Good, the food's here."

Her porcelain cheeks are tinted with rose, which is normal for just coming inside from the winter air. She looks fine now. Relief floods back over me, and I take my napkin and set it on my lap. "Yeah, you're just in time. Are you feeling better?"

"Much better." She picks up her soup spoon and scoops giant spoonfuls into her mouth in a very rushed manner.

"Isn't it hot too eat that fast?" I lower one eye and narrow my focus. Her eating pattern is a tad strange. I would have thought she'd eat in a more ladylike fashion, but I guess I'm no one to judge.

"I'm so hungry." She pauses and smiles at me before she hovers her face directly over her bowl and shovels in full spoons of soup.

Taking my fork and knife in my hand, I remember my manners as I carefully cut my steak. "Do you want a straw? It might be even faster." I risk a joke because I've never seen anyone eat like that.

She giggles, but still doesn't slow. Now, she's at the bottom of her bowl, and she drags her spoon along the bottom, scraping every last drop. "It was delicious." She sits back in her seat; a victorious expression washes over her face while she dabs the corners of her mouth with her napkin. "Best soup ever. Thanks for bringing me here."

I barely have my meat cut, and her gaze cuts to the front exit like she's waiting to leave. I motion to my full plate. "Are you in a hurry, or do you mind if I eat?"

"Oh." Her brows spring up. "Go right ahead and finish, but if you don't mind, I'm going to use the restroom."

Before I protest, she takes off through the dining room toward the front foyer where the restrooms are, and I stare after her.

Maybe she really is sick but is too embarrassed to say?

Or is she too humiliated to sit next to me because I'm so old?

My gaze drops to my steak again. It looked so juicy and mouth-watering when the waiter brought it over. It's served on an iron skillet and was literally sizzling, wafting off Cajun spices. It took every ounce of strength I had to wait until El was back before I cut into it. Now my stomach is in a knot, my appetite is gone.

What did I do wrong?

It has to be my age.

And honestly, who am I kidding to even drag this out? If I were her, there is no way I'd want to date me. I just need to get real about it.

The waiter comes up and leans over a tad. "Is everything all right with your steak, sir? I noticed you cut it but haven't taken a bite."

"It's fine." I stare at the chunks all neatly sliced, and I know what I need to do. I take my credit card out of my wallet and hand it to him. "I'm ready to settle up, and may I have a to-go box? My *date*—I mean, my dinner companion has gotten ill."

"Certainly." He disappears for a minute before returning with my card and a box. I transfer my meal and secure it in the box, and she's still not back.

I get she may want privacy, but what kind of man am I if I leave her here by herself if she is seriously ill? Maybe I should ask a waitress to check on her? I get up from the table, box in hand, and make my way back through the dining room. I can feel everyone's eyes on me. Living in a small town is hard, because people know your business. I'm sure they are all wondering who the female is.

Right as I get to the front foyer, El stumbles out of the ladies' room, a full layer of sweat on her forehead.

Poor thing.

She must be running a fever.

She really is ill.

Her eyes swell huge when she sees me, and she stutters, "W-What are you doing here?"

"I was going to send a waitress in to check on you." I gesture forward. "I can tell you're not feeling well. I'm sorry you're ill, but I'm happy to take you home so you can rest."

The back of her hand finds her shimmering forehead, and she attempts to wipe the sweat off her brow. "Ah, I didn't mean to mess up our date," she rushes out, her complexion flushing even more.

"You're not messing it up at all." I walk forward until I'm next to her and place a hand on her lower back to guide her toward the exit. "You can't help that you got ill. I'll take you back to the lodge."

"I'm really feeling much better," she rushes out. "Besides, I have at least an hour before—" her voice drops off.

"Before . . . you have a curfew?" I tease.

"No, just ignore that." She lets out a high-pitched laugh that does nothing to conceal her nerves. Then it makes sense.

Maybe she's not sick, but she's nervous?

She didn't get this way until we got to this restaurant. I *had* to bring her to the nicest place in town as I was trying to impress her. She has to notice everyone staring at us. All this just made her nervous.

"Really, I'm fine." She places a hand on my forearm and a sonic boom explodes. "I'm sorry I ruined our dinner, but I'm not ready to go home yet. I'd love a chance to talk some more."

"If you're sure." I linger on the word sure, giving her a chance to back out again, but she dials her gaze into mine. I feel an intense pull that says there's no way you are taking her home now, so I suggest something more casual than this, and somewhere we can be alone and away from all the stares. "How about we go on a drive through Evergreen Park?"

"That sounds lovely." She steps toward the exit, her voice pepping up.

I follow right on her heels. Now, let's try not to mess up the next half of the date.

# TWELVE

## Arielle

My back is a bay of sweat, and it's refreshing to step out in fresh air. I just completed the most epic bathroom performance of "Love Shack" that ever went down. There was even a granny in the last stall. Bless her heart, she didn't ask questions when she came out. She gave me a peace sign and washed her hands while I sang. Of course, I advanced to the next round. Now I have about an hour before the final, final showdown.

As ecstatic as I am that I won my battle round, it broke my heart to see Stallone standing outside the bathroom, looking so downhearted. I feel terrible for ditching him, but I honestly hadn't thought going to the bathroom would look so suspicious. He clearly is taking it personally, and I need to make it up to him. I link my hand into his arm and gaze up at him. "Tell me about your hobbies. What do you like to do for fun?"

"I'm basically your classic outdoorsman. I love to hunt, fish, hike, kayak, camp, anything of that sort. That's why I always found

Mapleton to be the perfect place for me to live. I have a cabin up in the mountains, and I can literally do it all in my backyard."

"That sounds amazing. I love hiking and fishing too, but I've never been kayaking before." I bat my lashes. "You might have to teach me."

"Well, kayaking is something I definitely prefer to do when it's a little nicer outside, and I'm guessing you'll be gone by spring . . ." His voice trails off, but his smile lingers on me.

I sigh, adding another inhale afterwards, bringing in enough cool air to relax me even more. "I don't know where I'll be this spring," I answer truthfully. We cross the street where he leads me to his truck parked right outside the coffee shop. It's so easy to get around here, and there's virtually no traffic since everything is within walking distance. It's the opposite of Boston. The air is so fresh and clean here, it's impossible not to take deep breaths. "I can't get over how cute this town is."

"Like I said before, it's the perfect town for me." He opens my door, and I hop in while he walks to the other side and gets in. Once inside, he starts the truck and backs up before picking up our conversation. "So, the same question to you." He nudges my elbow with his. The gentle sign of affection just gets me. I've always been a sucker for the little touches. "What are your hobbies?"

"I like to go out." I stare out the window, watching the cobblestone roads turn to gravel as he winds his way around the outskirts of town and heads to the mountains. I don't tell him that in the last year I've only been out with Tom, and I've done a terrible job of keeping friendships.

"Is that all?"

"Ah, family is a big deal to me. My brother, Christian, and I are close, and . . . I love music."

"What kind of music do you listen to?"

My gaze is still glued to the scenic drive. Since arriving in Mapleton, I've only seen the coffee shop and the lodge. It's breathtaking to see the mountains get closer and closer over the horizon. "Anything really, but I'm a sucker for the oldies, like from the sixties or seventies."

"For a second there, I thought you'd say oldies from the nineties, and I was going to stop you because that's my era. I grew up with that stuff."

I chuckle, sneaking a look at him. "Yeah, I think the nineties is old too, considering I was born in 2003, but I never really got into that decade. There's so much aggression."

"Not all of it." His lips pull to the side as if in a thinking stance. "The nineties also had great ballads. I mean, Celine Dion and Whitney Houston, Boyz II Men, all of that was the nineties."

"Yeah, I see what you're saying." I stuff my hands in my coat pockets as a cold shudder moves through me.

"Are you cold?" He immediately turns the knobs on the heater, cranking it up.

"Thank you." I look up at him, feeling our magnetism growing even stronger. "This is nice."

"Are you still feeling okay?"

"I feel great."

He slows to take a sharp bend in the road, and a vibration tickles my fingertips. My memory is instantly jogged. I was enjoying my date so much I forgot about the final battle round! I whip my phone out of my pocket, and my chest is filled with dread.

*I need to sing now!*

*Five hundred dollars that I could use is on the line. It won't make me rich, but it will help with all the lost wages.*

Christian always teases me about how competitive I am. I never really realized it until now. He's so right. I have this burning in my core that says I can't quit now. If I forfeit then my entire day's work will be lost, and I'm so close to being the ultimate champion. My hand finds the door handle, and I shoot a strained expression to Stallone. "Ah, maybe I need some air. Do you mind pulling over for a second?"

"Here?" One of his brows rises above the other as he steers the truck around the bend. "I can't pull over here, because it's too dangerous. Can you roll down the window until I can get to a better spot?"

My phone vibrates again, indicating my genre was named, and I drop my gaze to my lap.

**Genre: Nineties**

"Stupid nineties," I mutter, now afraid the app was listening to my earlier conversation. It had to be spying. *There's no way that wasn't a coincidence.*

"What did you say?" Now around the bend, Stallone slows the truck and pulls over to the soft dirt shoulder.

"Nothing," I assert louder, my fingers itching to open the door. If my calculations are correct, I only have about a minute before my song starts. A row of thick evergreen trees lines the ditch, and they'll be perfect to tuck behind. I need to run *now*. "You can stop right here. That's fine."

"Can I help you at all or—"

"Nope." I shove the door open, and drop to the ground, calling back, "I just need three minutes." I dart forward, but the ground is soft and muddy, and I cannot get my footing. I slip and slide all the way to the tree. Once behind it, I whip my phone out and stare.

**Song selection: "Truly Madly Deeply"**

*What kind of song is that?*

I might have heard that song before, but I hardly remember it.

*Stupid, stupid nineties music.*

*Every second counts. This app thinks it's going to pull one over on me because I don't know nineties music, but it has another thing coming.*

The timer is counting down from thirty seconds. This is serious business here, and I don't take winning lightly. I'm either first or last, and I won't be last. I open Google and type in the song title to get a peek at the lyrics.

"El," Stallone's husky voice calls from the other side of the trees. "Are you okay?"

My heart slams against a brick wall, and my eyes pop out of my skull. "Uh, why'd you follow me?"

"We're in the middle of the forest at night. I can't let you go wandering off. You don't have to be embarrassed that you're sick. I can take you home."

Thunk.

Thunk.

My heart slams against my rib cage at the same beat the timer counts down to my match.

*I'm busted.*

There's no way out of this, and I still don't know this stupid song. I will not lose.

"Look." I sidestep, coming around the tree and flipping my phone so he can see my app. "I'm not sick," I rush out as fast as I've ever spoken in my life. Hot shame floods my cheeks. "I didn't know what to say, because I spent all day singing karaoke into this app, and I'm in the championship round. It sounds stupid but I'm really competitive, and there is five hundred dollars of prize money on the line. I know it's not much, but I haven't been working all week, except for the coffee shop, but it's dead, and I've made no tips. I could really use the money, but I also didn't want to cancel our date, but I got thirty seconds until my round starts and I have to sing "Truly Madly Deeply," and I don't even know the lyrics—" I cut myself off, and a nervous giggle leaks out of my lips, as this really is the stupidest thing I've ever done. I ruined this date because of this stupid karaoke app.

His eyes glue to my phone. I'm waiting for a look of horror to flash over his face, but instead his lips bend into a smirk. "That's what this is about? Karaoke. Why didn't you say something earlier?" His giant hand flattens in front of me. "Give me the phone."

My brows furrow together for a moment before it sinks in that he's not mad at all. He has a full smile on his face, and he's ready to *help* me. "I don't think it works if you sing it. It must be my voice."

He swipes his hand through his hair. "I thought you were upset at me being so old." A giant sigh drops from his mouth, and he chuckles out loud. "If anyone can win at karaoke, it's going to be me. You hold the phone up to your mouth, but I'll sing in the background to help you find the rhythm. It's not a hard song—"

My app flashes, changing screens and I panic and cut him off, "It's starting!"

The lyrics scroll across my screen. Since I don't know them, I read them and try to find my pitch, but Stallone is right behind me, whispering the words to the melody and it helps so much. I feel dumb singing into my phone in the middle of the forest at night in front of him. Even if we make it past a first date—which I highly doubt after the way I've treated him—he'll probably never let me live this down.

My gauge quickly fills with green to indicate I'm winning. Then I no longer care how dumb I look.

*I'm winning.*

My confidence soars.

The headlights from the truck are the only real light, and it's enough for me to see his dark eyes staring deeply into mine. Our voices blend well together. Me, a solid soprano, and him a bass. The song ends with a long pause on the screen. I hold my breath, my gaze bouncing from Stallone to the screen. He's still here, which is mind-blowing to me, and he seems to be holding his breath, as excited as I am.

Confetti pops, and I squeal and pump my fist in the air. "We won!"

He throws his head back, letting laughter roll out, at the same time he scoops me up into a giant bear hug. It sends a whoosh right through me as our bodies are pressed together. All the air is wrung out of my lungs, and I can't help but freeze. After a complete twirl, he sets me down, and that's when I notice his nice pants are muddy. I motion to his pant legs. "How come you're all muddy?"

His smile never leaves his face. "I slipped when I was running after you." A slow chuckle starts from his lips. "I ran as fast as I could, because I thought you were dying."

My gaze slopes until I meet his, and a swelling starts in my heart. I put my hand on his forearm and stare into his eyes. Here's a man who ran through the mud to save me. When he finds out I'd been hiding this app from him, he sings Savage Garden to me.

It's all green flags for me.

"Stallone," I whisper his name. "Thank you for helping and for not being upset."

"You're welcome." His gaze softens, bright copper flecks dancing in his eyes. "I'm relieved everything is fine. I couldn't decide if you were upset that I was old or if you were sick."

"Neither of those." I let out a mischievous laugh. "I'm just broke right now and saw a way to make some cash. Now you know my secret. Plus, I'm the ultimate Karaoke Cash-oke champion."

"That's a good title to have." He holds his hand out to me, and I take it. Hand in hand, we both head toward the truck. "How about next time you want to sing karaoke though, you just tell me, and I'll take you out to a real show?"

"That sounds fun." My bottom lip rolls under my top teeth in disbelief. I got lucky with this guy. He's so fun and easygoing, yet he really was concerned when he thought I was sick. "Just know . . ." I pause and give him a challenging side eye. "You are not going to take my title from me."

"Just you wait." He throws his head back and laughs before giving me a stern look. "You think you're competitive? You haven't seen anything yet."

"I think I hear a challenge," I joke. "Care to make a bet?"

"Absolutely." We've reached the truck, and he opens my door for me, standing back while I hop in. "Not karaoke though. I get to pick the challenge, and it starts tomorrow."

My lips slide into a grin that fills my entire face. "Deal."

He shuts my door, and while I wait for him to return to the truck, my gaze drops to the ground. It's all fun to joke about, but I don't live here. It stinks to find someone I connect with so well, and I'm just going to leave.

He's quiet when he climbs in his seat and shifts the truck back into gear, steering back to town. Part of me wants to invite him back to the coffee shop for a drink and more conversation, but even though I have a key, it's not my store. I don't really know Graham or how he'd take it to have guests so late. I don't have any other ideas, and he doesn't offer anywhere else to go, driving me back to the lodge. He's quiet when he pulls into the parking lot. "Thank you for taking me out," I say as I turn to him to say goodnight. "I had a nice time, and I'm sorry for worrying you."

He slides his arm on the back of the seat, and it feels like a subtle invitation to move closer, but I'm not sure. "I had a great time too," he says as his eyes lock with mine. "If it's still okay, I'm going to text you tomorrow."

"I'd like that." I trap my bottom lip in my teeth and wait for him to say or do anything to indicate he wants me to stay, but he's still. After a quiet beat, I put my hand on the door handle, and push the door open, calling back, "Night."

"Night," he says as I shut the door, and I turn to go back into the lodge. I'm feeling a little down that the date is over. It's still fairly early, and I hope it wasn't me who made it end so soon. A tightness creeps into my chest, creating a pain in my heart different than anything I've experienced. It's like I miss him already.

# Thirteen

## Stallone

The next morning, my mind is quiet when I wake. Peaceful, and with only one thing on my mind. I can't wait to see Arielle. As soon as I'm back from walking Lucky, I turn on one stove burner. While I wait for my pan to preheat, I text her.

**Me: Are you ready for a little friendly competition?**

Little dots pop up on my phone screen, indicating she's typing back, and butterflies dance in my stomach in anticipation. I shuffle to the fridge for the egg carton and have enough time to crack two eggs into the pan before her reply flashes on my screen.

**El: You're not going to win at karaoke.**

Chuckling, I type my response.

**Me: Remember, I said no karaoke. I had something more adventurous but equally competitive in mind.**

Her reply is lightning fast.

**El: Like what?**

**Me: It's a surprise. Can I pick you up after work?**

**El: Yes, I close at 6 again.**

**Me: I'll be there.**

**El: Should I do anything to prepare?**

**Me: Maybe bring some tissues for when you lose.**

**El: Ha! Funny. I never lose.**

**Me: See you in a few hours.**

**El: Can't wait.**

I drop my phone to the counter and turn back to flip my eggs, chuckling to myself. She is just so much fun to be around. Now that we have the whole karaoke thing out in the open, I hope we can spend some real time together without so many interruptions.

I pull up to the Coffee Loft curb, and she promptly emerges, strutting over to the truck with her shoulders pulled back. When she opens the passenger door and peeps her head in, her huge messy blond bun drawing my attention, for just a moment before I level my gaze with hers. "I have no idea what you're up to." There's a chuckle braided into her words. "But I'm prepared to win." She slides into her seat and gives me a playfully haughty grin. "So you better be ready to lose."

"You think so, gorgeous? Remember, I'm the reason you won karaoke." I give her a solid thirty seconds to explain exactly how she thinks she can beat me at anything. She slowly straps the seat belt over her lap, not saying a thing, but her top lip is trapped between her teeth when she smiles. I struggle not to stare at her because she's so stunning. My pulse rockets through my veins, and I do my best to shift the truck back into drive and steer toward the mountains.

"I do think so," she finally replies, her eyes reflecting the last of the sunlight streaming in through the windshield. "I did my vocal warm-ups, my leg stretches, and I even skipped lunch in case this is an eating competition."

She could continue her smack talk, but my lips bend down from the guilt of not giving her at least a little hint. I sure didn't want her to walk around all hangry. "Not an eating competition. If you're hungry, we can grab an early dinner?"

"I'm good," she affirms, her eyes laser focused on where I'm driving to. "Depending on what the competition is, I may not want a full stomach."

I take a sharp left and steer up the narrow gravel road that leads back to my place. "I thought it would be fun to show you a little game I like to play when I'm bored at work."

"Game at work?" One of her feathered brows rises above the other until her face is a state of frozen confusion. "Aren't you a lumberjack?" The other eyebrow shoots up to match the height of the first, and she exclaims, "Tell me we are throwing axes! I've always wanted to do that."

"Oh, I don't know if I could trust you with an ax." I release one of my hands from the steering wheel and run it over my whiskers, and I teasingly give her a side-eye. Here's the thing, I've been throwing axes since I was the same height they were. There's no way she could win, but that's part of my plan. I'm going to set her up to lose, so I can win what I want.

"It's my surprise, isn't it?" She leans toward me, her eyes pleading.

"I thought it would be fun." I shrug, downplaying how excited I am to do this. "If you think you'd want to try it, I'm game to teach you."

"Oh, I'm game, but you don't have to teach me. I'm a natural at winning everything."

"We'll see about that." Pushing my tongue to the roof of my mouth, I raise my chin and take a sharp left onto the steep dirt road. The tires rattle in the worn ruts. Out of my peripheral vision, I see El casually grabbing the door handle.

"You really live out in the middle of nowhere." Her head moves in all directions as she scans the thick evergreens and steep sloped mountain banks.

"It may seem like that but it's not too far from my parents' house and my brother's. We all live on the same acreage, and it's honestly all I know. It's not that far from town, but out here in the mountains, it feels like I'm in my own world."

"It's so different from what I'm used to in Boston." Her gaze never leaves her window, and we round the last bend in the road, taking the turn to a clearing in the trees, which opens into my place. "This is not your house." Her gaze darts to me.

I press the brake to roll to a stop and shift into park in front of my garage. "I built it so I think that makes it mine."

"I thought you said you had a mountain cabin." Her gaze shifts from me to the house. "This is a mansion."

"It's bigger than I need, but I figured I was only going to build once and might as well have some room to grow." I grab my door handle and push open the door, calling back, "I can give you a tour if you want, but I'll admit about ninety percent of the house isn't even furnished yet."

She quickly hops out of the truck, and I wait for her to meet me by the walkway. We stroll up the pebbled path together. When I look over at her, walking by my side, my heart skips a beat. Usually, it's windier here than it is in town, but it's a rare moment where everything in nature is still, and to me it feels like a collective pause, as even the usually noisy birds are watching El—more than likely they are as mesmerized by her as I am. It feels awfully natural to have her next to me. Even if I am a little nervous to welcome her into my home. I never have guests, and I certainly don't entertain, but a niggling in the back of my head tells me this girl is different.

"Here's the plan." I motion to the back of the house, the side with the perfect view over the valley, where I have my practice target set up. "You can have as many practice shots as you want, but once we start the round, there's no starting over." My boots plod over the worn path. "It's not a competition unless we have a wager. What do you think we could bet?" I give her my mischievous smile, because I already know what I'm betting.

When she looks at me, it's pure magnetism, and I would probably agree to anything she'd say. My heart pounds against my rib cage, strong and steady. She hovers close by, bouncing her gaze to the target and then to me. "I don't need a practice shot." She raises her chin, appearing to analyze the target, but I suspect it's an act.

"Okay." I stare down into her eyes, and my heart flutters as I hold my breath. God made me a sizable man. It's not something I usually think about, but when I'm standing next to her, my body dwarfs hers. She's so stunning, I can't resist putting my hand on her lower back. When I'm this close to her, I just need to touch her. "And what should we bet?"

"If I win, you have to make me dinner." Her nose crinkles into the cutest pattern as she passes a sassy smile in my direction.

"I'll make you dinner if I lose." I nudge her shoulder, and I am instantly stilled by the spark that ignites in me.

"I won't complain about that." She gives me a gentle nudge back. "What happens if you win?"

So, I know what I want. I've never been so sure of something before that it's bizarre.

Standing outside my house with this woman I only recently met; a week ago, I'd have sworn I'd die a reclusive bachelor. As I stand here locked in an unwavering gaze with her, there's only one thing I want to do. It's something she put in my head days ago when she served me those sweet kiss coffees. With one brow cocked, I rub my hands together, drumming up the anticipation. "If I win," I lower my voice into a low rasp, "I get to kiss you like you're my girlfriend."

One of her hands smooths over her cheek, and she tucks her hand into her wild heap of hair, all the while her cheeks fire a bright pink wave. "El," I say softly, my tongue heavy, and her lack of reply causes my stomach to knot. "If you don't want—"

"Bet." She extends her hand like this is a boardroom negotiation. I take her hand in mine, knowing I'm going to win. This is clearly a setup. As I search her face for clues of unease, there are none. If anything, her gaze heats, and I'd say she's having as much fun as I am.

"Ladies first," I say through playfully gritted teeth.

She drops my hand, planting both of her palms on her hips with a take-charge expression on her face and impatiently looks at me. "Where's my ax?"

*Whoa, now that's not an expression you want to hear from a woman every day.*

*It's wild but yet hot.*

I walk to the porch where I keep several of my best throwing axes on a stand and run my hand along the row until I get to the lightest one. Her cyan-blue eyes track me as I walk the ax down to her and hand it over. "Can I walk you through a toss?"

She grabs the ax with both hands, her lips curling as she scrutinizes the ax. "This will do."

There's just enough of the sunset left to give us the light we need, and I stand back a few feet and hold my hands up to walk her through the motion. "First, you want to look at your target and never take your eyes off it. Then you raise your arms up slowly, keep your ax steady, and be careful not to drop it behind you."

She mimics my actions and then sets her gaze back on the target. My heart is ramming against my chest, and everything rolls out in slow motion. Her form is decent, but I still flinch when she releases the ax. It sails across the yard, snagging the target on the bottom right. "Not bad." I push my bottom lip out, pretending to be impressed.

Her face is a blend of doubt and triumph, and she steps to the side. "Your turn."

I rub my hands together again, teasing her. "Time to watch and learn." To make it fair, I walk up to the target, take her ax out and return it to the porch. I retrieve the heaviest one for myself and turn back to the target. "I'll stand way back here to give you the advantage." This is like taking candy from a baby. She must know this is a setup. I stand back, stretching both ways at the waist, building up the anticipation for her.

*One firm toss across the yard, and I'll finally know what it feels like to have those sweet lips on mine.*

My gaze wafts to her, and a beaming smile is spread across her gorgeous face. Shoot. Her button dimple on her cheek is even creased. My stomach wooshes. I'm such a sucker for dimples.

"What are you waiting for?" She bats her lashes at me, and I swear her dimple winks.

"Ah, nothing." I square my feet to the target and raise my ax, but a wave of guilt washes over me. I instantly lower the ax and turn toward her. I was only trying to impress her, but this isn't right. "Look, this clearly isn't a fair bet. I'm going to win."

Her bright eyes shine up at me, and the smile on her perfect-kissable lips doesn't deflate. If anything, they appear to plump up more, enticing me in. I can almost feel her sweet pink flesh when she lowers her voice, "That was always the point." She gives me a nonchalant side-eye, and the twinkle that sparks out of the corners of her eyes tells me she was here for the kiss too.

A shot of electricity shoots straight through my chest and doesn't stop until it zaps my heart, firing all my insides. My brain shuts off, and a pull of gravity draws my gaze back to her mouth. Her eyes widen, and I can't help act but out of pure instinct when she bats her lashes. She strides over to me. Even with her shoulders back, she's still at least a foot shorter than me. She doesn't stop until she's fully in my wide space bubble, close enough to nudge my elbow. "You know if you quit, not only am I going to think you suck, but I'm going to tell everyone you lost."

"Everyone? You don't know anyone here," I puff out, enjoying her sass. She's standing so near me, the heat of her body wafts off her, engulfing me, and makes it impossible to think about anything else than how perfectly kissable those lips are.

She's so close, I could lower my head straight down and land perfectly on her lips. She's unwavering, not backing up even a toe. She's practically begging for this kiss. I twist my lips into a line of flirtation and lower my head, speaking low, "I just need to make sure you aren't going to hold a grudge when I win, because I always hit my target."

A visible swallow rises and lowers in her throat, and she holds my gaze level with so much potency, adrenaline flits through my veins. I love the feel of her gaze on me, and coupled with the heat permeating off her body, there's so much magnetism drawing me closer. "No grudges." Her words release me from our hold, and I remember I'm holding an ax.

The way she smiles has my heart slamming against my rib cage. She has to know what's coming, and she clearly wants this as much as I do. I take a safety step to the side to clear space between us, and raise my ax. My hands warm as a blush flutters through my whole body in anticipation. I don't even need to watch, the ax lands in the perfect middle of the target.

I turn toward her, ready to feast my eyes on her beautiful smile. I shake my head, backing out of the competition. "It really wasn't fair," I say, but before I can continue, she closes the space between us. A hand snakes around my neck, and she pulls me down to her while she rises to the tips of her toes.

It's fast.

It's a little bit feral.

My heart expands, drinking her in as her body comes even closer.

Her lips capture mine, and she takes all the breath I have, erasing every ounce of insecurity I had over this bet. I wasn't taking advantage of her any more than she was of me. It's confirmed even more when I feel her smile into our kiss. Whatever this is, it's mutual. When she pulls away, she leaves me standing with my mouth dropped open.

"So much for being just friends." I reach up and physically close my mouth with my hand. "At least we got the hard part out of the way."

A serious line pins between her brows as she gazes back at me. I hold my breath as I wait impatiently to hear what she has to say.

She can't be mad.

She kissed me.

Her lips purse out, and I bite my cheek, waiting.

"Maybe it was meant to happen." A simple gesture follows, where she grabs my hand, pushing her fingers between mine, and smiles sweetly at me. My heart swells, feeling her hand in mine, and her gaze so steady on me it's as if she has nowhere else to go. "Now, let's see about that dinner you promised me."

# Fourteen

## Arielle

Stallone leads the way inside his house, and I struggle to keep my face neutral. This entire mountain is steeped so strongly in evergreen scent, and it doesn't dissipate when I pass through the threshold. More forest fumes waft around me as I take in his home. The exterior design resembles something similar to a log cabin, only so huge it could pass as a small lodge. Now, I see there is nothing rustic about the interior. It has dark wood floors and an open floor plan that leads to a modern kitchen, complete with stainless steel appliances and granite countertops. The wall across from the kitchen is replaced by floor-to-ceiling windows, opening to a view of the valley below. The window's so large, when I stand next to it, I feel like I'm standing outside. I step right up to the window and look down, scanning all along the valley. "This is a stunning view."

"It's my favorite thing about this place." He comes up beside me, his frame so huge I have to tip my head all the way to look up at him. His shoulders span wide and appear even broader, as his arms are so large he can't lower them to his body. Yet, I don't feel small standing next to him. If anything, it feels safe and shielded. Protected. He holds a lingering gaze on me that melts me to the floor. Ever since he brought up kissing me like his girlfriend, I find myself imagining what it would be like to be his girlfriend.

I can't imagine feeling any other emotions but loved and protected.

"What would you like for dinner?" He hikes a thumb over his shoulder, back toward the kitchen. "I have steak and beef thawed out."

"Oh." I pinch my lips together, as I love teasing him. "I only eat fish and chicken."

His eyes spring wide, and he starts a rebuttal, "I can make a vegetable stew—"

"I was kidding." I chuckle and clench his forearm, drawing myself a little closer to him. Man, it's strong and sinewy. I could certainly get used to these. "If you have beef, burgers are great."

"That's my specialty." He gives me a playful wink and crosses the room.

I back away from the window as well, following him to the kitchen. "What can I help with?"

"How about a salad?"

"I can do that." I gesture to the oversized fridge. "Can I take a peek?"

"Go right ahead." He opens the fridge, grabs a package of beef and holds on to the door until I come forward. I find the lettuce and cucumbers in the crisper and set them on the counter. A knife block sets next to me, so I pull out a smaller knife and locate the cutting board that pulls out from the counter. I pivot and set about washing the produce when Stallone fills in the silence, "So, we suck at being just friends, huh?"

I sputter out a laugh, but my heart doesn't think it's funny. It's the kind of laugh you have when you aren't sure what to say or think. "You started it with that bet."

"Not me." He shakes his head back and forth while he unwraps the beef. "You started it days ago with your sweet kiss coffee."

"What?" I pretend to be offended by lowering my brow and tilting my head away. "That was just coffee."

"Coffee with all the innuendo?" His gaze traps mine, and I don't turn away.

"Maybe." I shrug and raise my head to the cupboards above me.

As if reading my mind, he opens one, pulls out a bowl, and sets it in front of me. "Maybe?" His raised eyebrow challenges me. "Then you asked me to stay late first."

"I did." I nod and move the veggies to the bowl with my hands. "And I'm not the least bit sorry I did that."

He straightens his smile, boring a gaze into mine that seems to go right through me. "Tell me about your life back home."

"That's a weird thing to change the subject to."

"Not really." His tone is curt. "You're going back there tomorrow. Aren't you?"

"I-I am supposed to." All my replies fire out rapidly as a defensiveness rises in my chest.

"Answer my question. Are you going back tomorrow?" His voice is firm and insistent.

"Ah." A vision forms in my brain, bringing forth all the things that are in my life in Boston.

Tom. Definitely don't care to see him anymore.

My dad. He wouldn't be happy if I left Boston, but he couldn't stop me.

My job. I'm not even sure I have it anymore because I haven't showed up for days.

None of those things are enough to take me from the gaze that Stallone has on me now. When he looks at me, I feel like the most beautiful woman on the planet, and all I want to do is melt into his arms. It's more than just feeling beautiful though. I feel seen and respected, so much more than I have ever. My thoughts are muted but insistent with the biggest thing being that we both agreed from the start we weren't looking for anything long term.

"Would it matter if I didn't?" I level my gaze with his, and he wraps his arm around my waist, pulling me toward him with so much insistence I must place my palms on his chest to keep my balance. His hand finds my chin, tipping my face up with the same urgency, and his lips crash down on mine, leaving no room in my heart for doubts. When he pulls away, my fingertips rise to brush over my bottom lip that's still tingling. I wait for him to say anything to hint of how he's feeling.

When he speaks it doesn't disappoint. "It could matter."

I swallow, feeling my upcoming decision deep in my gut. I know what I want to do. I stare off past him, trying to think of what I'm going to tell my family. It's not even so much my dad, but Christian. He's so insanely protective of me, and when he finds out the reason I want to stay, he's going to chew fire.

# Fifteen
## Stallone

"I know you love coffee." I bring her a mug of the piping hot coffee I had made as we move to the couch for after-dinner conversations. She takes her mug, and I plop down beside her, taking up so much room, it feels like a love seat.

I'm not complaining.

We ate our burgers side by side, bellied up on my kitchen island. She didn't miss a chance to brush my shoulder or reach out to give me a soft touch. It's more than the flirtation we've shared before. Those little touches do everything to ignite a fire in my heart and bond me to her.

"You make great coffee." She hums between several slow swallows and focuses on the after the nightly news talk show that's on TV.

"It's the Keurig," I reply, but then our conversation wanes. The longer our date goes on, the more comfortable we are sitting in silence. It doesn't surprise me one bit when she slouches her body against mine, pulling her feet up under her until we are fully snuggling. I wrap my arms around her and it's a relief to feel her this close. She's relaxed, not the hyper- competitive woman she was on our first date. I take the moment to lean over and drop a kiss on top of her head. Her sweet honey scent consumes me, and I marvel at how I'm one lucky guy.

Speaking of Lucky, I let him in the house after dinner, and he took right to El, curling up on the floor by our feet. The three of us are the picture of happiness I always had in my head. Only now I finally see El's face in that picture, and it makes my heart pound so hard that if I didn't know it was happiness, I would think I was having a medical emergency.

I grab her free hand and playfully rub my thumb over hers. "So, what's your family going to say when they find out you met an old man?"

She tips her face up to mine. "You're not an old man, and it doesn't matter what they think. It only matters what I think."

The thing is, I want to believe her.

But she's so young.

Some would say too young, with wild oats left to sow.

But I believe her when she says she doesn't care, because she doesn't seem the type to care about sowing wild oats.

I'm in that place in life where I'm ready to make adjustments for someone special. I'm not so stubborn to think life must only be my way. If she wants to go slow, we will tiptoe together, relishing all the milestones we make. If she wants to move things along faster, and wants a family with me . . .

Then I'm an even luckier man.

I've never felt so still inside while knowing it's all going to work out.

I roll my bottom lip, trapping it in my teeth. It's crazy to feel this way so soon after just meeting someone, but I've never felt this kind of connection with anyone.

I'd say I'm falling for her.

It's clearly too soon to tell her that, but I have something else in mind. Something to show her.

"Hey." I drop my hand down to her hip and lean forward at the same time. "Come with me."

Her perfect brow furrows together into a quizzical look, but she doesn't hesitate to follow my lead. We rise off the couch together, and I take her hand and lead her to the French doors off the kitchen and onto the wraparound deck. I don't need to tell her why I brought her out here. The ladylike gasp that slips from her lips the second she sees the sky tells me she gets it.

"I've never seen stars like this before." Her tone is drenched in awe as her gaze glues upward, while she meanders all the way over to the end of the deck that overlooks the valley. Nothing blocks her view, and her expression morphs into one of childlike wonder.

I knew the stars wouldn't disappoint as the sky was cloudless all day. Normally, when I'm out at night, I enter a haze where I can't help but think this must be the most beautiful place on earth. Tonight, I just look at her. I walk up behind her and wrap both arms around her body. She doesn't flinch, but covers her hands with mine, and we freeze together looking up. She fits so perfectly into my arms that my heart skips an actual beat, making my chest ache, and I suck back a deep breath.

I never planned on Arielle.

I certainly wasn't out looking for something to consume my thoughts so much that it makes it impossible for me to concentrate on anything for longer than a few minutes, but I'm not going to run from this either. I dip my head down to rest it on top of hers.

"This is absolutely breathtaking," she coos after many long moments of silence. "I can tell why you love it here so much."

"One of the many reasons." The view from here never gets old, but a tinge of jealousy buds in my chest, as I can't help but wish I could see it for the first time again. Yet, I'm so grateful I can share it with her. "I grew up on the top of this same mountain. When I was a kid, I used to imagine that the stars would start to fall, and since I was so close, I'd be able to just reach up and catch one."

"I can see why. It does feel like we're right there with them. You're really lucky to live here." She turns her head, scanning in all directions, while pulling in a deep inhalation. "The air out here is so clean and crisp. I'm going to miss that too."

"I'm assuming it's completely different than what you have in Boston."

She answers me by squeezing my hands tighter, and I can feel her body slouch even more onto mine, creating a oneness that feels flawless. I would call this perfection. If there is anything I can do to get her to stay, even just a little while longer, I'm going to do it. I'm not the smartest guy on the planet, but I know a woman like Arielle is rare. Chemistry like ours is even rarer. "El," I rasp over the top of her head when my emotions bubble up so much, I can no longer contain them.

"Yeah." Her voice is soft and dreamy, like she's dreaming the things I refuse to let myself dream about. Like how I don't want her to leave, ever. In my head I see this play out like a movie. She leaves her place in Boston to stay here with me. It doesn't take me more than a second to make her my entire world, and it's not more than a month or two before we get married. I wouldn't be surprised if we had a little one on the way this time next year. That's the life I want so badly, but I don't dare to tell her that much.

"One thing I've learned in life is sometimes you have to take chances." I stall, take a deep breath, but that inhalation only pulls her sweet scent into my lungs, and it makes my knees shake. I risk another kiss, just ghosting my lips over the crown of her head, and I pray it's not the last time I get to do that. Swallowing, I say one mere sentence, but it's so powerful I feel as if I'm pouring my whole heart out to her, and my heart slams against my chest. "I hope this doesn't scare you, because we haven't known each other very long, but I'm falling for you."

I hold my breath, expecting a long pause and maybe even a little squirming, because I know I can come on strong, but I won't dance around for what I want. She does nothing of the sort. Instead, she turns around, her head tipped back so she can look all the way up at me, and she says with bold confidence, "I'm falling for you too."

I wouldn't believe something like this could happen so fast, but at that moment a seal is created in my heart, locking it off from anyone else but her.

# Sixteen

## Arielle

The next morning, I'm still in a haze of overflowing emotions from my date with Stallone, but I make it to the coffee shop right on time. While flipping the closed sign to open, a royal-blue streak running down the sidewalk catches my attention.

Christian.

In a blue warm-up suit, like the kind that was popular in the eighties.

Not his best look.

Pushing the door open a crack, I call out, "Hey, the eighties called. They want their clothes back."

"Funny." He gives me a pointed look and continues to stride forward.

"I told you I don't need a babysitter." My lips curl against my will, because even though he's here to take me home, it's still good to see him.

His knees rise to a ridiculously high angle as he marches forward until he grabs the door from my hand, pushing his way inside. "I'm not here to babysit you. I did a bunch of phone interviews for the manager's job. One of them is coming in for a second interview in person today. I think he's going to work out perfectly."

Christian's gangly legs cross over the threshold before I do, and he scans the place. "Graham never came back to work?"

"He's been coming in for an hour or two in the late mornings to check on things. He says he won't be returning full time until next week."

Continuing to make his way back to the coffee bar, Christian's gaze freezes on my roses, still soaking in the coffeepot. "What's going on with this decorating monstrosity?"

I quicken my steps and slide in front of the vase, hiding them from his view. "It's not decorating. They were a gift, and I didn't have a vase."

"Oh, no!" He sidesteps, reaching his hand around me, trying to get to the vase, but I push him back with my palm while he rants, "That dirty rotten Tom is not going to have his cursed flowers in my shop—"

"They are not from Tom!" I use both hands to hold him back. "I met someone."

His body goes stiff, no longer pushing forward while his gaze slides to me, a suspicious gleam sparkling out of the corner of his eye. "Tell me he's not a giant loser."

"He's not a loser at all." My brows furrow together, and anger bubbles in my gut. I hate that Christian treats me like I don't know how to make my own decisions. "He's a perfect gentleman, and you met him already."

"I met him?" he echoes, his hands planting on his hips. "Who are you even talking about?"

"You saw him here. That man who came in with the flannel shirt and beard."

Christian's jaw dramatically flops down. "Tell me you're kidding."

My cheeks are hot, but I don't back down. "We got to talking, and he asked me out on a date, and we really enjoy being around each other."

"El! How can I ever trust you?" His eyes roll to the ceiling before they slam back at me. "I leave you alone for a few days, thinking nothing could possibly go wrong, but you somehow manage to start dating an ogre."

"An ogre?" My head jolts back as I'm offended for Stallone. "That's awfully mean and shallow of you."

"Why?" Christian's eyes bug out of his head. "You just got out of a horrendous relationship. Why would you do this?" He gestures forward, demanding I speak, but then adds, "Oh, wait, is that what this is? A rebound thing? Something to even the score with Tom?"

"No." I struggle to put into words what happened these last few days. "This has nothing to do with Tom. I know it sounds weird, but Stallone and I have made a connection, and it feels like I've known him my whole life."

"Stallone?" Christian snarls his lip and acts like he's going to vomit by dropping his jaw. "Is that even his real name?"

"Stop." My voice is quieter than usual, as I don't have it in me to argue with Christian over a guy he's never even spoken to. The front door swings open, and Graham shuffles through with two sacks in front of him. I'm grateful for the interruption, planting my attention on him. "Did you find a good sale?"

"Diapers," he huffs and heaves the sacks onto the bookstore checkout counter. "And a bag of cabbage. Apparently, that helps with nursing 'issues.'" He makes finger quotes while shaking his head, and then drops his hands to rifle through some papers on his desk, pulling out an invoice on the bottom. He advances toward his computer and clicks the mouse to turn it on, while adding, "I need to double-check something that was bothering me."

"How's the baby?" I ask, already feeling the stress wafting off him.

"He's really great." Graham's gaze stays fixed on his computer; a smile never leaves his face. "He's healthy, and I feel blessed everything has gone well. How are things here?"

"Great." I nod, even though he's not looking at me. Christian cuts me off before I can expound.

"Interesting." He parks his hand on his hip again as that seems to be his new favorite place to rest it. "It's been really interesting. I was back in New York for a few days, and El here has started dating someone. Do you know anything about some stupidly named Stallone guy?"

"Christian," I scold, but they both ignore me, as Graham is also happy to gossip in front of me.

"Stallone Hart from Hart Logging?" Graham's gaze cuts to meet mine.

"Sure." Christian locks on Graham with his impatient glare. "We will go with that. Who is he?"

My face burns, and I feel like a small child whose parents need to discuss my inappropriate behavior in front of them.

*Only I did nothing wrong.*

Graham's slow shrug draws out the suspense, while Christian and I both stare at him, waiting. "Stallone's been a regular here for as long as I've been here. Not much of a talker. I've always seen him as a loner. I'm surprised he went out with you. How'd you get him to do that?"

"He asked me." I stare forward, feeling like that should be obvious.

"Interesting." Graham stuffs his invoice back into a file drawer and returns his gaze with a thoughtful expression. "You do know he's super rich, right?"

"Not really." I'm definitely not going to admit to Christian right now that I've been to his mansion. He'd come unglued.

"Yeah, he's made a fortune with his wood business. Course, it was his dad's before his, and if I remember the rumors I've heard correctly, it might have actually even been his granddad's company first. He seems like a good guy," Graham says with thoughtful inflections. "I'm just surprised he asked you out, because he seemed to be over dating after his last breakup . . ." Graham's voice trails off while he opens another file drawer and runs his hands over the top of it looking for something. When he finds what he wants, he grabs it and closes the drawer.

Christian doesn't wait for us to have privacy. His gaze slams back to me and he lets out a noisy huff. "Seriously, El, please tell me this is all a joke about this guy."

"You don't want me to be happy?" I'm not even trying to argue. It's absurd he thinks he gets an opinion about this. I went on two dates with the guy. That's it. It's not a big deal. It's not like we eloped. A naughty chuckle bubbles in my gut as I visualize how fun it would be to tease Christian that Stallone and I eloped.

"Of course you're not happy." He gestures forward wildly. "You just went through a horrific breakup. This is just a distraction." He squares his stance, his face transforms into a stoic expression. "Trust me, El. What you need is to come back with me and spend some time healing and don't go on any dates for at least a month, or two."

I try to set my mind on Tom, but it won't stay there. I can't even think about him if I want to. This has nothing to do with Tom or what I recently went through. I don't know how to convince Christian of that.

My nervous gaze pulls to Graham. He's more thoughtful as he overhears our conversation, but he doesn't back away when he catches me looking at him. "What do you think?" The question is out of my mouth before I can second-guess allowing an almost-stranger into my personal life.

His brows raise as he hangs onto my gaze, and he asks, "About Stallone?"

"Maybe it's about him," I bumble around for words, "but it's also about me and what I want. I don't want to go back to Boston. I like it here, and yes, okay..." My voice rises as I circle back to my earlier thought. It appears my thoughts are growing less cloudy by the second. "Maybe, by doing what I want, I can say it's about Stallone. So, what if I want to get to know him more? That doesn't make me a bad person."

"Whoa, I never said it did." His kind chuckle erases some of the tension. "I just wanted to make sure I knew what we were talking about." He lowers his gaze to his papers, moving them into a straight pile. His voice is firm when he asks, "Do you think you could love him?"

"Whoa, whoa, whoa. Don't say that!" Christian butts in, physically inserting himself between us with his eyes glued to me. "You don't have to answer that. That's a dumb question." He flashes a look of annoyance at Graham. "Of course she doesn't love him. They just met."

"I didn't ask if she loved him. I asked if she *could*. There's a clear difference." Graham crosses his arms against his chest, seeming to stand even taller. "I met my wife when I was in high school. We didn't find a way to be together for many years, but in our years apart, I always knew I *could* love her if I was given the chance. I knew it from the first time I saw her."

"You're not helping," Christian mumbles, turning his back to Graham. When he looks at me, my chin quivers. I know exactly what Graham is saying. I'm not that inexperienced to say it's love, but every part of my heart twists when I think of him. I am certain if I gave it a chance, I could love him. "El," Christian's coax is softer this time, as his gaze paces my face which I know is not hiding my emotions. When I say nothing, he repeats softer, "El."

I step forward, sharing all my vulnerabilities with him and whisper, "I think I can."

His eyes take an arc roll before he grunts, "So, what are you telling me? You want me to leave you here?"

I shrug, completely unsure what the days before me will offer, but I know I must try. "I'm saying I want to stay for a while. I actually think I'd enjoy being a barista. It has to be better than working for dad. You don't have to hire anyone. At least not now. It works out that I can stay here and see what this thing is."

"You're for real about this?" he says, voice oddly quieter, and it's evident this is finally sinking in for him.

"I am."

"Okay, then." He shakes his head, backing away. "I'll finish this week's order, but then I'll leave the rest up to you." The thing with Christian is, he's always been dramatic, but something happened when he met Portia. He gained a sense of urgency where when they are not together, he just seems edgy. I know the impatience he shows me is because he really is in a hurry to tie up his ends here to get home to her. It was never his plan to leave me here, and it is unsettling to him.

What he doesn't know is, the same urgency he always has to return to Portia is one that now pounds in my chest. As I sit here at the coffee shop with a full day before me, all I can think about is getting off work so I can see Stallone.

That's not love.

But it's something.

And I can't wait to see what it turns out to be.

# Seventeen

## Stallone

I clear my throat for the second time as I stand outside the coffee shop. The sign has already been switched to closed for the night. Through the window, I can see El is alone again, but for the life of me I can't go inside.

With her hair up in one of the wild messy buns, that always leaves a few wispy strands to fall down to frame her face, she floats around the coffee bar, wiping off the counter. Her expression is soft, and under the muted Coffee Loft lights, her skin has a soft glow. I catch my breath in the back of my throat as I marvel at how she's absolutely ravishing.

Never in my life did I think a woman like her would have eyes for someone like me. I reach out to grab the door handle but freeze again. This is so different than the other days I met El at work. Before it was a mere flirtation. Something changed yesterday. Now I feel like I have something to lose. It's so early in this situationship for me to ask for her to give anything up. We hardly know each other. Yet, the magnetism has only grown stronger. My palms tremble as I finally find the bravery and pull open the door. I heave a sigh of relief that she left it unlocked. She was clearly waiting for me.

At least, I hope.

Her gaze locks on mine, and if I didn't know better, I'd say it's a tad frantic. "Stallone."

Man, I love the way my name sounds when it falls from her lips. Her one-word greeting is enough to make my heart slam against my rib cage. "Hey, gorgeous."

Her palms find the coffee bar in front of her, and she playfully leans forward while batting those gorgeous dark lashes at me. "What can I get you?"

"You know what I want." I stride forward, my steps growing longer the closer I get to her. "I came for one of your sweet kisses."

She doesn't flinch or pretend to not understand. Her gaze softens even more as she steps out from behind the bar, and she rushes forward to meet me halfway. I scoop her up in one swift motion, lifting her off the ground, and her lips find mine with perfect rhythm. The coffee shop could implode into a giant fire, and I wouldn't even notice as my eyes turn into literal hearts, and the only thing I'm able to focus on is her.

When I set her down, her eyes stay locked on me. She teasingly smiles and says, "Is that what you had in mind?"

"That'll do." Pushing my lower lip out, I nod. "But I might need seconds in a little bit."

Her soft giggles cushion my heart, and she pivots on her heel back to the bar. "Did you actually want a coffee too? I'd love to spend some time together."

"If you have time." It's an uncertain reply, and my voice cracks as I feel nauseous just coming flat out and asking her if she's leaving. She has a whole life outside of this place, and she told me from the start that she wasn't looking for anything.

She turns toward me, grabs both of my hands, and stares up at me. The lighter hue of blue fires sparkles out of her eyes. "I have time. I told Christian I was staying for at least a little while. I definitely want to see where this goes." Her tone is plumb full of certainty. "Unless you're busy." Her gaze hovers over mine, and nervous reflections shine back at me.

Was she afraid I didn't want her to stay anymore?

"El," I speak as boldly as I can, "I have all the time in the world for you. There's nowhere else I'd rather be." I move in close, wrapping my arms all the way around her into a tight embrace, and slowly lower my face down to her, ready for another kiss.

Thud.

Thud.

*Ugh.* I moan in my head.

I don't even have to look to know who's there, but both our gazes pull to the front window. Someone is watching us—or should I say—watching El. Lucky has jumped out of my truck again, and his nose is pressed against the glass, eyes locked on El. "Not again," I whine.

I swipe my hand through my hair and look back at El. "I think someone else is happy you're staying too."

Her eyes pump so much power over me, I am frozen when she says, "So we agree? We're going to see what happens. One day at a time . . ."

*So that's how this goes...slowly, but promises of heaven just by being near her.*

"I'll give you any day you want, but I think we need to do it a little differently."

She swallows before she replies with a now shaky breath, "What do you mean?"

I take a grandiose step forward, leaving no space between us and no room for doubting. "I think we should take this one sweet kiss at a time."

My hand finds her hip. She rises to the tip of her toes, clenches my shirt in a way that steals my breath, and she tugs on it, pulling me down. We find each other with perfect timing, and I close my eyes, melting into her softness. There isn't any way for this situationship to get better than this. I'm going to spend each day proving to her she made the best decision to stay here by showering her with all the kisses and affection she could ever want.

My lips pull tight as they tease a smile, but I don't break our lip-lock.

*Thud*

*Thud.*

El breaks out into a giggle, and pulls back, "Let Lucky in. I'm sure I can find him a pup cup."

I give her a pointed stare, as I'm not sure she has any idea what she's started here with Lucky. This could surely turn into a habit. "Are you sure you really want to do that?"

"Yeah." She nods a slow confirmation, adding a wink. "We have something to celebrate."

"Okay, coffees for everyone, but don't you dare give him caffeine." I stride back to the door, bracing it open for Lucky. He doesn't wait for the invite as he barrels through the door and goes right to El.

# Eighteen

## Arielle

## Just two weeks later

"Hold your oar out in front of you like this." Stallone straightens his arms, shoulder width apart, and continues calling back his instructions from his place in front of the kayak. "Turn it gently like you're pedaling a bike with your hands." I lift my oar, mimicking his moves, ungracefully smacking the side of the kayak with my oar. "Smaller movements," he coaches as his oar grazes over the smooth river water, and we glide forward.

Correcting my pattern, I try to steady my oar, but I'm all over the place. "This is a lot harder than it looks." A chuckle leaks out of my mouth right as I tap the kayak again.

"You'll get the hang of it."

I sit back on my legs, tipping my head back to see the top of the nearby mountain. Everything is still snowcapped, and I wouldn't have believed they would be even more beautiful from this view on the water. It's what my father used to call January thaw. A nice random day in the coldest month of the year, where it's actually nice enough to go outside without a coat. Stallone picked me up from work with only one thing on his mind. Well, maybe two. He didn't forget to kiss me hello.

"So, this morning on the way to work"—Stallone's voice takes an even tone, and I lean forward, hanging on to his every word— "Ryson asked me what happened to me."

"What do you mean what happened? What's wrong?"

"Nothing's wrong." He continues to propel the kayak smoothly along the water with ease and precision. "That's what he was hinting at. He said I changed, and I told him about you."

"You did . . ." And just like that my heart crawls up in my throat with all the nerves. Stallone and I have been spending all our time together—just the two of us. One thing we haven't done is complicate things by including extra people. Sure, Christian knows about us, but it's not like I tell him personal things. I could. I trust Christian more than anyone, but it's more about protecting my heart. I'm still so confused as to what we are. "What did you say?"

"I said that I met someone, and we've been spending a lot of time together. He asked me if you were my girlfriend."

"What did you say?" I struggle not to squeak because I'm actually quite curious too. It's not a term we've used yet.

"I said, 'She lets me kiss her like she's my girlfriend.'"

My lips spread wide across my face, and I shake my head. "That's really all you care about, isn't it?" Our laughter synchronizes for a beat before it falls away, and we are left with only the soft whooshing of the oars in the water. "I ah, had an interesting conversation today too."

"Oh yeah?" He tilts his head back ninety degrees trying to sneak a side-eye on me.

"Yeah, Graham asked if I wanted to rent the apartment above the bookstore."

"He did?" He hangs on to the word did, dragging it out to last at least three syllables. "What did you say?"

"Well, I asked for a tour, and he let me take a look. It's small and very outdated, but he only wants six hundred for it. He said I can go month to month." I swallow, feeling the hugeness of this announcement deep in the pit of my stomach. "I told him I'd take it."

"Are you for real?" He twists in the kayak as best he can, meeting his gaze directly with mine. "You're moving here?"

"If you want me to..." I love looking into his eyes. They don't make brown eyes like that anymore. Full and honest, bearing so many emotions in the reflections that never disappoint.

"W-well, y-yeah." He seems to stutter a bit before his words come out. "I want that more than anything. You know what that means."

I tap my finger to his chin, holding it there in pause. "Ah, it means you are invited to help me move all my stuff."

I linger on how it's crazy his smile is both serious and teasing at the same time. "Absolutely I can help you move, but if you move here, I can't continue kissing you like you're my girlfriend. That's seriously messed up."

"What?" My eyebrows bead together as I know he's setting me up for a punchline. I already know what it is, and it makes my heart beat fast.

"It means you *are* obviously my girlfriend."

"I agree." I smile sweetly and lower my lashes. I've been waiting to make this official. It's exactly what I've wanted, and I couldn't have asked for a sweeter way to be asked. I can't help but feel my life is unfolding exactly the way I dreamed it would.

Dear Reader,

Thank you for reading Truly, Madly, Steeply Brew.

I wanted to add a note to say, if you enjoyed Graham, he has his own story already. You can find it on Amazon, and it's called *Kissed by My Billionaire Boss*.

If you missed Christian and Portia's Story, that one is *Pardon My French Press*.

# Introducing
# Mountain Brew

The Coffee Loft is back with another collection of cozy, stand-alone sweet romcoms—this time served with an extra shot of rugged charm!

Wrap yourself in flannel, breathe in the crisp mountain air, and settle in with a new brew. Mountain Brew is bold and smooth, just like the men who drink it.

These bearded mountain men may look rough around the edges, but one taste, and they're *irresistibrew!* Get ready to fall for flawed but lovable heroes, laugh-out-loud dating disasters, mixed signals, surprising twists, and heart-stopping grand gestures guaranteed to make you swoon. Grab your favorite table over in the corner and prepare to be swept off your feet by these unforgettable mountain men.

Find the series here: https://books.bookfunnel.com/thecoffee loftseriesmountainbrewcollection

Do you want to see what other books we have in this series? We have two more series to enjoy. Find them below:

Fall Collection: https://www.amazon.com/dp/B0CXQBFPH K

Winter Collection: https://www.amazon.com/dp/B0CG2MQP2J

# About J.P. Sterling

J.P. Sterling grew up watching old reruns of Lucille Ball and Mary Tyler Moore and fell in love with wholesome entertainment and slapstick comedy. She loves leaning into the over-the-top humor and full circle moments, especially if it means the underdog gets to shine.

Aside from writing, she's also a wife and homeschooling mom, a holistic dietitian, a former college professor and lover of all-things dark chocolate.

*No swears. Just kisses. No Blasphemies. *

Let's get social!

Hey you amazing reader! You are invited to join my private reader group for all-things clean books and friends.

Enter the group here: https://www.facebook.com/groups/1500850764081965

Other places to follow me:

Instagram: https://www.instagram.com/stories/authorjpsterling/

Facebook: https://www.facebook.com/jpsterlingauthor/

Amazon: https://www.amazon.com/stores/author/B01N9TJXJN/about

# Also by J.P. Sterling

**_Christmas Shenanigans_ (All Standalones)**

_Mingle All the Way_

_Tis the Season to Get Married_

_Let's Not and Sleigh We Did_

**_The Coffee Loft Series_ (All Standalones)**

_Pardon My French Press_

_No More Mr. Chia Guy_

_Truly, Madly, Steeply Brew_

**_Sweet Hockey RomCom_ (All Standalones)**

_The Pucker-Up Pact_

_Shot Through the Heart_

_Come and Get Your Glove (Coming 2025)_

**_A Modern Fairy Tale Series_ (All Standalones)**

_Royally Rugged_

**_Bosses and Billionaires Series_ (All Standalones)**

_Maid for my Billionaire Boss_

_Upcycling My Rig-Pig Boss_

*Kissed by My Billionaire Boss*

*Marooned with My Celebrity Boss*

***A Heart that Dances Series***

*Dancing on Broken Ankles*

*The Stars We See*

*A Heart that Dances*

*A Heart that Loves*

***Water and Stone Duet***

*Ruby in the Water*

*Lily in the Stone*

# Mingle All the Way

J.P. Sterling

# Contents

# ONE

# Jade O'lette

*Schreeeeeech. Schreeeeeech.*

Yanking the covers over my head so hard that I almost disjointed my shoulder, I held my breath and tuned into the I'm-clearly-a-ghost-scratching sound outside my bedroom window. My lungs screamed for oxygen, and I inhaled a deep breath of stale hot air. Suddenly, the discounted price on my new rental house made *so* much more sense. I had suspected something like this since it was an older neighborhood. Not only a little old, but we're talking colonial times. That's what the realtor called this house. A colonial. All I saw was thirteen hundred dollars a month rent in a city where nothing was under two thousand. I signed on the line so fast that I practically left a smoke trail behind my pen.

This was my year of saving money, as I did whatever I could to cut corners. If I did the mathing correctly, at the end of next year I could pay off all my debt. All my student loans, plus the credit card debt I had acquired after unexpectedly losing my middle-school teaching job last spring. Having been locked into my old rental agreement and without a job, I drained every penny out of my savings, and then some. I did what I could to honor the contract, but even though I eventually found a job as a barista, I didn't make the same money as I had teaching. I fell further behind every month. Or at least until I found this budget rental at the exact time my previous rental contract expired.

Speaking of the discounted house, this was my first night in the house, and I'm not sure I signed up for a ghost. Unless he was like Casper, who transforms into a hot date for the dance. Christmas was around the corner, and I could use an escort for my work Christmas party.

"I'm beautiful, strong and brave," I whispered. It sounded dumb, but I had listened to this podcast where the dude said to repeat what you want to be. I'd been doing it for almost a year now, and bad things kept happening. It clearly wasn't working, but I was terrified of stopping. *What if it got worse?* "Oh, and rich," I added.

*Schreeeeeech.*

"I heard you!" I forced a brave voice as I peeled back my blanket, peeking out. "I know you're here, but I'm trying to sleep. You can cut it out now."

*Schreeeeeech.*

Tapping my finger to my chin, I mused. He's clearly a male ghost because he's pretending not to hear me.

*Maybe I'll have a closer look.*

I eased one foot off the bed, softly hitting the bare wood floor, and gently shifted my weight onto that leg, careful to not make a peep. Not sure why I was worried about disturbing mister-clamorous-hot-invisible dude when he obviously wasn't worried about *his* noise level.

Casing the four hundred square foot studio apartment, which was my part of the house, for a weapon, I settled on the broom stowed in the closet. Now to make my legs carry me across the room. I eased one foot before the other, tiptoeing across the squeaky wood floor. I opened the closet door, and my gaze unexpectedly landed on a pair of over-sized, glow-in-the-dark swimming goggles.

*You never know . . .*

Without a second thought, I tugged the goggles over my head, not taking the time to smooth out where the headband created a huge bubble of long dark hair above my head. I grabbed the broom, and a flashlight from the shelf, and Nancy Drew'd my way over to the window. I paused for a beat, swallowed the lump in my throat, and slowly exhaled. Breathing was so nice. Then I gradually peeled back the curtain . . .

*Schreeeeeech.*

"Ahh!" I jolted, my feet cementing to the floor in fright. My heart motored away, and even though I wasn't in danger, the moment's intensity left me lightheaded.

The neighbor's titanic tree branch dangled like creepy, giant fingers trying to claw into my room!

I breathed out a heavy release as the twiggy branch scraped against the metal siding until it thumbed off the side of the house.

A stupid branch! I held my chest, waiting for my heartbeat to slow.

A light switched on in the upstairs room in the house across the alley. Before I had time to think, a man stepped out on the upstairs veranda. He wore red flannel pajama pants and a white T-shirt. His hair was dark, with the perfect wave at the tips where it was slightly overgrown past his ears.

He was hot.

Somewhere in the universe, a calendar was missing their Mr. December.

My jaw fell. I could see him, but did that mean he could see me? I was standing here in my Christmas jammies and swimming goggles . . . I panicked and jerked the curtain closed. With a cringed expression on my face, I motored back to bed, yanking the covers tight around me, and rolled over on my side.

Now that I knew a ghost wasn't ready to wrap his fingers around my neck, I was finally ready to sleep.

Did Mr. December see me?

Nah, I'm sure he didn't.

The goggles. I forgotten I had them on, and they pinched the back of my neck. I started to yank them off, but my hair pulled with the elastic band. Wincing, I sucked in a hard breath. Get a grip, girl. I grabbed the front of googles and gave them an impatient tug over the back of my head. Now, I could finally rest. Squeezing my eyes shut, I tried not to think about the hunk across the alley, or how ridiculous I must have looked to him, no sir.

*Schreeeeeech.*

# Two

## Evan Gabbert

I had been watching my program when I heard a woman cry out, the shrill tone sent chills up my spine, and I leaped out of bed and fled to the veranda. The sea creature from the blue lagoon stared at me from the vacant apartment across the alley. I rubbed my eyes as I struggled to open them wider and took another step closer. "Ouch!" I slapped my mouth, suppressing my holler of pain. I had stubbed my toe on my other toe. Who does that? Apparently, I do.

*Man, I need to lay off the Discovery Channel.*

Or maybe it was the hot wings? I swiped my forehead with the back of my hand, checking for a fever. Serrano peppers always had that nightmares-and-night-sweats-cleansing effect on me.

No fever. I must be sleepwalking again.

I rubbed my eyes, trying to wipe my nightmare away, and when I reopened them, the creature was gone.

It worked.

"Evan!" My mom's "I'm-about-to-go-ginger" voice called up the stairs. Most people called the attitude of a redhead feisty. After having lived with a redhead a good portion of my life, I would say it's more special than that. "Ginger" deserved to be a verb. "Honey!" Her puffed curls crested the steps, and she emerged with Dolly, her hairless dog, cradled in her arms. "What in mistletoe mania are you screaming about? You scared Dolly half to death. I thought someone was breaking into the house."

I cocked my head to the side. "Scared?" My eyes landed on Dolly. She was wrapped in a hand-knitted baby blanket that matched her collar. Looking relaxed, her eyelids visibly drooped. She didn't look scared to me. This was obviously more about my mother. I stepped away from the window, my voice dropping into a mutter, "I, uh, thought I heard something and tripped on my foot."

"Evan." Her words came out smooth and empathetic. "This is not the first time you've woken up with these issues. You are spending far too much time watching those alien shows." She flicked her hand toward my TV, where it incriminatingly displayed *UFO Witness* paused on my big screen. "I'm worried about you. This isn't normal. You're in your thirties and living in your child-hood home. Maybe I'm making this too easy for you—"

"Mom." This was her failure-to-launch speech, and I under-stood her plight. Still living at home, I was the nerd that the nerds made fun of, but I wasn't ashamed. I owned it.

It wasn't like I still lived in the basement and slept all day.

I recently moved *upstairs*.

I worked and paid rent.

I wasn't lazy.

I had lived on my own for most of my twenties. It was phenomenal, until I had one of those life-altering defining moments that made me hate corporate America, at the exact time my engagement to my ex-fiancée imploded. I pledged to put myself first, get out of the rat race and work for myself by opening my own computer repair shop. However, the first year was painfully slow, and I moved back home to make it work.

Living at home with parents was sort of a trend my generation was starting to normalize. Unless I wanted to have three side hustles and never sleep, I couldn't afford the cost of housing anymore. Long Island is one of the most expensive places to live. With my rent payment, Dad was able to work less overtime driving a city bus and finally save a little extra for retirement. I saw that as a win for all of us. Dad appreciated the money, but he never would admit that to my mom.

Not to mention, the extra money had improved my dad's health in more than one way. With his evenings free, he started walking. He lost a few pounds, which in turn helped his back. Mom began walking with him, and for the first time in a long time, they are enjoying each other, and I even see them holding hands.

"Please don't think I mind that you're here." She took a step forward, while rubbing Dolly under her chin. "But I worry that you're putting your life on hold because it's too easy here. Don't be afraid to make mistakes."

"Mom." I started but then halted as her eyes filled with tears of worry. She'd sacrificed so much for me. It wasn't worth arguing with her. Not in the middle of the night anyway, when we were both overtired. I pulled my lips into an understanding smile. "I appreciate your concern."

Her shoulders raised and lowered as she took a deep breath, cueing for her change of subject. "I forgot to mention I'm hosting an early Christmas dinner here, with your grandma and cousin Rob—"

I cut her off with a stern glare. I never wanted to hear a word about that jerk. Rob had always been the golden child in our family. It traced back to his mother being my grandmother's favorite, and my grandmother never bothered to hide her favoritism. When his parents died in a car accident, Grandma swooped in to raise Rob, and no matter how mean he was, Grandma put him on a golden pedestal.

Rob and I were only three weeks apart in age. When we turned eight, Grandma gave me a transformer, while Rob got a go-cart. When we got our driver's licenses, grandma let me pick her up and bought me lunch. Rob, on the other hand, got a new car.

Looking back, I understand my grandma was merely filling in for his parents, and my young brain never understood that. What still bothered me was Rob had made a game out of showing off the disparities. He got enjoyment from "winning" over me. I learned to ignore him, but ignoring my enemy turned out to be my biggest mistake, which still haunted me to this day.

You know the saying, "keep your friends close, but keep your enemies closer?"

He screwed me over in a way I could never forgive.

"I know what happened between you two," she said, shutting off my "I-hate-Rob" spiral. "I agree with you, it's best to avoid him. However, Rob specifically asked if you'd be here. He's flying in for just a few days. Maybe he wants to make amends? It would be nice if you could try to forgive him. After everything that's gone on in the world these last few years, maybe we could all get together for your grandma one more time. You know she isn't going to be around forever, and it means a lot to her. And it shouldn't be that bad. Maybe you can bring a date?" She held her hand out in pause, gesturing forward like I should get the hint, before she tacked on, "Maybe you should try a dating service to get you out of this rut? You never know."

I raised my eyes heavenward. She was giving up on me. Before I could stop my word fart, I blurted out, "I can bring a date. I have a girlfriend."

"Oh?" Her over-tweezed eyebrow quirked. "This is news to me."

"Yeah, we kept it quiet until we knew we were serious." My eyes didn't blink as I let out another lie. I was half amazed about how easy it was to lie, and half scared I had this amazing skill.

"You're serious?" Her voice turned up at the end into a happy squeal as she reached out and cupped my cheek with her palm, letting her hand linger while her smile grew, reflecting almost a giddiness. "I'm going to mind my own business, but I can't wait to meet her. Night, Evan." She backed out slowly, rubbing under Dolly's chin again, even though Dolly had nodded off already. Right before she exited, her eyes landed on my open laptop, seeing a half-completed application for an engineering job at NASA. Her eyes flashed to me, before slamming to the heavens. "NASA? How are you going to keep your girlfriend happy if you're up in orbit, pooping into a vacuum cleaner?" she muttered as she padded back down the hall. Her voice got even quieter, but I heard the faint, "Grandbabies, Evan, that's the goal, not the stinking moon. . ."

I wasn't slighted that she dissed NASA, because my mind was racing.

No, not racing. Crashing like a forty-two-car pileup, and I was in the center in a Ford Pinto!

*What did I just do?*

I slammed my hand to the side of my head, trying to stop the building pressure. Where was I going to find a girlfriend?

I couldn't back out now! My mom was so happy. She would be crushed. No, now I was committed to this. The thought of Rob coming here all smug. Clearly, he was coming here so I couldn't avoid him anymore, but I wasn't a fool. He'd be rubbing his perfect I-just-made-partner-at-my-law-firm life all up in my face.

Bringing a date would be mandatory if I wanted to survive Rob's fat "I'm-winning" mouth, and it would also make my mom happy. The problem was I didn't know any available women. I worked alone at my own computer shop. In the summer, I'd go to the beach, but it wasn't exactly beach weather. Hence the Alien show marathon.

Where was I going to find a date in two days?

My eyes surveyed my room, landing on my collection of micro, self-built robots, all the way to my full-sized R2D2. Hmmm. I tapped my finger to chin. He might look cute with a wig. . .

# THREE

## Jade

Late. Late. Late. No, not that kind of *late.* Trust me, these choco-late cravings told me I was right on time on that schedule. Oh, and the fact that I didn't have a husband and cute little house with a white picket fence assured me more. I was late for work. "Phew," I took deep breaths as I ran around searching for my boot. Dressed as an elf, I wanted my black boots to match my green dress. My boss, Portia, encouraged us to show our Christmas spirit. When I discovered the Christmas spirit made me extra tips, I was all in. I had quickly become obsessed with dressing in costumes.

How my boot had gone missing in the twelve hours I'd lived in this place, was a mystery I couldn't solve. I didn't even unpack, and here I was, losing stuff already. With no furniture except a bed, it couldn't get stuck under anything. Undoubtedly there must be a black hole in the apartment. It's not even an actual apartment, just a back room of this house remodeled into a studio. Everything is contained.

There's no place for footwear to hide!

Centering myself in the room, I turned in a circle, scanning the floor. Bed. Wall. Bathroom door. Another wall. Tiny kitchenette. Exit door. Bed again. No boot!

I scratched my head. Maybe it got sucked into a void?

I'd have to stop at the store on the way to work and grab a new pair. There was a Budget Shoes for Less across the street from my coffee shop. I'd used all my savings for the two- months' rent and security deposit on this apartment, and all I had was twenty dollars. Good thing today is payday. With my winter boots not an option, I slipped into the only other pair of shoes I had unpacked—my sandals. I threw one arm in my jacket, not wasting time to slip in my other arm, and hurried out the door.

Icy air slammed into my face, stealing my breath, and freezing dampness seeped through the slits of my sandals. If I wasn't having the best day before, all I could say was one word.

Snow.

So perfect. I forced my lips into a sarcastic grin and slid across sidewalk, toes stinging and red by the time I reached my car and grabbed for the door handle. Thankful to make it across without falling, I pulled on the handle and found it frozen stuck. I yanked more than a gentle tug, but nothing budged. I didn't have time for this! I grasped the handle with both hands, anchored one foot on my car, and pushed off, feeling the ice crackling. It was working!

I held my breath, and dug deep for one final heave, and at last, it flew open. I scurried inside with toes so numb I couldn't even feel the cold anymore. I really hoped for an upfront parking spot at the mall, or I'd risk frost bite with these temps. This was clearly some kind of torture. I started my car and waited for the engine to warm up. Not that I cared about engines, but that's what my Midwestern dad always told me to do.

After four minutes, my car still had its freezing vibrations thing going on, but I got impatient because I was going to be late. "Sorry, car," I breathed out. "I know you hate driving when you aren't warm, but I have to get to work." My toes were not even close to normal flesh toned when I applied my brake and shifted the gear into reverse, but I didn't have time to waste. I glanced over my shoulder, assessing my exit strategy. I had parked in the alley, where my landlord had told me to park, because the street had No Parking signs.

It was fine when I pulled in, but the neighbors across the alley had several cars, and they had crowded in, parking at weird angles. I cranked my wheel, ready to Houdini out of this parking situation. I pressed down on the gas, but the car didn't move. My tires spun. Clearly, I was on ice. I dug my teeth deep into my bottom lip, as this morning was overwhelming me. I put my car into drive and tried to pull forward, but my tires whirled again. I didn't even move an inch.

Okay. I blew out a frustrated breath, one that made my bottom lip flap. Then I put my car back into reverse and pressed harder on the accelerator.

*Too hard!*

The ice created a launch pad, and my car flew back, out of control. I "can't-handle-my-life" screamed and slammed on the brake. Unfortunately, the soles of my sandals were slick as snot. My foot glided right off the pedal, and I slammed into the neighbor's car!

Stunned, I stared forward, terrified to turn around. The car was obviously empty. At least I didn't have to worry about hurting anyone, but this was not good in so many ways. Due to my recent financial emergency, I had gotten behind on *all* my bills . . . including my car insurance.

It was first on my list to pay!

I even had the check made out, but it didn't change the fact it had lapsed over a month ago. A dollar could only go so far. If I didn't have it to spend, I couldn't poof it out of thin air. I took a deep breath, wriggled my toes, and stretched my neck. I was fine. And really, I wasn't going that fast. How bad could the damage be?

I was about to ease out of my car to assess the damage, when a guy with red flannel pants and white shirt came flying out of the neighbor's house. *What are the chances?* Blush crept up my cheeks and I facepalmed. The *same* Mr. December who I saw last night. His dark brows furrowed tightly as he plowed through the snow. He was clearly enraged about me hitting his car.

This day—this month—this life—had been too much! I thought I had finally caught a break by finding this budget apartment. Evidently my bad-luck streak was never going to end.

Fanning my face with both hands, I struggled to cool the sting in my eyes.

"I'm beautiful, strong, and brave," I said out loud. Even though my brain told me not to say it, I added, "without car insurance."

I don't cry.

Unless I do.

I swallowed the lump in my throat and opened my car door.

# Four

## Evan

## Five minutes earlier

Drawing my second spatula, I stood on guard like a knight in a duel as I slipped it under my jalapeno-and-cheese-six-egg omelet and carefully balanced it. The tension in the air was thick. I held my breath as I prepared for my double-spatula final flip. The capsaicin was pungent, wafting under my nose, making my mouth water. Just moments away from breakfast perfection. To complete this final spatula rotation, it would have to be quick and smooth. On three. One. I stepped closer to my pan, ensuring I was perfectly squared. Two. I swallowed and inhaled a deep breath. Ah. The fumes were so delicious. My tastebuds were begging for a taste.

Three . . .

BANG!

Startling, I dropped my spatulas, my omelet ripping as it cascaded down, and plopped right on top of my foot, sizzling on impact.

"Ahcha!" I yelled, as I kicked the smoldering-torch-of-delicious-ness off and fought back tears of pain as my foot scorched crimson. I still didn't know what died outside, but with my injured foot, I was pretty sure I had *egg*sterminated all hope of ever winning the World Cup. Not that I played soccer, or even had a ball. My sport was surfing, but . . . I could have at least dreamed about playing soccer before this *egg*sult.

Forget soccer.

My foot blazed!

I ran-hopped out the backdoor, not stopping until I plunged my foot into the fresh snowbank. I was freezing, dancing in place, but my burned foot thanked me. I quickly packed the top of my foot with snow and pivoted to return inside when something appeared out of place . . .

"What the?" I called out, feeling the burn in my foot now fleeting to my chest. I instantly forgot about my foot and ran to my baby! A Chevy I hadn't seen before, had rear ended my classic Mustang. I slid over to the bumper, my anger was boiling over.

This was my *baby*.

The car I spent my high school years restoring with my dad. It was really the only time we had ever spent together, and so all of my memories of him were with this car. I never even drove it unless the weather was perfect. "What happened to you?" I asked my car in a voice filled with concern.

A shuffling noise pulled my gaze from my car and onto a lady with braided pigtails and brightly painted makeup, slowly pacing toward me, tears running down her face. Her arms wrapped across her chest protectively. When her eyes met mine, she seemed to struggle to hold my gaze because she kept blinking. As mad as I had been, my anger melted away because she looked so afraid. She bit her bottom lip and paused before finally speaking in a tiny voice. "Is this your car? Please don't call the cops."

My eyes slid back to my car. I built this car to be a tank. This elf had managed to hit my bumper perfectly, placing a nice dent in the center, but in reality, it was only a bumper. Nothing that couldn't be easily swapped out. Her car took the brunt of the damage, as her fender was smashed. I didn't want to tell her that's what Chevies do, but it made me smirk a little as I stood. Struggling to balance on my good foot, I said, "Ah, yeah." My eyes narrowed as my brain caught up. I'd never seen this woman here before, but clearly, she had moved into the apartment across the alley. Which meant that creature I had seen last night—yeah. My cheeks heated despite the icy air. Perhaps my mom had been right about me needing to cool off the alien shows?

"It is my baby—I mean car." Hating to see a woman cry, I kept my tone even. I definitely didn't want to be responsible for new tears. "It doesn't look *too* bad," I tacked on calmly, then nodded toward her car. "Your car is much worse. It's not even drivable."

Her eyes skirted to the fender, brows pulling up high, and her hand flew over her mouth, "Oh no!" she exclaimed. "That's not good."

I staggered forward and ran my hand over her wheel housing, confirming what I had thought. "All you need is a fender." I inspected the dent, pressing against the tire, which wasn't flat. "It should be easy to fix. Your insurance company might not even require more than one estimate for this because it's such a clean dent. You only need the one part—"

Her chin started to quiver, and new tears budded in her eyes.

I rushed to ask, "What did I say?"

Judging from the way she rapidly shook her head, I thought she was going to go into a hysterical wail. Instead, she said in a voice that was barely above a whisper, "I didn't pay my insurance bill."

"OOOh." I stretched out the word to sound like it had five syllables.

"I'm not a bad person," she swiftly continued. "I lost my teaching job, and everything piled up. I had to pay double the rent to get into this apartment. It was either put a roof over my head," she bobbed her head toward her car, "or *insurance*."

"Right." I wouldn't say I came from a place of extreme privilege, but I always had parents who had my back. Exhibit one: I was living with them. I wasn't in a place to judge her.

Her eyes were wide and vulnerable. She sounded as if she'd been down on her luck. My gaze paced back to my car, and it was . . . fixable.

Nothing I couldn't buff out.

I was also fairly handy, and in a position to help her. "Well, you can't drive your car like that." I pointed to the fender rubbing on the wheel. "I can pound this out for you, to make it drivable, but I would feel bad knowing you were still driving without insurance—"

"Are you calling the cops?" She sucked back a loud breath that sounded like a hiccup, but I gathered it was actually her fighting back new tears.

"No," I reassured her. "I'm going to help you. I'm not a mechanic, but I can replace a fender for you. I'm a bit of an inventor and know a guy who sells me used parts for things. I should be able to get you a deal on what you need, and I can fix it for you."

Her eyes paced over my face like she was lost and looking for a way out. "Why would you do that?"

*Why would I do that?* I mused, as I was happy to help her.

Here she was, just a single woman down on her luck.

Wait a moment . . .

Single?

She didn't have anyone to call to help her. So, that meant she had to be single. Right? If she'd had a boyfriend, she clearly would have called him to help her. She didn't call anyone. So, she was single. It was perfect math. A single woman was exactly what *I* needed. Maybe if I helped her, she could help me? It made sense enough to me to try. Not wanting to come on too strong, I tried to downplay my offer by tossing a shoulder up. "It looks like you need a break."

"I do." She exhaled slowly. In a calmer voice, she tacked on, "I get paid today."

I nodded, refocusing on how she was dressed as an elf. "Is there somewhere you need to be?"

Her inhalation was so loud I thought she was choking, but somehow, she wasn't, exclaiming, "I'm so late for work! I'm going to get fired." She spun on her heel as if she was going to run back to her driver's seat.

I called out, "If you give me a second to grab some shoes, I can give you a ride." Her eyes latched back on me as if she was checking to see if she had heard me correctly and I added, "I would feel better to see you get there safely."

"I hate that I have to accept your offer when you have already been way too nice to me." Her lips curled into an appreciative smile.

My pulse started to pound harder when I realized what was happening. I had literally been sent this perfect single woman gift at the exact moment I needed her. I tossed up a lazy one-shoulder shrug. "It's my day off, and it's my pleasure." I motioned to the Jeep, parked next to my Mustang. "Let's take my Jeep. It's my winter car. You can hop in, and I'll grab shoes and I'll be right back."

"Thank you." Her voice was so sweet, it made me pause and look back. In the commotion of everything, I hadn't noticed how pretty she was. Now that she wasn't crying, her eyes brightened, shining on me, making me feel good about being able to help her. It was Saturday anyway, and I had less than two days to find a girlfriend. She was obviously put here for a reason. I shrugged my shoulders, pulling up one side of my lips. "Don't mention it."

# Five

## Jade

With short winter days, it was already dark by the time I finished my shift. The air was crisp, but at least no new snow was forecasted. I stood outside the coffee house, a coffee cup in each hand, scanning the curb for my ride. The hot guy from next door had taken my number when he dropped me off at the shoe store this morning and made me promise to text him when I got off work. I insisted I could call an Uber, but he reminded me I was broke.

He instantly won that argument.

I wiggled my toes, feeling the squish in my new boots. I had found a pair on clearance that was a half size smaller than what I needed, but the price was in my budget. I had reasoned it would be fine. Not like I had to stand on my feet for an eight-hour shift or anything.

Since I was late for work, it had been only *seven* hours.

Clearly, my feet were fine*ish*.

And at least I still had a job. I was lucky because Portia, my nice manager, had been working. If it had been, Christian, the new owner, I don't think I'd have been so lucky.

A bell-ringing Santa stood next to me, shaking his bell. I avoided looking at him. However, it felt awkward, and I suspected he had telepathic powers that sensed the loose change in my coat pocket. I shimmied my drinks into one hand and dug in my pocket, pulling out some lint and the forty-seven cents I had gotten as change from the shoe store.

Holding my cinched fist up, I scooted over to the bucket, and fed the coins one by one. Santa, who looked nothing like classic Santa, donned purple dreadlocks hanging out of the bottom of his backwards ball cap and a pierced lip. He smiled at me with even teeth peeking out. "What's your Christmas wish?"

"Huh?" I blinked as his question sparked my focus on all my current issues and run of bad luck. "It depends. How many wishes do I get for forty-seven cents?"

He chuckled. Not the typical full belly roll you'd expect from Claus. It was more of a sarcastic smirk. "It's not the amount that matters." As I was about to stroll away, his gaze latched onto me, like he expected me to actually tell him my wish. I snickered dismissively but he continued to stare. "Oh! Um. Yeah. So since you're taking orders, and if the price is right, I want bad stuff to stop happening to me long enough to get caught up from the bad stuff that has already happened." I curled my lips into an uneasy smile. He didn't reciprocate the smile, so I figured I had asked for too much. "Okay, then." I sidestepped back to the curb, right as Evan rolled up in his Jeep.

I opened the door, and got in, taking a moment to notice he was dressed in jeans and a cotton zip hoodie. That was innocent enough, but it was the crooked smile on his face that stuck out the most. Even though I hadn't seen many of his smiles, something about the way it curled higher on one side told me he was up to something. I dug into my bottom lip with my teeth, fighting to keep a straight face while my nerves tugged in my gut.

Proceeding with an air of caution, I slid in next to him, handing over the extra cup of coffee. "I made coffee as a thank you. I wanted it to be a surprise, so I guessed at your order."

He quirked an eyebrow while staring at the cup, not daring to touch it. "Oh really?"

Sitting this close to this handsome man didn't make me nervous at all. Okay, maybe a tiny bit nervous. Definitely excited. "Yeah, when you work as a barista, you hone a talent for being able to tell people's coffee orders by how they are dressed."

"And my red flannel pants tipped you off?"

"Well, partly." I pushed the cup further in front of him. "Please, take this. I promise it's good." I was unsure of how much I wanted to disclose about my secret skills. He finally took the cup, and I explained, "The red flannel said you like cozy, so I assumed you preferred a hot drink. It's later in the day, so I went with decaf."

"I can live with that," he hummed out, his lips tight as if he was waiting to seal his approval.

"I didn't peg you for a chocolate guy. I went with a caramel macchiato because they make a nice dessert drink, and I figured you'd already eaten dinner."

He pushed his chin forward. "I'd say you got one of my top three favorites."

"See?" My smile grew as he took a sip, a pleased grin spread across his face. "What's your top favorite?"

"I actually prefer iced, but it's freezing out, so the hot coffee is nice." He took another sip before setting it in the cup holder. As he pulled the Jeep away from the curb, he flashed me a teasing smile as if he was purposely stalling. "Thank you. You didn't need to get me anything, but in case there's a next time, I love chocolate peanut butter frappes."

"Well, who doesn't like chocolate peanut butter?" I chortled. "But that's one of those drinks that's totally more dessert than coffee. I bet you think it's extra protein."

"It can be—"

"Nope," I popped the p. "We don't use real peanut butter. We use syrup, but a lot of people think it's healthier. Most coffee shops use syrup unless you pay extra." I relaxed in my seat. Evan headed into the intersection, but instead of taking a left to the freeway toward our homes, he went straight, leading out of town. "I knew you were a serial killer!" I blurted out.

"What?" He chuckled, flashing me a confused look, but instead of denying it, he played along, "How'd you figure it out so fast?"

"That's not the way to our houses." I gestured to the road, my smile seeding even more. After our award-winning embarrassing meeting this morning, I had no pressure to impress him because he'd already seen me at my worst. I only had up to go. I held up a detective finger. "You were too eager to give me a ride home. I figured something was up. You're taking me to your abandoned farmhouse with a secret underground chamber where you take all your victims."

He kept one hand on the wheel, continuing to watch the road, but snuck a glance at me. "You like horror movies, don't you?"

"Like them, hmm," I mused while pressing a finger to my lip. "I like to figure them out."

"Oh, you're one of those people who talk constantly while you watch them?" He shot me an accusing glare, but the smile on his lips told me he was still joking.

"I can be quiet." I sealed my lips tightly and turned to peer out my window, attempting to figure out where we were going. We were obviously in an industrial area of town that I'd never been in, and it was looking very deserted. "So, which movie are we doing today?"

He let out an easy laugh I was beginning to recognize. "None. We are going to see my friend, Rash. He sells used car parts and has a fender for you."

"Woo. Wait. What?" I blinked cautiously, my gaze slamming back to him. "You have a friend named Rash, and you say that like it's normal."

"It's not abnormal." He kept a straight face, but I gathered he was messing with me. Instead of being nervous, I bit back a smirk. This had to be one of the strangest two-minute conversations I'd had. We'd clearly skipped normal small talk, and somehow bounced town, hunting for a man named Rash. It should have felt foolish, but my mind ruminated on how he had spent his time searching for a cheap fender when he didn't even know me.

Plus, I was the one who crashed his car . . .

*Who is this guy?*

"Can I ask how much this fender is going to cost?" I asked in a serious tone, even though I really didn't want to know. Maybe

I wanted to know a little. It was a bit like getting a Pap smear. Necessary to endure, but I mostly just wanted the uncomfortable part over. "I did get paid today, but in case you haven't figured it out, I'm what you call a nillionaire."

He chuckled his easy grin again. Now, I not only recognized it, but was beginning to enjoy it. "No money?"

I shot a finger gun at him. "Ding, ding, ding."

"I didn't ask about the money," Evan replied to my previous question. "Rash isn't much of a talker. He just told me to come on out." Evan turned onto a narrow road leading up to a small square house sitting next to a large industrial shop. With the only light coming from the glow of the TV from a darkened window, and a small house light above the shop, it was *extra* creepy dark. Evan slowed as he approached. The tires bouncing around the snow ruts were the only sound. To fill in the silence I whispered, "Why do I feel like this is a bad sequel to a series where I never watched the first movie, so I have no clue what's going on?"

Rash must have seen us approach as he was standing on his step—*with a saw.*

Swallowing, I was so out of my comfort zone, I sat stiffly, waiting for cues from Evan about what we would do next.

"Name that movie." Evan's smooth voice rolled out.

I pointed an accusing finger toward him. "Don't even."

Evan rolled down his window, and called out, "Hey, Rash. How's it going?"

Rash staggered up to the Jeep, nodding at each one of us. "Not bad." Other than the dark goatee that wrapped his mouth, he was bald, but he had kind eyes that he latched onto me. "You need a fender?"

"Yeah. I have a Cobalt," I squeaked out.

"That's your first problem." A smile crept on his lips, putting me a little more at ease as he leaned on the open window. "What year?"

"Ah, 2015."

"I got a fifteen." He ran a hand over his already smooth goatee. "If you got cash, I could do seventy-five bucks."

"Deal." I spurted back quickly before he changed his mind. The price was right but oddly, I felt like we were doing something illegal, which felt adventurous, and made excitement bubble in my chest.

"You guys can pull up next to the door." Rash motioned to the shop. "If you want to come in, you can, but there's no need." He flashed his hand saw at us. "It's still on the car, so it will take me a moment to grab it."

"We'll wait out here," Evan quickly agreed, and rolled up his window as he drove the Jeep forward. "Now that we know what movie this is, we might need some snacks."

I laughed inwardly, but not in an amused way. "I can't even think about it." Most of the mental tension which had built up all day was now released. This fender would cost me a fraction of what I had thought since Evan was fixing it for me. I still had no idea why he'd agreed to help me. I stared at Evan, feeling like I'd made a new friend. I wasn't sure how I'd ever repay him, but I would try. "I have no idea why you're helping me so much . . ." I paused for beat. "I'm sure you're busy, but if there is anything I can do for you, don't hesitate to ask."

His cheeks twitched, teasing he was going to say something. I was sitting so close to him that I could see a glimmer of something in his eye. My eyes narrowed, inspecting him. "There is something, isn't there?"

He blinked, but didn't pause. His words fell out in rapid fire, "I should keep my mouth shut because I don't want you to think I'm some weirdo."

"No," I pressed. "You dragged me out here to meet a guy named Rash, with a saw, and I haven't left yet. How much worse can it be?"

He let out a heavy sigh, that opened his thoughts to me. "So, you know how you didn't pay your insurance, but you were still driving, and that didn't make you a bad person?" He gestured toward me. "We're on the same page, right? I totally get you were in a bind."

"Right?" I scratched my chin, wondering where he was going with this. I hoped he wasn't still thinking about calling the cops . . .

"I'm sort of in a bind, too." He raked his hand through his hair and slid it down the back of his head until it hooked on his neck. "I could tell the truth to get out of it, or make something else up, but there's this guy who drives me crazy. It's my cousin, Rob, and he's coming over for Christmas dinner tomorrow." His face pinched like he was sucking on a sour lemon. "He is one of those cocky guys who always wins. And I hate that about him. And he has this fiancée, and I don't even have a girlfriend, but I accidentally told my mom I did, and before I could take it back, she told my grandma—"

My hand flew over my mouth, and I blurted out, "But you don't have a girlfriend!"

He tossed up a one-shoulder shrug. "Not unless you can count my life-size R2D2."

My volume ticked up a notch as if from the delight of cracking a mystery. "You want me to come over for dinner tomorrow and pretend we're dating."

"I mean . . ." He lifted his shoulders, holding them in pause. "Since you're right across the alley and can't drive anywhere anyway—it makes sense." He dropped his shoulders, tilting his head toward me while he tacked on, "My mom makes awesome lasagna."

*He was asking me out!* My inner self turned a few amazing cartwheels.

*Not a real date.* Now, I slumped in my seat.

*But I didn't care about the logistics.*

I hadn't been on a date in months, and he was asking me on a fake date! My heart pounded against my ribcage, and I quickly nodded with a full smile on my face. "I'll do it."

He gave me a suspicious side eye. "You will?"

"Yes." I held up my finger. Not in hesitation, but I was curious. "On one condition."

His expression deflated into a frown. It happened so suddenly, and he was overly animated about it, it made me want to laugh when he groaned out, "What's that?"

I did the gossip lean in. "Tell me, what's up?"

His brows furrowed down. "What do you mean what's up?"

"What's the deal with Rob? Why don't you have a girlfriend? You know, give me details." I left out the part about how he was obviously gorgeous. He should have women flocking to him. At least until they learned he lived with his parents, but I'm sure there had to be a reason for that. I was intrigued.

He made one of those coughs that sounded fake, but as his eyes almost bugged out of his head, I knew he wasn't choking. "Do you think it's that easy to summarize?"

"I don't think it's hard. I mean." –I gestured with to myself with both hands— "I don't have a boyfriend because I dated this guy for a year. We were the fun couple who always went out and met with friends. It was a total blast. When I lost my job, he ditched me because I wasn't *fun* anymore." My suppressed anger over my financial situation started to bubble up, so I quickly cut myself off. "That's my story." I pointed to him. "Now you go."

"He sounds like a total jerk." Evan's voice was softer, as he held my direct gaze a little longer than what would have been expected, before saying, "I'm sorry that happened to you."

"No big deal." I shrugged with my face. It probably would have needed to be over sooner or later. My unemployment helped me figure that out. I really couldn't care less about him. "It's your turn."

"I was engaged." His voice floated out as if the words were too sour to hold in his mouth.

"Woo. *Engaged*?" I tucked my leg up underneath me and pivoted in my seat to get a better look at him. "That's deeper than I thought. What happened?"

"Two years ago, I was doing everything my parents wanted me to do. I was living on my own, working at the big office corporate America gig, which I hated. And I was engaged to this girl I met at church. You know the story. It was like a movie." He flicked his hand out in a gesture. "She had the perfect family, and my parents were friends with her parents. We had chemistry together, so I asked her out. We hit it off, fell in love, and it was perfect. After we dated for a year, everyone kept asking when I would propose. I didn't think there was a rule that I had to set an expiration date on that sort of thing, but that's what everyone wanted from me, so I did."

His words fell away, and his facial expression was locked forward, as if he was concentrating on something outside the car, in the distance. He was quiet for a long time, I started to wonder if he forgot I was here. His Adam's apple bobbed before he finally continued, "I felt as if I was watching my life play out more than I was living it." He finally skirted his gaze back to me. "Have you ever felt like that?"

"Lately, I have been in survival mode, dodging one curve ball after the next. I don't feel like I'm watching, as much as I am reacting," I held an air of teasing in my voice, but he maintained his serious expression.

"Sometimes you don't know you're on the wrong path until something opens your eyes. For me, that something was as simple as finding an incriminating text message on her phone from my cousin Rob. I swore it was a joke that Rob had set up to get to me, but when I confronted her about it, she didn't deny she'd been seeing him."

"Oh." My lips made a perfect circle as I connected the dots. Evan's heartbreak of betrayal had to have been unbearable. I was oddly honored he was able to be this vulnerable with me. That had to be brutal to talk about. "No wonder you don't want him to win. He stole your fiancée. He's not a nice man."

"My ex." His lashes lowered back to his cup that he'd retrieved from the cup holder and picked at the edge of his lid for a long moment. "I have no idea why I told you that."

"Because I made you tell me why you didn't have a girlfriend," I quipped, then added in a forced cheerful tone, "I'll go to dinner tomorrow, and we'll totally show Mr. Not-so-Nice."

His eyes narrowed, skeptically. "Are you sure?"

"Yeah. Like you said, I can't drive anywhere anyway. Now I definitely want to help you show up your cousin." A loud pop sounded, causing us both to startle, and out of reflex, I grabbed the dash with my free hand. "What was that?"

"The shop door slamming." He motioned forward with his finger. "Rash is coming back."

"That didn't take long at all." I breathed a sigh of relief as I had almost completed the Saw encounter, and I hadn't even screamed. This day, that had started awful, kept getting better.

"No, it didn't." He opened his door, calling back. "You can stay inside. I'll load it in the trunk, and then I'll take you home."

"Thank you," I said, but I don't think he heard me as he had shut his door. I glanced in rearview mirror as he handed Rash some cash. I hadn't given Evan any money. Now, I'd have to pay him back. I was starting to feel like a burden with all these favors. Then I remembered our fake date tomorrow.

Goosebumps trickled down my spine.

It wasn't a real date . . . so I shouldn't be excited for real. Right?

# Six

# Evan

After busting out a couple of last-minute, running-into-my-ex pull ups on my door frame, I dropped to the floor and opened the bi-fold closet doors. Scanning the pile of board shorts on one side and stretchy waistband pants on the other, I got overwhelmed by my lack of options. I wasn't one of those guys you'd call fashion . . . whatever. I don't even know the word for a guy who cared about clothes. I liked comfort.

The knot in my gut told me tonight I needed to level up and wear dinner-appropriate pants. While I did have a pair of once-worn funeral pants, I avoided those like the plague. The doorbell rang and the bottom dropped out of my stomach. I was more nervous tonight than when I had an actual date. It had a little to do with Jade, as I hoped I didn't come off as some creep. She really did seem awfully sweet. However, most of my anxiety had to do with how I was lying to my entire family and hoped not to get caught.

Part of me couldn't believe I was attempting to pull off a fake date. Never in a million years had I thought I could find a date on such short notice. And then have her actually agree to this shenanigan. I still don't believe I asked. Before I knew what I was doing, the words tumbled out of my mouth. *She's the crazy one to agree to this!* Crazy, or maybe just fun? I rubbed the side of my recently shaved face. She seemed to be a fun-loving spirit who was willing to help, and I didn't hate the thought of spending time with her.

*Maybe it would be fun?*

Distant laughter cut through my concentration, cueing for the arrival of my cousin.

No, *not fun.*

Then, a softer giggle I had memorized followed.

Holly was here.

My heart was put in a chokehold.

I had clearly forgotten the effect Holly had on me.

How could she come to *my* house, with all *our* history? Never in a million years would I go anywhere to intentionally see her again. My mom wasn't one to meddle in my life, but it was out of character for her to go along with it. Even though a massive boundary had been crossed, I didn't blame my mom. This was clearly the finagling of Rob. He was up to something. How Holly went along with it was also beyond me. Evidently, Holly was as big a piece of work as Rob.

My eyes paced between the board shorts, and the stretchy pants as my adrenaline ramped up. "Whatever," I muttered as I pulled the funeral pants off the hanger and started to leave to shower. A niggling you-want-to-dominate voice in the back of my head piped up, and before I lost my nerve, I quickly turned back, snatching the matching funeral shirt, and tie. "This is unreal. I'm dressing up to eat in my own kitchen," I murmured while I crossed the hall to the bathroom.

"Evan!" My mom's perfect-hostess voice called from the bottom of the stairs. "Everyone is here."

I hollered down, "I'll be five minutes." I got into the shower as quickly as possible. It wasn't until I dropped the soap for the second time, I self-assessed something was up with my grip. It was undoubtedly medical because it wouldn't be anything else.

It clearly wasn't seeing Holly again for the first time in two years. Or seeing Rob *with* Holly.

And it obviously had nothing to do with my fake date because . . . well, I was totally calm about that.

Okay, I was lying to myself, and it was D. All of the above.

By the time I dressed and successfully managed not to strangle myself with my tie, a cool sweat beaded down my lower back.

So much for the shower.

I slathered on another layer of deodorant and was about to call it good when the doorbell rang again. I bolted down the stairs as if taking hurdles, dodging my mom's poinsettia plants that were lined up, one on each step. Mom said the plants were festive. I referred to them as a fire hazard. Desperate for my mom—or anyone for that matter— not to get to Jade first, I flew to the foyer, slamming my entire body against the door just in time.

When I yanked open the door, I was instantly confused. The Jade I remembered wearing braided pigtails and painted rosy cheeks, wasn't here. This Jade had her hair down, pulled to the side, with soft waves and muted makeup that left me staring at her as if I was seeing her for the first time. Sure, I'd thought she was pretty before, but now she was stunning. Seeing her like this made me want to stand up taller and find random reasons to flex my biceps.

"Hey," her voice came out hushed and unsure.

"Hey…" I totally squeaked like a prepubescent boy on that one. Wincing, I inhaled deeply and tried again. "How are you?"

"Good," she quipped, gazing past me into the Christmas-cluttered foyer.

"G-Great." I stumbled over my fat tongue as I opened the door wider, now feeling like a complete tool because I'd clearly forgotten how to speak. "You can come inside."

"Is that Jade?" Mom's voice was noticeably closer, as she was already in the foyer. A dying-to-know smile was pinned on her face.

"Yes." I shimmied closer to Jade, not sure how to act. We hadn't discussed any ground rules, but I had to make this somewhat convincing. I put my arm around Jade's back, pulling her to my side. I prayed that she wouldn't slap me, but she didn't waste a beat, and slid her arm around me as well. A swirl of sweet vanilla, better than any frosting I'd ever smelled wafted under my nose. Obviously, it was Jade's perfume, but I had a hard time pretending not to notice. "This is my mother, Pearl—" My voice dropped off. Both Jade and my mom had gemstone names.

That was an odd coincidence that I'm sure had nothing to do with anything…

It's not like we were meant to be soulmates or anything.

My dad rounded the corner with an easy grin and waved toward Jade. I motioned to him. "My dad, Tony."

Dad was bald, thirty pounds overweight, and he had on his ugly Christmas Rudoph sweater he wore every year. Rudoph's nose lit up with an actual real Christmas bulb. The first year he had it, I was only ten years old, and it worked well, staying fully lit. Over the years, it must have developed a short in the wiring because now it would randomly blink, or go ominously dull at the most random times, like it was possessed. The thing used to give me nightmares as a child, and I can't understand why Mom hasn't "lost it" in the wash by now. He obviously still loved it, and true to fashion, Rudolph's nose creepily winked at Jade when Dad leaned in, shaking her hand. "Nice to meet you, Jade. Welcome to our home." I wasn't at all worried about Dad liking Jade or vice versa. My dad had practically earned a Ph. D in people skills for all the years he drove a city bus. He always put everyone at ease and could smooth out any turbulence.

"Thank you," Jade responded, standing a little stiffly with her eyes locked on Rudolph's creepy winking nose. This had to be awkward for her, and I vowed to do anything possible to help her feel comfortable. I was about to invite her further inside to take a seat, but something happened. I didn't even have to look; my body was so attuned to my ex's Holly's scent. Her smell was a tad spicy, like amber musk, instantly warming my lungs. Come to think of it, it was a great prelude to being stabbed in the back.

Holly had entered the room. I didn't think it was possible for anyone to ever glow up more than she had already been. She was just one of those women born with a face of a seraphim, but I grinded my back teeth trying not to notice how huggable she looked in her cream sweater dress. Her turquoise eyes radiated with so much blue and green sparkle; you'd think you were lost at sea.

I wasn't playing my C game tonight. The only way to win was to pretend she didn't affect me. I planted my gaze on her and smiled as if I was on top of the world. "Holly." Her eyes were like a vortex that sucked me in, and I struggled to remember what I was supposed to be doing. Thankfully, Jade dug her fingers into my back, giving them a twisty squeeze, busting me out of the Holly vortex.

That was close. I shook off my tingles and I pointed out the rest of the crew. "This is Rob." I did a double take after barely looking at him the first time. Rob had a mustache. That was new. It made him look older. Furrier. Did Holly like that?

I tried not to stare, sweeping my gaze at my grandma, adding, "Grandma Clementine." Grandma leaned over her cane, peeking in from the other room as if coming all the way into the foyer was too much work. I doubted she could even see Jade since she was so nearsighted, she usually carried a magnifying glass in her apron pocket. I didn't blame her, though, we were extra crammed in this Christmas village foyer. I set my eyes back on Jade. She had a mischievous sparkle in her eyes, oddly putting me at ease. For the first time, I felt this could work. "Everyone, this is my girlfriend, Jade."

I had rehearsed this moment in my head so many times over the last twenty-four hours, but the way Jade Hallmark-movie smiled at everyone, and then latched her eyes back lovingly on me, beat anything I could have imagined. She was obviously playing to win, and a massive rush of relief rushed into my lungs.

My mom spoke waving her spatula in hand like it was traffic flags. "Dinner will be ready in a few minutes. Why don't you all have drinks in the living room and get to know one another."

Rob almost pounced on my mom. "I'll help you serve drinks, Pearl."

"Thank you, Robby." She called him by his childhood nickname and placed a hand on his shoulder, pausing in thought before motioning to the China cabinet in the adjacent living room. "Glasses are in there. The drinks are in the kitchen." Her inquiring eyes shot to me. "Evan, can you help Rob?"

"Suuuure," I called after my mom, who had already left the room with Rob on her heels. My dad and grandma wandered into the living room, and Holly was left standing next to Jade. I hated to leave Jade by herself with Holly. Not because I didn't think Jade could hold her own, but I was oddly feeling vulnerable with Holly so near me. I could handle Rob being Rob. That was a guy rivalry thing, but Holly . . . I breathed out, feeling the sweat build in the creases of my hands. If anyone could tell that Jade was a fake date, it'd be her. She knew me, and all my mannerisms more than anyone. I couldn't let her see she was having this effect on me. I leaned over and whispered in Jade's ear, "I guess I have to compete for best host with Rob. Are you okay talking to Holly?"

I thought she might snicker, but instead she threw her head back and laughed as if I'd said the funniest thing in the world. Out of the corner of my eye, I could see Holly watching us. Jade didn't take her eyes off me as she wrapped her other arm around me and drew me closer, bringing her lips to my ear, and whispering back, "Don't worry about me. I have seen this movie before. I know *exactly* what to do." Before she pulled away, she shocked me by pressing her lips to my earlobe for a quick in-Holly's-face nibble, and an electric shock jolted the side of my head, stunning me into a system malfunction.

I couldn't even turn my head. I was utterly immobilized!

She had a flirty we're-going-to-win smile on her face before she winked and took a few steps toward Holly. She quickly started a conversation by complimenting Holly's dress. Together they entered the living room, leaving me struggling to feel my face.

That was *not* what I had been expecting!

"Evan!" Mom called from the kitchen. "The wine is waiting for you."

I ran my hand along the side of my face, feeling it tingle as it slowly thawed. Then followed her voice to the kitchen.

Maybe this wasn't going to be so bad?

Rob cornered me by the island, with a glass in each hand. "Hey," his voice was hushed while his gaze was locked on the closed kitchen door. "I ah, wanted to bring something up while I had you alone."

I grabbed the closest wine bottle, and corkscrew, as I was anxious to do anything other than look at Rob's arrogant skinny face in my personal space. "Yeah," I muttered as if his mere presence was putting me to sleep.

"I know we had some issues in the past and all, but I was hoping we could put everything behind us. I ah, think things worked out for the better this way anyway. For both of us."

"You don't say." I jabbed the corkscrew in the cork and twisted it, funneling my frustration with Rob into each turn. I used all my strength to shove that thing deep into Rob—I mean, the bottle. Man that was satisfying.

"Yeah. I mean, you and Jade." He motioned to me, and then hooked his thumb back to himself, adding, "Me and Holly."

"Right." I gritted my teeth and yanked on the cork, pulling it out in one piece.

"I uh, wanted to come on this trip for one main reason." Rob shifted on his feet, leaning back on his heels as if he was pumping up his ego even more. "You know we got engaged, and I want to ask for your blessing. We are going to get married no matter what you say, but I don't want family gatherings to be awkward."

I lowered one eyelid, trying to calm the twitch that was starting to develop in my eye. It had to be because I was holding back my desire to slam my fist into his face, and it was building too much pressure. Now my ear was ringing because I clearly didn't hear him correctly. Did he just say he wanted my blessing? My anger boiled up my chest, and out my arm, triggering my fingers to curl into a fist. I'll give him a blessing—

"Boys!" My mom's cheery voice rang out. She had popped the top half of her body though the swinging kitchen door, appearing so joyful, even wearing her Christmas red lipstick, something she never did. She always said redheads can't wear red, but boy, did she look festive today. "What's the hold up on the drinks?"

I blinked once to refocus. Then added a second blink to shut off my anger. I couldn't do this to my mom. Rob wanted me to punch him to ruin my mom's dinner and make me look bad. This was a trap Rob had set to show the family I was the bully. I was on to him, and frankly over it. "I'm so over Holly, you can marry her in my living room for all I care." Jerking my head toward the door, I quickly filled the glasses with wine and said, "Let's go."

# Seven

## Jade

I led Holly to the plaid sofa next to the Christmas tree. It appeared Evan's mom still took the time to decorate the tree with the homemade ornaments from Evan's youth. My eyes caught an especially cute one, a paper stocking with cotton balls glued above his picture. He had a fun haircut with bangs in the front, and what looked like lightning bolts shaved into the near-buzzed sides. Clearly, he wore the getting-ready-to-rock-on look, and it was adorable.

I glanced back to Holly. If I'd met her on the street, I wouldn't have taken a second look, but everything about how she stared down her perfect nose at Evan, made me wish I had met her at work. I would totally pretend to spill iced coffee all over her. I couldn't imagine being in Evan's position and having to entertain his family with his cheating ex-fiancée.

I don't know why it bothered me so much.

Evan was hardly a friend, having known him for only two days, but he'd been extremely nice to me. I got the impression he was one of those nice guys who got walked on often. As I stared at Holly, I knew who'd done the walking.

Correction: traipsing.

"So . . . Holly." I flashed her more teeth than a smile. "I love your hair color. You must tell me your stylist's name. She did such a great job on your highlights." I bit back the part about how I could still tell she wasn't a natural blonde, but I didn't want to be a mean girl. That wasn't why I was here.

She stayed quiet, but smirked when Rob returned with two half-full glasses of red wine. He handed one to me first and passed the second one over to Holly while barely acknowledging her. He promptly squeezed between Holly and me, planting his gaze on me. "Tell us, how did you meet Evan?"

Evan appeared in the doorway with another wine glass, handing it to his grandma. His eyes locked on mine, and he nodded slightly as if yielding to me. "It's such a funny story, but actually, I crashed into his car." Running a hand through my hair, I tucked it behind my ear and pulled a bigger smile on my face. "It truly was fate stepping in, though, because ever since that happened, we've been inseparable."

Rob's eyes stayed dialed in on me. "And how long has that been?"

My eyes narrowed as his tone wasn't that sincere. I was careful not to name a time frame because I wasn't sure if Evan had given one. "A while."

"It doesn't matter." Evan swooped in, sitting next to me on the couch. Now we were all squished on the couch, sitting four people wide, with Rob and me still hip to hip in the middle. I leaned on Evan out of need for space and because I didn't want to feel Rob's boney hip. Evan tacked on, "I feel like we've known each other our whole lives, right Sugar Boo?"

He cringed as soon as the terrible nickname came out of his lips. I bit back my giggle by sipping my wine, with my shoulders noticeably shaking. Like he was trying to stifle me, Evan placed his hand on my knee. A shiver shot right through me, instantly melting all my humorous thoughts. Goosebumps traveled up my leg, and didn't stop until my cheeks flushed.

*Yikes!*

I took his hand into mine, lacing my fingers with his, and winked. "Right. Sugar Boo." I didn't feel like laughing anymore. Maybe I had been single way too long, but I hadn't ever experienced instant chemistry with someone just from them touching me.

Evan's grandma sat in an armchair near the stone fireplace and spoke in a voice that was deeper than what you'd expect for someone barely five feet tall. "Are you from here?" Her eyes locked on me. Everyone's eyes followed, including Evan's. Wow. I hadn't noticed how seriously dreamy his blue eyes were. Like right out of a photo-shopped magazine. "No." I wagged my head briefly, trying to pull my gaze away from Evan. "I actually grew up in the Midwest."

Rob leaned over, physically butting his perfectly aerodynamic face in. "I adore the Midwestern states. They are so wholesome. And how did you end up on the East coast?"

"Well." My gaze slid to the side, mentally retracing my life. "I graduated college with a degree in history, but no plan. I heard about the New York City teaching fellowships and applied." Although it was Rob who had asked the question, I shifted my gaze to Evan's grandmother, engaging her. "If you have a bachelor's degree, you can apply even if you don't have a teaching license. If you get accepted, you are hired to teach in an underserved public school while taking master's classes in education—"

"So, you're a teacher," Rob cut me off again. Even though he was sitting on the same couch I was, he stretched his neck as if he was hard of hearing and had a nosey-all-in-my-business expression that reminded me of a dog salivating. He clearly wasn't trying to hide the fact he was taking social scores.

"Er . . ." I bit my lip, pausing. I wasn't sure how much acting Evan wanted me to do. Was I supposed to make up a fabulous career or tell them the truth? The truth would be more believable. "I was," I affirmed before adding, "unfortunately, the district had cuts, so I was dismissed from the program before I could complete my master's degree. Without access to the program, my teacher's license is invalid. I'm taking some time to figure out my next career move right now." I rubbed my ear, pretending to adjust my earring. "I work at a coffee shop called Coffee Loft on Huntington Avenue at the moment."

"Coffee?" Rob's brows sprang up, his smirk seeding on his lips. "I served a lot of coffee in my internship days." He cackled as if he was competing in some annoying duck call contest. "Now that I'm a partner in my law firm, I won't be doing that anymore."

Evan squeezed my hand hard, sending me a be-tough signal.

I fought the urge to say something snarky. I was saved by Evan's mom calling from the kitchen, "Dinner is ready!"

Everyone filed into the kitchen, leaving Evan and me to loiter in the back. As we stood, he stayed in character by not dropping my hand. He leaned in, whispering in my ear, "You're doing great. Just one more hour."

I had half-forgotten I was only supposed to pretend to care about this interaction because it had somehow gotten personal. I wanted to wipe that smug grin off Rob's face. Rob had become a weird placeholder for all the random people who'd been jerks to me in the last year. All the times I walked away and never had the chance to fight back.

I wasn't only fighting for Evan anymore.

This had gotten personal.

# EIGHT

## Evan

"If tomatoes are fruit." Jade set her fork down from her final bite of lasagna. "I'm voting ketchup and all tomato sauce in general are smoothies, which therefore means—"

"Don't even say ketchup is a healthy food," I placed my palm on the table between us, cutting her off with a teasing tone.

Pulling both perfectly groomed brows up defensively, she went on, "Who said that was what I was going to say? You wouldn't let me finish."

My grandma was chuckling, and even though she had her share of wrinkles, I could easily pick out her dimples. She was enjoying this way too much, so I gave her a playful glare. "Grandma, you cannot pick Jade's side on this. We are blood."

Jade and I had been bantering back and forth the whole meal. She was so witty. She had my parents and my grandma laughing the entire meal. Rob and Holly, who sat directly across from us, didn't say a word as they sullenly ate their food.

I had never seen my grandma so amused in my life. Grandma raised her hands like she was under arrest. "I never pick sides. I was merely laughing. Besides." Her lashes lowered, but they didn't completely conceal the humored sparkle in her pale blue eyes when she pretended to mutter. "Tomatoes are a vegetable."

"Oh!" Jade's jaw dropped all the way down. "You did not just say that."

Grandma tucked her bottom lip in, but it only fed her giant smirk. "They are a vegetable, or why would you put them in salad?"

"To make salad not toxic," Jade disputed, and the whole table, minus Rob and Holly, laughed.

Holly drained the last of her wine. As soon as her empty glass returned to the table, Rob retrieved the wine bottle and tipped it over to fill her glass. "Easy there," I teased Holly in the first direct comment I made to her all night. "We don't want a hair-holding situation again." Sitting next to Jade must have inflated my ego because I was never one to be confrontational. I held Holly's gaze as if I was daring her to remember our first meeting.

My parents had been bugging me to ask her out for months. When I saw her at a party, I started to pay attention to her. She wasn't much of a party girl. She quickly got ill, and all her friends ditched her. I found her on the deck, barfing over the railing, and made myself useful by holding her hair.

That's all I ever was to her . . . useful.

She used me until she ran out of uses.

Jade's hand randomly touching my thigh pulled me from my memory. She had an earth-to-Evan smile on her face, and she was laughing as she said, "I volunteered to help with dessert. Can you help with the cheesecake?"

I heard what she had asked, but I clearly wasn't functional. Her hand was still on my leg.

*She should not be allowed to touch me without proper warning!*

I wasn't emotionally immature or anything, but her touch was the antidote to Holly's memories. It set off a tsunami of shimmers that rocketed through my body, sending me back into failure-to-operate mode for the second time tonight. "Ch-cheese," I stuttered, still feeling the tingles resonate in my limbs. S-Sure." I slid from my chair, wholly shocked my legs could still do the leg thing. "I'll h-help you."

We ducked into the kitchen together, giggling like two partners in crime. As soon as the door was shut, Jade locked her eyes on me. "Boy, you got it *bad* for Holly. No wonder you had to deploy the fake date."

"What are you talking about?" I scoffed while I moved to the fridge, grabbed my mom's five-pound, cheery cheesecake, and set it on the counter.

"Your mom made that." Jade's eyes drifted to the cake as she thankfully dropped the previous topic. "That looks better than the ones we sell at the Coffee Loft. She should totally make these for us."

"You should tell her that." I grabbed the plates and forks and set them on the counter, while scanning the wall magnet for the perfect knife. "She's always wanted to have her own bakery."

"Tell her that?" Jade grabbed a fork and dug it right into the center of the cake. "I'll take orders."

I barely heard what she was saying because my eyes were locked on her fork sticking out of the center of the cake. "You can't eat out of the middle, you, you uncivilized person!"

She scraped off a layer of cherry filling and brought the fork to her mouth, clearly not sorry for ruining the cake.

"Who are you?" I kidded, pretending to be repulsed because I was actually disgusted, but didn't want to act like I was not cool. I slid the cake closer to me and positioned myself between the cake and her. "You can't eat the cake like that, you hog!"

"It's so good." She swiped the fork in her mouth. "You should try it."

"I'm going to try it like a normal person." I picked up the knife and sliced twelve perfect slices, making sure to keep the part Jade had eaten all on *her* slice. We had all the slices dished out on plates, lined up ready to serve.

And that's where it all went south.

I'm not a waiter. I should never be allowed to serve any food.

Lesson learned. I'll jot that down somewhere in my free time.

I tried to balance a plate on my arm like those fancy servers do, but it didn't even last three seconds before it flipped off my arm, plopping the cake down on the floor.

That should have been the end of it—but Jade . . . she wore a rascal smile, and she should clearly have taken all the blame. The spark was in her eye as soon as the cake splattered. She needle-nose-dolphin dove, swiping the biggest chuck right off the floor with her bare hands.

She was savage.

Also maybe a little unstable.

I didn't have to wait to see where this was going. This wasn't about a three-second rule. I'm no idiot. I grabbed a piece of cake from the counter and smooshed it into the side of her face while she struggled to get off the floor. She screamed, but her terror quickly transitioned to deep belly laughs which only set me off into the hugest rush of laughter I'd ever felt.

But I had an issue.

*She wasn't done!*

She grabbed my leg. That was her best defense. She was weak. Undoubtedly, she had no idea who she was up against. As she swiped the cake from her cheek, she tried to stand, but now the floor was slick, and she slipped. That didn't stop her from reaching all the way up and smashing a handful of cake right into my chest. "Stop!" I called between fits of laughter. "Truce. We must stop. People need to eat this cake."

She was finally able to find her footing, but she acted as if she didn't trust me when she took a stance against the wall, staring me down. "Truce?" she echoed.

"Yes." I motioned to the floor smeared in cheese and cherry filling. "My mom is going to kill you."

"Me?" She motioned to herself. With her plaster of cream cheese and cherry filling on the side of her head, she looked like she had been raised from the dead. I couldn't stop another fit of laughter.

Her eyes slid to the side. She was obviously trying to create a diversion as she planned her next attack. I wasn't letting her get away with that. I saw my chance, quickly swiping another slice from the counter. She was already running toward the exit. I was fast, grabbed her arm, pulling her back. I was *not* as smooth as I had planned because she slipped again. She dominoed me down with her, but not before she smashed the cake that I held right between us. She landed on top of me in the perfect little cheesecake human sandwich. She didn't move. Her dark hair cascaded down, framing her face.

I held my breath.

My heart motored rapidly from the laughter to the food fighting, and then there was the way her eyes hooked mine. Her eyes were kryptonite, blasting all memories I had ever had of Holly, and instantly filling that void with something I hadn't even seen coming.

"Evan!" My mom's voice sliced through the air like a hot knife on butter. "My cake!"

Jade's eyes bugged out of her head as she scampered to get off me. Humored tears ran down my face by the time I had finally managed to stand up, and then I saw them . . .

The cherry-on-top moment I couldn't have made up.

My whole family crowded at the door. They apparently had seen Jade and me lying on the floor together, rolling in cheesecake.

Grandma was almost choking with laughter. So was my dad. Holly was stoned-faced and backed out of the room with Rob on her heels.

When I locked my gaze back on Jade, she gazed at me as if we had suddenly created our own secret club. A world where only we understood the language, and everyone else didn't matter. Like a camera snapping a picture, my heart twisted as it captured this moment perfectly, saving it. I bit down on the side of my lip, as my heart continued to swell. Before I had a chance to rationalize it, I gave up. Jade was too powerful. This was the exact moment I started to fall for Jade.

# Nine
## Jade

"Did you see your mom's face?" I winced while ducking into Evan's Jeep, freshly changed into new jeans and an oversized comfy sweater. I took a moment to notice he had recently updated the air freshener in here, as Christmas tree pine smell permeated the air. It was festive, and I liked it. But it didn't do enough to wash away my guilt.

I had left the party right after the cheesecake brawl, because there was no way I could clean up without a shower. As soon as everyone else left, Evan texted me to meet him in his Jeep to get my car from his shop. "I could cry. She was so mad at me."

"She wasn't mad at you." He tilted his head to the side as if he was mulling something over. "Well, she was upset her cheesecake was ruined, but I told her what you said about selling them, and she was totally flattered. I think she'd be interested."

"Really." I pulled my door shut and buckled in, my nerves calming down. Not all the way down, but enough so I didn't hyperventilate. "Did she say so?"

"She didn't say it directly, but she's not the type to admit that. She's always been overly modest. Her cheeks got a little pink, and she started wiping the already spotless kitchen counters. That's what she does when she's wanting to overthink things."

I bit back a smirk, clearly seeing the path to make it up to her. "I will ask my boss tomorrow when I go to work."

Evan started the Jeep, letting it idle for a moment. "Are you ready to see your car?"

"Yeah, I am. I can't believe you fixed it already," I rambled into the change of subject. "That was amazing service."

Putting his car into gear, he backed out saying, "It wasn't a big deal."

I didn't realize prior to now, I had a thing for voices, and Evan's baritone voice made the tips of my lips turn up. It was unlike anything I had ever heard. I wouldn't call it raspy, but it had enough hoarse intonations that it was unlike anything I'd ever heard. I could easily listen to it for hours. I sighed, relaxing in my seat, when my memory pulled something up. "Oh." I held up my finger to interject in the silence. "I still have to repay you for the money you gave Rash."

"No." He shook his head admittedly. "Don't worry about it. You did an amazing job acting. I would pay a thousand dollars to see Holly and Rob's faces in the kitchen again . . ." His voice trailed off into a hearty laugh.

Even though I loved to see him happy, it stung a little. I went over there intending to play the role of the girlfriend. However, I didn't act. I was myself the entire time. He was still laughing as he turned the corner, and I added, "It was funny to see Rob. His face was so red. I felt sorry for Holly, though."

His brows bent down harshly, and he nearly shouted out in disgust, "Why?"

I tucked my hair back behind my ear as I thought about why, but I couldn't pinpoint it. "The look on her face wasn't shock like everyone else's. If I had to guess, I would think she still has feelings for you."

Evan threw his head back and guffawed, then rolled right into a chuckle. "Fat chance there. She burned that bridge a long time ago."

I wasn't convinced. I had been around plenty of mean girls in my life, and I recognized the look of jealousy. "How so?"

"She was my fiancée." His voice was filled with conviction as if he was going into battle. "I didn't easily let her go. I was a month away from saying vows to her. What kind of man would I be to give up? I had already made up my mind for better or worse with her. I reached out to her more than once, asking if there was something I did that made her cheat. She made it clear that she had zero feelings for me. It's hard to think about that now, but I didn't see it as dodging a bullet. I'm glad I'm not in that place anymore."

I bit down on my lip, running her expression over in my head. Something else was going on with her, but I couldn't place it. "Maybe she's jealous?"

Evan turned into an alley behind a brick building and killed the engine, completely ignoring my question. "Here we are."

"This is your shop?" I quickly unbuckled and jumped out of the Jeep.

"Not a shop." He waited for me at the door, and he punched numbers in the keypad. "It's a research lab."

"Oh." I pinned an amused expression on my lips, and we slipped through the door. At first glance, it looked like a two-stall garage, with my car in one bay, and stacked boxes along the wall in the other bay. There was a small bathroom in the corner, and a long worktable in the middle. Where it got interesting, was the row of life-sized robots standing in front of my car. "What are these?" I asked while slowing my steps.

"That's my research." He walked over to one and did some sort of weird sign language in front of it, and it immediately powered on. "This is Greta."

"Greta?" I stared at her, not sure if I should shake hands, she looked so real. "What kind of research?"

"It's always been my goal to work for NASA someday, but they've never asked me for an interview. So, in the meantime I've been experimenting with programming robots to do all sorts of fun things."

Planting a new smile on my lips, I was intrigued as this was not what I had expected to find from a thirty something who lived with his parents. "What kind of things?"

He wagged his head back and forth. "Here, Greta," he spoke to her slowly, "can you pick up my friend and put her on the chair?"

Greta swiveled without a sound and started rolling toward me. I took a giant step back. "No, don't pick me up." I shooed her away, but, before I knew it, she gently picked me up, squeezing her robot arms all the way around me like a clamp. The transition was relatively smooth, but I freaked out and tried to break my arms free. It didn't work, and she squeezed tighter. I stiffened and waited for her to glide to the chair. When she lowered her arms, they must have gotten jammed, because she didn't open her grasp. I was left levitating above the chair. "Ah, Evan," I squeaked out, my eyes on the chair, as I struggled to break out of her super huggie hold. It was no use. My arms were stuck. "How do I get her to let go without dropping me?"

"Greta," Evan cut in. "Let go of Jade."

"Security breached. Alarms engaged," Greta stated. "System shutting down."

"Don't shut down!" He yelled and slid in front of Greta, flinging the front control panel open, and hummed, "Hmmm, this isn't good."

"What's not good?" I tried to see what he was looking at, but Greta's hold on me was too strong. I couldn't bend forward at all.

"I'm not sure, but you must have resisted her enough for her to feel threatened. I've programmed her to shut down if she feels attacked."

"If she feels attacked?" I squawked, all the blood rushing out of my face leaving me dizzy. "What about me?"

His eyes locked on the exit. "I might have to pull up the code, but my laptop is at the house."

"Oh, no you don't!" I blurted out, before he had a chance to ditch me with Greta. "You are not leaving me."

"Ah, give me a sec." He got up, and ran into the other room, swiftly returning with a cord, and plugged it into his phone. "I might be able to do this on my phone."

"Can you just pull me out?" I waved my arms like I was drowning. My stomach quibbled. I didn't want to be stuck in this robot hold anymore.

"Well, I can try . . ." One side of lips curled up as if he was priming me for bad news. "She has been programmed to resist such things. She might let go, or she might squeeze you to death."

I stiffened, not even wanting to breathe now that I understood the severity of her sensitivity. "You're kidding, right?"

"Ha." His nervous sputter told me he wished he was. "Maybe we could trick her?"

"This isn't funny," I cried out, wondering if this was ever going to end, but now I was terrified to fight back.

"Relax, I have an idea." Evan's grabbed the other end of the cord and plugged it into Greta's back. "I think I can switch her to auto repair mode, and she should reset to baseline and let you out."

"Or?"

Evan didn't reply to my super-important inquiry. Instead, he hunched over his phone, typing in something I couldn't see. It was creepily quiet, as he worked, and I tried to ignore the sound of my panting. It was getting harder to breathe in this hold, and the harder I tried to stay calm, the quicker my breath ran in and out. "Ah, just another minute—" he muttered, as he moved to adjust something on Greta's back.

"System restore activated," Greta announced as she powered back to life, swiveled to face the opposite direction, raised both arms above her head—with me *still* in them—and opened her grasp. I was not prepared for the instant release, tumbling right out, but I was never happier to land flat on my face. I spread my arms out wide and gave it a nice hug.

"Wow. That was slick," I joshed, so glad to be out of her grasp. Not taking any chances on having her pick me back up, I army rolled to the side, fleeing far away from her, and scrambled to my feet, protectively backing up all the way against the wall. "I can see why NASA doesn't call," I said sarcastically, still panting to get my breath. Now that I was safe, I found the whole thing silly, and the release of adrenaline left me giggling.

"Yeah, we are still working on some things. I'm sorry about that." He flipped Greta's off switch again, and propped one hand on the wall next to me, leaning his weight on it casually. Never noticed before, but suddenly, I was an expert in leaning. He was great at it. He had this tilt in his gaze that made him even more intriguing. "We still have a long way to go but we'll get there."

"So, this is your job?" I tried to mimic his lean, but my arm was shorter, and it didn't have the same effect. Plus, my hand was sweating from being squeezed and began sliding up the wall, making me look super awkward. I quickly stood up straight, squaring my body with his. "I thought you installed Windows for people. You NASA science these robots?"

"That's my avenue. I do install Windows for some people. The laptop market is more lucrative than my mad scientist inventions. Some stuff pays the bills, and some stuff fuels my soul."

"I love that." My lips parted in awe as I could picture him spending long days, and even nights in here, getting lost in his element and having it out with Greta. Even though it had some glitches, it made me a little envious. I had a job, but I never had a thing that made me, me. I tried every hobby and sport, but I was never more than okay at anything. "I wish I had that."

"A mad scientist laboratory?"

"No, a passion that identifies me." I had my gaze locked on Greta. One part for security reasons. The other part, growing envious. "I never really had one thing."

"Maybe it's still coming," he said matter-of-factly as he opened a door that led into a retail space. Then he waved me forward. "Come on. I'll give you the rest of the tour."

"There's more?" I pretended to spin on my heel and head for the door, calling out. "Not a chance! I can't handle any more robots."

Before I took even a tiny step, he reached back and grabbed my arm, trapping me. An instant sonic boom exploded from his grasp and slammed into my heart. "No more robots. I promise."

I resisted staring at our hands because the physical explosion had been enough without me having to see it. Now, I was wishing I had a system restore button to reset my heart rate because something unnatural was happening. I couldn't ignore the pounding vibrations. Somehow—it was not luck, because I didn't have any of that—I managed to meander to a storefront, all the while I was still aware, okay, hyper focused, of the fact that he still held my hand. Maybe he'd forgotten he was holding it? Or forgot Rob wasn't here. I barely was able to pull my gaze away from him, to survey the store. It had normal computer displays and customer service areas. Everything was clean and modern. "This is very impressive," I managed to casually muster up. I hoped it was casual anyway.

"I don't know if I'd say it's impressive, but it does fill the space." He finally released my hand—to my huge disappointment, and he walked farther back into the hall to open another door, with stairs. "Up here is more storage, but you can follow me." He ascended the narrow stairs, speaking to me over his shoulder as I followed. "When I purchased this building, I had planned to remodel it into living quarters, but as you can tell," He flipped on a light switch, revealing open beams. "it has not gotten done yet."

Pacing forward, I took in the space. It was huge, with so much potential for a fantastic loft apartment. Spaces like these were a rare find. I knew that because I had spent months hunting for a nice apartment. He was sitting on the Bermuda triangle of available rental space. "Look at the view of the park!" I motioned out the large window at the literally picture-perfect overview of a small creek, and magnolia tree. "This is beautiful."

I felt him move in behind me. I didn't look back, but he was close enough I could feel the warmth of his body fill the air. Not sure why that made my toes curl under, but it didn't help when his voice came out softer than normal in his reply. "I thought so, too."

Dying to see his expression, I search for his face in reflection from the window. With his lips pinched tightly together, it didn't disappoint, as it clearly hinted, he wasn't telling me something. I was insanely curious to know more about him, pressing, "How come you never finished it?"

"I didn't decide not to." He sighed, not like he was giving up, but more like he was about to get transported into some sort of a dreamland. "It's still on my to-do list, it just fell to the bottom. I know I'm a little old to live with my parents, but things got complicated."

When I had first realized Evan lived with his parents, I had envisioned this dude who held down the couch all day next to two-day-old pizza boxes, but Evan wasn't like that at all.

He was sort of like me.

We were both trying the best we could.

He backed away from the window, and as he did my heart rate slowed to a more normal pace. When he nodded toward the stairs, he said, "I'll grab your keys. I know you said you have to work in the morning."

"I do." Reality slammed back into my brain, flashing a giant neon sign counting down the possible hours of sleep I could still get, and it wasn't enough. "I open at six."

"Ouch." Evan descended the stairs. "Sorry to keep you so late, but I figured you needed your wheels."

"It's okay. I haven't been sleeping well anyway. There's this branch. Actually—" I paused. "It's your mom's tree. It scratches on my window all night."

"That was totally you in the window the other night." He blurted out, his smile spreading across his face into a wonderful playful one. "I had convinced myself I had a nightmare. What was on your head?"

"Goggles. I was wearing my detective gear." I laughed because even though that was only two nights ago, it felt much longer than that, with so much happening since then. "I'm sure I looked like a nightmare."

We both chuckled, letting the incident go. I didn't need to explain myself. Perhaps it was because I'd already embarrassed myself so many times in front of him, he just understood me. It was a weird moment, where I felt like the easiness that we had when we hung out with each other was something special. Now we were downstairs, and he passed through the garage and pulled my keys off a hook, tossing them at me. I should have warned him never to throw stuff at me. Back to my thing about trying every sport and not finding one I was good at. I couldn't catch them, and they landed right by my feet.

"Sorry," Evan said, instantly leaning forward to retrieve them. "I should have given you a think fast."

"It's okay." I picked up the keyring before he could and fiddled with the ignition key.

"How come you're wearing sandals?" Evan's gaze was still on my feet. "It's like ten degrees outside?"

"It's dumb really." I gave him a dismissive wave, but I continued because we were at that point in our friendship where I was totally fine with making fun of myself. "I lost one of my winter boots. When I went to buy a new pair, they had the size six on sale. I didn't think a half size would make a big difference but after wearing them all night at your house, I needed to let my feet relax."

His head took a curious angle, and he was quiet for a moment before saying, "So . . . you met my family, you've seen my business, you even met my ex-fiancée and heard my whole dating history. Aside from the make and model of your car, I know nothing about you."

"That's not true," I took a defensive tone. "You know where I live." I held up a finger, popping up another finger each time I counted off something. "Where I work. I told you about my recent boyfriend. I think we're even."

"What about your family?" His chin moved forward, as if he was taking a stubborn stance. "You said they are in the Midwest?"

"Yeah." I pursed my lips out, thinking of something interesting to say but everything was pretty average. "Not much to tell there. Mom. Dad. Married. Like you, I'm an only child, so they weren't happy when I decided to move a thousand miles away. I think they are still waiting for me to fail, but they never say a disapproving thing. When I lost my fellowship, they pleaded with me to return. I don't feel like I fit in that small town anymore." I paused, remembering the blue-haired ladies who always gossiped at the diner. There wasn't anything terrible they'd ever said about me, but I felt gross knowing how much people talked in that town. "There's no sob story there. I was looking for a way out. Then I got laid off, but I like working at the coffee shop. It's nowhere near the stress of teaching. And it's crazy, now that I've decided I love dressing up in character every day, I'm fantastic at my job, and get amazing tips. The pay isn't that much less than teaching." I let my gaze fall on my fender. It appeared nothing had ever happened. "You did an awesome job." I quickly changed the subject, thankful to have it off of me. "Thank you."

His lips curled until the small lines by his eyes creased, and that's how I knew he was truly genuine. "You don't have to say thank you. I'm definitely the one who got the better deal." He chuckled again, like he couldn't stop seeing Rob's smug face in his head. "The pleasure was all mine."

He held his gaze on me, and it started to feel like there was something woven into the words he wasn't saying. I wanted so badly to flirt, but I wasn't sure where we were with that, so I simply said, "I had fun getting to know you."

"If you need anything, I'm right next door. Or maybe we can hang out again sometime?" He leaned in closer to me. Slightly. Or maybe I just imagined that part? Okay, I was hopeful, but I was definitely sure he was flirting when he threw in his last comment. "Perhaps walk over instead of driving, though."

It was my turn to throw my head back and laugh. Then I smiled at him, hoping to express my heartfelt appreciation when I said, "Deal."

# TEN

## Jade

My car drove beautifully, but I still underestimated the time it took to get across town. My manager, Portia, had already switched the closed sign to open when I arrived late. Not that it mattered. Portia was the manager who was everyone's best friend more than a manager. She worked the early shift every day until she could build her matchmaking business. She was amazing at setting people up, and spent more time asking customers about their love interests than making coffee. Her eyes scanned my outfit before she pushed the door open. "Cute Antlers. You're really into this holiday stuff, huh?"

She reminded me to adjust them, and as I straightened them, I replied. "I'm into tips. They are almost double when I dress up. This is the latest costume I found at Goodwill last week. I'm not sure yet, but I think it will be even better than the elf."

I followed her back behind the counter, and we both grabbed aprons and put them on. "Are you still struggling?" Her brows dipped, but she kept her gaze low as if she was allowing me some privacy. "I thought the new apartment was supposed to solve all your money issues."

"It will," I assured her. "But it will take a few months until I get ahead, and now this weekend, I'd like to send gifts home to my parents, but I'm afraid it's already too late."

I didn't think it was possible, but her brows fell even more. "Oh, I forgot that you don't have family here. It's a bummer you can't visit for the holidays." Her head jolted back, and her eyes opened wider. "You should let me set you up for a Christmas—"

"No, no, no." I wagged my finger at her, then turned my back and went down the line, switching on the espresso machines. "I'm completely okay with being single." I turned the coffee grinder on, and refilled it with beans, fully done with that conversation, but Portia pressed on.

"I know you needed some time after your last breakup, but it might be good to get out there again. I just recruited another cute guy from the hardware store. He would be *perfect* for you. When's the last time you went on a date?"

I stared forward, recalling the weekend. I wasn't sure if I could credit myself for going on a date. It was a fake date, but in an odd way it had felt real. I had woken up this morning, thinking about how sweet Evan was for fixing my car, and I still giggled every time I thought about the cheesecake, and Greta trapping me. Portia was probably right about it being way too long to wait after a breakup, but right now, I wasn't interested in dating. But the fake dating was fun. Fewer expectations. "I don't know, Portia. I'm not the single-and-ready-to-mingle type." To bring my point home, I reached into a bag of chips I had stashed below the counter for snacking, retrieved one, and popped it into my mouth. Speaking through a mouthful, I said, "I'm more in the single-and-ready-to-Pringle stage."

She snickered, then opened the fridge to open milk cartoons. "Some people walk around with rose colored glasses; you are the opposite. You walk around with gray ones."

It was my turn to snicker, because she had a point. "Yeah, gray, clouded, scratched, and sat on."

She moved to the dessert case, filling it with fresh muffins, which reminded me of Pearl's cake. "Say," I began. "Are you open to sampling some delicious cheesecake as prospect to sell?"

Her eyes became "are-you-kidding-me" narrow. "Is cheesecake ever a question?"

"Right?" I grinned, excitement budding in my chest. I desperately wanted to make amends with Pearl. "I thought I'd ask before I sprang it on you."

"You can spring cheesecake on me any time, but remember that new owner, Christian, took over yesterday and he now has the final say, and well, we both know he's . . ."

"Blah."

"I meant to say a grump, but blah works, too." Her gaze skirted to the counter, and she swapped her sympathetic expression for a "may-I-help-you" grin. "What can I get you today?" she asked the customer.

"I'm actually here to see Jade, if that's okay."

I hadn't even heard anyone come through the squeaky front door, but my ears perked, immediately recognizing Evan's voice. I spun on my heel, finding him standing just on the other side of counter. He was back to wearing jeans and one of those relatable millennial-hoodies that made him look snuggly. Though he was smiling, there was strain in his eyes. "Hi," I greeted him, suddenly questioning my decision to wear antlers. At least my embarrassed flush wouldn't be apparent under the red-painted cheeks and nose. "You're up early today."

"I wanted to catch you before you got into your morning rush." He held up a pair of black boots, the tags still on, and placed them on the counter. "And I got you these."

My eyes cemented on the shoes. They were obviously genuine leather and expensive with the size 6 ½ sticker still attached. As sweet as that was, my intuition told me they came at a price. I took a step closer to the counter and lowered my voice. "What's up?"

Rubbing the side of his face, he also took a step forward. "My cousin Rob texted me. I think he suspects we aren't really dating. He had all these questions for me. Not that it's any of his business." A disgruntled expression took over his face.

"So not his business," I filled in the pause with conviction.

"Right?" He gestured toward me. "I was worried he might come in and ask you the same questions, to see if we had the same answers. I mean, he asked me what we liked to do for dates, and I made the mistake of telling him that you love movies, and then the next thing I knew, he asked if we'd want to double tonight."

I let out a graceful snort as the thought of going to a movie with Evan's ex-fiancée was absurd, but his lips didn't even bend. "Wait a second. You told them we would, didn't you?"

His lips curled into a cringy smile "I'll buy you another fender.".

I let out a forced laugh as the thought of getting into another car accident was overwhelming. "Hopefully, I don't need another one for a long time." Evan didn't have to offer me anything. I enjoyed spending time with him, and I had nothing to do tonight. "I'll go."

Now, his lips curled into a real smile, one that I definitely loved. It held relief, as well as mischief . . . and maybe a hint of flirtation. Or maybe I was hoping for flirtation?

"Do you think we can rehearse a little this time? I didn't realize how hard it was going to be.

I matched his mischievous smile. "I get off at three."

A string of chatty female customers entered the front door, lining up behind Evan. He checked behind his shoulder, and then stepped to the side, clearing the way. "The movie's at seven, but I'll come over early."

"Sounds good." I motioned to the espresso machine. "Did you want a coffee?"

"Nah. I'm good. I was only here to see you."

I blinked, feeling that in my soul. I understood he was here for this whole business transaction, but somewhere inside me, it felt fantastic to be wanted. It had been forever since I had a guy visit me at work. Why couldn't this be real? I resisted the urge to slam my head into the wall mournfully. Instead, I held up my hand and wiggled my fingers in a feminine wave. "Okay. I'll see you later." I went right into taking customer orders. I worked my entire shift, but I couldn't tell you one thing a customer had said. I was so distracted, thinking about my fake date.

I wasn't ready to date.

So not ready.

But fake dating was exciting.

When my shift was over, I counted my tips, and it was the most I'd ever made. "Two hundred and thirteen dollars and seventy-five cents," I called out as I split the equal piles between Portia and me.

"I guess Rudolph is the way to go," Portia said.

"I guess." I stowed my neatly organized stack of bills into my wallet and held onto the change as I made my way outside and scouted for the bell-ringing Santa. He was always there, and I knew I couldn't walk away without at least dropping something into his bucket. Today, Santa was short, with big chocolate eyes, and braces on his teeth. He also was going for the clean-shaven look as he only had a Santa hat and no beard. I smiled at him and pushed my quarters into the slot one by one.

"What is your Christmas wish?" Santa asked, while sliding a candy cane out of his bag, presenting it to me.

My brow quirked. Did they get paid to ask that because that was the exact same thing the dread-lock Santa had asked? "Um, well," I mused as things were looking up since I was last asked that question. I had a stack of tips, a fixed car, and even a fake date. I wasn't going to push it by getting too excited and I kept my same wish. "I wish that bad stuff stops happening to me so I can get ahead of the bad stuff that has already happened."

"Merry Christmas," he said with a definitive tone and pushed the candy cane closer to me.

"Thank you." I received the gift and called back, "Merry Christmas to you, too!" My phone started to vibrate in my pocket, and I pulled it out to answer, noting the caller ID. "Hey. Mom."

"How are you doing?"

"Not bad. Just leaving work." I pulled my keys from my purse, jingling as I strode to my car with a little pep in my step. "What about you?"

"Same old, but I was calling to tell you that the middle school had an opening to teach eighth grade history. I mentioned to Principal Ron that you had a history degree you aren't using, in addition to teaching experience. He said he'd love to see your application."

"Mom." I started, then stopped, giving myself time to think. "That's very thoughtful of you to think of me, and you're right. I do have a history degree, but I live here."

"Right," she quipped, "But you're working at a coffee shop."

Flashing my eyes heavenward, I inhaled a deep breath. I reached my car, unlocked my door, and got inside, remaining quiet the entire time. Once I started my car, I finally said, "I know it wasn't your plan for me, but I like working at a coffee shop. The amount of stress I had teaching wasn't good for me. I learned I wasn't meant to teach tiny, or even mid-sized humans."

"Well, it doesn't hurt to put in an application," she pressed. "Have you applied to any other teaching jobs?"

I could have restated that I had a job, or explained to her again that my teaching license wasn't valid without the fellowship program, but she obviously wasn't hearing that part. She never heard that part. "Mom, I gotta go," I rushed out. "I'm about to pull into traffic and want to pay attention. Love you, bye." I didn't feel bad when I ended the call, because I had learned my mom and I had different visions for my life. I wasn't going to change her mind, and it would only hurt our relationship if I tried. I loved my mom, and for the sake of our relationship, I avoided certain topics altogether.

I was about to put my phone down, but it quickly lit up with a text.

**Evan: I may have run into Rob again. I might need to go over some notes with you. Can I come over early?**

I didn't even try to hold back my chuckle. The poor guy was in over his head. It's a good thing his cousin lived out of state, and he'd be leaving soon.

**Me: I'll be ready.**

I set my phone down in the center console, letting my eyes linger on Evan's text. For the first time in a long time, I had plans to go out. Sure, it wasn't a real date, but that didn't mean I couldn't enjoy the movie and have a good time. Evan was handsome but he didn't act like it, which made him even more attractive. Plus, he made me laugh. Not just a little laugh. I can't ever remember a time recently I laughed until I cried. Extra plus, he was super sweet, fixing my car. That made me heart him so much.

My gaze drifted to the side.

If I didn't know better from how my nerves fluttered in my stomach, I'd think I was going on an actual date. I shook my head and put my car in gear, pulling out of my parking space. I didn't need to have these thoughts.

But then again, he was single.

And I was single.

Maybe I was ready to mingle?

# Eleven

## Evan

Chainsaws are just big butter knives, right? I checked over my shoulder as if I had expected someone to answer that. Then I stared at the tool I had borrowed from my parents' garage. It wasn't one of those loud, gas-powered ones. This was compact and battery operated.

Sensible.

It's no secret I leaned more toward tree hugger—with my zip hoodies and Hey Dudes—than lumberjack, but Discovery Channel was my jam. I watched every season of American Loggers, and I had the major points noted.

Chainsaw.

Red flannel shirt.

And lack-of-shaving-effort facial hair.

Safety goggles. I chuckled, as I positioned my goggles over my eyes, remembering Jade in hers the other night. She was adorable.

Inhaling deeply, I filled my lungs and straightened my spine.

I was ready, but there was a slight catch.

I HATED heights.

Not a little bit bothered by them, but full-blown anxiety attacks.

I was going to push through it because I'm doing this for Jade. She's going out with me again tonight, and it's only fair I repay her in some way. Because she wouldn't do this unless she had a reason to.

Would she?

Tilting my head, I lingered on that thought. I enjoyed spending time with her. Better than enjoyed, I was looking forward to seeing her again. Everything from her mischievous, fun smile, to how her presence had this warming effect on me.

A car alarm blared from somewhere in the neighborhood, and pulled me from my thoughts, reminding me I had a job to do. Without another moment of contemplation, I stuck my foot on the lowest branch. I slowly lifted myself as I tested its strength under my weight.

It held. I let out a sigh of relief and gave the tree a friendly thank-you pat.

It was a girthy branch. It didn't creak as I brought my second foot up and balanced my weight. Lucky for me, I knew the branches of this tree by heart. Not because I climbed them. Remember, the heights thing. Nope, I used to hide behind this tree daily in my youth when we played hide and seek. Back in the days before the internet, where you would get lost outside every day, until your mom screamed at you from the porch with her curlers in. The lamp posts were our alarms, and our bikes were our preferred method of transportation.

A lot has changed since then.

I hoisted the saw over my shoulder and gripped the branch above with my free hand. That branch was like a titanium beam; it was so sturdy. I pulled myself up with ease. I was getting the hang of this working by the sweat of my brow thing. I cocked my head to the side, stretching my neck out. It felt good to be active in the fresh air.

Manly.

And so easy.

All I had to do was shimmy over and saw off the low-hanging branch, and I'd be golden with plenty of time to get ready for my date with Jade. It felt good to say that, too. "I have a date with Jade," I said aloud casually, and I scooted one foot in front of the other. "Because I do that now. I date again."

*Snap!*

I jerked my foot back, as I apparently had gone too far. I was in between two branches now. Standing on one, but I also had another thick branch at my shoulder level I used as a guardrail.

Safety first.

I breathed, knowing this was only going to take a moment. "Just a quick snip," I hummed out loud as I steadied my weight on both legs and focused on maintaining balance as I found the power switch.

The saw powered on with no problem, and I eyed the narrowest part of the branch for the perfect place to slice. I needed to get a little lower. I crouched, feeling the stretch in my hamstrings, but it was a good stretch. I lowered my saw to the branch, bracing for impact. It was slick and made a nice clean cut; nothing jerky, or dangerous, at all. I cut halfway through the branch as they do on AxMan, and then gravity took over, and I could feel it giving out on its own. I retracted my saw and held onto the branch over me as I watched it break.

It fell brilliantly to the ground, not hitting a thing. Clearly, I was such a natural. I could give a YouTube tutorial on this. Or maybe even a weekend side gig? I'm sure there are plenty of elderly ladies who need a big strong man to take down their low-hanging branches. I straightened the collar on my flannel shirt, thoroughly impressed with myself. Leaning over, I inspected what a clean cut I had made.

Maybe I could have been a surgeon?

Who knew I had this talent?

I couldn't wait to tell Jade she could sleep now, and I quickly—too quickly, maybe a little carelessly—stood up, and smacked my face right into my rail branch. I wasn't positive, but mostly sure my tooth cracked. It was evident when I saw something white fly out of my mouth. Pushing my tongue forward into the massive gap in my teeth that wasn't supposed to be there.

Yep, now I needed a dentist.

But it was after office hours, and I had a date. Pushing my tongue back into the gap, I tried to measure the size of the hole. I wonder if she would even notice?

Who was I kidding? It was right in the middle of my face!

Of course, she would notice. It's not like I had time to grow a mustache. My eyes swelled as the lumberjack facial hair suddenly made so much sense. What I wouldn't give for a big burly mustache to hide behind right now.

Rubbing the barely-there stubble on my chin, I had a thought. I didn't have time to grow one but there were other options. A smirk grew on my lips as I lowered myself onto the next branch. I had an idea. A brilliant idea, and just enough time to execute it.

# TWELVE

## Jade

I was feeling good about tonight. Dressed in jeans and a fitted knit shirt, I was comfortable. I wasn't overdoing it by trying too hard. However, I won't pretend I'm not excited for tonight. I thought about Evan and how he looked at me when I fell on him in the kitchen. I couldn't deny there'd been sparks.

If the chance arose, I was going to tell him I started to have feelings for him.

The doorbell rang and I pushed through the nerves, pinned a smile on my face and opened the door. My gaze skirted to the side, landing on Evan oddly leaning on the door frame with one arm like he was having a hard time standing. "Good evening," his voice rolled out as if he was out of breath.

He was wearing an ugly red Christmas sweater with pine trees on it, and huge pants with gold suspenders. I blinked, trying not to stare. What happened to his hoodie? I shifted my gaze to his face, and almost jumped back. I didn't want to offend him, but I had no idea what that thing was on his face. Facial hair didn't grow that fast, and this was so puffy it didn't look dead! I fought the urge to swat at it with my purse to make sure it didn't bite.

He had a full beard and mustache a shade too light to match his hair, so it was clearly fake.

Was that supposed to be attractive?

I guess it was a style choice. Not one I would make personally, but I wouldn't judge.

Maybe he was dressing this way for Holly? Maybe this was her jam?

Rob had a mustache, so maybe this was his way of competing? I bit my lip, reminding myself this whole fake dating thing had always been about impressing Rob and Holly, but I couldn't deny that my gut twisted. "Ah, heeey," I finally managed to say. It came out as if it had three syllables, with each syllable higher than the previous octave. I clenched my purse close to my body, all my previous excitement for the date draining. Perplexed, I pushed through it. "I'm ready."

He finally stood up straight, taking his arm off my door frame. "The movie tonight is the Grinch. I got tickets online, but then saw they were having a contest for the couple who dresses up as the best character from the movie. I couldn't let an opportunity to win against Rob go by, and I already knew you love to dress up. However, I didn't have much time, so I went with Bricklebaum. What do you think?"

Letting out a huge sigh of relief, I almost chuckled when I finally understood this was a costume. Actually, now that I didn't have to pretend not to be alarmed, I assessed it, and he looked perfect. "Ah,

I couldn't even tell you were wearing a costume for a moment," I admitted truthfully.

"I didn't want you to stress about finding something on short notice, so I got you something, too." He retrieved a bag I hadn't noticed before by his foot, and he pulled out items one by one: a yellow sweater, matching earmuffs, and a pink scarf. He paused after each item as if he were waiting for me to solve the mystery. When the last item was out, he said, "You can say no, but I thought you'd make a great Izzy."

My lips fell slightly agape, as I let it sink in how sweet this was for him to plan my costume. I didn't even know what to say. "Ah, why Izzy?"

His lips pinched together, and it was obvious he was holding back a laugh. It went on forever, and I was convinced he'd never tell me what was up. I was about to twist his arm to squeeze out his joke, he managed, "You already have the goggles to pull this off."

"Of course." I easily made fun of myself. He was right. It was perfect, and a huge smile grew on my face because this sounded so fun. "Give me a second. I'll grab them." I excitedly stepped back from the door, and hurried to my closet, retrieving the goggles, not wasting a moment to pull them over my head. I knew Evan would be smiling when I looked back at him, and his grin did not disappoint. There was no way we could ever be serious about this, and I loved it. I snatched the button up sweater from him and slipped it over my shirt. A rush of laughter fell from my lips as I grabbed the earmuffs and scarf. I had the hardest time keeping a straight face. "Oh wait!" I whipped around and ran to my dresser. "I have pink pants!" Snatching up my pants, I rushed to the bathroom and quickly slipped them on. We were both fighting back giggle fits when I was finally dressed and pulled the door closed behind me to walk to his Jeep.

"So. Tell me." I swallowed, trying to be serious, but it was hard to take him seriously when we were both dressed like this. "What are the things I need to know about *us*?"

"Yes, I thought we could rehearse a few things, and we could come up with the perfect relationship." He opened my car door for me, which I thought was sweet, but I still couldn't look at him without laughing. "When is your birthday?"

"July 3rd." I slid into my seat.

He cringed and immediately rebutted. "I accidentally let it slip that we always go skiing on your birthday weekend. I don't even ski, but he doesn't need to know that part, but how does February work?"

He shut my door before I had a chance to reply, ran around to his side, got in, and picked up the conversation where he had dropped it. "We could plan a Valentine's getaway every year."

"That sounds sweet and very couple*ish* but." My brow arched, as I was stuck on the first thing he said. "What do you mean we always go? Didn't we just start dating?"

He started the car and backed out. "Right. We just started dating because that's the only thing that makes sense as to why my parents recently met you, but I thought it would be cool if maybe we've known each other for years. Like maybe we made an annual ski trip with friends, keeping in touch and I'm the reason you found the apartment across from my house."

"Oh." I stared forward as that sort of made sense. "That could work, but how did we know each other? I grew up in the Midwest, and you were—"

"Coding camp."

My forehead started to tighten, as all of the sudden this started to feel more like a job than a date. I was given an assignment and needed to study. "Color coding?"

"No, computer coding. My friends and I always went to a coding camp in the summer, and you were there. You were the only girl in the class. All the guys had a crush on you, but you always sat by me. I thought it was because I had the best snacks. I brought the double pack of chocolate peanut butter cups in my bag, and I opened them to eat, and I looked around for someone to share them with. In a perfect meet cute, I looked to my left and there you were."

I still struggled to take him seriously because I couldn't stop staring at that bush on his face. It took every ounce of strength I had not to look directly at it when he tried to make eye contact with me. This whole thing was ridiculous, yet adorable. I never in a million years even thought I'd find a man who loved to dress up as much as I did. "Isn't that a commercial?"

"No, I think that was the Oreo commercial where the girl split it. This is way more original." He turned left, entered the freeway, and sped up. "I got a little carried away trying to make it believable."

"I guess." I didn't think I was that gullible before but as I sat next to Evan and soaked this all in, I began to wonder if maybe I had missed some warning signs. At this point, I thought I might be going against my better judgement to agree, but I was already in his Jeep, heading to our date. "Okay . . . You like chocolate peanut butter, which makes sense, but I can't code."

He waved dismissively. "It's fine. Nobody is going to ask you to."

"If I knew how to code, does it make sense that I work at a coffee shop?"

"How about, you forgot everything when the chalkboard fell on your head."

I double-blinked, feeling a light headache coming on with all these details. "Say what?"

"It could be the real reason you quit teaching. The school was dilapidated and falling apart."

I eyed the freeway speeding by, admitting it was tempting to jump out to avoid the hole of doodoo getting deeper and deeper. I honestly couldn't tell if he was serious or not. We had come from giggling like kids over our costumes to needing to plan the Geneva convention. The only explanation I could think of for his odd behavior was this whole Rob thing. He really was stuck on winning. "When does this end?"

"Let me check." He held his phone up to eye level while keeping one eye on the road. I still was unable to not see that stupid thing on his face. It wasn't even proportionate to anything realistic. This had to be a prank.

"Let's see, your birthday . . . got that," he mumbled. "Job, coding camp, peanut butter cup, meet-cute."

"Wait for a second," I blurted out, feeling fear creep into my chest. "You forgot; I told them we met because I crashed into your car! Now, none of this backstory makes sense."

"And he busted me on that," he blurted out, holding up a finger and tacked on, "but I was quick and blurted out that's how we reconnected."

"How many questions did he ask? It sounds like an interrogation?"

"He is a lawyer."

My gaze dropped to my lap, and I played with the hem of my sweater. "Do you think he knows? Maybe, that's why he had all the questions."

"No, he can't know. I was so smooth. I never even flinched."

My eyes hooked his mustache, which was starting to go a little slanted, with one side bending up. Swallowing, I thought about what I was getting into. Everything about the tone of the evening had changed in the last fifteen minutes. Before, Evan was this sweet guy who offered to fix my car, and now, he was wearing a disguise while we made up false identities.

Something in the back of my head niggled at me, as Evan was acting so completely insane right now. "Have you ever thought of taking a less passive aggressive approach to winning with Rob?"

"What do you mean? Like punching him in the face," he spurted out. "Sure. Everyday."

I started giggling, wanting so much to rip that slanted mustache off Evan's face.

Had we taken this too far?

I was about to find out.

# Thirteen

## Evan

By the time I found a parking spot, I was sweating so profusely that my mustache was sliding down my lip. Do most people add glue? I used the included double-sided sticky tape, but apparently it wasn't enough. The package had no instructions or even a warning label about how hot these things were. I should have worn shorts. Plus, I think I had an abnormally small upper lip pallet thingy because even with it sliding down my lip, I had difficulty breathing through my nose.

Too late, though. I couldn't take it off now, because that would be totally weird. There was the issue of my chipped front tooth. It didn't hurt even though it cracked right through the center. Luckily, I found the part that broke off, and dropped it in a cup of water now marinating at home, per Google recommendation until I get into the dentist.

I smiled at Jade as we got out of my Jeep and beelined to the theater. Tugging at my collar, I regretted wearing this furnace sweater, but I had to have the whole 'fit' or it wouldn't look right. I was loudly mouth breathing as I opened the door for Jade.

"I'm really sorry about this." She strolled through the entrance and peered back, waiting for me. Her eyes were slightly narrow, and laser focused on my upper lip. Perhaps she suspected something was up? I couldn't be certain because she had a pleasant smile on her face. I prayed she wasn't miserable, because at this point, I really wanted to impress her, but I had a sinking feeling something was off about her. I just didn't know what.

"It's okay. I was looking forward to a night out." She smiled at me slyly and stood close to me. Not just a little close.

*Date close.*

My eyes scoured the room, searching for Rob and Holly. Maybe Jade was being extra prepared, but I saw no sign of them. Taking a cue from her, I grabbed her hand. She didn't flinch as she received my hand in hers.

We had the perfect arm lengths for holding hands.

"They leave town tomorrow, so this will be the last time for sure we have to do this, and I hope I can make it up to you."

Before she could reply, Rob's boisterous voice sliced through the air. "Hey, cousin." I turned toward them, careful to give them my new Bricklebaum gaze, but they both stopped dead in their tracks.

Rob was dressed as the Grinch, which frankly didn't surprise me, but Holly didn't have a costume. I'd assumed she would dress as Cindy-Lou Who, with her long blonde hair, but she would have to at least braid her hair to resemble Cindy. She wasn't even wearing pink or anything remotely passable as Christmas. She had on a long black sweater dress, and heels, and her hair was pulled back in a messy bun. I tried not to stare, but she must have sensed my confusion because she pulled up one side of her lips into an awkward smile the way she always did when she was insecure. "I didn't know I needed to dress up."

"Oh, no." My jaw fell, as I recalled I had texted Rob about the contest, assuming he would tell Holly. "I didn't think I needed to tell you because I told Rob."

Her eyes slid to Rob, who didn't even defend his choice to not get her a costume. He raised his chin and guessed at our costumes. "Mr. Bricklebaum and Izzy."

I didn't want to draw attention to my tooth, so I ran a hand over my beard smoothing it and casually said, "Glad you could tell."

"It's not hard." Rob's laugh rushed out. "My first guess would be a woolly caterpill—" Holly elbowed him hard, cutting off his words, and his face instantly flushed red. Holly didn't bend a lip at him as she crossed her arms and stood a good foot away from him. They resembled sworn enemies standing like that, rather than two people who were supposedly newly engaged. "Oh, before I forget." Rob reached into a small shopping bag he had hooked on his arm, and pulled out a set of stuffed antlers, presenting them to Jade. "I saw this when I grabbed my costume. I had assumed you'd dress up as the dog. I had pegged you for an animal lover and thought it would be funny if I gave you the antlers like the Grinch does in the movie."

"Ah." Jade let out a low nervous chuckle. "Nope, not a dog. Sorry." She turned her shoulder away from Rob, leaning closer to me.

I was completely disgusted, though not surprised, Rob forgot Holly's costume while trying to suck up to Jade. That's just the tool he was. Feeling completely offended for Jade, that Rob would even think of getting her a gift, I leaned closer as well, asking, "Are you ready to go into the theater?" I wavered a little at the end because I wasn't sure if I should add a nickname or other term of endearment. I decided to leave it open. I wasn't the best at fake dating, but Jade on the other hand, was a fantastic actress.

She stepped closer to me, erasing the small gap between us. I could smell the swirls of her warm vanilla scent again. Man, she smelled amazing. When she latched her lashes back up on me, she had her competitive expression. Wrapping her free arm around my waist, she said, "I'm ready to snuggle you."

Her touch was smoldering. The mere friction of her hand wrapped around my waist sent a spark right through my body, and I instantly started sweating even more.

It wasn't as bad as that time I accidentally sat on my welding torch, but close.

If Rob wasn't buying this act, then it couldn't be helped, because even I had a hard time discerning what was going on. The heated way Jade studied me made me forget we were faking this.

Give this girl an Emmy.

I guided her forward, not glancing back at Rob or Holly because I had an impossible time breaking my gaze from Jade. We must have looked like a pair of love birds who couldn't get close enough. As soon as I sat down, she scooted so close to me, I easily slipped my arm around her. Her look-of-love performance put me at ease. I had almost forgotten we weren't even on a date. Everything about her was so perfect. From how her petite little body fit perfectly in my arm, to the way the top of her head brushed against the bottom of my chin. Man, did I mention she smelled amazing?

The only bad thing was the mustache was a little more animated than the instructions had mentioned. It had a life of its own. A life filled with dancing all over my face. Maybe it's because I was sweating so much from this sauna sweater, but every few minutes the 'stache would creep down to my top lip. I was smooth though, and I placed my hand on my chin, tilting my head away from Jade as if deep in thought. As soon as my head was at the perfect angle of an isosceles triangle. I would casually rub my chin, and discreetly push my mustache back into place.

It was an art.

And I was Picasso.

The perfect fidget device.

I was preoccupied with keeping my 'stache on my face, and fielding those dreamy looks Jade kept flashing at me, I never even once looked over at Rob or Holly. I had forgotten they were even there.

We were halfway through the movie, and I had completed another successful angle-tuck-and-slide 'stache sequence as I turned my face to snuggle her. The top of her head was like the warmest little nest made just for me. I nestled into it, and then it happened . . .

The corner of my 'stache got stuck to her hair!

I gave my head a backward tug, but her hair pulled tight and she jolted slightly.

Not good!

Nightmare!

I scooted closer, giving her hair some slack. I was so close to her now there wasn't even a slice of air between us as I hovered my face over the center of her head, assessing the situation. It didn't seem to bother her, though. She only cuddled tighter to me.

I didn't mind that part. Though the face trap was a tad disturbing.

Yep, I had trapped a lock of hair like a mouse's tail right to my face.

I flexed my lip up and down, side to side. I couldn't get her hair to fall out.

I poked my index finger underneath the edge of my mustache, trying to brush the hair out. It was hopelessly stuck to my face. Two seconds ago, it was sliding off my face but now it wouldn't budge.

I had to do something.

I was in a hairy situation.

Someone was going to notice soon.

I could pull her hair and pray she didn't notice or I could rip my 'stache off.

Ripping my mustache off would hurt. I eyed the top of her head. Maybe she wouldn't feel anything if I ripped it out fast enough? I wrapped my fingers around the edge of the 'stache, ready to pull. It was the only way to free us. I held my breath, counting to three. One. Two. Three. Then like a perfectly executed dance sequence—okay, not even close—I yanked. She yelped, jumping to her feet right in the center of the theater.

The mustache stuck to her hair and boomeranged back at her like a giant wooly caterpillar in flight. Waving her hands in the air, she sucked in a squealing breath, and I plugged my ears, waiting for it . . .

"Ouch!" She yelped from the tug on her hair. All the eyes in the theatre were on her. She had gargantuan air sacs for lungs that belted on forever like an opera singer singing her last note. In a moment so fast, I didn't have time to think, I wrapped one arm around her waist, swooping her into me and planted my lips right on hers, silencing her scream.

She was the most brilliant impromptu actress, not missing a beat, kissing me back as if my lips were the only thing that could save her life.

Taking my chance, I slid my hand up to her hair, snatching the 'stache back before breaking the kiss. Breathless, my eyes dropped to hers. It didn't take me more than a second to know she hadn't faked that kiss. The inflections in her eyes were honest and dialed into me. If we weren't standing in the back of a movie theater, I would have . . . I'd . . . I don't know what I would do because this wasn't part of the plan.

I inhaled measured breaths as I stared back at her. I didn't have the words to explain what had happened. I held up the mustache and shrugged.

Someone behind us yelled at me to sit down. I wanted to sit down, but my face was like a used circus stage. Half sticky, and slimy from the glue mixed with sweat. The other half burned from where it was ripped off. I'm sure my lip was swollen from the tree branch, in addition to the chipped tooth. I was feeling overly exposed. I held the stache again and leaned forward, whispering in her ear, "I'll explain after the movie, but I need to go wash my face. I'll be right back."

Nodding softly, her eyes never left me. As I walked away, I did some math. The looks she had been giving me all night, plus the

way she kissed. . . I had a hard time thinking she could really be
that good an actress.

I entered the empty bathroom, and crossed over to the sink,
squinting through the pinching as I ripped off the beard and
splashed cooling water on my face. I used a paper towel to wipe it
off. I was a mess. My hair was drenched from sweat, shining like I
had gelled it. The stupid sweater was an abysmal failure. I had no
idea what I was thinking, but now that the mustache was gone, the
sweater had to go, too. I slipped it off and threw it in the trash.

There I was.

Me again.

Except for the fat lip and tooth stub, but really it wasn't that
bad.

Now to explain to Jade what had gotten into me.

That meant I had to confess to cutting down her tree, but I was
oddly excited to tell her that. Then it struck me. I had completely
removed every ounce of Holly from my heart.

She didn't have a hold on me the way she had before.

Something had happened.

I didn't even have to think twice about what that thing was.

All I thought about as I stood here was getting back to Jade.

And it felt amazing.

Basketball tossing the paper towel into the trash, I flinched when
it landed six inches away. Nobody saw it. It didn't count. I re-
bounded it, dunking as I hurried out of the door.

It was much better with the costume off. I could breathe again.
Rushing around the corner, I didn't even notice when I almost
walked right into Holly.

"Oh, hey," she blurted as if she was trying to get my attention.

I checked behind her, looking for Rob, but she was alone. I motioned down the hall in the direction I was going. "Hey, I'm headed back—"

She pushed her hand forward, touching my arm. I was frozen. "Can you wait a sec?"

"What is going on?" I asked, but then my eyes sprang open wide when I noticed the tip of her nose was red, as it looked like she had been crying. She must be upset with Rob. I mean, who wouldn't get annoyed by him? She chose him though. It's not like their relationship was any of my business. I placed my hand on hers, mostly to remove her hand from mine. I tried to think of the perfect something to say that told her I didn't want to be dragged into her Rob's drama. It's not that I was heartless, but I was not the right person. Maybe I could send Jade to talk to her about this stuff, or better yet, she could talk to him. "Holly, I think this is something you need to talk to Rob about—"

"Rob just stole Jade," she blurted out, sealing her eyes on mine in a way that told me she was a thousand percent serious. "They just left together."

"What?" I scoffed at her weird diversion, totally ready to blow off this ridiculous assumption, but Holly went on rambling, "Rob does this thing where he pursues a woman so subtly, but with so much vigor. He did it to me, and I've been watching the signs this whole time, and he just did it to Jade. It's a game to him to steal your girlfriends. When he did it to me, I got confused, and as soon as he had me, it was like I was his trophy. All he wanted to do was put me on a shelf and brag to everyone that he stole me from you. I realized it wasn't about me, it was this weird thing about you. He's awful. I've been wanting to tell you for so long. Rob would check my phone, but I came back to find you to warn you, so you can stop Jade before she ruins her life too."

"Ah . . ." My gaze quickly fell away from hers as I tried to think of what to say. It was the oddest thing I had ever experienced. Was she saying this to get me to distrust Jade? But then my mind planted on the weird gift Rob gave Jade, and all the weird extra attention he gave Jade at my house. Could Holly be right? No way. This had to be some skit for me to doubt Jade. "I need to find Jade," I said, my gaze skirting to the side at the rush of people exiting the theater. The movie was over. It would only be a moment, and Jade and Rob would be looking for us. "Come on." I nodded to the crowd. "Let's not leave them waiting."

But they weren't waiting.

They weren't anywhere.

After waiting for the slew of people to pass in front of us until the last person was out of the theater, Rob and Jade never came. I took a frantic lap around the theater, thinking maybe they were somewhere, but they were gone. "They left without us."

I looked at Holly, who swallowed, nodding through it like it would help her to breathe. She looked broken. I could only imagine how horrible her life was with Rob. He clearly tricked her, but she had a chance to start over.

"Something bad had to have happened," I added as I checked my phone, already en route to my Jeep. There was no way Jade would ever leave with Rob.

Unless Holly was right.

Did Rob steal Jade?

He had done this before.

That was not going to happen again! I steeled my chin, scanning the parking lot until I spotted my Jeep but not Rob's rental car. I dialed Jade's number, pressing my ear to the phone, and called after Holly, "I'll give you a ride to my grandma's if you want. It's on my way, but we must hurry. I will not let Rob get to her."

# Fourteen
## Evan

I pulled into my grandma's narrow driveway and didn't put my Jeep in park before announcing, "Here you go."

Holly stared forward. Her fair-skinned cheek twitched as if she was feigning deep in thought. I didn't want to waste time because I had to get to Jade, but I couldn't push Holly out the car door. Maybe I could offer to walk her to the door? That might get her out of here faster.

Too late.

Rob manifested on the front porch, strutting towards us with his shoulders back, obviously displaying his lofty sense of superiority. Just one time, I wanted to punch him in the face. My nostrils flared, unbidden. If I found out he did anything or said anything to Jade, I wasn't going to be able to hold it back.

Holly finally moved, getting out of my Jeep, and I already put the Jeep in reverse when she ran past Rob, not even acknowledging him. That jerk didn't even try to talk to her either, he just kept pacing toward my Jeep.

On any other day, I could have let it roll off my back.

Not today.

I shifted the Jeep into park, and rolled my window down, calling out, "What did you say to Jade?"

"Maybe if you'd pay more attention to your woman, you'd know." His head bobbled, as if it was too fat to stay balanced on his scrawny shoulders.

I wrung my hands together, fighting back every urge I had to not strangle him. It didn't make sense Jade would ask him for a ride home. He had to be lying about something. The problem with trying to talk to a liar, though, is they aren't going to tell you the truth. My attempt to give him a chance to be honest was clearly futile.

I was done wasting time with this cantankerous jerk. I needed to find Jade. I had a mission. A mission Rob insisted on interrupting when he blubbered out the stupidest thing, "Looks like you lost another girl, huh?"

"What's that, Robby?" I didn't think twice before I jumped out of my Jeep, pulling my shoulders back. "You need help shutting your mouth?"

I grabbed his shirt collar, roughing him closer to me and jerked my fist back, ready to flatten his smirk. My heart swelled, as this was going to be better than a decade of therapy. The front door opened, Grandma hollered out, "Oh, heavens, Evan, no!"

My fists shook, but I didn't want to give my granny a heart attack. I flattened my palm and raked it through my hair, the tension seething in my fingers. "You're so lucky you got saved by a ninety-year-old lady," I whispered under my breath, as I ground my molars.

"Rob," Granny called out, her voice taking an inquiring tone. "Something's wrong with Holly. She's in here packing and crying. She said you're a loser, and a jerk. You'd better come talk to—"

"Coming!" He cut her off, sprinting forward as if he was a scared cat with his tail between his legs. I could hear Holly screaming in the background and it was getting louder. Before Rob could duck inside the house, Holly was on the porch, not slowing her steps. Her brows beaded together, her entire expression is thunderous. "I was just coming inside to check on you," Rob squawked out.

"Don't bother." Her boots clicked across the wood planks on the porch until she stopped in front of Rob. "I'll tell you exactly how I feel about you right now." Raising her hand, as if she's ready to spike a volleyball, she swiped at the air until her palm loudly cracked against his cheek.

I couldn't help but sputter out a laugh. It was all coming full circle, and I didn't even have to break my fist to make it happen. Talk about a Christmas miracle. Now, I needed to get to Jade.

# Fifteen

## Jade

I kept my phone silent and all the lights in my apartment dark as I hid below the window and peeked. Evan stood in his window, staring this way with his phone attached to his ear. My phone had been blowing up continuously, since I had left the theater with Rob. I just needed to get away. I had lost myself in the date. Somewhere between arriving and settling in, I had forgotten we were faking it, and I one hundred thousand percent felt we were on a real date.

It was the start of something.

While I waited for him to get back from the bathroom, I went to refill my drink, and Rob came out. He told me the reason he didn't get Holly a costume was because he had found messages from Evan on Holly's phone. They were planning on getting back together. Rob was upset, but still came to the movie to see if they'd confess. When they didn't, he was so disgusted, he had to tell me the truth.

Faceplanting into the palm of my hands, I cringed. How could I be so stupid? This whole thing was a sham to make Evan's ex-fiancée jealous. I knew THAT from the beginning. Of course, he was fine using me to make Holly jealous.

My ears literally burned from embarrassment as I thought about how I had kissed Evan.

When Rob dropped me off, he felt so bad for me that I was sucked into this drama, he offered his Grinch costume, since he knew I loved dressing up. It felt odd, but I took it, knowing I had to work in the morning. Maybe a part of me wanted it to spite Evan.

Now, I crawled on the floor to my bed, careful not to cross in front of my window. I should have known better than to get involved with the man next door. Now I was a prisoner in my own home. I slipped into the bed, pulling the covers tight and shut my eyes and waited for the rhythmic-not-lullaby-branch thumping to cement my headache.

But it never came.

I yanked the blanket back, and sat up, listening. The wind howled as if it was getting ready for a kite festival, but no thumping.

What happened to my branch?

I got up, beelined to the window, and did the fastest peak and sneak I could, confirming the branch was *gone.*

There was only one person that would have chopped down that branch.

Somewhere inside me, my soul screamed. Life wasn't fair. I'd finally found the most amazing and conscientious man, and he was in love with the mean girl who didn't deserve him.

I flung back down on my bed, flopping a pillow over my head. Now it wasn't the sound that kept me awake but the absence of it. Not because I had gotten used to it, but because it reminded me of Evan.

# Sixteen

## Jade

I was late to work the next day, but it had nothing to do with a lost shoe, a crashed car or even a branch that kept me up all night. For the first time in a while, everything was fixed. At least the logistical stuff was, but I couldn't say the same about my heart.

Dressed in the Grinch costume Rob had given me, I truly felt drained of all Christmas spirit, and I dragged my feet. My heart was clouded, and I didn't even rush the last steps into the coffee house. Santa was set up in his usual spot, and I somberly waved. "Hey, Santa."

"What's your Christmas wish?" His smile was jolly underneath his classic Santa white beard.

I paused, wondering why these fake Santa's felt they could ask me personal questions all the time. It's not like we're friends. "What's with the invasive question?"

"Socratic Method."

"Socrat—what?" I quirked a brow at him.

"Socrates believed everyone with a problem already knew the answer, as long as you asked them the right question."

I parked one hand on my hip, and barked out, "Who said I had a problem?"

"People are scared to ask the question because they are afraid of the answer." He winked at me, sending a shiver down my spine like something I had never felt. "It's okay. I already know your wish." He nodded to the shop. "He's here."

"Who's here?" I asked haughtily, stretching my neck like a crane trying to see through the tinted glass windows. "If who I thought he was talking about was in there, then clearly Santa was senile.

Evan was not my Christmas wish.

I stomped forward, zipping through the door, hoping Portia wouldn't notice I was late, but then I dug my heel into the floor halting fast. Portia wasn't behind the counter. *Christian was here!* He instantly squared his body with mine, checked his wristwatch and flashed it at me.

"Sorry, I'm late." I beelined back to the pantry and grabbed an apron, tying it on, while speed walking to clock in. "Where's Portia?"

He walked in front of the computer, partially blocking it from me. "I switched shifts with her." His eyes were narrowed, and he held his lips tight.

"Oh." I deadpanned, not having time to examine my thoughts before Christian continued.

"I cross checked your schedule with your time ins, and I don't think you have ever been on time."

Cringing, I forced a breezy tone. "I had a rough week. I moved across town and still struggling to find the fastest way—" My voice dropped off, because he stuck his hand in front of the computer screen, blocking it.

"Don't bother clocking in." His voice was even. Stern.

"What?" I whispered.

"I'm sorry," he firmly continued. "We need to cut payroll."

"I'm great with customers," I squeaked out, placing a hand on my chest. "I dressed up as the Grinch."

He paced to the counter, removed an envelope and handed it to me. "I'm sorry, but we've been too slow."

"Christmas is tomorrow." My words were more matter-of-fact than sad. I was so totally stunned, my feet glued to the floor. How would I be getting fired again?

He motioned to the envelope. It wasn't lost on me that his Rolex glinted in the light. Being an owner of a chain of coffee shops, he never spared himself luxury. It wasn't fair. My measly wage was nothing to him. He didn't care. "That's your last week's pay, and a small severance pay."

Blinking back tears, I slid one foot away, as I didn't want him to see me like that. "You said I was free to go, right?"

His lips thinning into a straight line, but I didn't believe for a moment that he had real empathy for me. "I'm sorry, but I'll be a good reference for you."

"Don't bother," I spit out and spun on my heel practically running, adrenaline pumping through my legs right back out the door I had just entered. There was fat ol' Santa sitting smugly on this stool. "Hey you!" I called, not caring that I was picking a fight. "You lied! You said my wish was inside." I flashed my envelope at him and spat out, "But I got fired."

He smiled at me, lifting his chin the slightest bit in motion. "Look behind you."

I threw my hands up and spun on my heel. "Are you nuts—" My voice dropped off because there was Evan. The last person I wanted to see right now. "Santa. You're killing me," I called over my shoulder, but as I turned, the sidewalk was empty. My eyes about bugged out of my head and I called out, "Santa!?"

"Who are you talking to?" Evan asked in a weary tone.

"Santa was right here two seconds ago." I motioned to the perfect open space.

Evan's lips curled at the corners as if he was sharing a secret. "Jade—"

"Don't tell me I'm crazy because he was right here."

His shoulders bounced slightly as if he was stifling a chuckle. "I'm not going to tell you that."

"Why are you here? To rub it in my face that you got your girlfriend back. Do you want congratulations?"

One of his brows was raised above the other. "What are you talking about?"

"Rob told me you were getting back with her."

His expression sparked as if he had solved a riddle. "That's why you left and are avoiding me?"

"Well, of course it is. I felt like a fool. Bad things always happen to me. I can't believe I got sucked into your weird game."

"What do you mean bad things always happen to you?" Even though I was nearly screaming at him, his voice got even softer, carrying the empathy I'd been dying to have from ANYBODY in my life.

I pressed my palms against my chest—my hands trembled so badly I knew he could see—my heart pounding hard against them. "Have you met me? I just got fired. AGAIN! It's Christmas Eve, and I have no money. Then there's you." I gestured toward him frantically. "I thought I had made a new friend but it became clear to me that you were only using me to get back with your ex—"

"That's not true." He took a step closer and put his hand on my forearm, squeezing it so firmly, I struggled to get away. "I'm not back with her. Stop saying that. I don't ever want to be with her. I want someone else."

"Well, good for you." I didn't even know why I was talking to him. This whole encounter was ridiculous. So embarrassing, and I was over it. I took a few steps off the sidewalk. Evan released his grip on my arm. In a way, it felt as if my heart left go of the pull it had toward him.

He called after me, "Jade, this may suck to hear, but maybe the reason bad things happen to you is because *you're the good thing that has to happen to someone else.*"

Halting my steps, I wanted to scream, "What does that mean?" When I spun back on my heel, I saw moisture in his eyes, and my gut fell. I was silent on the outside, but my heart sent sirens on the inside. His gaze danced around my face, and I waited for him to explain but he didn't. He moved forward, erasing all the space between us. I froze as he slowly lifted his hands to my face, brushing his thumb over my lips.

His eyes entwined with mine as I searched for an explanation. When he finally spoke, his voice squeaked, "I wish we could go back to the beginning, to when I first saw you."

"Why?" I stared forward with my resting Grinch face, waiting for him to blame this whole thing on me.

"Because I was so wrapped up in trying to beat Rob and Holly that I almost missed *you*."

"I don't understand."

"You were game to engage in my random shenanigans, and along the way I had the most fun I've ever had. I almost missed it, though. I wish we could start over, and I would never ask you to be my fake date. I would ask you to be my real date."

My heart pumped full of all the swoons I had never had. Had Santa been totally right? I let my lips curl into a giant smile while I curled my toes pinching them tight. "What are you waiting for?"

His gaze continued to dance across my face. He looked at me the way I needed to be looked at. Like he was really seeing me. As if his entire world would collapse if I merely suggested I didn't want him. "I wish for that, too," I replied, knowing with all my heart I wanted a chance to get to know Evan for real. To date him for *real*. It was my final Christmas wish.

# Epilogue

## Jade

I stood behind the Formica counter at the new shop above Evan's mad science lab, tallying the number of cheesecakes I'd sold that week. "Forty-two orders were picked up, and I have another eleven presold for next week."

The smile on Pearl's cherry-painted lips only grew bigger as Evan did the rest of the math. "At fifty dollars a cake, you two made over two thousand with only word-of-mouth advertising the first week."

"That's not bad for a side hustle with no business plan, or even a name." I was proud of what we'd thrown together in the last week. It started as a late Sunday idea that we tossed around. Evan immediately volunteered space in his shop loft for a small commercial kitchen. Everything was modest and done on a budget, but I was amazed how we all pulled together and made it happen.

"Yep, just two chicks bootlegging cake from a computer shop loft," Evan teased, while taking a moment to look at each of us.

"Hey, wait a second," I interjected. "What about Two Chicks Cake Shop?" I wrinkled my nose, letting the name ring in my head. "Is that any good for a name?"

"I like it," Pearl immediately agreed. "I can even visualize some-day when we get our own building, we'd have a cute logo with two chickens and barn house decor."

"No, Mom." Evan chuckled, giving his mom his easy grin to let her down gently. "Chicks like women, not birds."

"Oh!" Pearl's eyes rounded. "That makes even more sense. Here, I thought it was something to do with your Discovery animal shows."

We all shared a good laugh, but Evan didn't let the comment die. "I can't even remember the last time I watched one of those shows."

"Really?" His mom's gaze angled in a disbelieving way.

"Yeah," Evan assured her, moving toward the display cases. "Look at everything I've been doing. I work all day. After work, Jade and I remodeled the loft. It's been one thing after another."

"Sorry to keep you so overextended," I teased, with a faux hurt look on my face.

"I didn't mean it like that." Evan slid his arm around me, pulling me into a side hug. "I was saying a lot has changed in the last two months." He leaned his face closer to my ear, and whispered, "But I wouldn't change any of it for the world."

A trickle of goosebumps swirled through me as I felt the same way. I had no idea how I had finally broken my bad luck spree. "Hey, I have an idea," I piped up, as an idea to make Evan happy came into my head. "It's Friday and work is over for the week.

Let's celebrate by having one of your famous Discovery Channel marathons. All the alien shows you can cram in."

"Count me out," Evan's mom proclaimed. She dramatically grabbed her coat and slipped it on. She leaned in for a fast hug around Evan's neck. "You two knock yourselves out. I'm ready for bed."

"Love you, Mom," Evan called after her as she was already halfway toward the exit.

"Thanks for a great week," I said, still in disbelief we'd pulled everything off.

"See you both on Monday." She waved goodbye with the jingle of the old-fashioned doorbells signaling she was gone.

Evan turned to me with a gleam in his eye. Not just any gleam. My favorite one. Wrapping one arm around my waist, he pulled me in close to him, and he whispered, "Thank you."

Tilting my head to the side, I gave him a humored expression. "For what? Offering to watch your alien shows with you?"

He rolled his lips inward, drawing attention to them. I had to fight the urge to give them a little smooch, but I waited patiently for him to finish his thought. "For, everything. I don't think I've ever seen my mom so excited about something. You just came into our lives and made it better for everyone. It's like you were the missing piece we didn't even know we needed."

My cheeks blushed as Evan was giving me credit for something I didn't do. They were the ones who did all the heavy lifting. I merely walked beside them and that wasn't a herculean task, because I much enjoyed the view of my handsome boyfriend. "I can't take all the credit." I playfully batted my eyes, adding, "Santa helped."

"Was it Santa?" Evan's eyes narrowed. "Because I seem to recall everything being traced back to that first slice of cheesecake."

"Ah." I threw my head back, and laughed, recalling that day at Evan's mom's. He was right, that was the start of it all. You're right," I agreed. "From now on, the answer to all our life's problems is cheesecake."

Evan nodded, his lips spreading into the most sensational grin, as he leaned down and pressed a kiss to the tip of my nose, and whispered, "Cheesecake is life."

# Bonus Epilogue

## One year later . . .

"I can't believe it's the last time we clean this place." I dropped my stained rag into the laundry bin in the closet, and soberly turned back to Evan; my arms hung loosely at my sides. "I have no idea where the last year went."

Evan pushed the last tray of cake pans farther into the dishwasher, and shut the door, rocking back on his heels as his gaze regarded mine. There was a slight turn on one side of his lips, but he remained quiet, which frankly drove me nuts. I hadn't seen him all day, as he was working his job. He had arrived to help me clean and perform the emotional lock up. I had spent the day naturally over caffeinated—well, some parts my natural personality and some parts supplemented with caffeine—wanting to chatter about my anxiety. Of course, I recounted all our funniest, scariest, and most random memories about owning this little cakeshop to myself.

It was a little lonely, and so hard to believe it was all coming to an end. Not the way we had dreamed either. We weren't expanding. We weren't moving into a beautiful new building with a coffee bar for me to run. We were shutting up shop. Forever.

Evan's dad retired and to everyone's surprise, including his own, he bought a condo in Florida. It didn't take Pearl more than a moment to trade in her bakery days for a bathing suit and cabana. It turned out Evan never had to move out because his parents moved first. After Thanksgiving, they swiftly crammed thirty years of memories into a U-Haul and gifted the whole house to Evan.

Pearl wasn't available to be my business partner anymore. I didn't feel right using her recipe. That wasn't the total truth either. Turns out, I didn't have the special something to make these cakes. I swore she never gave me the correct recipe because whenever I tried, something was off. I teased it was her special essence, but either way, the cakes were never the same. Frankly, I lost my passion for it once I learned she was leaving.

So, I hit a crossroads with my career again. I swear if I never have to worry about money again in my life, I'd be one happy chicken. Yep, I dressed as a chicken today. We went with the Two Chicks Cheesecake name, and well, the costume was amazing for tips. I fluffed my feathers and went to grab my mop bucket to stow away. As I wheeled it back to the janitorial closet, I savored the glossy tile, and shiny stainless-steel countertops *one more time.*

I had to let it go.

All of it.

I was going to miss this little bakery with its cheesecake charm smells—dark chocolate, and salted caramel, unliked anything you'd find at a market.

Another dream bites the dust.

Unemployed again right before Christmas.

"Something happened today." Evan came up behind me, leaning with one hand on the wall. He stood, framing the hallway, causing my breath to hitch in my chest. *He was still a phenomenal leaner.*

"What's that?" I jimmied the mop bucket into the over-stuffed micro closet and quickly closed it before it rolled back out. It was a slick trick I'd learned earlier this year, and it made me smile to think this was the final time I'd have to do it.

"It started last week when my dad reconnected with an old friend at his retirement party. It turns out, he knew someone who worked for NASA."

"Oh yeah." I slid my over-sized chicken feet forward, until the tips of my toes bumped into the tips of his toes and rapped both hands smugly around his waist. I gazed up at his handsome face, thoroughly inspecting it for the things he wasn't telling me. Yep. He had a squiggle of indistinguishable line right above his brow. I was going to need more details to draw this out of him. "And then what?"

"My dad put in a good word for me, and that guy passed it forward, and I guess I have an internship."

"Say what?" I sputtered out a cough of dust that must have been marinated in my throat since I mopped. "You have a job at NASA?"

"Not just any position. They need a robotics specialist." His lips pitched together, as he cocked his head to the side. It was a flawless expression among many that I loved to stare at. "I accepted."

"Are you kidding me right now? Wait . . . you didn't show them Greta, did you?" I wagged my head back and forth, stalling my reaction as I inspected his expression for signs he was teasing. "Because Greta might not help your case."

"No, I'm totally serious, and I want you to come with me." The spiral of light that rippled through his eyes told me exactly how he was feeling. He leaned forward, tilting his chin down until he was kissing close. I didn't mean to ruin the moment—okay, I'll blame it on my nerves. When he leaned over something caught my eye behind him.

There was a lone cheesecake sitting on the counter that Evan had been standing in front of earlier. We never brought cakes back to the dish area, as they all got stored in the front freezer. Even then, I clearly remembered we sold our last cake. I put it in the box myself. "What's that cake doing there?" I didn't pretend for a moment that Evan wasn't up to something.

If he expected a cake brawl for old time's sake after I meticulously shined this kitchen, well, he knows me better than I know myself because I'd do it. In fact, I was one step ahead of him, sliding my talon toward it. I'd learned some hacks about cake brawls. The trick was to take all the ammo and attack first. As I slid in next to the cake, I was all hands, ready to sweep it up in one big chunk for some facetime. I quickly halted on my heel when I saw what was placed in the center of the cake. "Evan . . ." My voice decreased in volume so much it dropped into a whisper all the while the intonations increased in urgency.

"I know you don't have a problem digging into the center of a perfect cheesecake." He crossed the room, closing the gap between us.

"I do actually." I eyed the cake with the perfect princess cut solitaire diamond ring in the center, but my fingers trembled enough that I didn't want to touch it.

Evan was one step ahead of me, and carefully pinched the ring between his fingers, bringing it out of the cake without getting cake on it. It was obvious to me now; he had selected a cake without topping on purpose. He brought the ring close to his body, holding it protectively. He turned it over a few times and was so quiet, I thought he'd changed his mind. I ran my tongue along my lips, hydrating them, waiting for the best part but Evan didn't budge. This was the part he was supposed to get on one knee! Was he waiting for me to do it?

I wasn't ready for that!

I stared at his hands as they turned the ring over. When I gazed back at his face, he wasn't smiling. He'd clearly lost his nerve, or changed his mind, but I didn't want this to get anymore awkward and blurted out, "It's okay if you don't want to."

"What?" He blinked, nostrils flaring just enough to pin my feet to the ground. "Why would you think that?"

"It's just that you were hesitating—"

"Taking the moment in," He cut me off. "Wanting to remember this forever."

"Oh." I curtly made an actual O with my lips, feeling silly now, and threw out an excuse, "My nerves have been a wreck all day." Before I could ramble on about how I spent the whole morning slurping my coffee from the pot with ice and a loppy straw because I was hopelessly trying to do fun things to avoid the tears, he finally took a knee.

And I cinched every muscle I had in my body tight, holding everything in, so I wouldn't accidentally ruin *this.* I fought all day not to cry. I wasn't strong enough to handle this. Tears pricked at the back of my eyes, and I willingly blinked them down my cheek.

"I know we haven't talked about this much, but this month has been hard for me with all the changes. My parents moved. For a moment, I wondered if I should go, too. They are the only real family I have; I quickly stopped those thoughts when I realized I'd have to leave you. I was worried after you lost your job that maybe you'd want to move back to your family. That thought horrified me, too. I don't ever want to be away from you, and I realized we are each other's family. It's time we make it official because I don't want to imagine my life without you." He displayed the ring in his flattened palm. With his free hand he picked it up and held it out. "I love you, Jade. Will you marry me?"

"Yes." I squeaked out, but when I reached my finger out to receive my ring, yellow chicken feathers broke my tunnel vision. I giggled the sweetest giggle, already knowing this would be my best memory here at the bakery. "You had to do it when I was dressed as a giant chicken? Didn't you?" I managed to spread my fingers out and he finished slipping the ring on my finger while I added, "You couldn't tip me off to wear a nice dress or something? Can you imagine how this engagement selfie is going to look now?"

A rush of laughter fell from his lips, but I moved in to stifle it with a kiss. When I pulled back, I gazed down at my ring on my finger, fully taking it in. All the bad things that had happened to me led me to this moment. I wouldn't change any of it. "I love you, fiancé." I flashed the ring back at him, wiggling my fingers as I tried to get used to this engagement thing. I already know it would be the best thing to ever happen to me.

"I love you, too." Evan slipped his hand into mine, weaving his fingers perfectly through and we left our little bakery. Once outside, Evan rolled up the little tattered cloth Welcome rug for the last time. Unlike other nights where it was brought inside to be used again the next day, tonight he tucked it under his arm. "I'm keeping this for your next adventure, whatever that ends up being."

Suddenly I wasn't sad about losing the bakery. I had something much sweeter. I was beautiful, strong, brave, and now, *engaged*.

### Thank you for reading Mingle All the Way!

*Guess what? If you liked this coffee shop romance, I have another one coming next year. It's an enemies to lovers, slow burn, coming in Jan 2024. Available for preorder now. https://www.amazon.com/dp/B0CG2NRLJ7*

*Did you know Evan started as a side character in my Maid for My Billionaire Boss book. You can find his cameo here: https://www.amazon.com/dp/B0BSDSM3ST*

# 'Tis the Season to Get Married Excerpt (Name change: previously listed under a Holidaze.

## Charlotte

So, do I want to be in a serious relationship?" I nodded in answer to Nick' question, setting my seconds-after-another-friend's-per-fect-wedding-mocktail glass down to clear my hands so I could better defend myself to my best friend, Nick. We were sitting near a window at the bar in Sterling Lodge, the *same* lodge where my three best friends held their destination weddings.

They all chose the town of Amesbury because, "it held the perfect winter wonderland background for a beautiful Christmas wedding." Amesbury was so secluded and charming it was named the number-one spot to have a Christmas wedding. I'd bought so many weekend packages to stay here as a bridesmaid, I was pretty sure I deserved a free upgraded bride package any day now—I just needed to find a groom.

"I do." My adrenaline ticked up—like way up—all the way up to my neck. I continued to use my hands to illustrate my point, something I always did when I got emotional. Placing my flattened palm on my chest to stifle the rush, I continued, "Do I want to go to vineyards and apple orchards?"

"—I love apple orchards," Nick cut in. "They have the best hard cider."

"Cheers to apple orchards!" I pinched the stem of my glass between my fingers, and tapped it with his, then lowered it to my lips so I could take another generous sip of my mocktail, made with their famous poinsettia infused tonic water. As I came up for air, I finished my sentence right where I had left off. "And hayrides with pumpkin spice lattes, sharing fluffy blankets that are perfectly coordinated to match our turtleneck sweaters, and do all the other insanely cute stuff?" I paused, but did not let him answer. He didn't need to tell me how he was feeling because I already knew. We were both tired of people acting as if I didn't know *all* our friends were marrying off at increasing speeds. That didn't sound like something I should be upset about, but no matter how much they insisted they would still make time for a night, one-by-one they disappeared into the baby-raising abyss.

I shifted in my seat, scooting closer to the edge. Sure, I'd get an invite to birthday parties, or a family picnic—and I enjoy supporting my friends in that way—but it was *painful* to always show up alone, when all I wanted was to be able to do what they were doing.

*I saw all my friends getting married.*

*Of course, I saw them!*

"I do," I rambled out. "I want all of that. But do I want to go on dates with every loser I barely know, just to suffer through hours of awkward conversations, only to find out he is a player like the rest of them?" I sealed my lips tightly and wagged my head back and forth.

No words are needed.

"I know what you mean." Nick leaned forward as he picked up my comment perfectly, like I knew he would. He always understood what I was going through. "I'm no Michelangelo's David but I want to find *one* woman who likes to cuddle on the couch, without having to twist her face into fourteen versions of duck lips so she can take the perfect ego-feeding selfie." He gestured toward me. "Is that too much to ask?"

"Oh, I hate selfies." I seethed, remembering his recollection of his last date. "When I'm on a date, I want to look at the other person, not stare at an isolated reflection of myself. I mean, I've been doing that long enough."

"Agreed!"

"Is it too much to ask my fairy Godmother to hurry and change a pumpkin into a carriage to transport me to the ball to meet my prince already?" I whined, but it came out forcefully like it was wrestling with a groan.

"Well, I hate to inform you." Nick rubbed his chin, cueing his transition to an armchair therapist, "nor do I want to be *that* guy who points this out, but you used your pumpkin in a latte for the hayride. I don't think you can ride in your pumpkin and drink it, too." His phone dinged, drawing his attention. "Uh, I'm sorry, Char. This is work." He placed the phone next to his ear, tacking on, "This will just be a second."

Grinning, I dropped my eyes back to my drink, rotating the glass slowly with my thumb and forefinger, wistfully dreaming of my prince. *What in the world was taking him so long?* I was at the stage in life, where I would be okay with backup prince number one—or even number two—if he had his act together.

I wasn't even sure if I believed in soulmates. At this point, I would be perfectly fine making a home with my soul neighbor—just as long as he didn't hog the covers at night, or listen to talk radio in the car. Well . . . technically, I could always bring earbuds. Maybe I could make an exception for the talk radio if he didn't complain about my bare feet being on the dash while I rode shotgun. *They always get too sweaty with shoes on!* They much preferred riding in the daylight.

Yeah, talk radio for a barefoot swap. That seemed like a logical compromise. Oh! And he'd have to listen to "Blue Christmas" by Elvis, on repeat, from Thanksgiving to Christmas, while also singing harmony, but he could totally have the other forty-eight weeks after that for his talk radio. Except for the obvious Elvis week where "Can't Help Falling in Love" would have to blast on all six speakers with the window rolled down to hear it outside of the car so we could dance under the stars—but that would be a given. If

I had to explain dancing under the stars to any man, he definitely wasn't soul neighbor material.

Actually, since I'd been waiting so long, scratch everything except the dancing under the stars.

Dancing under the stars was a very reasonable condition that should be a cinch to finagle. Then, off to happily-ever-after land, and I wouldn't have to spend the rest of my life alone.

Nick set his phone screen down, leaning back into our conversation. "Sorry about that. Where were we?"

"I don't know," I started, ready to give up on love entirely so I could be finished dating. "Find me a dude who needs a maid but promises to take care of me forever—or something close—and I'd be happy to fill that role. I want to be done with dating." I pushed out my bottom lip and plopped my chin to rest in my palm. "It's such a waste of time."

Nick stretched one arm up and dropped it to scratch the back of his head. "I feel like I can put in another year, or two, tops, just to see if there are any stragglers who like to cuddle, but I'm going to end up where you are here shortly if all I get are duck lips."

"Another year and you'll be thirty," I commented, letting my eyes smack him with that reality.

"It's *adomania*." Nick's words came out soft, barely above a whisper, while he stared wide-eyed at me.

"Is that another word for a birthday?" I hiked a brow, letting a smile take over my face as I marveled at his rare talent for knowing the most unknown words that perfectly summed up every conversation. I called him the word whisperer. He hated that nickname, but that didn't stop him from going out of his way to find the most obscure words.

"Nah, not birthday." He blinked a couple of times as if he was trying to refocus on our conversation and then planted his gaze back on me. "It means your future is coming too quickly."

I let the definition ring over, and I had to admit he'd done it again. He'd summed up this entire conversation with one word. "It's perfect, 'adomania.'" My voice floated, as if it was still holding awe. He nodded gently, and I nodded back, our smiles synchronizing before I added, "Can you imagine how hard dating is going to be in our thirties?"

"I can imagine it will be pathetic—"

"So pathetic," I finished his thought like always. "Here we are, two amazing people,"—I straighten my spine, feeling an ego boost coming— "and nobody wants to spouse us up."

"Everyone must be blind." His words were laced with a low sputtering chuckle.

"Obviously." My eyes made a giant arc around the top of my lid as I strove for the most perfect eye roll ever. "I mean, look at you," I gestured to him with both hands. "You're like what? The most genius CPA on the planet?"

He shrugged only one shoulder, as if he were more-or-less accepting that as a compliment. "More like an office manager."

"Just call yourself a human calculator with all those skills." Exhausted from a full day of wedding party activities, and overly emotional, my words were starting to slur now, but I didn't care because I had a point to prove. I licked my lips, trying to remember what that point was . . . I wasn't sure, so I took another sip of my drink and stared at him until he came into focus. Then I remembered! "Oh, yeah, so what do you make a year, six figures?"

"Low six."

"Right!" I pointed at him accusingly because it would make him laugh. "You're rich!"

He snickered, as it was becoming obvious to both of us now that my "medication" was kicking in, but I continued as I still had a point to prove. I clumsily gestured at him again. "And you're buff! I've seen you with your shirt off, and you have two shadows of abs in there. Sometimes." My own laughter cut off my words as I giggled intensely and fondly looked back at my best friend. He was laughing, too. Not looking even slightly offended because he knew it was true.

Wrapping my fingers around the stem of my mocktail again, I lifted it to my lips and finished the rest, before setting it down, and seeing my glass was now empty. It was a little blurry, but I could mostly see it, and it was most definitely empty.

I was tired of being a glass-is-empty person. It was painful. Part of what one gets out of life is what they put into it. At some point, I would have to accept the plight I was given. It was then I made my decision. Letting out a sigh steeped in desperation, I put a voice to my decision, "If I'm not married—or at least engaged by Christmas—I'm forever giving up on dating—for eternity."

Nick quirked a skeptical brow. "This Christmas? That's eleven months."

"It seems like the only realistic thing to do. I could use all that time for a new hobby, or something." I pursed duck lips to remind him of his own fate, then tacked on, "Want to join me? We could make a pact."

"I don't know." He nervously scratched the back of his head. "I mean, I really like to cuddle."

I glared at him through my one good eye, which was less blurry than the other one. I picked up my glass to take another drink, but found it empty, which made me sad. I didn't want to be sad because I had a plan. Or more like a pact, and I was trying to snatch a partner for my pact. I flashed him more duck lips and said, "Quack," which sent us both into another rush of laughter.

"Okay," his voice sobered up, and he latched his eyes onto mine. "I'm done with duck lips. If I am not engaged by Christmas, I'll be done dating too, and we can do hayrides together."

"Wait." My eyes skirted the room, trying to see where that idea came from. "What did you say?"

"I said, I'm in. I agree with your pact. I'll give up if I'm not engaged by Christmas."

"No, no, no." I wagged my finger in the air. "What was that other part?"

"We can do hayrides together?" His voice teetered up, ending his statement as a question.

"Together?" I hiked a brow at him, feeling his vibes. "Are you saying, when we give up trying to find other people, we will just be together?"

"Well, I mean, if we are both single . . . it makes sense that we hang out, no?"

"Wait for a second. I'm getting an idea." I leaned forward, trying to pull him into my excitement. "If we aren't married by Christmas, then *we should get married to each other!*"

I could see him mouth the words "marry each other," but it wasn't audible. Then his eyes sprang wide as they hooked mine. "Yeah, that's the best idea ever!"

"I know!" I sprang to my feet, exclaiming, "I'm getting matching turtlenecks just in case! What's your size?"

"Large," he answered in a definitive tone and added, "I'll book the honeymoon suite here at the lodge—just in case."

"Right." I nodded, finding it perfectly acceptable. Then I leaned forward, extending a playful fist toward him. Somewhere over the years of wasting time together, we had accidentally made our secret handshake, and I was ready to deploy it. "Okay, Nick this is it. I swear if I'm not married by Christmas, I will meet you here in Amesbury, and marry you."

He balled his fist and pushed it out toward me for a bump, then we both made a half heart with our fingers and connected it in the middle. Nick didn't waste a second to confirm, "Deal."

***Coming to Kindles November 7, 2023***. https://www.amazo n.com/dp/B0BRVQJWGC

# About J.P.

Hey you! Thanks for being here.

Let me introduce myself.

I write wholesome stories and adore all things slapstick humor and heart strings.

Growing up, I binged on classic comedy like Lucille Ball, and Carol Burnette. It was a great escape from reality, even when the plots were farfetched. I discovered my love for writing slapstick comedy after motherhood and I haven't looked back.

Aside from writing, I'm also a wife and homeschooling mom, a holistic nutritionist, a jewelry designer, a professional archivist, former college instructor and lover of all things dark chocolate.

Author Clean Code: I like to make my stories about the story and not about a bunch of profanity, mature content, or graphic violence that are only there to shock you. I write my stories to be family friendly.

I also just launched a private reader group on Facebook. I can't wait to welcome you there. This is where we share all the things humor and heartstrings. This is my exclusive group of readers who are first to get access to all my books, giveaways and more.

Hop on in my reader group here: https://www.facebook.com /groups/1500850764081965

For free audio books please visit:

https://www.youtube.com/c/JpSterling

Find me on Instagram.

https://www.instagram.com/authorjpsterling/

Sign up to my free monthly newsletter to get the first look at my new books, free book offers and random updates.

https://landing.mailerlite.com/webforms/landing/q9c0v3

# Also By J.P. Sterling

Tis the Season to Get Married (releasing 2023. Previously named Holidaze)

### *The Coffee Loft Series*

Pardon My French Press (Coming Jan. 2024) https://www.amazon.com/dp/B0CG2NRLJ7